Threads of Betrayal

Monica Koldyke Miller

To Shirley + Al,
Hope you enjoy the book!
– Monica Koldyke Miller
1/31/13

ISBN: 1-4750-7744-0
ISBN-13: 9781475077445

Acknowledgments

A heartfelt thank you goes to my family who've supported me with unwavering faith and encouragement throughout this process.

To Laurel Steill, who after becoming my teacher became my mentor, friend and an unrelenting inspiration to develop my abilities.

To Bobbi Ray Madry, who took my writing to a higher level and whose belief in my potential gave me the courage to realize my dream.

To Les Edgerton, for his insight in creating a unique 'hook' and his complement that "you can flat out write."

And, a special thanks to my 6th grade teacher, Mrs. Rindfusz, who after telling a shy 11 year old "you write the most interesting sentences," opened a whole new world of possibilities.

Lastly, to God, who listened to innumerable prayers and in his timing removed all obstacles. To you I give thanks most. When I asked for an eagle, you gave me a hawk.

I will never forget any of you.

Prologue

Spring of 1860, Burnsfield Lumber Office

Reagan sat near his father's desk, hat in one hand and papers in the other. Outside the office door, the whine of saw wheels kept a constant vibration beneath their feet. "According to these reports, there's enough unclaimed tracts along the Cattaraugus River for several camps. If we get someone up there, we could begin harvesting this fall," said Reagan.

"Send Bradley," Thomas said to his son. "He's quick, but thorough."

"I'll do that." Reagan stood. He put on his hat, but instead of leaving, shuffled his papers, glancing from them to his father.

"It's been five years since I've taken over logging operations," he blurted. "You said once I had that experience, we'd become partners."

"Now isn't a good time," Thomas said, frowning. "As you know, we had to use our own lumber to rebuild after the mill burned down. We broke contracts in order to use that lumber, and it put us behind. I need to concentrate my efforts on finding clients."

"That's why it's time I became partner. I'd like to begin soliciting contracts, as well."

Reagan saw Thomas pursing his lips, something he often did when agitated. He almost knew beforehand, what Thomas's words would be.

"Right now, I need your efforts put into cutting timber. There'll be time for that once we've got enough tracts to keep the mill running for more than a summer." He then opened a ledger and began scribbling. "We'll talk about this next year when things have calmed down."

"That's what you said *last* year."

"That was before the fire," Thomas said. "We lost a lot of revenue. Now that we're up and running, I'm trying to regain what we lost."

"Why not let me take time from logging to see if I can help?"

Thomas opened a drawer, his eyes sweeping its contents. "Because, Reagan, it's not that easy. We've discussed this before. When I think you know enough, I'll let you give it a try."

When I think you know enough, I'll let you give it a try.

As those words echoed in his ears, it was as if a curtain parted, revealing a play of Reagan's past. He suddenly realized his father had used those words often, usually when he tried doing something other than what Thomas wanted.

He had always viewed his father as a shrewd businessman, cautious but wise and so accepted his caution without question. It occurred to him, he now looked at a man who for years had no equal, who found he liked it that way and so kept Reagan busy, never progressing beyond Thomas's restrictions.

He recalled the time he tried overstepping his father's rules while at a logging camp. At fifteen and nearing his father's height, he chafed at being kept from working as a chopper. His mind became set on felling his first tree. Telling no one, he had taken an axe and walked the woods, picking a pine away from the track being harvested. He worked swiftly, envisioning his father's pleasure at his newest skill. He didn't see Hank approach with a gang of swampers as he drove a wedge into the back cut after chopping an angle to direct the tree's fall.

Cupping his mouth, Reagan called his warning a second before Hank came into view.

"Timberrrr!"

The man looked up when a rifle-like crack pierced the air. Twisting in a slow pirouette, the pine broke free, followed by a whoosh that scattered swampers back into the woods.

"Look out!"

Reagan had slammed into Hank and together they tumbled to safety as the tree crashed, hard. Someone yelled for help while men rushed to lift Hank to his feet and had him dusted off by the time Thomas reached his son. By his tightened jaw, Reagan knew he had made a mistake.

"What the hell were you doing?" he said, yanking him upright. "That was foolish and you know it."

Reagan's ears reddened and he slapped away his father's hand. "Why? I just felled a tree. Can't you see I'm ready?"

"You're not ready until I say you're ready. What you did just proves my point." Thomas scooped up Reagan's hat and slapped it on his head. "Every man here knows you don't chop alone."

"You started younger than me," Reagan said stubbornly. "When do I get to chop trees?"

Thomas sighed before resting a hand on Reagan's shoulder. "Listen, son. Lumbering is dangerous. I have a lot to teach you. When I think you know enough, I'll let you give it a try."

❧

Reagan said nothing as he turned and left Thomas's office. The desire to prove himself formed like a lump in his gut. It grew larger and harder with every step until it near choked his craw. He would show his father he knew *damn well,* enough. Not only would he make a contract, it'd be the biggest contract ever. He knew of a broker. He'd contact him and set up a meeting before leaving for New York. After that, Thomas could no longer say he wasn't ready to be his partner.

chapter I

Summer of 1860, Cantonsville, Ohio

Reagan sat slanted across the carriage seat, his arm flung against the windowsill. His fingers drummed in cadence to the rhythmic hoof beats as the coach traveled the rutted dirt road. Though his destination was less than a mile away, his stiff collar and merciless heat made the trip difficult to bear.

Reaching inside the pocket of his gray frock coat, he withdrew a small white envelope. *Another wasted evening,* he thought, staring at the invitation. He sighed and placed the envelope back into his pocket. Having just returned from the forests of New York, he would've preferred working at the lumber mill. The company's dwindling list of business deals pressed a more urgent need for finding clients than attending a debutante's ball. Yet obligations between the family business and the Bruester Bank and Trust made his attendance necessary. Ever inventive, Reagan had formulated a clever plan of escape. He would act properly attentive and fulfill his duty before making a swift departure after dinner.

As the coach neared Cantonsville, Reagan pondered several solutions to his problem. His earlier contact with a broker had proven useful when he had been informed the Marine Dock Company needed lumber. Anxious to demonstrate his ability to generate sales, he solicited a contract on his own and foolishly told Thomas the deal was done before the contract was signed. Initially furious, Thomas yielded by granting Reagan limited authority on obtaining future contracts that carried both their signatures. Reagan agreed, and the mill ran for weeks, piling lumber on the warehouse dock before the client declined the offer. Reagan had gambled new contracts would arise to cover his error. They had not and he grew worried. He could tell his father of the lost contract, which if not replaced, could jeopardize the business. He could say nothing and ask for an extension of funds from the bank. Or, he could find another contract before Thomas found out Reagan had invested nearly all his own money for this latest land deal. No matter his choice, he was sure to experience his father's displeasure at this turn of events.

Reagan ran a hand through his recently clipped hair. He recalled his mother's mortified reaction to his appearance when he arrived home earlier that day. With feigned protests, he had tolerated her relieving him of his shaggy condition. Combined with his clean shave and perfectly pressed suit, he now looked more the aristocrat and less a lumberman. Reagan sat up and straightened his coat. He would work on his problems later. Now, he had to get through the evening.

The carriage came to a shaded drive and joined a line of surreys unloading guests in front of the Bruester mansion. The three-story manor, built of stone and covered in English Ivy, harbored the oldest family in Cantonsville; something the resident matriarch took pride in.

Reagan alighted before approaching the open doorway where George and Emily Bruester were greeting their guests. The childhood ditty "Jack Spratt" sprang to mind as he viewed the oddly paired couple. In her youth, Emily had been quite beautiful, but little beauty remained as her once trim figure now strained her gown. Her raven hair streaked with gray was arranged in a pompadour designed to diminish her considerable size. Wearing an immaculate white suit, George appeared almost diminutive next to his wife. His fringed, balding pate glistened as his eyes fell on their newest guest. He held out his hand, smiling widely.

"Reagan, we're so pleased you came. Emily feared you wouldn't be attending."

With amazing alacrity, Emily flicked open her fan to cool the flush creeping up her neck. "Having received no response, I assumed you were still traveling."

Reagan grinned, handing her the envelope. "My error completely. I overlooked posting the reply in time. I wanted to keep this engagement, especially since I've neglected making your daughter's acquaintance." Reagan decided it best to twist the truth for propriety's sake. Despite having reached the age of thirty-two, he felt no hurry to marry and had never been interested in attending the balls for the daughters of his business associates. Instead, he preferred seasoned balls where he could portray the gentle suitor, enjoying the challenge of pursuit.

"You remember me telling you about Amanda, don't you?" George continued. "Since her return, we've been desirous of our daughter rekindling friendships as well as making new ones."

Reagan smiled. "I'm sure she's delightful. I'm looking forward to us forming a friendship of our own." For some time he had been aware of the animosity Emily harbored toward the Burnsfield name. Though beyond his understanding, Reagan sensed the dislike lay rooted in a long-ago slight. His invitation had been the result of a chance meeting between the Burnsfields and the Bruesters at the theater where conversation turned to Amanda's return from a Baltimore college. George had insisted the Burnsfield son should be invited to her coming-out ball.

With as much grace as he could muster, Reagan disengaged himself from the Bruesters to mingle with other guests.

"Lumberjack!" Emily said, sniffing.

chapter 2

AMANDA BRUESTER SAT at her vanity while Gertrude, her personal maid, curled her hair into ringlets. A younger maid, Betsy, knelt while attaching stockings to garters under her chemise. Standing to allow the corset to be tightened, Amanda clutched the dressing table as the stays cinched her waist. "I'll not have a full breath," she gasped, "or be able to swallow a morsel if you don't loosen those laces!"

"Now, Miss Mandy, you know how important this night is. Your mum made it clear you're to be the most fetching lady at your coming-out ball."

Amanda groaned as the matronly servant knotted the corset securely. "I'll impress them all right. I'll swoon from lack of air."

"Huh!" Gertrude said as she helped Amanda into a corded petticoat. "Fact is, all those girlies ought to be turning green with envy about the time you come prancing in. You're gonna steal all the gents from under their up-stickity noses." With a finger above her lip, Gertrude tipped back her chin and took mincing steps around the room.

Despite her nerves, Amanda laughed at the image of all her feminine guests walking around with their noses pointed in the air.

Betsy giggled as she tidied the room. "You sure could prune the bushes, Miss Amanda, and leave only one rose for the plucking."

"Stop it both of you. I'm not looking for a husband."

"Harrumph!" Gertrude made a face, her hands planted on her hips. "Your mum's looking *for* you. She's eying the gents up one side and down the other, most likely checking their bank accounts too."

"Shhh! Someone might hear you."

"Don't you worry. Your mum's busy greeting and inspecting the potential sons-in-law. I think she got her eye on a couple of them by the way she gloated over those acceptance cards."

"They're R.S.V.P.'s," corrected Amanda, drawing on her slippers. "Mother is..." she searched for the right word, "...used to managing these things."

"Bossy's more like it." Gertrude wagged a finger. "Your mum's been bossing your papa as long as I've known her. One of these days your papa's going to put his foot down. The only reason I'm still under this roof is because I want to witness that blessed event."

"Enough. Betsy's liable to think you're not respectful of Mother."

Though a dozen retorts danced on her tongue, Gertrude thought it best to say no more as she took a lavender gown from the wardrobe.

Betsy's hand flew to her bosom. "Oh, how lovely!"

"It is beautiful," Amanda agreed, stepping into the dress. "And expensive. Mother insisted the gown come from Paris so it couldn't be copied." While Gertrude fastened the hooks, Amanda adjusted the sash attached with an amethyst brooch. Larger versions of the pin gathered the hemline, revealing a deeper violet hue underneath.

"Well, I say it's stunning," Gertrude said, stepping back. "I know you didn't get a say in its choosing, but in this instance, your mum showed a flair for fashion."

Inspecting herself in the mirror, Amanda saw her likeness replaced by the image of a woman who appeared more poised than she felt. She noted the bodice concealed little of her bosom and tugged at the lace. Yet, the cloth resisted her efforts and she relented lest she damage the appliqué.

"There's one more surprise." Amanda caught her breath as Gertrude opened a jewelry box. Nestled between violet-hued earrings lay a diamond and amethyst necklace. Gertrude assisted Amanda in putting on the jewelry, answering the unspoken question in her eyes. "These were gifted to you from your Aunt Ella. She wanted to present them herself, but an unexpected engagement kept her from coming."

"Aunt Ella must've taken great pains matching jewelry to the gown," Amanda said. "She always seems to discover mother's best kept secrets."

Gertrude nodded. "I always liked that woman. She's one lady that ain't afraid of your mum." Gabriella Bruester, the never-married older sister of Amanda's father had given welcome reprieve to Amanda during an otherwise lonely childhood. Whispering secret confidences, Gabriella had often conspired in mischief making, much to Amanda's delight and Emily's eternal disdain. It sorely chafed Emily she couldn't forbid the close contact Gabriella had insisted on by frequent visits with her niece.

Gertrude gave Amanda's arm an affectionate squeeze. "Mandy, darling, you've become a fine woman. I couldn't be prouder if you were one of my own."

Betsy sniffed the stoppers of several perfumes before handing a vial to Gertrude. "This smells like the rose garden when it blooms."

"There." Gertrude touched the fragrance behind each of Amanda's ears and across her throat before turning her toward the door. "Now you're ready. Show them what a fine lady you've become."

"But, I'm so nervous."

"Go on, I say! You'll not be hiding in your room while guests are waiting."

Amanda slipped on a pair of lace gloves. "What if I do something foolish?"

"You'll do just fine." Gertrude patted her shoulder. "Your heart is good. They'll see that right off."

Amanda drew a breath. "I suppose it's time."

chapter 3

REAGAN HAD BEEN conversing with another fellow on whether slavery should be allowed in the territories. Though Reagan didn't disagree with the man's belief of abolishing slavery, he took the opposite view to add a bit of lively conversation to an otherwise dull evening. Suddenly, a murmur rippled among guests and Reagan turned to see a young woman through the doorway, descending the staircase.

As she entered the parlor escorted by Emily, the girl's beauty caught Reagan by surprise. Her gown appeared magnificent, fashioned solely for the purpose of revealing her feminine assets. He joined the quickly forming queue where Emily presented her daughter, his gaze traveling admiringly over her bosom and narrow waist. When his turn arrived, Emily paused before managing a reasonably pleasant tone of voice.

"Amanda, this is—"

"Reagan Burnsfield," she finished, extending her hand.

If it were possible, Amanda appeared even more beautiful up close. Her eyes were pools of liquid indigo that studied him under perfectly winged brows. Her skin appeared dewy and her black hair tumbled in ringlets past her shoulders. Reagan took her hand, abandoning all thoughts of an early departure. "It's a pleasure making your acquaintance. I hope this will be the start of a lasting friendship."

Amanda nodded. "I'm pleased to meet you too." For years, she had overheard Emily's tirades about that 'Burnsfield brat' and searched for the renegade lurking behind his polite manner.

"I'm flattered you know me, though we've never formally met," Reagan said.

"Of course, I know about you," Amanda blurted. "I've heard about those scrapes you got into—"

"Amanda!" Emily gasped. "I'm sure Mr. Burnsfield doesn't wish to be reminded about such foolish tales!"

Reagan laughed good-naturedly. "It's quite all right. I'm sure the stories were true. However, I can assure you I've long since abandoned such behavior."

Amanda blushed. "I'm sorry. I shouldn't be repeating gossip."

"Nonsense. You couldn't sully my name any more than I have already. And, to show I take no offense, I insist on a dance this evening."

The kindness in his voice caused Amanda to meet the warmth of his open regard. "Certainly," she said as impressions of being held by him flitted through her mind.

Having turned the incident to his favor, Reagan touched her fingers to his lips before joining those already introduced.

Moments later, a hand clamped on Reagan's shoulder. "Well, if it izzn't that bushwhacker Burnsfield! Why aren't you in the backwoods cutting that scrub you call timber?"

Half turning, Reagan grinned at the dapperly dressed fellow and clasped his hand. "Beauregard Barrington, you sorry excuse for a gentleman! How did someone of such questionable heritage get invited?" He leaned forward and whispered. "And where did you find your newest conquest?" he asked, smiling at the young lady Beau had his arm around.

"Sacrebleu! You cast aspersions on my dear ma mère. She'd be wounded to hear you say such blasphemies."

"I think not. I never see you work at your father's hotel. Like all Frenchmen, you spend your time enjoying your lady friends."

"Tis true! Ma mère is most proud I favor her looks and temperament, rather than my English sire."

Reagan folded his arms, considering his friend. "And yet, that very same woman has uttered such insults that your companion would blush if she ever heard what your dear *mama* has called you."

Beau grinned cheerfully. "But, it was all in *French*."

"Still, I've been around long enough to grasp your mother's tongue, and believe me," Reagan said, jabbing Beauregard's chest. "It wasn't pretty."

Pulling his lady companion close, Beau whispered loudly. "Do not believe this jack-a-napes. It's no secret he can twist anything to his advantage."

"Now who's insulting my heritage?"

"La pomme ne tombe pas loin du tronc. The apple never falls far from the tree." Beau shrugged. "Can one truly depart from one's destiny?"

"I can't vouch for French *sots*, but my fate is shaped by my hands only." Reagan refolded his arms, raising a brow. "And, if I recall, many were the times these hands had to save your hide when your wit superseded your sense."

Beauregard laughed, displaying white teeth. "Go fishing with me next Sunday and we'll put them to good use. Quick! Dinner is about to be announced. Will you come next Sunday?"

"Only if you clean and cook what we catch for supper," Reagan said. "Your hands are small, but they're as nimble as your tongue."

Beau grinned as a servant opened wide the dining room doors. "We'll let the chef at father's hotel prepare them," he said. "I've better things to do than handle cold fish."

Once everyone was seated, Reagan noted the most eligible bachelors were strategically positioned near Amanda. Leroy Spelding, the son of a business partner at the Bruester Bank and Trust, held the enviable space to Amanda's right. His pale hair combed straight back accentuated his long nose and wide forehead. He seemed to think his profile gave an aristocratic appearance and bestowed Amanda with its effect throughout the meal. Across the table, Reagan decided to content himself with Mayor Hampton's daughter, Elizabeth, to his left. Though barely in her twenties, he recalled she had assumed at her mother's death hostess duties to her father's many gatherings. Yet, despite their conversation, Reagan found himself continually drawn to Amanda's beauty.

"Reagan, you've not heard a word I've said," Elizabeth pouted, tapping her fork in annoyance. "I asked whether you were interested in attending the dramatic Carnival." She shot a glance at Amanda who held captive Leroy's attention. "It seems everyone is quite taken with Miss Bruester."

"My pardon," he said, dragging back his gaze. "I fear I've become besotted while surrounded by all this beauty. Please allow me to make amends."

Elizabeth searched his face hoping for evidence of a budding attraction. For years she'd secretly desired Reagan's notice, never getting more than the same regard he gave to anyone. Determined not to lose this opportunity, Elizabeth coquettishly lowered her lashes. "Why, if you're truly repentant, Mr. Burnsfield, then of course I forgive you. You may make amends by honoring me with the first dance."

Though Reagan had already intended his first dance to be with Amanda, he hid his chagrin. "It'll be my pleasure," he answered.

chapter 4

After dinner, Amanda's guests retired to the parlor with sherry offered to ladies and stronger libations for men. From across the room, Reagan observed Lorelda Hargrove and Camilla Muelder standing on either side of Amanda. Reagan guessed Lorelda to be nearing her thirties as she typified the never married who were still invited to coming-out balls. Thick set with sparse brows, Lorelda could never be considered pretty. But as fireflies are drawn toward fire, Reagan suspected Lorelda's sole purpose was to be positioned near enough to the flame to attract a firefly of her own.

On the other hand, Camilla was a honey-gold beauty with sparkling green eyes that never ceased moving and whose laugher lilted like music. Though younger than Lorelda, Camilla tolerated and even encouraged Lorelda's presence when the two happened upon the same gathering. If Lorelda suspected her friendship being used to bring out Camilla's beauty, she never let on.

When strains of music beckoned from the ballroom, Leroy, who had been standing near Amanda, became the first to extend her his arm. After she accepted, he escorted her to the dance floor. He turned with a flourish and lifting his leg, displayed what could best be described as a gallop-turn-gallop across the floor. As he reached the far side of the room, other couples joined in, obscuring his clumsy stride and Amanda's pained expression.

Elizabeth spied Reagan walking toward her through the crowd. She subtly lifted her shoulders and by the time he drew close, her neckline had slipped, exposing more cleavage.

"Will you honor me with this dance?" he asked.

"Of course," she said, taking his arm. "I've been waiting. And, you must tell me all about your timber trade. From what I've heard, it sounds most exciting."

Reagan laughed. "Not nearly as exciting as being here," he said. "All winter with a bunch of men, isn't much fun."

"Then, I consider it a privilege to raise your spirits," she said when they entered the ballroom. "In the future, I hope you'll allow me an opportunity to do so again."

On the dance floor, Elizabeth pressed close, inviting a daring view of her bosom. Yet, as they waltzed her ploy went unnoticed and she felt an urgency to snatch his attention.

"I'm so enjoying myself," she said, sighing. I wish Daddy would give balls like this."

"Doesn't the mayor often entertain?" Reagan asked. "He seems to keep busy."

"Those are just stuffy dinner parties for Daddy's old cronies," she said. "I mean *real* parties."

"Oh?" He smiled politely. "I recall Beau mentioning your presence at most events. Maybe you could have your father plan one like those."

Softly, as if it were accidental, Elizabeth's fingers stroked the back of Reagan's neck. "Daddy never cares about including my friends. What I meant, is throw a ball where I can invite only those whom I wish to entertain." Her elation was short-lived and her heart became scored when Reagan looked sharply toward Amanda as Leroy swept her by in a whirl of legs and elbows.

"It seems Miss Bruester has fascinated the lot of you," she said, a snarl creeping into her voice. "And no wonder, wearing such scandalously revealing attire."

"My pardon," Reagan said. "They looked as if they were about to stumble into us. But even if I *were* staring, you could hardly blame Amanda."

"Why not? That dress is designed to seize a man's eyes. I'm shocked she's even wearing that rag."

Reagan didn't speak for a moment and when he did, his voice sounded tight. "Perhaps you'd be doing Amanda a kindness to inform her of her blunder."

"Oh dear! I didn't mean that how it sounded," Elizabeth said, eyes rounded. "I only meant that one's clothing should reflect one's breeding. Amanda must not realize how tawdry her dress looks. At least, I thought Emily should've known. Please, can you forgive my clumsy words?"

"But of course," Reagan said. "Let's forget about any unpleasantness and enjoy our dance."

When the music ended, he returned Elizabeth to her place and though she hoped otherwise, Reagan didn't solicit her company again.

It was well into evening before Reagan found an opportunity to claim his dance with Amanda. Finding her resting on a bench with Beauregard nearby, he took her hand, purposely bumping into the confrère.

"At last, Miss Bruester, a moment when you're not otherwise engaged. May I now have the pleasure of my promised dance?"

"Monsieur Burnsfield, how rude to interrupt," Beau sputtered. "Even an oaf like you can see I'm her escort."

"But, where's your enchanting partner?" Reagan asked, nudging Beauregard farther away.

"Powdering her little nose! Stop that! Look, you *are* an oaf. My shoe has a Reagan-print on it."

"That's because you have very big feet for such a little man. Look." With a foot, he tapped Beau's shoe. "How do you keep from stepping on the toes of all your sweethearts?" He made a show of looking around. "Where did you say she was?"

Amanda touched Beau's arm. "It's all right, Mr. Barrington. I did promise Mr. Burnsfield a dance."

"As you wish, demoiselle," he said, relenting. "Your pleasure is mine."

Grinning at Beau, Reagan helped Amanda rise before tucking her arm under his, striking an unhurried pace. "My mother once told me that her life was never the same after her coming out ball. So, I'm wondering if anything's changed now that you've been presented."

"Well, let's see..." Amanda counted out her fingers. "I've been introduced to so many people and my head is awhirl with jumbled names." At Reagan's upraised brow she quickly added, "Yours excepted, of course."

"Of course," he agreed.

"My feet are protesting the miles I've surely danced." Amanda's second finger took its place beside the first. Reagan consolingly patted her hand and then left it there, deciding he liked the feel of it.

"I've learned there's more than one way to do the Highland Schottische." Up went the third digit. Reagan kept silent about Amanda's miserable luck in finding Leroy her partner when the lively dance began.

"My nerves have calmed considerably," Amanda declared, her little finger making a quartet.

Reaching the dance floor, Reagan took her into his arms. "That, my dear, is because of the repetitious nature of balls. With time, your confidence will grow."

As they swept the floor in perfect cadence, Amanda enjoyed a strange sense of ease in his presence. He didn't exhibit the stuffy mannerisms of her other partners nor did he list why his family name was as distinguished as hers. If anything, he seemed like a man who simply enjoyed her company. "You must've partaken in too many balls to dance this well," she accused, her eyes sparkling.

Reagan wiggled her middle finger. "It only seems that way because your toes are quite numb by now."

Amanda laughed. "By morning, I'll know what it's like to have bruised and achy feet."

"The remedy is to soak them in hot, salty water and a massage to end it with," said Reagan. "I highly recommend it."

At that moment Leroy and his partner whirled by. Craning his neck in their direction, Leroy didn't see a third couple, Beau and Camilla, until too late. As Leroy and Beau collided, Reagan pulled Amanda close and spun away.

Beau teetered on his heels while letting loose a string of French pejoratives. Leroy, red faced and sputtering apologies, righted Beau and Camilla before dancing away with his partner.

Reagan had prolonged his embrace until Amanda's sachet enticed his eyes downward. From his vantage point he fairly devoured the sight of her breasts pressed against his chest. Though he'd maintained a cool reserve while keeping her at arms length, he found it impossible when right below his nose. "Madam," he uttered, feeling his lower belly tighten. "You're a vision of loveliness I'll carry with me forever."

Staring upward, Amanda's heart thudded. "Sir, you can release me. I believe the danger is past."

Reagan's eyes smoldered as he met her gaze. "My dear, your beauty stirs the imagination. I simply made the most of a circumstance because I'm ill advantaged to every swain who's known you longer."

Amanda felt his hold loosen and she quickly put safe distance between them. "A gentleman doesn't take advantage of a lady or a circumstance," she said sharply. "I'm shocked you admitted such a thing. Yet, you can repair your wrongdoing with an apology."

Reagan swung her in a dizzying whirl before grinning. "It's a logical request and I'm happy to do it. I should show remorse, but in truth, my only regret is not making your acquaintance before now."

"Considering your past reputation, I doubt that would've been a possibility," she said. "Perhaps, the gossip is true after all, and I should be wary."

"I've been reformed, remember? Although," he lowered his voice, his eyes once again dipping to her décolletage, "you sorely tempt me to break my promise. Had I known what a delightful morsel you'd become, I'd have come sooner to sample your sweetness."

She became startled as pinpricks followed his gaze over her bosom and when his insinuation sank in, Amanda stiffened with fury. "You think me a temptress?" she choked, pulling away. Her thoughts became jumbled as her initial impressions of him blended with the rake he now appeared to be. This night she had been torturously cinched, trod upon by privileged oafs and now leered at by the one man she thought a gentleman. *This was too much*!

Reaching back, she soundly slapped his face. "I see the tittle-tattle is true after all, Mister Burnsfield.

I fear I've misjudged you. You're a scoundrel of the first sort!"

Dancers halted at the commotion while musicians spluttered into silence. A murmur erupted among those clamoring for a better view as a hush descended around Reagan and Amanda.

Having witnessed the slap, Emily hurried toward the couple now the center of everyone's attention. Her breath labored as she realized the appalling situation. That her daughter had dishonored a guest was disgraceful enough, but in front of all her peers! Emily didn't doubt that before night aged into day, the story would be spread throughout the city.

Without further words, Amanda lifted her hem and fled the ballroom. Emily, having no choice but to follow, hurried after her just as Beauregard skidded to a stop beside Reagan.

"Oo la la!" he whispered. "I think I'm in love!"

Reagan rubbed his jaw. "I'm not sure you'd survive that one's love. She packs quite a wallop."

"Where are you going?"

"To find Mr. Bruester and extend my apologies," he said. "Go back to your dance. Camilla is waiting."

chapter 5

THOMAS BURNSFIELD LOOKED up when his office door opened. "Good morning, Father," Reagan mouthed around a cheroot.

"Since you weren't yet awake for breakfast, I assume the Bruester ball was worthwhile after all," Thomas said.

"Intriguing," he said, removing his cigar before taking a seat. He changed the subject by withdrawing several sheaths and a map from his satchel. "We were right about unclaimed timber along the Cattaraugus River. Bradley registered enough land tracts for several camps."

Reagan anticipated his father's pleasure at his successful mission. Not since taking over registering land tracts had he accomplished such a windfall for the company. He hoped the acquisition would soften news of the withdrawn contract for he'd decided to tell Thomas of the loss today.

Thomas scanned the map. "Well done. We'll start the first camp this fall."

A knock on the door interrupted their conversation moments before the office manager, Irwin Bates, entered. "There's a gentleman here to see you. He says he's from the federal government."

"Give me a few moments, then show him in," Thomas said.

Reagan stubbed his smoke. "I'm sorry, did you have an appointment?"

"No. I wasn't expecting anyone." Removing papers from his desk, Thomas rose and drew up another chair. "If you recall, we've supplied lumber in years past for government steamboats. This may be another such order."

Bates opened the door allowing the agent inside. "Mr. Burnsfield, this is Mr. Raymond Follet."

"Good morning." Follet smiled, extending his hand to Thomas, then Reagan. "I hope my visit isn't an inconvenience."

"Not at all. Please, have a seat."

"Thank you, kindly." Follet sat down and appeared to be busily groping his pockets until he heard the door latch. Quieting his hands, he looked from Thomas to Reagan. "Gentlemen, as a matter of concern, I need to ask that this visit remains private. Not even your man Bates can reveal my identity. Will this be a problem?"

"You can rest assured, Mr. Bates has never breached a confidence," Thomas said. "And neither will we."

"Good. Just a formality, of course, but one must ask." Shifting his weight, the agent cleared his throat.

"As you've surely seen in the papers, there's been increasing hostility between the states ever since Kansas turned bloody. This has the president deeply concerned. After taking counsel with his cabinet, he's decided to fortify our departments in the improbable event of war. It's only a precautionary step but must be kept quiet because the southern states would view his move as aggressive. In the end, we fully expect and pray it'll be a needless arrangement."

"Couldn't Buchanan simply explain his reasons?" Thomas asked. "Secrets have a way of coming back to haunt you."

"It's a ticklish situation. There are those in congress who wouldn't understand the president's actions. The hornet's nest, shall we say, is stirred up enough. With all this talk of secession, it's his hope these operations stay out of newspapers."

"I see." Thomas opened a ledger, his fountain pen poised. "Which department do you represent, Mr. Follet?"

"Both Secretary of the Navy and Department of War." He reached inside his coat pocket and withdrew a folded parchment, handing it to Thomas. "This is an outline of our requirements." While Thomas scanned the paper, Follet turned to Reagan.

"I understand you've recently acquired a large land tract," he began. "Congratulations."

"I didn't realize our company affairs ever made it to Washington," Reagan said.

Follet chuckled. "It's in everyone's best interest to know each others qualifications. If you can meet our needs, we're prepared to award you the largest contracts." He then turned to Thomas. "Also, once you sign, you'll be our sole provider unless and until you couldn't handle any further needs."

"I see," Thomas said again, tapping his pen.

"Perhaps you don't have sufficient resources...?"

"We have resources," Thomas cut in, handing the paper to Reagan. "We'll start immediately. We have a million feet of timber on our docks. We can ship the rest after next spring's harvest."

"Very good." The agent produced two agreements and waited while Thomas and Reagan read the contracts before they signed. Follet offered his hand. "I'll be in touch. Until then, it's been a pleasure."

After the agent left, Thomas placed the contracts in his safe. Worry marked his face.

"Is something the matter, Father?"

"This just makes war seem all the more likely," Thomas said. "Looks like we got these land tracts just in time. I'm leaving it to you to fill these contracts by spring."

Reagan nodded, deciding not to tell Thomas of his own botched contract. The government's order would gain him time. And though these contracts were larger than the one he'd lost, if he didn't replace it, Thomas might never trust Reagan again.

chapter 6

THE CANTONSVILLE PICNIC made a place for friends to gather, eat heartily and doze through the Mayor's annual speech. A platform built in the meadow near the river would refresh the marching band after its trek from town square. And since the picnic marked the end of summer, the townspeople enjoyed a more relaxed atmosphere than any other time of year.

Katherine Burnsfield removed two bread pans from the oven, setting them to cool before retrieving a basket from the pantry. She had finished stacking plates when the housekeeper entered the kitchen.

"Tea is being served in the parlor and Mr. Burnsfield asked to see you," she said, holding open the door.

"Thank you, Sarah," she said, stretching her back. "I didn't realize how late it was." Soon after, Katherine entered the parlor to find Reagan browsing the bookshelves and Thomas reading *The Cantonsville Daily.*

Amy, their daughter of seventeen looked up from the loveseat. She wrinkled her nose. "Mother, must you wear that shabby thing? If anyone saw you in it, I'd just die."

"Well, young lady, instead of doing embroidery, you could help me," she said. "Let's see what *you* wear in a hot kitchen."

"Enough." Thomas held up his hand. "I didn't call us together to hear my two favorite women squabble. I wanted to speak with everyone, so please sit a moment."

Amy scooted over, making room for Katherine as Reagan shelved his book. He then kissed Katherine's cheek and settled into a chair, lighting a cheroot.

Thomas folded his newspaper. "I've been concerned with what's happened at Harper's Ferry and have decided we won't be vacationing in Charleston as planned."

"Oh Daddy, I told everyone we were going to see some real plantations. Lucy Barnett's family traveled there without harm. Surely, we could too."

"That was before Brown's raid. Ever since, the papers have warned other raids are likely. Anyone traveling south could be accused of inducing a slave insurrection. With those kinds of rumors, I'm taking no chances. You ladies will simply have to content yourselves with visiting Philadelphia this year."

"So you think violence will worsen?" Katherine asked.

"I'm not sure. But, it's not worth risking our safety. Charleston will be there next year and the year after that."

Reagan twirled his cigar, causing smoke to spiral like a corkscrew. "I bet those southern boys would take one look at Amy and beat a path to her feet. Maybe we should wait till she's married good and proper rather than chancing a Dixie son-in-law."

The jest missed its target as Amy's sullen expression didn't change. "That's all right, dear," Katherine said as she brushed back her daughter's hair. "We could go shopping like your father suggested. You've wanted new clothes and this would be the perfect opportunity." She looked expectantly at her husband.

"Yes, I suppose, if you promise not to spend all my money," Thomas said, smiling.

"But, I'll look like a ninny to all my friends. I said I'd bring back souvenirs."

"You can tell your friends of our change in plans at the picnic..." Katherine began.

"Oh no!" Springing upward, Amy's sampler fell when she grabbed Katherine's hand and pulled her toward the door. "I forgot the picnic's *tomorrow*. I don't know what to wear!"

After they departed, Reagan picked up the embroidery hoop. "Dinner's sure to be delayed," he said, chuckling. "I hope you realize Amy's hopelessly spoiled."

"I know. I've probably ruined her," Thomas said, grinning. "But then again, I've had no trouble with any man wooing her with his paltry fortune."

"Would you like a drink?" offered Reagan, opening the sideboard. At Thomas's assent, he poured sherry into two glasses, handing one to his father before retaking his seat.

"I guess I never wanted to believe it'd go this far," said Thomas, swirling his drink. "The war, if there's to be one, could light a bonfire if it's discovered we supplied lumber while others were seeking resolutions."

"We're breaking no laws," Reagan said. "I can't see many getting upset about a business deal."

"It's more complicated than that." Thomas got up, tossing the paper into the hearth. "John Brown has become a martyr to those who believe in abolishing slavery. Yet, there are just as many who believe the South has every right to its way of life. Like Mr. Brown, they may be willing to take the law into their own hands. Those are the ones I worry about."

Reagan stubbed his cheroot, stretching his long legs. "I suppose there's always that chance. But as long as we're careful with whom we deal, I see no problems in doing business with the government."

"Just the same, I'm not mentioning it to Katherine. I think it prudent you do the same."

"The election itself may make the point moot," Reagan said. "From what I've read in the papers, there isn't one candidate that'll satisfy either side. Not even Lincoln, though most consider him a dark horse."

"Lincoln!" Thomas snorted. "What do we know about him except he's against slavery spreading to the territories? The very thing the South wants most."

"If war is coming, we might as well turn a profit," Reagan said. "If we don't supply the lumber, someone else will."

Thomas nodded while looking into his drink. In the deepening dusk it appeared like blood and he inwardly suppressed a shiver.

chapter 7

THE CANTONSVILLE PICNIC was about to begin. The band assembled in Town Square while youngsters ran among waiting wagons. From buckboards, bonneted girls dangled their feet while adolescent males jostled each other. On his horse beside the family surrey, Reagan searched for the Bruesters, catching sight of their fringed surrey as the band struck up a tune.

Reagan had looked forward to this day for no other reason than to initiate another encounter with Amanda. Having earlier sent a note of regret for his behavior at the ball, he now believed he could seek her company.

What had started as a ballroom diversion had turned to a hindrance when he couldn't banish her from his mind. Often, he found himself reliving their one shared dance, her beauty awakening lustful cravings that had to be beaten back with iron will. Frustrated that a mere chit, barely out of adolescence could so plague him, Reagan thought seeing her again might cure his fascination. He must know if she were worth pursuing or would become a preoccupation that quickly faded.

It took nearly an hour for the procession to reach the meadow along the river's edge. As the band neared the pavilion, wagons fanned out forming a ring around the platform. While horses were unhitched, baskets were unloaded and children dashed away to play. The womenfolk hastened to claim areas under the willows while toddlers amused themselves on hastily unfurled blankets.

After hobbling his horse, Reagan searched among the crowd until he spotted Amanda shaking out a blanket. He decided his memory hadn't been faulty and her beauty just as flawless as he'd recalled. He leaned against a nearby tree watching as she assisted Emily to a seated position before she turned toward two women walking by. Though the women were shabbily dressed, Amanda smiled and lifted her hand in greeting. It became obvious he wasn't the only one watching when Emily tugged on Amanda's purple-sprigged dress.

"Amanda, get my fan and parasol from the surrey. And stop gaping!" Though spoken low, Emily's rebuke caused startled looks from the two passing by.

"I'm sorry. I wasn't aware..."

"Remember your station! Why must I keep reminding you? You're a Bruester and shouldn't appear familiar with anyone except those of similar birth. It's only proper."

"Mother, please," Amanda whispered. "Others might hear you."

"Never mind them. They're just envious," Emily said, lowering her voice. "Amanda, you don't understand. When I was your age, I too had notions and fancies for the common man. But, they were foolish dreams. You're too young to know who's best for you and as your parent I should be the one to guide you." Emily's voice grew hard as she eyed her own wedding ring. "And here you are, ruining all I've sacrificed for since you were a child. Now, get my things and tell your father to stop talking horses, I want him here."

Amanda hastened to do her mother's bidding, her steps taking her directly toward Reagan. As she rounded the tree, he stepped from his vantage point.

"Why, hello Amanda," he said. "I almost didn't see you. But, since you're headed somewhere, may I escort you?"

Having her gaze on the ground, it took several seconds for Amanda's eyes to travel up the long legs and broad chest before reaching Reagan's face. Her cheeks flushed as the night of the ball flashed through her mind and the same exhilaration filled her as when he asked her to dance.

"I received your apology, which caused no small stir with Mother," she said, stepping around him. "I told her I'd simply overreacted to your teasing. So, no other amends are necessary."

Amanda hurried off, but Reagan caught up with her, touching her arm. "I ask only for a moment," he said.

She stopped abruptly. "You have some nerve, Mr. Burnsfield. Though manners dictate I accept your apology, it doesn't mean I'll give you another chance to be rude."

"Allow me to make amends..."

Amanda poked a finger in his face. "You spoke that night as if I encouraged such comments!"

"Not at all..."

"I suppose it never occurred to you a lady wouldn't permit a second chance. I believed you honorable, but you betrayed my trust."

He grinned suddenly, rubbing his jaw. "And, you properly chastised me. You have permission to smite me twice if I ever forget to be a gentleman again."

Even as her anger kindled, Amanda was reminded how handsome he was. His white shirt, open at the collar and turned at the wrists revealed a man unafraid of labor. Lifting her eyes, Amanda met Reagan's amused look as he caught her examining his person. "If you'll excuse me, I must go," she said.

Reagan held up both hands, dismayed by her stubbornness yet delighted at the challenge. "A truce!" he pleaded. "Please, let's start anew." Lifting his hat, he bowed with a flourish. "How do you do? I'm Reagan Burnsfield and it would be an honor to assist you around these woods." Rising, he covered his heart with his hat, being rewarded with a roll of her eyes. "My greatest desire," he continued, "is to see you forgive the braying ass before you, who most humbly asks your pardon for his behavior."

Amanda's pique ebbed at his ridiculous stance and she played along, hoping none would see their foolish behavior. "Oh, for heaven's sake! Pleased to meet you too." She gave a brief curtsy. "Now put on your hat before someone sees you."

A distinct clearing of someone's throat caused both to turn. "Every time I see you, you are pursuing the affections of my next paramour, no?" Beauregard stepped close, forcing Reagan to step back.

"Hey!" Reagan said, pushing none too gently on Beau's chest. "Don't you have enough diversions of your own?"

"Ah," the Frenchman said, lifting Amanda's fingers. "This rare flower is too delicate to be handled by a rough lumberman like yourself. Gladly will I sacrifice my other enjoyments to instruct Miss Bruester on the finer delights of amour."

"Why Mr. Barrington, I had no idea of your interest. We spoke only once the night of my ball."

Beauregard assumed a humble stance. "Ce n'est que le premier pas qui coûte. It is only the first step that is difficult."

Amanda laughed gaily. "Though I enjoy your banter, it's been said you only use your mother's tongue when flattering a lady."

"My dear, do you doubt my sincerity? Ask Reagan if my heart did not pit-a-pat so, that I dared just one approach at your ball."

"If memory serves me," Reagan said, his eyes boring into the smaller man. "Most of your evening was spent firmly wrapped around another 'delicate flower'."

Beau sighed. "Alas, that one discovered my interests ran also toward her cousin. Both had brothers who convinced me my love for one as well as the other was—shall we say—unhealthy?"

"Within a fortnight I wager you'll have a new interest to entertain with your vast charms. If you'll be so kind to excuse us, *I* was escorting Miss Bruester."

Amanda touched his shoulder. "Mr. Barrington..."

"S'il vous plait, all my friends call me Beau. It'd greatly please me if you'd be my friend." Inclining his head, he gave Reagan an elfish grin before allowing the couple to continue.

"Do you have something against Beau?" Amanda asked. "Twice you've chased him away when he's been nothing but a gentleman."

"I caution you. If you think me a scoundrel, you'll find Beau has the reputation of a rogue." Reagan firmly clasped her elbow as they came upon a patch of weeds. "Many young ladies have had their hearts—and worse—stolen."

Lifting the hem of her skirt, Amanda picked her way through the nettles. "At least he doesn't insult a lady in her own home."

"Nay, he does far worse. He overcomes a woman's natural defenses with his glib tongue and fervent attentions."

"Beau's *your* friend. Do you counsel all the women he fancies?"

"Only those innocent of the ways of men. Beau has a tendency to trifle with women's affections. I wouldn't see you so abused."

Through the trees, Amanda could see George speaking to Thomas while hobbling their horses. Drawing near, she kissed her father's cheek. "Papa, I came to get mother's things and ask you to return to the picnic."

"Forget that a moment," George said. "Come say hello to Thomas Burnsfield."

Offering her hand, Amanda was amazed at the resemblance between Reagan and his father. It crossed her mind that Reagan would look equally handsome in his later years. "Hello, Mr. Burnsfield, it's a pleasure to meet you."

"It's a pleasure indeed," he said, clasping her fingers. "I see Reagan accompanied you. I trust he's being a gentleman?"

Amanda couldn't tell if Thomas knew of the incident at the party, or if the gossip had somehow escaped his ears. She desperately hoped her father hadn't mentioned the event.

"Why yes, so far," she said. "If I find him lacking, I'll be sure to inform you."

Thomas nodded. "Please do. Once I finish thrashing him, I'll turn him over to George."

George's pleasant countenance grew stern as he grasped his lapels. Though no accusations were uttered, Reagan felt the intensity of both men's regard.

Amanda reached for Emily's things in the surrey. "I really must take these back. Shall I tell Mother you're coming?"

"Yes, yes, I'm coming," George said, winking. "It seems I never have a minute to myself."

Thomas laughed, slapping him on the back. "I know what you mean, George. Although Amy's decided she'd rather spend the day with her friends, I'm usually hemmed in when my family's about."

As they returned to the picnic area, Thomas noted the erect strength of his son's back. Though powerfully built, Reagan walked more like a sleek cat than a lumbering bear. It brought to mind that their plans for the lumber camp had been accelerated to fill the government contracts. Even now, wagons loaded with provisions were being secured in a warehouse.

A small, dark corner of Thomas's mind kept turning over the sobering events of recent days. According to the papers, many Southern newspapers advocated secession when it became clear Lincoln was the front-runner. When Lincoln refused to alleviate the South's fear of having slavery restricted, alarm bells rang in Thomas's mind. He felt Follet's appearance at his office indicated how far the North would go in controlling Southern discontent. Despite his decision to accept the contracts, his conscience remained troubled.

With spaces under the trees nearly filled, Leroy Spelding had squeezed his blanket close to Emily and now sat with his bony legs bent like twin arches. Grinning as he spied Amanda, his smile faded when he saw Reagan walking beside her.

"Good morning, Emily." Thomas paused politely as Amanda offered her mother her belongings.

An unsettled look passed over Emily's face before being replaced with her usual brittleness. "Hello, Thomas," she said, slapping open her fan. "You're looking well."

"Amanda's a delight," Thomas continued, "and as beautiful as I remember you at her age."

"That she was," George said, giving Emily a peck on the cheek before sitting beside her.

Amanda sat down, ignoring Leroy's stare as Reagan and Thomas joined Katherine on a nearby blanket. Closing her eyes against light filtering through the trees, Amanda felt the sun suddenly blocked.

Peering upward, she became startled at seeing a green-eyed stranger standing over her.

"Derrick. Why you scoundrel. You came after all." George burst skyward, rapidly pumping the man's arm. "Heavens, I had no idea you'd come this soon. But no matter, you're here. Emily, this is Derrick Banning whom I met while doing business in New York. The moment I arrived, he introduced himself as my escort, assigned by my investment firm. While there, Derrick showed me the sights as well as superb places to dine. In return, I offered him our hospitality."

Emily assessed the nattily dressed man from his stylishly thin mustache to his fashionable suit. She recalled George's venture had culminated in an alliance between the Bruester Bank and Trust and the renowned Bank of New York. Extending her hand, Emily gave her most charming smile. "How do you do, Mr. Banning? Won't you join us?"

"I'd be honored," he said, glancing at Amanda.

With his attention directed at her daughter, Emily made introductions before resuming the conversation. "Tell us, Mr. Banning. What brings you to visit us now? Isn't this the busy season for lending and real estate investors?"

"Why, you're correct, Mrs. Bruester. You prove my theory that behind every successful man is an intelligent woman." Sitting straighter, Emily beamed while he took a seat. "I was due a vacation when Mr. Bruester extended his invitation, so I didn't wait long to visit. Arriving in Cantonsville, I found only your servants at home. They informed me of your quaint summer ritual." He paused as he looked at Amanda. "I hope I'm not intruding and my apologies if I startled your daughter. But, Mr. Bruester described her so enchantingly, I knew I could find you by looking for her."

"You're too kind, Mr. Banning. I'm afraid papa has a mote in his eye when it comes to me," Amanda said.

"Now Amanda, you're my heart's pride. I'm sure Derrick agrees with my right to speak highly of you."

"Of course," Derrick said. "If only I were married, I could boast as well. Unfortunately, I've yet to find a wife."

Emily's face brightened. "Do you have relatives west of Pennsylvania, Mr. Banning? If you do, then perhaps you could visit us more than just this once."

"I'm afraid my family hasn't ventured beyond New York. Which is a shame, now that I see how pleasant a small town can be."

"Our city may be smaller than grand New York," Emily said, the tempo of her fan increasing. "But Cantonsville has all the amenities."

"That's true," George affirmed. "We have theaters, dining halls and so forth." He licked his lips in sudden thirst. "Amanda, break out the tea. It's hotter than..."

"George!" Emily looked horrified.

"Well, darling, it is. And, I didn't get my sarsaparilla this morning, either."

Opening the hamper, Amanda poured drinks from the iced pitcher while Emily continued. "Perhaps your family would consider a holiday here as well," she suggested. "We'd love to meet them to get better acquainted."

"I'll pass on the invitation. Although my father rarely travels, I could try persuading him."

"Life's too short to never pause and smell the roses," George said, smacking his lips. "I never believed in working oneself to an early grave."

"I agree." Derrick stroked his lip, his gaze passing over Amanda. "I pause to admire beauty whenever I happen across it."

"And I appreciated your services while doing business in New York," praised George, remembering. "Why, Derrick never left my side, dropping me at the bank then picking me up each day."

"Your generosity exceeded mine," Derrick said. "For I merely gave direction, but you insisted on paying for all engagements."

"Bah, t'was nothing. The venture was exceedingly successful. I spent a pittance of what I profited by my investments."

"It seems your picnic is about to start," Derrick said. He stood and touched his hat. "If you'd excuse me, I need to refresh myself. I left my bags with one of your servants and I'd like to get settled."

"You may stay as long as you wish," Emily said. "Please inform Wills, our butler, you're to occupy the guest rooms."

Derrick raised Amanda's hand to his lips. "Until this evening."

After he left, Emily fluttered her fan. "He's such a nice gentleman. I hope he finds his stay agreeable. Don't you agree, George?"

"Certainly, dear, I'll do my best to see he has a pleasant stay."

"We must all do our part. After all, he's used to the highest accommodations," Emily said, looking pointedly at her daughter. "Amanda, this'll be a golden opportunity to employ all the graces you've learned at school."

Though it remained unspoken, Amanda believed she'd just been assigned the first of many grown-up duties she was now expected to perform.

chapter 8

REAGAN SPENT THE day after the picnic in the study. On the desk before him were lists of expenditures lying next to a map.

"Hello, Reagan," Thomas said as he entered then leaned over his son's shoulder. Spying the figures, he plucked up two sheets. "What's this?" he asked, scanning the first page.

"Those are supplies I'm taking to New York."

"And this?" Thomas raised the second sheet.

"That's the new equipment I'm ordering since we've none to spare from our other camps."

"But son, you've already exceeded the original budget. Bradley's to receive one fourth the land anyway, so why so much equipment?"

Reagan took a deep breath. "Because, I purchased Bradley's share."

"You did what?"

"I bought his portion with my money. I am however, using company money for all the rest."

Thomas stared at his son. "I can't believe you'd spend the camps allotment without even discussing it with me!" he said, choking. "Did you forget our agreement?"

"I can explain-"

"You're damn right you will!"

"There's something I should've told you months ago," Reagan said, leaning back. "The deal I made with The Marine Dock Company fell through. I tried finding another buyer, but it seems no one else needs lumber right now. If it weren't for the government contracts, we would've run short of revenue."

"I don't understand. That lumber was transported last month. If the contract fell through, then where did it go?"

"I found an exchange broker from Chicago who was willing to take the lumber. At a substantial loss, however."

Thomas's stunned expression prompted Reagan to continue. "I went to the Bruester Bank and Trust and took out a loan to cover expenses. It's been deposited into our account. I'm sorry. I thought I could fix my mistake before it went this far. It'll never happen again."

"Why didn't you tell me sooner? Perhaps, we could've found a solution by now," Thomas said, tossing the papers. "With the country in turmoil, now isn't the time for added expenses."

"Our solution is to produce more lumber," Reagan said. "With Bradley's cut we can set up one major camp and several smaller camps farther inland. Once we sell the extra lumber, I'll be able to repay the loan and replace the lost revenue." He touched his father's arm. "I intended to tell you once everything was in place.

"That's all well and good, but how will more lumber help if we don't have a buyer?"

"Because Follet's last missive promised additional contracts if we had more lumber to sell," Reagan said.

Crossing his arms, Thomas sat on the desk. "The mill is running continuously now. Come spring, the added logs will bog the river and rot before they're processed. How do you propose we mill the timber before it molders?"

Reagan smiled. "We're going to build another mill."

Thomas blinked, almost falling off his perch. "*Another* mill? Good Lord! Building another mill would drain our finances and if war came, our operations would slow right along with the economy."

"I believe it'll be the best investment we ever made. The amount of lumber Follet wants should keep us busy for a year, even with both mills running. After that, we could well afford a break in production."

"You know Reagan, without these contracts you wouldn't have considered a second mill. What'll we do with the other mill once the demand ends?"

"Once the war is over, I expect there'll be future contracts for rebuilding whatever gets destroyed. By then, we'll be solvent enough to sell our pine at the lowest price."

"That's possible," Thomas said. "However, even that won't last forever. The demand is bound to fall off."

"When that happens, we'll shut down whatever lines are no longer needed. It'll be no different than our existing mill. So, what do you think? Can I wire Follet and tell him we'll accept more contracts?"

Rubbing his lip, Thomas mulled over the idea. "I'll give my consent on two conditions," he said finally. "One, you send me the blueprints and await my approval. And two, you stop this flagrant spending. You may have taken out a loan, but we produce lumber, not currency."

Reagan grinned. "The blueprints will be ready next week. We should be able to break ground this fall."

Thomas sorted through the scattered papers. "I'll approve the additional monies once I've reviewed it on paper." He tapped a finger on the desk. "From now on, I'll expect a written proposal before you take any more liberties with the company's future." With that final admonishment Thomas left with an uneasy feeling about the enormity of the deeds taking place.

chapter 9

As September waned, the early morning chill often preceded midday heat, making it a difficult choice between wearing a thin frock or heavy cloak. Even more problematic to the citizens of Cantonsville were speeches of traveling orators who spoke in support of their presidential candidates. Crowds cheered if in agreement, but just as frequently disagreements broke out moments before fists found their marks against boisterous jaws. Whether the nation moved toward war or peace depended on the four-way contest of the presidential elections. Mindful of his heavy investment, Reagan judged that his fortune would be guaranteed with a Lincoln victory. He determined that when the time came, he would cast his ballot for the backwoods Kentucky lawyer.

The same day Reagan received a shipment of building materials, hired workers laid cobblestones from the road to the new mill site. The plans called for the site to be farther from town than the old mill but close enough for short travel between the two mills.

As news of the construction spread, Reagan found that paying his accounts off before the required dates kept prying questions at bay. Soon, money flowed out as fast as it came in.

A few weeks later, Thomas sat down to review the latest invoices. Within minutes he had angrily left his desk to seek out his son. He found him on a knoll overlooking the mill site. For a few moments neither spoke as they observed the work in progress.

"It's cold," Thomas said, frowning. "Too chilly for this time of year."

"I take it you didn't come to see the mill," Reagan said.

"I went over the budget this morning."

"Oh. Yes, well I can explain that."

"Can you?" he bit out. "I distinctly asked you not to squander our money. Yet you disregarded my wishes. I happen to know your personal funds are nearly gone. The business allotment is *completely* empty, and what I loaned you is surely spent by now! Is it your purpose to run our business into the ground? Because personally, I don't know where you're going to get the coin to finish this project. Furthermore, I don't find this the place to discuss the issue, but since you're just as scarce at home as the office, I'm forced to seek you out!"

"I planned to go over the figures with you today," Reagan answered calmly.

"Then let's retire to a place more private."

"There's something I must do first. When I return, I promise to go over everything with you."

Thomas labored to restrain his fury. "I don't care what damnable plans you've made! I want an explanation. If not in the privacy of my office, then here, now."

"First of all, I've no intention of ruining the company," Reagan said, glancing at his father. "In fact, I'll have all the money we need by Christmas."

"How? Our coffers are nearly empty!"

"By marrying it."

Had Reagan suddenly sprouted horns, Thomas couldn't have looked more shocked. "You-you're what?" he said, lifting his hands. "Your mother keeps dinner warm every night because you haven't the courtesy to show up. You've abandoned all other work save this mill, and now you're telling me you're getting married? Reagan, what's gotten into you?"

"That's the business I have to tend. You see, I'm going to marry Amanda Bruester. Once we're wed, I'll be able to tap into her dowry. And, if that proves inadequate, as George's son-in-law, I'll obtain additional loans from the Bruester Bank and Trust." He raised a brow. "Are you satisfied now?"

"Marry by Christmas? Hell, Reagan, you haven't even begun courting the girl, and it's now October. Furthermore, it seems Mrs. Bruester has other plans for her daughter. Have you forgotten their guest, Derrick Banning? He's being introduced to all their friends and seems firmly wedged in Emily's good graces. How do you hope to woo and then wed Amanda in the space of two months?"

"Don't worry. I'll find a way," Reagan said as he mounted his horse. He then rode away, leaving Thomas more exasperated than ever.

chapter 10

CRISP LEAVES WHIRLED around Reagan's feet as he sounded the knocker at the Bruester home. A manservant soon led Reagan to the parlor where a piano ceased playing when he entered.

Emily sat on the divan stitching a sampler while Derrick leaned against the piano where Amanda sat, her hands against the keys.

Gabriella Bruester, George's older sister, balanced a cup of tea in a nearby chair. "Well, if it isn't the handsome son of Thomas Burnsfield!" Fixing her gaze on Reagan, the elder set her teacup down. "Do come in and join our little gathering. My niece was just entertaining us with her musical talents."

"Please, have a seat," Emily said, jabbing her tapestry with sudden, unnecessary enthusiasm.

As Reagan took a chair, Gabriella gave an audible huff. "Really, Emily, you're manners are slipping. I don't believe these men have been introduced. Reagan, this is Derrick Banning, an associate of George's. It seems they became friends while my brother did business in New York. Derrick's been visiting these past weeks, though I daresay, his employer must be the lenient sort to let him miss so much work."

"How do you do?" Derrick nodded before smiling at Gabriella. "I've notified my employer about extending my stay. He's agreed, due to the venture I'm pursuing."

The meaning wasn't lost on Reagan as Derrick's eyes followed Amanda while she rose to pour tea for their newest guest. "Beauregard tells me you'll be leaving soon," she said, handing Reagan a cup.

Emily brightened. "You're going away? Will it be a long absence?"

"I'm afraid Beau's tongue waggles more for entertainment than accuracy," Reagan said, inwardly fuming at Beauregard's meddlesome nature. "I'm returning from camp next month."

"What sort of camp?" Derrick asked, eyeing Reagan's hands.

"I believe it's called a lumber camp," Emily said. "Mr. Burnsfield cuts down trees for his livelihood."

Gabriella squawked, thumping her cane on the carpet. "Emily! I'll not stand having honest labor disparaged. Some of my best investments were in the founding of that company. Thomas Burnsfield and his son have a very prosperous lumber business."

"Thank you, Madame Bruester," Reagan said. "Father always appreciated his early financiers."

Derrick inspected his own manicured nails. "But of course, lumber is a most necessary resource. Without that," he smirked, "what would we sit on?" Grinning at his own cleverness, Derrick was rewarded with a burst of tittering before Gabriella's glare silenced Emily.

Knowing Reagan would be traveling soon, Emily more calmly plied her needle. "How is your dear mother?" she asked. "I haven't seen Katherine since the picnic."

Reagan took a polite sip of tea before answering. "Very well. In fact, mother sent me to ensure Amanda received her invitation for tonight's dinner. One was sent, but we haven't received an answer."

"We received Katherine's card," Emily said without looking up. "However, Amanda draws so many requests, it's impossible to accept them all."

"Mother expected as much. That's why she decided a personal invitation was in order. Amy's anxious to meet Amanda since she was too young to attend the ball. This would give them a chance to become acquainted. Don't you agree, Mrs. Bruester?"

With Amanda dutifully responding to the many engagements since her coming-out ball, Emily had deliberately kept tonight open for a quiet evening and could think of no excuse to deny his request. "Why of course," she said, smiling weakly. "We're delighted Amanda will be received into your home."

Amanda sipped her tea, wondering if Reagan was up to more folly. Inwardly, she welcomed a reprieve from Derrick, her increasingly attentive guest. Of late, he had pressed her for more than polite companionship, which Emily seemed too willing to allow.

“Please thank Madam Burnsfield for her invitation,” Amanda said. “I look forward to meeting your entire family.”

“I’ve interrupted long enough,” Reagan said, nodding toward Emily before standing to take Gabriella’s hand. “It’s been a pleasure, madam. Can I call upon you to further our friendship?”

“Harrumph! If it weren’t for my niece, I’m sure you wouldn’t grace my parlor. But for Amanda’s sake, I say come anytime.” Gabriella inspected Reagan from head to heels, noting the powerful frame beneath finely cut clothes. “And tell Thomas he’s been neglecting his benefactors if he’s allowed his son to grow into a man and not keep me informed! I expect an invitation within a fortnight so I can meet the rest of your family.”

“I’ll relay the message,” Reagan assured before extending his hand to Amanda. “Until this evening?”

When he touched her fingers, the memory of sturdy arms guiding her across the dance floor replayed itself in unbidden pleasure. The path of her imagination was less than ladylike as she wondered what it would be like to be kissed by him. Suffused with warmth only he seemed to cause, Amanda withdrew her hand.

Gabriella noted the exchange and promptly decided Reagan possessed even more determination than his father had as a young man. For the first time in many years, Gabriella felt pity for her sister-in-law, for it seemed Emily was destined to again feel bitterness against a Burnsfield.

The spinster remembered a youthful Emily Winfield who had been openly courted by the timorous Bruester heir, but secretly yearned for the handsome upstart whose empire would be built on the foundation of ready lumber.

chapter II

PLEASED BY REAGAN'S announcement that Amanda would be their dinner guest, Katherine hoped her son's enthusiasm would remain strong and not fade like it had with previous interests. As a mother, Katherine knew he was admired for his tall form and attentive manner and that he had no trouble finding women with whom he could share social events. However, she'd noted their idle chatter soon wearied him and his attention eventually waned. Despite his trifles with the fairer sex, his penchant for protecting those unable to defend themselves only increased his attractiveness. It had also led to Reagan's friendship with Beauregard Barrington.

Katherine remembered that as a teen, Reagan had happened upon Beau being thrashed by two tormentors. He had halted the scuffle, but not before blackening both their eyes for attacking the smaller boy. Henceforth, Beauregard had considered Reagan his brother, shielding the hard-knuckled lumberjack from the slights of others with his razor sharp wit. As their friendship grew, so did their camaraderie; whether hunting or playing cards, both appeared well suited to the other.

Promptly at six, the Burnsfield carriage stopped in front of the Bruester manse. The driver placed the step for Reagan who a few minutes later brought Amanda to the carriage.

"My dear," he said, extending his arm toward the empty carriage. "Your envoy has arrived."

She laid a hand on his sleeve. "Are you to be my guard of honor? I thought Amy would've accompanied you."

"Honor and I alone, will have the privilege of escorting you," Reagan said while aiding her into the carriage. Settling into the cushions of the opposite seat, he allowed himself a more personal appraisal of Amanda. If possible, she seemed lovelier with each encounter. "Have I told you yet today, how beautiful you are?" he asked, striking a sincere tone.

"Be careful, sir. You're dangerously close to where you erred the night of my ball." She canted her head, eyes twinkling. "Poor mother couldn't take another refusal from me to explain your offense."

"I never did thank you for that courtesy," Reagan said. "Without that kindness, I'm sure you wouldn't now be gracing my presence."

"Mayhap, it was a mistake," Amanda teased as the coachman climbed aboard, swaying the carriage. "I only spared myself the embarrassment of repeating your words." Instead of replying, he only smiled, leaving Amanda to wonder if he were really sorry for his behavior.

Responding to the slap of the reins, the horses launched forth, causing Amanda to suddenly pitch forward. Reagan instinctively caught her by the arms, holding her upright between his knees as she stared at his mouth, now close to hers.

"Oh!" she whispered, her gaze slowly rising. It was one thing to banter lightly at arms length, quite another to feel his warm breath caressing her cheeks.

Time swept by as Reagan's gaze became trapped in her vivid blue eyes. Ensnared by her perfume, he neither drew her close nor set her aright as he fought the urge to kiss her softly parted lips. Though courting Amanda had turned into a business venture, images of her soft and yielding invaded his thoughts even as his mind urged restraint. Had the prize been less crucial, he might've risked the trespass. With reluctance, he set her onto her seat where Amanda busied herself straightening her skirt.

"I-I'm so sorry! I didn't mean to topple onto you," she stammered.

Reagan chuckled as he flexed his now empty fingers. "Rest assured, madam. The pleasure was all mine."

Mortified by the rush of pleasure she had felt in his arms, Amanda fixed her eyes on the passing scenery. She had earlier decided to feel no more than polite disinterest when he was near, not realizing how impossible it would be when her heart fluttered at every new encounter.

"Why don't you tell me about your house guest, Mr. Banning?" Reagan said, breaking the silence. "I've heard he's a broker trying to establish business dealings with your father's bank."

"That's true." Amanda looked relieved by Reagan's change of subject. "As you know, father met him in New York. Recently, Derrick proposed some kind of venture between The Bank of New York and the Bruester Bank and Trust. Though I don't know the details, I heard father say it's something he'll consider."

"What about his family? Doesn't he have obligations at home?"

"Derrick's told mother on many occasions he'll receive his inheritance when he turns thirty. Until then, he works to support himself though his father still manages his finances. I suppose being an heir is what allows him to extend his visit. That, and the hope of a new business deal."

Reagan perceived the swain also had more than a passing interest in Amanda. "Surely his business here doesn't occupy his every moment. What does he do with the rest of his time?"

Amanda gave a short laugh. "I've been charged with entertaining Mr. Banning. Mother feels it's a good lesson in hospitality."

"Can't he find his own amusements?" Reagan burst out. "A gentleman shouldn't expect his host to provide for his every waking moment."

"Derrick's been introduced to several families and at times accompanies father to the bank. So, I'm not perpetually engaged. However, if I recall, I *have* met a man who was exceedingly indelicate, who took advantage of my dance with him."

"Which you promptly corrected," he said with a smile. Reagan again shifted conversation and Amanda listened as he described his upcoming journey as well as the progress of the mill.

On reaching the Burnsfield home, Reagan assisted Amanda from the carriage and into the hall where Katherine and Amy awaited.

"Welcome to our home," Katherine said, signaling a servant to take their wraps. "Reagan informed me this afternoon that I'd sent you a dinner invitation, though I've no memory of picking up a pen."

"Why Mother," Reagan cut in. "You've said many times that I could extend an invitation in your name. Does it really matter who did the asking?"

"Of course not. We're delighted Amanda's here. Right now, your father's in the study," Katherine said. "He's asked that you see him as soon as you get home. Hurry now, or dinner will be delayed as I told Thomas he had til half past six. In the meantime, we'll take Amanda to the parlor."

Turning on his heel, Reagan headed down the hall and into the study. "Hello, Father." He withdrew a match from a nearby tinderbox before retrieving a cigar. "You wanted to speak with me?"

"You didn't return to the office," Thomas said, lowering his paper.

"Yes, I know. I had to pack. Besides, I had that engagement I spoke of earlier." Reagan took a seat, grinning around his lit cigar. "By the way, Amanda is dining with us tonight."

"So I've heard." Thomas looked accusingly at his son. "I think this scheme of yours is preposterous. I've a mind to put a stop to it."

"I wouldn't do that if I were you," cautioned Reagan as he exhaled an aromatic puff. "Our future rests upon my success."

"Damn you for putting us in this situation! How do you think Amanda would feel, knowing you wanted to marry her for her dowry?"

"I don't intend on telling her *that*," Reagan said, studying his cigar. "I need a wife. I want a family. And, coincidentally, I have use for Amanda's dowry. Besides, it'll be repaid soon enough."

"Suppose she doesn't wish to marry you," Thomas said. "What if her heart's set on someone else?"

Derrick Banning's smirking visage loomed in Reagan's mind. "That's a possibility, of course. I've got the impression the Bruester houseguest is after the same prize. But, I will win."

"Dammit, Reagan, this isn't a game! Amanda deserves a husband who'll love her, not what's in her bank account."

"Do you think I'm blind?" Reagan said, looking amazed. "Amanda's beautiful. She lacks none of the qualities I would naturally seek."

"When I said love, I wasn't referring to the marriage bed," Thomas said. "Attraction eventually wanes and then you're left with each other faults and all. Being ill matched will make your union a weight to be born rather than a journey to be shared. I've seen what that kind of marriage can do to a person."

Reagan blew smoke in a lazy spiral that partially hid the disappointment on his father's face. "Love wasn't necessary when nuptials were arranged in times past," he reasoned. "Marrying Amanda would give me everything I want. The rest will come later."

"It's not that I disapprove of her. I simply have no desire to see her innocence ruined." In the silence, the mantle clock chimed. Thomas rose, feeling a heaviness that was becoming all too familiar. "For now, I'll hold my peace. Come, let's see if the rest of the family approves of your choice."

Entering the dining room, Reagan noted an additional place setting and turned to see Beauregard escorting the women from the parlor. Beau beamed as he spied the pained look on Reagan's face.

"Ah, my friend. You'll not believe what I found completely unguarded in your very own parlor!" An eruption of giggles served only to encourage the Frenchman, causing him to become even more animated. "Three gems of such exquisite splendor," he said, capturing Amy's hand. "This blossom has eyes the color of the tiger. And such magnificent hair!"

As Amy gasped in delight, Beau ogled one eye and began circling Katherine. "Telle mère, telle fille. Like mother, like daughter." Blushing, Katherine smoothed her hair as Thomas chuckled nearby. "Oui! Mr. Burnsfield makes me a ve-rry jealous man!"

"But this one." Beau's eyes shone as he stopped near Amanda. "Hair the color of onyx and a smile to capture one's heart." Stepping near, he splayed his hands. "As I live, I must know if your attentions are already taken!"

Reagan couldn't believe his ill luck. It seemed the wily Frenchman was eternally thwarting his purposes. Though Beau had never before pressed one of his love interests, Reagan feared his friend was about to mount a vigorous offense. All the signs were present, the rapt attention, flattery, and ingratiating charm, which until now had only amused Reagan.

"Hello Beau," Thomas said, smiling. "It seems you've discovered a gold mine of feminine beauty." He kissed Katherine's cheek before putting his arm around her waist. "I trust you'll direct your attention to the *unmarried* ones?"

Beau touched his hand to his heart. "My admiration for monsieur's lady won't let me overstep my bounds when there are ample diversions to keep me occupied."

Everyone laughed except Reagan. "You must join us Beau," Katherine said. "I've taken the liberty of placing you beside Amanda. How fortunate you came to visit on the eve of Reagan's departure."

"If you insist," he said, a pleased look crossing his face. "I'd be delighted to stay for dinner."

A helpless frustration gripped Reagan. Not only would Beau be an unwanted distraction, the Frenchman could very well press his own intentions on Amanda while he sat nearby.

Reagan approached the table and held out Amanda's chair. "For our guest of honor," he said. Graciously accepting, she failed to see Reagan glaring at Beau or Thomas's smile as he seated Katherine.

Unperturbed, Beau seated Amy before taking his place beside Amanda.

"How's your father these days?" asked Thomas, pouring a glass of wine. "Has he finished renovating the Barrington Hotel?"

"Mais oui," Beauregard said. "With our new kitchen, you must come and experience real French cuisine. Papa's hired a new Master Chef whose talent rivals those in New Orleans."

Thomas poured wine into Katherine's glass before handing the bottle to Reagan. "I've sampled spiced dishes in French Quarter bistros. It's some of the most unique food I've ever tasted."

Reagan filled his goblet before splashing a small amount in Amy's glass. Smiling in petty satisfaction, he set the wine out of Beau's reach, forcing him to stretch for the bottle.

Beau poured a glass for Amanda before pouring a sizable amount for himself. "Bah! The Creole's mutilate the delicacy of artful cooking. Their seasonings burn the tongue and water the eyes. It's a disgrace to all who are French!"

"But isn't Cajun the common method of French provincials?" Reagan goaded, enjoying Beau's agitation.

"Oui, common is correct!" Beau snapped his fingers. "Like that, vulgar and unrefined." Seeing Reagan's overly cheerful expression, Beau calmed his voice. "That's why I insist you sample the finest food in all of Cantonsville." He gestured around the table. "Ma mère will post the invitations." Grinning at Reagan, he continued. "So sad you'll not be joining us. You will be gone, no?"

"Not for long. Perhaps you could wait for my return."

"One never knows when Reagan returns from the timberline," Beau said, waving. "Of late, his work is more important than his friends. We'll proceed without him."

"Between building the new mill and outfitting camp, I've a great deal to do," Reagan said, smiling tightly. "Surely, you can understand it requires my time and attention."

"He who chases two hares, catches neither," Beau said gaily. "A lesson I've recently learned with the Barrett cousins."

Reagan chuckled with the rest, but soon felt vexed he couldn't capture Amanda's attention. Amy peppered her with endless questions about her ball while Thomas and Katherine kept a steady dialogue about her school years in Baltimore. Throughout dinner she proved the perfect guest, giving heed to whoever spoke, then graciously responding. He recognized his mother's approval and saw that Amanda had equally charmed Thomas. She looked comfortable even around Beau's fawning overtures. Something had to be done!

"Amanda plays the piano beautifully," Reagan blurted as dinner ended. "I think it'd be nice if she played for us." Hoping Beauregard would excuse himself, Reagan gave his friend a look with unmistaken meaning.

"Well then, if everyone's finished, let's retire to the parlor," Katherine said, laying down her napkin. "Will you be joining us Beau?"

Ignoring Reagan's look, Beau nodded. "I'd be delighted."

As Thomas escorted Katherine through the doorway, they failed to see Reagan round the table and nudge the Frenchman aside. "Excuse me!" Knocking away Beau's hand, he grasped the back of Amanda's chair.

"Reagan!" Amy gasped. "What's gotten into you?"

Amanda also looked at Reagan. "I believe I was in perfectly safe hands with Mr. Barrington."

"I'm afraid I must insist," Reagan said to Beau. "Miss Bruester has been entrusted to my care, not yours."

"But, of course," Beau said, turning toward Amy. "I'm delighted to assist my little dove." But once he and Amy entered the hall behind everyone else, he voiced his displeasure.

"Amateur!"

Amy glanced at him curiously. "Is my brother always this rude to you around ladies?"

"Only when he's around this one, ma petite," Beau said, indicating Amanda with his uplifted chin.

Lowering her voice, Amy whispered. "Did she *really* slap Reagan at her ball?"

A wide grin split Beau's face. "Most soundly!" he sighed. "T'was the highlight of the evening and a memory often enjoyed."

"By the look of things, he deserves another whack," she said. "I can't believe his behavior."

"Don't be overly concerned," Beau said, patting her hand. "It's a disease I've experienced many times myself. Your brother is infected, though he doesn't yet know it. I'm only helping to open his eyes. Someday he'll thank me. But as yet, he thinks me his enemy."

"Let's hope you cure him. I've never seen him so agitated," she replied.

Once everyone was seated in the parlor, Amanda took the piano bench and tested the keys. In a nearby chair, Reagan envisioned his courtship slipping away with each passing hour. He wasn't amused at the interest Thomas paid at his lack of progress and imagined there'd be precious little help in the matter from him.

"What shall I play?" asked Amanda.

"Do you have any favorite pieces?" asked Katherine.

A popular tune soon filled the room with a melody that had everyone humming and tapping their toes. Beauregard, in a show of genteel flair bowed to Amy before taking her hands. In brotherly fashion, he demonstrated a few steps and then picked up the pace to match the tempo. Amy giggled as she spun around the room completely unaware of the scowl forming on her brother's brow.

Sinking deeper into his chair, Reagan watched the unfolding gaiety and silently cursed for tomorrow he'd leave with no advantage gained. It was one thing to match wits with an outsider like Derrick Banning, quite another to be bested by his own friend. He knew there was no accounting for Amanda's heart. If she found appealing Beauregard's flattery, his own overtures might lack sufficient charm.

Amanda ended with a flourish while Beau spun then whirled his partner in a final pirouette. Amy clapped her hands as the Frenchman bowed his thanks before turning to Amanda.

"Such gifted fingers!" he quipped, bringing her hand to his lips.

Amanda laughed. "My music tutor would disagree, having declared my abilities unfit for any respectable parlor."

"Nonsense! That was wonderful," exclaimed Katherine. Recognizing Reagan's gathering fury, she gave him a warning frown. "Do play another piece, won't you Amanda?"

Amanda smiled as the mantle clock chimed the hour half past eight. "Although I'd love to, I must be getting home."

"Surely you could stay for some fresh tea. It's become our favorite after-dinner pastime," Katherine said, leaning forward.

"Oui mademoiselle, do not depart," Beauregard urged. "You could play another tune while we wait for refreshments."

"Yes, stay," said Amy, joining Amanda on the bench. "I could learn another dance."

"Another time, I promise," Amanda said. "I had a lovely time. Thank you for having me."

"We'll expect you again," Katherine said warmly. "You're welcome anytime."

"I'll tell our driver to bring around the carriage," Thomas said, rising. "He's in the kitchen with Sarah."

Reagan nearly vaulted from his seat. "Have him ready the surrey instead. I'll be taking Miss Bruester home."

"But ami," Beau said, grinning. "If you use the smaller conveyance, how can I join you?"

Reagan's face darkened. "If you've lost the buggy you came in, our driver's still available."

"Non," Beau said. "On second thought, another time. I'm looking forward to Madam Burnsfield's tea."

"Reagan dear, sit a moment," Katherine said, patting the sofa cushion beside her. "I've yet to hear of the plans for your trip. We were so engaged at dinner, I forgot to ask. Amanda, this chair next to the sofa is more comfortable than the bench. Why don't you rest yourself while we wait?" As Reagan joined her on the sofa, he found Amanda sitting near him for the first time. "Thomas, tell the driver to put warm furs in the surrey," Katherine continued. "It's a bit nippy tonight."

"I'll be right back," Thomas said.

As he made his way to the kitchen, Thomas wondered if Reagan could actually succeed in making Amanda his daughter-in-law. The thought did not displease him even as a distant recollection stirred, one that had taken place almost two score ago. Though faded, he recalled the bitter memory of having his own proposal rejected because he had little wealth. Her words still echoed in his mind, "...Papa said he'd disown me! If I defy him, I'll lose my inheritance!"

"I can replace anything you have," Thomas had reassured her. "Not right away, but in a few years."

She had shaken her head. "It's too humiliating. We'd live like paupers! You must go and ask Papa again!" He had pleaded, but nothing could convince her he could restore her position if she were cut from her father's will. Unable to bear being rebuffed again, Thomas had eventually found solace in the arms of another.

Strands of nostalgia tugged at Thomas's heart as he mused how Emily's daughter could still become his own after all.

chapter 12

BEAUREGARD JOINED THE Burnsfield's in the hall as they bid Amanda farewell. While a servant brought their wraps, Amy touched Amanda's arm. "I don't know what you see in my brother," she said, wrinkling her nose. "But, I hope you come again even if he stays gone all winter." Catching her words, Reagan swatted at his sister's backside but she avoided the cuff by skittering behind her parents.

Beau took advantage of Reagan's distraction and lifted Amanda's hand. "It's my good fortune to have enjoyed your company once again. Au Revoir, mademoiselle."

"Good tidings to you, Mr. Barrington," Amanda said as she accepted her jacket. "It's been a pleasure."

Beau grinned at Reagan over his shoulder. "Don't be gone overlong, my friend. I fear such a flower of savoir vivre will not long last."

Reagan furrowed his brow, thinking, *the little weasel is practically proclaiming his intentions!*

"I consider myself duly warned. Now, if you'll excuse us," he said, giving a halfhearted smile. "We'll take our leave." He led Amanda to the porch, listening with satisfaction as the door closed behind them.

"That was quite an experience," she said, feeling the cold settle over her like an icy shawl. "I had no idea an evening could be so extraordinary."

Reagan assisted her into the surrey. Then climbing in, he unfolded a fur pelt, spreading it over her knees. "I have to confess, I was unhappy to find Beau a guest at our table," he said.

"Seething seems a more accurate word, Mr. Burnsfield. Why, you were wretchedly rude during dinner as well as in the parlor."

Relaxed now that he had Amanda to himself, he smiled while snapping the reins. "Was it that noticeable? I'm afraid I'm not a gracious loser when Beau intrudes where he's not wanted."

"Intruding? Mr. Barrington was merely being clever and charming," she said as he eased the conveyance into the lane.

"As charming as a cobra," Reagan snorted. "As long as I've known him, Beau's sown mischief. But until now, I've never felt the bite of his foolishness."

"After tonight, I'll not be surprised if you've so offended him, he'll not visit your table again," Amanda said, her fingers sinking into the fur. "Why, he must think you've taken leave of your senses."

"Hardly. I doubt that anything can insult your Mr. Barrington, especially when it comes to his trifling with every pretty skirt he sees."

"I can scarcely be considered a-a twitching skirt," she said, her voice growing irritated. "I certainly didn't encourage Mr. Barrington to be ought but himself."

"Well, you didn't dampen his tomfoolery in the least! I won't be surprised if he pursues you while I'm gone."

"What if he does?" Amanda's chin rose. "Who are you to say yea or nay to whomever I choose to entertain?"

"I only wish to protect you from scoundrels," he replied. "Beau fancies himself a ladies man. It's my duty to warn you."

"I've yet to see the menace, Mr. Burnsfield. You have a lot of gall for someone who's turned his foot at every corner."

Reagan gripped the reins tightly. "It's no secret the man dotes on every female he sees. Yet, none hold his favor for long. I hope you realize his attentions are nothing more than passing interest." He glanced toward her as if expecting her to agree, but was met with stony silence. Reagan realized his words weren't serving his cause and tried again. "Amanda..."

"You insolent whelp!" she cried, drawing away. "You strut and preen in front of me like a rooster, all the while accusing a true gentleman of buffoonery!"

Viewing her up thrust chin, Reagan perceived he was the cause of his own undoing. "I apologize madam for putting you in a temper," he said, sighing. "I'm at a loss for my ill manners."

"Ill manners aren't the half of it," she sputtered. "You treat me as if I were some kind of possession."

"No, you're more like a gem of exquisite beauty," he said softly. "I'm forever losing my head in your presence. Can you forgive me?"

When she didn't answer Reagan reached over and laid his hand over hers. "Amanda, you're shivering!" he burst. "Why didn't you tell me you were cold? Come closer where I can keep you warm."

"I'm close enough, thank you," Amanda said. "I might find your protection as insufferable as your words.

"This is ridiculous. Come here," he said. "There's no sense in you catching your death." He drew Amanda against him, feeling an undeniable rightness in holding her. "Now, stay put until I get you home."

Amanda willed herself to ignore her quickening pulse. Sitting stiffly, she listened to the hoof beats that steadily drew her home. But even after she felt warmed by his nearness, her heart still thumped at a maddening pace, betraying how little she controlled it. She thought to bolster her resolve by mentally listing Reagan's faults and her reasons for rejecting him. Yet strangely, her ire gradually ebbed and within his embrace she felt only contentment. As she relaxed, she rested against his shoulder and thus nestled, the buggy's motion lulled her into a drowsy state and her eyes slowly closed.

Reagan felt her snuggling against him and taking advantage of the moment, redirected the mare. It wasn't until the surrey began to undulate with the gentle rise of land that Amanda sensed a change and sat upright.

“Where are we?”

“I thought a ride to the river would be nice before going home,” Reagan said.

“It’s late. Mother will be worried.”

“I wanted to speak with you and I’ve had no opportunity all evening.” He drew in as they reached the river’s edge, resting the reins on the dash rail. “I ask for only a moment.”

“Then, a moment I’ll give you,” she said. “Afterward, I’ll expect you to take me home, straightway.”

Reagan took her hands into his. “As you’re aware, I’m leaving tomorrow and won’t return until just before the elections. When I do, I hope to convince your parents of my sincerity in courting you. Until then, I ask that you don’t troth your heart to another.”

“Are you speaking of Beau?” she asked tartly. “If what you say of him is true, he’ll be on to another long before you return.”

“Not just Beau, but anyone who’s interested in courting you,” Reagan said. “I realize from the beginning, I’ve handled myself badly. I’ve been reckless and uncouth—”

“And boorish and rude,” Amanda cut in.

“Yes,” Reagan said, laughing. “I seem to put my foot in my mouth at every turn. As you can see, I’m less than perfect. But, I want to make amends. I’m not so much a cad as when I’m around you, I lose control of my sensibilities. So, please, let me prove myself worthy to both you and your parents.”

She smiled in the darkness, her ire forgotten. “Even if I overlooked your churlish tendencies, I doubt my mother will. Your chances of gaining her consent are slim, I'm afraid."

"That's why I'm here," he said, stroking her fingers, "to rid whatever doubts she has, so I may court you."

The small caress provoked shards of pleasure, causing Amanda to withdraw her hands. "But what of me? Doesn't it matter what I think?"

Realizing he'd been granted a measure of concession, Reagan lifted Amanda's chin. "It matters very much," he whispered.

All at once, Reagan forgot this was about saving his business. He became enthralled by the moonlight in her eyes and as her breath forged a path over his mouth, it seemed natural to close the distance between them. He slid an arm around her and slowly, warmly brushed her lips. He intended only a small kiss but her parted mouth trembled, prompting him to linger. As he traced his tongue over the edges of her mouth, his hand slid down her back and pressed her close.

The sensuous contact caused strange yet wonderful yearnings within Amanda. She let his lips move over hers as she experienced these new sensations. She found it decidedly pleasant as a fluttering ripple began in the pit of her belly, radiating upward and outward. Its pleasure dulled rational thinking and caught in its trap, she melted against him.

Emboldened by her unresisting form, Reagan daringly slanted his mouth over hers, plundering that which he had only sampled. The sudden fervor and unexpected intrusion of his tongue caused a swift response. Amanda drew back, wedging a hand against his chest, her heart leaping to a dizzying pulse.

"Reagan..." she gasped.

Horrified at the pleasurable warmth that flooded her being, she turned her head, exposing a more delectable target behind her ear. There, the scent of her perfume clouded his judgment and like a man long starved, the taste of her only whetted his appetite. Much time had passed since he'd felt the gratifying release only a woman could provide and now, he wanted more. Reagan deftly plucked the buttons of her jacket, forgetting everything except his need to possess her. Like liquid fire, his lips scorched her throat while he ran a hand inside her jacket, causing it to part.

Amanda never imagined a man could create such physical craving for she knew not what. Her heart thudded as she falteringly allowed his mouth to explore hers once again and not until she perceived a hand pressed to her waist did she awaken as if from a stupor. "Stop! Please stop!" she panted, pulling away. "We mustn't do this..."

Her panicked voice became a splash of cold water and though his belly roiled with desire, Reagan wrested control of himself, releasing her. "Amanda! I...my apologies," he said, drawing in a ragged breath.

Amanda had no time to respond as the mare snorted at sounds of loud splashing. Both peered toward the river where moonlight revealed a tree limb drifting toward shore. Another splash, closer this time caused the horse to prance and Amanda fearfully clutched together the edges of her jacket.

Reaching under the seat, Reagan withdrew a revolver and cocked the hammer. He pressed his lips with a finger, motioning for silence before backing the surrey behind a nearby willow.

Within moments they heard voices, hushed yet excited as three ghostly shapes rose from the branches. A prickling ran over Amanda's scalp as she watched the figures hunch together, talking in an unfamiliar dialect. When the forms slinked from the waters edge and out of sight Reagan released the hammer, replacing the gun to its former place.

"Do you suppose they were robbers?" Amanda whispered.

With his passions sufficiently cooled, Reagan chuckled at her childlike conclusions. "There's only one reason for a person to risk a night river crossing. We probably just witnessed escaping slaves from the South."

"Slaves? Why would runaways come to Cantonsville?"

"Obviously, there are those who oppose slavery enough to aid them along the way."

"Poor souls! It's so cold. Shouldn't we try to help them?"

"They seem to know where they're going and wouldn't likely trust strangers. The best we can do for them is to tell no one what we saw," he said. "Otherwise, by law we'd be compelled to turn in any fugitives."

"You're right," Amanda said. "I'll forget we ever saw them."

Reagan snapped the reins, crossing the meadow before spying a line of torches along the riverbank. Pulling up sharply, he veered off the path when a gunshot sounded, followed by shouts as several men with firebrands encircled three figures cowering in the dirt. Upraised torches revealed dark skinned people in filthy, ragged garments. But with hats covering their faces, it was impossible to tell whether male or female lay prone on the ground.

"What's happening?" Amanda whispered.

"Slave catchers," Reagan spoke low. "Most likely bounty hunters."

"Ho! Whut have we here?" A towering figure suddenly loomed from the darkness and as the mare skittered sideways, the monstrous apparition grabbed her by the bit, yanking cruelly. "Whoa there," he growled. "Settle down, yu damn animal."

Amanda gasped, for though the voice was human, the wide, fur-clad shoulders gave the figure a beast-like appearance.

With darkness still shrouding the conveyance, Reagan reclaimed the pistol, holding it within shadows. "Your business isn't with us," he stated. "Release the mare and we'll be on our way."

The gravel-voiced man paused before answering. "Me'bee, me'bee not. Whut ya'll doin' here? Helpin' some nigra's perhaps?"

"Nah," Reagan drawled. "I'm just taking my lady out for a ride." He then put urgency into his light banter. "We should return before she's missed though. I'd be obliged if you'd let us pass."

"Well now," the giant said. "Ah wouldn't be doin' mah job if'n Ah didn't make sher yu wuzn't re-eely comin' fer these here fug'tives. Ted! Bring yer light over here!"

As Ted approached, his light fell on the giant, revealing bearskin pelts covering massive shoulders beneath collar length hair. Though the giant's hat prevented a satisfactory look at his face, it was apparent by the stubbled jaw he didn't often use a razor.

Holding high his torch, Ted peered into the buggy. He missed the subtle movement of Reagan's gun, hidden at his side. His unwashed body emanated a foul stench as he poked around Amanda, lifting the fur pelt. She reacted by slapping his hand. Laughing, Ted pushed up his hat, exposing greasy hair. "Look'ee here, boss," he cackled, ogling Amanda's loosened coat. "'Pears they's doing more'n just taking a ride!"

"Is that so?" The large man pushed the smaller one aside. "Mayhap yu wouldn't mind sharing, seeing how yu prob'ly had a taste a'ready."

Looking intently at Amanda, he didn't see the hardened look in Reagan's eyes or the determined set of his jaw. Suddenly a loud click brought the giant's attention to the gun barrel pointed directly at his chest. Reagan's voice grew deadly as he dropped his friendly guise.

"I'm not of a mind to share anything, especially my lady."

Just then two bearded ruffians approached, guns drawn. "Trouble, Jebediah?"

"Nah," he said. "Appears a bit unreasonable, is all." He rubbed his chin. "We's not wanting to keep the filly, just borree her fer a little fun." At Reagan's continued silence, Jeb pressed more forcefully. "Seeing how we got yu outnumbered, yer sher being stupid!"

The two miscreants crowded Ted, leering at Amanda as she clutched Reagan's arm. Images of forceful defilement raised her gorge and she felt threatened by a thorough retching.

"Ah'm conducting lawful business, yu understand," Jebediah said, licking his lips. "Just t' assure yu'uns ain't involved with these slaves, we'll hafta search ya, real careful-like!"

"Yee-haw!" Ted jumped up and down, peeling his gloves and tossing them to the ground. The others laughed and nodded, eying Amanda.

"Shut-up, Ted!" Jebediah thundered. "Since Ah'm in charge, Ah'll be the one to give the laidy the once over." He jerked his thumb toward the buggy. "Yu men c'n make sure the gent ain't got nuthin' else but his pig-shooter, a'fore we let's 'em go. He ain't gonna use it with so many of us."

"Me too, Jeb!" Ted frothed angrily. "I gits to search her too!"

One of the men reached out and boxed Ted's ears. "Hush, you fool," he rasped, lowering his voice. "We'll gits our share once we got th' feller tied up."

As the men crowded in, Amanda sobbed, burying her face in Reagan's shoulder. Her fear grew with her certainty of being trapped with no hope of escape.

"One step closer by you or any of your men and the first bullet's yours," Reagan said. "And just so you know, I never miss."

Jeb paused. He wasn't used to hearing the calm certainty in Reagan's voice. From an early age, he had bullied many a dandy with his size alone. This man's refusal to be intimidated caused him to reconsider.

Reagan's gaze never wavered as he indicated the slaves still crouched on the road. "Don't you have more pressing business at hand? Or do you waylay all innocent travelers?" Jebediah glanced back as if recalling the captives for the first time. "Perhaps, I should notify the sheriff," Reagan continued. "He'd be interested to know who's prowling our woods."

With the chances of fulfilling his lechery growing dim, the blackguard tired of the game. He wasn't willing to test the mettle of the one holding the revolver. Even if he moved suddenly, he doubted he could outrun a well-placed bullet. Jebediah decided however, if the opportunity ever presented itself, he'd put the arrogant bastard in his place.

"We're well within the limits of the law," he spat. "These are fugitive slaves Ah wuz hired to hunt down."

"Then, my suggestion to you is to get those poor souls fed and someplace warm. Mishandling someone else's property could cause you trouble, especially when I report how poorly you secured your charges."

Jeb knew it wasn't uncommon to find resistance from locals despite penalties imposed on any who hampered his duty. He had dealt with such before, losing his bounty to incompetence, real or otherwise, of lawmen called upon to incarcerate his captured slaves. Masked men would burst into a poorly guarded jail, releasing the prisoners while the sheriff was conveniently absent. The lawmen never seemed to find the captives, professing ignorance of local abolitionists who might do such a daring deed.

"We wuzn't r-eely gonna hurt yer laidy none, mister," Jebediah said. "Just makin' sher yu ain't breaking the law."

"Tell your men to move back," Reagan ordered.

"Do's he says!" the giant snapped.

After backing away, the bounty hunters pulled a buckboard next to the captives and forced them inside. Urging the mare forward, Reagan didn't release his gun until he was satisfied they weren't being followed. When Amanda couldn't stop weeping, he pulled a hanky from his pocket, placing it in her hands.

"It seems I'm in peril whenever I'm with you, Mr. Burnsfield," she said, daubing her cheeks. "Is this an omen I should avoid your company?"

"On the contrary. It means you need constant protection," he said, smiling. "But for now, we need to get you home."

Arriving at the Bruester manse, Reagan aided Amanda to the door. "I'll call again in two fortnight," he promised. "Until then, I suggest you stay out of the woods and within the vicinity of your father's pistols."

"Perhaps, I need a gun of my own if I'm to defend myself from scoundrels. Would you then teach me its use?"

"From all but one, my sweet," he said, bending near. He had hoped for another kiss. But, before their lips could touch, the door opened, flooding the entrance with light. Reagan straightened as Wills, their manservant, stood observing him. After seeing Amanda safely inside, Reagan left the porch and hoisted himself into the surrey. Gathering the reins, he slapped the mare.

"Giddap!"

With more surety than ever, Reagan felt convinced nothing would persuade him from his purpose. Amanda would be his bride.

chapter 13

REAGAN DONNED HEAVY trousers and a flannel shirt before eating a breakfast of cold ham and biscuits. Hearing a rap at the door, he admitted his foreman Danny O'Reilly and led him to the study where a map had been laid out.

"We'll take supply wagons north til we get to Meadville in Pennsylvania," Reagan said, tracing the route with his finger. "Then, I'll head to Jamestown for the new equipment while you continue north with the wagons, crossing Elk Creek, near McKean." He tapped the spot, indicating the small town. "We'll meet up in Stockton to travel the last few miles to the Cattaraugus River. Is everything clear?"

"Yes sir! Sounds like a plan," Danny said, running fingers through his coppery hair before donning his hat.

"Good, then let's get going." Reagan folded the plat, handing it to Danny before checking his pocket for his own map.

As they headed for the door, Reagan went over preparations in his mind. He had stowed a small trunk of belongings in one of the wagons, and in his saddlebags he carried contracts for the equipment. He had earlier sent a crew to slash a road into the forest so by the time he arrived the men could begin erecting camp.

Reagan was only mildly surprised to see Katherine near the entrance, a shawl draped over her shoulders. "Good morning, Mother. I thought I said last night, you needn't see me off."

"Morning to you, Danny," she said, ignoring Reagan. "How's your mother these days?"

Danny doffed his hat. "She's in good health, thank you."

"Mother, go back to bed. It's too early to be about."

Katherine frowned as Reagan retrieved his coat. "You know I always see my men off, no matter the hour."

"Yes, I know," he said, kissing her cheek. "Tell papa good-bye and give Amy a kiss. And keep an eye on that Beauregard Barrington. Tell him if he gets fresh with Amanda, he can expect dire consequences."

"Really, Reagan," Katherine said. "I'll do no such thing."

He shrugged, winking at Danny. "All right, then. Kiss *Papa* for me and tell *Amy* good-bye."

She threw up her hands. "Oh you! Go before I swat you." She waited until the door closed behind them before she ascended the stairs.

After Reagan saddled his horse, the men departed. They rode in a thickening fog, their breaths forming vapors that wafted before them like puffs of smoke. When they neared the warehouse, a milk cow tethered to a wagon bellowed as she spied two apparitions approaching in the mist. Sleepy loggers barely noted her cries while hunched in wagons, waiting to get underway.

Danny spoke to the driver of the lead wagon before hailing the others. The string of wagons burdened with supplies and men then headed in the direction of the rising sun.

Reagan separated from the caravan at the Meadville crossroads, reaching Jamestown the sixth day. After registering at the Madison Hotel, he ordered a bath and sizable meal while a message was sent to Mr. Price, the equipment contractor who had been awaiting his arrival. The next morning he left with three wagonloads driven by hired muleskinners. When he arrived at Stockton he found Danny at the livery, inspecting harnesses.

Lifting a patched bridle, Reagan stretched the leather. "These ought to do," he said. "Have the animals been checked?"

"The mules are shod and we greased the wheels just this morning," Danny said.

Reagan loosened the cinch before easing the saddle from his horse. "Since everything seems ready, I see no reason why we can't leave within the hour."

"So soon? The boys were expecting a night on the town."

"Why didn't the men have their fun last night?"

"We arrived late and were plumb tuckered. We just unhitched the livestock and piled in for the night."

"Don't they know we're going to a lumber camp?"

"We weren't expecting you until tomorrow and thought there'd be time." Though he, like Reagan, abstained from such entertainment, Danny never forbade the liquor or brothels that would hereafter be available only on days of pay.

Reagan poured oats into a bucket and set it before his horse. "The men are rested, that's all I care to know. Anyone who thinks differently can collect his wages and be done with my outfit."

"Sure, boss," Danny said. "We'll be ready."

By afternoon, a disappointed and much subdued crew traveled north. With little else to do, many pressed their faces against upturned collars and slept. Finally, late that night, the group reached their destination, the mouth of the Cattaraugus River.

chapter 14

AWAKENING TO THE breakfast horn, Danny tumbled from his resting place. He could see others vacating straw filled wagons where if cold, they had at least been asleep. Near the fire, he accepted a cup of coffee from Theodore, the cook's helper.

The cook then handed him a plate of food. Danny easily recognized the short-cropped hair sticking from underneath a mannish hat.

"Morning, Hattie," he said. "We're sure lucky to have you again this year."

The leathery face split into a wide, toothy grin. "If'n I didn't, half these boys would leave a'for the next dawn," she cackled. "I come every time Mr. Reagan asks, because I complete the operation!"

"Who-doggie," hooted a large lumberjack who had drawn near. "You call this slop cooking? My horse could do better'n this!"

His laughter turned to yowls of pain as Hattie slapped his ear with a calloused palm. "I don't take guff from anyone, especially the likes of you, Billie Greely!"

"Git 'im Hattie," encouraged another. "That lummox is always shootin' off his mouth."

"Yeah," spoke a third, grinning. "Everyone knows Hattie ain't no beauty, but she's *some* cook!"

Danny settled on the ground, spooning beans into his mouth. "You fellows best leave Hattie alone," he said. "Otherwise, you're liable to find a ladle bent over your skull. Now, fill up your plates or forget about eating."

Hattie's coffee washed away the last dregs of sleep as men crowded around the fire, devouring fresh biscuits and beans. Soon, the rising sun revealed they occupied a large, flat clearing. Coupled with its close proximity to the river, Danny knew it to be an excellent choice to make a campsite. Once breakfast was over, Reagan gave instructions before leaving to map out land tracts where trees would later be felled.

With cheerfulness of the Irish, Danny set about his work. He first directed clearing underbrush and laying corner logs for various buildings. Next, the men framed the cook's shack; a large building that housed long tables where the men would eat. Another smaller addition would be added to store meat and supplies. After digging a depression in a nearby creek, men inserted a wooden box for a water supply while others retrieved bucketfuls of mud from the river. As the buildings rose, a mixture of clay and grass had to be chinked between logs to lessen coming winter drafts. Commanders and axes sounded through the air, only to cease briefly as the men bolted down their noon meal.

The structure of two bunkhouses facing a second pair of bunkhouses began the next day. The loggers lined the low, squat buildings with double bunks and a bench, placing iron stoves in each cabin for heat and light. The roof was made of wooden shakes lined with tarpaper. Afterward, criss-crossing beams would be used to dry boots and wet clothes. After three days of hard labor, the men slept gratefully in their bunks.

As the days wore on, the camp's design unfolded. Reagan's cabin-office and livestock shed formed the bottom of the U-shaped campsite. Lastly, the filer's shack and outhouses would need to be finished before hard winter set in. But for now, the time for cutting timber was upon them.

Under Danny's direction, a gang of swampers cleared away brush to form open spaces where trees would fall. Reagan checked each logger's skill by overseeing the placement of back cuts forged with crosscut saws. Once down, fallers would pair off to chop right angles into tree trunks, their powerful blows swinging alternately to avoid each other's axe.

By late afternoon, the cry of "Timberrrr!" caused men to scurry from falling trees. Swampers chopped off branches before buckers sectioned trees into logs. Oxen, mules and horses hauled logs onto skidways formed along new roads. As the men dropped into a routine of eat, sleep and work again; trees were felled, bucked and stacked.

Reagan worked equally hard, relieving more than one out of shape logger even when he felt the strain in his own limbs. Nightly, he fell into bed too tired to think about the thorny matters gnawing at him.

A month later, on the eve of his return home he sat with Danny in his cabin.

"I want you to start this section of land next," Reagan said, marking the map.

"Sure, boss," he replied. "As long as the snows hold off, we'll be in good shape come spring."

"Which is exactly why I want a step up of work." Reagan's voice took a tone usually reserved for disciplining an errant shanty boy. "The men are fit. For every two trees felled, I now want three. Tell the boys their effort will be rewarded."

Danny looked surprised. "But, they're already working hard. Progress is safe and well paced," he reasoned. "Surely..."

"And, they can work a little harder. I don't ask anything from my men I wouldn't do myself." Leaning against his chair, Reagan ignored the ache in his muscles. Constant work had hardened his body into the powerfully thewed frame of a seasoned lumberman. "Of all crews, mine are the highest paid. So I expect more. Is that understood?"

Danny's eyes glowered. "Perfectly," he said. "Three trees for every two." Rising, he folded his arms over his heavily muscled chest. "Hell!"

Reagan refrained from uttering a rebuke. He sighed, rubbing his eyes. "Let me ask you. Do you have a better recommendation?"

"As a matter of fact, I do. If it's so important to increase output, hire more men. It's unwise to push the boys too hard."

Reagan nodded. "You're right. I can surely find men needing work in nearby towns. Take a day to build extra bunks so they'll be ready when I return."

Afterward, Danny left for his bunkhouse. He prayed Reagan would find additional men. Otherwise, a mutinous wave from the shanty boys would certainly disrupt their smooth operation.

chapter 15

REAGAN PACKED FEW belongings for his journey home. For the past week, he'd been consumed with thoughts of furthering his marriage proposal. Yet, every idea he conjured up was soon discarded. Short of compromising Amanda's reputation, he could find no grounds for a swift courtship. And, by the time he reached Cantonsville a few days later, he had gotten no closer to securing Amanda for his wife.

After tending his horse, Reagan entered the kitchen through the garden door the same time Katherine emerged from the pantry.

"Reagan, you're home!" she said, wiping hands on her apron.

"Yes, I am," he said, giving her a hug. "I'm starved. Is there anything to eat?"

"Of course." Katherine's nose wrinkled as she scanned his frame. "But, I want you to bathe first. You look as if you've not sat a bath since you left."

"Yes, ma'am!"

"And don't forget to shave," she lectured as he headed toward the hall. "Or else you shan't eat until supper time." Her stern look vanished the minute the door closed behind him. It was good to have him home.

After his meal, Reagan pushed back his plate. A bath had eased his sore muscles while clean clothes served to refresh his mind. He claimed he needed to keep his beard however, and allowed only a trim amidst Katherine's sighs of exasperation.

Later, the dining table had been cleared as he recounted to Katherine the camp's progress. That accomplished, it wasn't long before his thoughts led to his last encounter with Amanda.

"Mother, I was wondering. Have you heard of anyone in Cantonsville being involved with escaping slaves?"

"There've been whispers of comings and goings for years, but no real proof that I'm aware."

"Such as...?"

"Well, for instance, Henrietta Livingston claims she hears strange voices and mysterious sounds passing by her bedroom window at night."

Reagan looked askance. "Doesn't the widow Livingston also say her dead husband speaks to her while she sits in her parlor?"

"Henrietta's a bit queer, that's true. But aside from her attachment to her departed Frederic, she's as sane as you or I."

Reagan smiled tolerantly. "Ma, she speaks to a ghost. How can you believe anything she says?"

"I've known Henrietta my whole life. She's like an aunt to me. Besides, she mentioned these things even before Frederic's death."

"What things?"

"Henrietta's afflicted with insomnia, and thinks fresh air is the best cure. So, she always keeps her window open. She says many nights she's heard what sounds like wagons passing by and people whispering in a heathen tongue. Sometimes, sounds of animals-"

"And spooks and fairies and forest sprites, I'll wager," scoffed Reagan, dismissing the account as anything connected to the flight he had witnessed a month ago.

"I should've known you'd ridicule that poor woman!" Katherine stood, glaring at her son. "Have you no sense of propriety?"

"Now Ma, I didn't say she didn't hear *something*. I just don't think what she heard was fleeing slaves. After all, it'd be safer to hide in the Negro settlement than in town." Reagan recognized the provoked gleam in his mother's eyes and stood as well. "I didn't mean to imply..." he said, laughing, "...that Mrs. Livingston had lost her marbles!"

"Oh you! You never take anything seriously," she said, seizing a broom near the fireplace.

Reagan raised a finger. "Now, just a minute..." As the bristles neared his face, he caught the handle, lowering it. "As I was about to say, Mrs. Livingston most probably heard the routine passage of wagons, and her imagination stretched the sounds into something more sinister."

“I won’t tolerate you ridiculing helpless women,” Katherine warned. “Is that understood, Mr. Smarty Pants?”

“You’re right,” he said, setting the broom aside. “I shouldn’t tease you about your friends.” He kissed her brow before turning away.

“Now where are you going?” she asked.

“To the construction site,” he said. “But, I’ll be home for dinner.”

At the new mill, Reagan canvassed the completed foundation before going inside. Few recognized the tall, bewhiskered man in workman’s garb as he inspected whipsaws and mill irons. He stopped to observe a saw wheel being bolted in place. Once started, the sharp-toothed blade would only halt to be sharpened or repaired.

Reagan envisioned the path the logs would take as they wound their way through the mill. He could almost smell the sawdust and feel the vibration of machinery as timber became lumber. But without buyers, he knew the planks would remain stacked on docks.

Reminded once again of his growing debts, Reagan decided to pay Amanda a visit. He thought he had arrived too late when on the road, the Bruester carriage passed by him. But his disappointment turned to hope when he saw through the window only George and Emily inside. Believing Amanda at home, he hurried the rest of the way and crossing the porch, knocked.

“May I help you?” asked Wills, who answered the door.

“I’m calling on Miss Bruester.”

"Unfortunately, you just missed Mr. and Mrs. Bruester," he said. "Perhaps you could return at a more convenient time."

Reagan smiled. "I fear you've misunderstood. I wish to see Miss *Amanda.* If I'm not mistaken, she's home." As if to prove his theory, a feminine hand drew back drapes from a nearby window.

"I'm sorry," the butler said. "Since neither parent is here, it's unlikely Miss Amanda would welcome an unexpected guest." Stepping back, he was about to close the door when interrupted by Amanda's voice.

"Wills, Mr. Burnsfield and I have already been introduced."

"But mistress," he objected. "You haven't a proper escort."

"Mr. Banning can certainly provide the accompaniment I need. Please, let Mr. Burnsfield in at once."

Reluctantly the butler stepped aside, allowing Reagan to enter.

"We were just about to have tea," Amanda said. "Won't you join us?"

"I'd be delighted." If Reagan noticed Amanda's heightened color, he didn't let on as he doffed his hat and coat, handing them to the servant.

"We'll need additional refreshments brought to the parlor, Wills. Please see to it at once."

After a moment's hesitation in which the servant pondered his continued employment if he refused, Wills turned to do her bidding. "Very good, Miss Amanda."

"Milady." Reagan extended his arm. "Allow me."

"I think you frightened poor Wills," Amanda said as he led her down the hall. "He's not accustomed to bearded men in less than formal attire. Please forgive his misgivings."

"Madam, I have no quarrel with any whose job it is to protect you," Reagan said. "And, the reason I haven't shaved is because I'll soon be back to camp."

"How long have you been home?"

"I arrived today." At her surprised look, he added, "I wanted to see you, and considering your lingering guest, it wasn't a moment too soon."

Amanda laughed. "Mr. Banning seems determined in arranging business with papa's bank. Though obstacles have come up about codes and rules I know nothing about, Derrick's persuaded papa they can be overcome with time."

As they neared the parlor, the door was suddenly yanked open. Derrick scanned the newcomer from head to toe before his eyes softened in recognition. "Why Reagan, is that you? I feared some ne'er-do-well had forced his attentions on Amanda."

Although meant to put Reagan ill at ease, the lumberman only seemed amused. "Rest assured, she's safe for the time being," he said.

The implication wasn't lost on Derrick who, though annoyed, swept his arm invitingly. "Come join us, won't you? I hope you'll accept my stead in the Bruester's absence." He then retreated to the settee; the only place two people could sit together.

Reagan waited until Amanda sat next to Derrick before settling into a chair. A maid entered with a platter of cakes, setting them beside a tea service. Amanda knew exactly how Derrick liked his tea by stirring in two lumps of sugar before handing him the beverage.

"I believe you prefer your tea plain, Mr. Burnsfield," she said, pouring two more cups before offering him one.

"Thank you. So kind of you to remember."

As he accepted the brew, Reagan's fingers lingered against hers, branding her with a warm caress. Amanda was instantly reminded of another time where his touch had stirred her senses. Her cheeks became stained as she sought to change the path of her thoughts.

"Your taste seems rather simple," she said. "I'd have thought you'd prefer something to soften the tea's bitterness."

"Your presence is more than enough to make anything taste sweet," he said, smiling. "Gladly I'd drink several cups if in doing so, we shared the occasion. It's my loss I'll soon be returning to camp."

Derrick eyed the exchange; vexed he had to suffer courting from Reagan as well as others interested in Amanda's hand. He considered Leroy's awkward posturing more of a nuisance than a threat, for Amanda only tolerated those visits with polite interest. Derrick realized she only became flustered in Reagan's presence and he craved to prove himself superior.

Adjusting his tie, Derrick smoothed an imaginary wrinkle on his fawn trousers. "I daresay I must compliment the tailors of your fine city. I found this magnificent suit while exploring your shops, proving

New York isn't the only city with modern fashions." Reaching inside his vest he withdrew an expensive watch, checking the time. As he replaced the timepiece, he stared at Reagan's flannel Mackinaw. "With your travels, I'm sure you haven't time for clothiers. If you like, I could make some recommendations. Although sadly, there aren't any more suits like this for sale."

"I know," Reagan said, sighing. "Bostwick's showcased your suit last season and marked them down to make room for newer fashions."

Derrick's face darkened. "But, have you viewed the upcoming styles? A good clothier would know which trend would be most in demand."

"The fashion plates I *have* already seen," Reagan said. "For years, Ives Du Monde who's employed at Bostwick's has allowed me to view the styles before making suggestions for my wardrobe. However, I much prefer the patterns he creates. It makes for more unique attire." Pausing, Reagan allowed the insult to hit its mark before softening the slur. "But I have to admit, you wear the ensemble extremely well."

"Why, I think it's a right stylish suit," Amana said, laying a hand on Derrick's arm. "I don't believe I've seen another like it all summer."

Pleased, Derrick smiled. "My dear, you could charm the profit from the stingiest merchant. I must call upon your help at my next outing."

"I'm afraid I'm not well versed in men's apparel," she said, withdrawing her hand. "I can only say whether or nay the clothes are becoming."

"Your presence would be all that's required to get the best price," Derrick said, stroking his mustache. He leaned forward as if an idea just struck him. "In fact, we can try out my theory the day after elections. The shops will be open, and with the money I save I'll purchase the bonnet of your choice."

"It sounds lovely. However, I promised Aunt Ella I'd spend a few days with her," she said, smiling brightly. "Perhaps another time."

Reagan maintained an impassive countenance as he mulled that bit of news. It would be difficult to press his courtship the few days he'd be home if Amanda's time was taken with Gabriella. The only consolation, he thought, was if he couldn't avail himself of her presence, then neither could the tenacious Bruester houseguest.

"So, Reagan," Derrick said. "Are you home for the holidays? The weather can be treacherous this time of year. It'd be a good idea to leave before snowfall."

"Quite simply, I've returned to vote. Can I assume you'll be going home to cast yours?"

Derrick stretched an arm along the divan near Amanda's shoulder. "My employer's interests outweigh my personal affairs. Besides, I don't care who wins the elections." As if wanting to change the subject, he cleared his throat.

"Amanda dear, please offer our guest some pastries. He's surely missed such tidbits while he's been gone."

Reagan declined her offer with a shake of his head. She then turned the platter to Derrick who took his time choosing. When he popped a sweet into his mouth, Reagan felt the need to wipe the contented look from his face.

"The last time I visited, you spoke of having business plans. How are they coming?"

Derrick managed a long-suffering grimace. "Proposals have a way of dragging on, I'm afraid. With the uncertain times, the firm I represent has become hesitant to start the venture. They remain interested, however, and asked that I stay until determining their next course of action." Derrick agitated the spoon inside his tea before tapping it against the cup. Setting it down, he reached for another small cake, disposing of it in a single bite.

"I see." Reagan shifted in his chair, intensely interested. "What's the name of the institute you work for? As I've had dealings in New York, perhaps I could be of service to you."

Suddenly, Derrick began to choke. Gasping for air, his face turned an alarming red while his Adam's apple bobbed rapidly. After a fit of coughing, he managed to clear his throat by swallowing some tea.

"Excuse me," he said, inhaling deeply. "I don't know what came over me!"

Amanda pressed a napkin into his hand. "Are you all right? Can I get you anything?"

"I just need to catch my breath," he begged, dabbing watery eyes. "Please, pardon my clumsiness." As Amanda poured fresh tea, Derrick coughed discreetly and took several small sips. "My dear, can you ever forgive me? I'm afraid I've spoiled our tea."

"It was an accident. Thankfully, you're all right. Mother would've been horrified had anything happened to you."

Derrick turned to Reagan, his eyes strangely averted. "My apologies, sir. I'm embarrassed by my ill manners."

"Think nothing of it," Reagan said. "But perhaps it's time I leave after all."

As he rose, Amanda stood also. "May I accompany you?"

"It'd be an honor," he said, extending his arm. When Derrick came to his feet, Reagan continued. "If you'll excuse us a moment, I wish to have a private word with Amanda."

"Of course," Derrick said, forcing a smile. As they left the room he approached the door, straining to hear their words.

"So tell me, how long will you be staying with your Aunt?" asked Reagan. "I'd hoped to give you a tour of the mill."

"A few days, I'm afraid. I promised Aunt Ella I'd spend time with her."

"Circumstances have a way of working for the good of all," he said. "If not this occasion, then soon we can arrange another time."

When they neared the entrance, Reagan took her hand. "I bid you adieu. I hope you'll have a pleasant stay at Gabriella's."

"I'm sure I will," Amanda said as Wills appeared, holding Reagan's outerwear. She tarried until Reagan departed then returned to the parlor finding Derrick bent to the task of rekindling the fire.

"The servants have become lax in their duties," he chided, dusting particles from his clothing. "Were they in my employ, I wouldn't hesitate correcting them."

"Shall I call for Wills?" Amanda said, hiding her exasperation. Of late, Derrick became querulous at the slightest provocation, especially when he didn't get his way.

"That won't be necessary. It's a man's duty to handle these things." He indicated the sofa. "Let's at least finish our tea, my dear. I too, have something to discuss."

Derrick's wolfish gaze swept Amanda while she retook her seat. Unleashing the imaginings of his mind, he felt the familiar ache of desire as Amanda nervously picked up her tea.

"What is it you wished to discuss?" she asked.

He approached and sat beside her. "You're very beautiful," he breathed, touching her fingertips. "Until you choose, you'll never be free of suitors. You know how I feel about you, how right we are for each other. We could have the perfect marriage if you'd just accept me." Rattling her cup against its saucer, she tried to drink, but Derrick took her cup and placed it on the table.

"Derrick..."

"I know you have feelings for me, Amanda. I can see it," he said. "You only become confused when others come courting. But they're not worthy of you."

Amanda looked away. "Derrick, I-I've told you before, I don't have those kinds of feelings for you."

"You've not given me a chance!" he accused. "You've not dealt with me like your other callers, though I've been more than patient."

Amanda rubbed her brow, a phobic feeling constricting her chest. "You're not like others, Derrick. You're always here..."

"Why do you refuse my courtship?" He leaned forward, taking her hand. "Even your mother considers me a suitable match. My intentions are honorable, and yet you treat me like a brother."

Amanda fought the urge to withdraw her hand, allowing it to lie limply within his fingers. "I don't know why," she lied. "As long as you live in this house, it's impossible for me to think of you as anything other than a brother."

Moments elapsed while Derrick stared, digested her words. "Yes. You're right," he said finally, a smile crossing his face. "I see how this situation could become...unhealthy."

Perplexed, she searched his eyes for hidden animosity. "So, you understand?"

"I see it's time for me to stop imposing on your family. Perhaps then, you can view me in a proper light. I'll take up residence in town," he said. "Then, you wouldn't deny me the pleasure of calling in the customary manner, would you?"

Amanda smiled in relief. "No, of course not." Taking up her tea, she decided she could manage his advances once she was no longer obliged to play hostess, unaware of his scheme to make her his wife, no matter the price.

chapter 16

WITH THE MILL closed for Election Day, the Burnsfields enjoyed a leisurely breakfast. Reagan had been listening to his sister's banter when he caught a disapproving look from Katherine while scratching his whiskered jaw. He grinned as he continued to scratch.

"Really, Reagan, that thing makes you unfit for our table," she said.

"Why mother, I think he looks dashing," Amy said. "Not every girl has a brother who's the talk of the sewing circles. Just the other day, I heard Rebecca say-"

"Amy Burnsfield," Katherine admonished. "Young ladies do not gossip."

Reagan raised an eyebrow. "What did Miss Rebecca say?"

"She said..."

"Amy! I'll not allow such talk." Katherine then switched her complaint toward her son. "Don't incite your sister so. It's difficult enough to instill decent goodness into the child without you encouraging the contrary."

"I thought she was about to give me a compliment," Reagan said, shrugging.

"Do something," she said, turning to Thomas. "Your children are impossible."

Thomas wiped his mouth before clearing his throat. "If there's to be any questionable talk at our table, you're to pass the rumor to me," he said, giving each a stern look. "Afterward, I'll decide if it can be shared."

"Thomas!" Katherine looked aghast as everybody burst into laughter.

"Now, Katherine," he said. "You're sounding a little priggish. I'm sure Amy wasn't about to say anything unsavory, were you?"

"No Papa, of course not."

"From now on, be considerate of your mother's feelings. She works hard to prepare an enjoyable meal, part of which is gentle dialogue. Besides, it's not attractive when one gossips. You should pay attention to your mother's example."

"Yes Papa, I'm sorry."

Noting Reagan's finished meal, Thomas scraped back his chair. "Are you ready? The polls are being held at the saloon this year."

"Yes, I am," he said, emptying his coffee cup.

Once on the road, Thomas experienced a sense of blame about accepting the government contracts. With every step of the horse's hooves, his mood only worsened and not even the gay red, white and blue banners decorating the tavern could alleviate his guilt. Inside, colorful streamers were attached to the bar as well as the table facing the door. Two men sat in attendance verifying names and handing out ballots.

"Good morning," one said as they approached.

Thomas smiled with effort. "Morning Heustis. I see you got the early shift."

Heustis checked off their names while the other attendant handed each a pencil and three ballots. "Yep. Figured it's too early for the fistfights to start. The mouthier ones ain't up yet." He grinned, pointing to several deputies leaning against a wall. "Course, if'n it's not, these guys will knock some sense into their empty heads."

As Thomas and Reagan took positions at the end of the line, three boys too young to vote, entered the saloon. Finding it less than exciting, they swaggered to the bar and loudly demanded to be served.

The bartender, with his elbows propped on the countertop, didn't move. "You boys know the saloon's closed," he said.

"Aww, just one little drink?" begged one, leaning in. "Since we're not gonna vote, none should mind."

"The bar is closed," he repeated.

"Ye're no fun," another said. Hitching up his pants, he puffed out his undeveloped chest. "This ain't th' first time I've had liquor, neither."

When the bartender continued to ignore them, the smallest spoke up, raising his chin to get a better view. "Ain't you got nuthin' fer us, Mister?"

Sighing, the bartender reached under the bar and pulled out three glasses, banging one in front of each boy. He went into the back room and returned with a crock. After pouring a cloudy liquid, he set the jar down and folded his arms.

"Well, you wanted something. Now you got it."

The urchins looked at each other before picking up the glasses and drinking.

"It's cider!" squeaked one.

"Thanks, Pops," the oldest said, pushing himself upright. Clinging together, the boys began to sing as they staggered out the door.

"Pops!" the bartender muttered, gathering empty glasses.

When Thomas reached the booth he felt his own need of a drink, thinking the sooner he left, the better he'd feel. After marking his ballot, he emerged to see Reagan speaking with George.

"Good morning," Thomas said, dropping his ballots into a box. "Are you here to observe or vote?"

"Neither. I saw your carriage outside and came to invite you to Mayor Hampton's tonight. The telegraph office is staying open and Sam's been assured it's the first place they'll send the results before closing for the night."

Thomas was about to decline when Reagan spoke. "It sounds just like the diversion we need, eh father?"

George smiled. "Great. We'll be gathering around seven. I've got a few more to round up yet. Of course,

Katherine's invited also." As he turned to leave, Reagan touched his arm.

"Mr. Bruester, if you have a moment. I'd like a word with you."

"Uh-oh!" George said, winking. "When he calls me Mister, he's up to something." Slapping Reagan on the shoulder, George headed for the door. "Speak with me tonight. I'll have more time."

Despite Thomas being unusually quiet on the ride home, Reagan felt buoyant that he had laid another brick toward his goal. The most delicate piece however, had yet to be formed. He simply had to find a way to capture Amanda's betrothal.

chapter 17

The Burnsfield carriage slowed as it waited its turn to approach the Hampton residence. A riderless horse was tied to the rear of the carriage. Though curious about the election results, once Reagan received permission to court Amanda, he intended leaving the party.

Elizabeth stood at the door, smiling as their newest guests crossed the threshold. "Mr. and Mrs. Burnsfield, Papa will be glad you came." Turning to Reagan, she offered her hand while her eyes swept his stylish suit and perfectly knotted cravat. "Reagan. It's been too long since I've had the pleasure of your company."

"You look exquisite," Reagan said, taking her hand. "The mayor must be proud he has such a striking hostess."

"You're too kind," she said. She then turned to Thomas and Katherine who had handed their wraps to a servant. "I had such a wonderful time at Amanda's ball and nearly swooned at Reagan's ability to dance."

Katherine smiled. “He must’ve inherited a bit of his father’s magnetism. As I recall, my first dance with Thomas was equally inspiring. Let’s hope he uses it wisely.”

Appearing beside Elizabeth, Mayor Hampton beamed. “Welcome! George said he’d snared the Burnsfield clan.” He scanned the hallway. “But where’s your lovely daughter, Amy? Not taken a chill, I hope.”

“Oh, no,” Katherine said. “She’s spending the night with a friend. It seems their talk centers around the season’s fashions and the subject of boys. She’s decided both are quite beyond her understanding.”

The mayor laughed. “Unfortunately, given a few more years, that’ll completely change.”

Thomas nodded his agreement. “So far, we’ve avoided the pitfalls of young infatuations. But tell me,” he said, indicating Elizabeth, “how have you managed to keep such a beautiful daughter unattached? I must know your secret, so I can keep Amy into my old age.”

“That my friend is a mystery even to me.” Hampton cleared his throat. “However, I fear someone may’ve caught her eye, for she’s been unduly distracted of late. I can only lay blame to some swain who’s captured her fancy.”

“Papa!” Elizabeth reddened, glancing furtively at Reagan.

“All right, daughter. I’ll be quiet and leave you to your duties. No telling how much longer I’ll have the privilege of having you in my home. Come,” he said, offering his arm to Katherine. “I have guests anxious to speak with your husband about Douglas's chance of winning the Southern vote."

As the mayor escorted the Burnsfields to the drawing room, Elizabeth laid a hand on Reagan's sleeve. "Please forgive my father. He can be frightfully indelicate."

"Let's just say that for tonight the mayor is only a father and enjoys teasing his daughter," he said warmly.

Elizabeth sparkled as she tucked her hand inside Reagan's arm. Knowing he would be among the guests, she had chosen a flattering muslin gown decorated with braids and tassels. Though modestly designed, the gown accentuated her form and she hoped, would snare Reagan's eyes.

As they entered the drawing room, Reagan noted among the guests George Bruester conversing with his business partner, Ezra Spelding. Leroy stood nearby, looking dejected as he sipped wine. After a quick sweep of the room, Reagan saw that Amanda was absent and surmised she had made good on her promise to visit her Aunt Gabriella.

"Ah, my friend!" Beauregard approached, smiling widely. "You came to see how Ohio votes." He made a show of kissing Elizabeth's hand. "Belle amie, have I told you how exquisite you look this evening? Don't you agree?" he asked Reagan.

Reagan wondered what was wrong with Beau. Of late, his interruptions were becoming an annoying habit. Subduing the urge to put the Frenchman in his place, he instead smiled at Elizabeth. "As a matter of fact, those were the very words I used when I came in this evening."

Beau winked. "Then we are in agreement again Monsieur, no?"

"Gentlemen, all this praise mustn't keep me from my duties. Beau, if you'll please excuse us, I have to get Mr. Burnsfield some refreshment." Touching Reagan's arm, she tried directing him toward the sideboard.

Beauregard held up a hand. "Please, allow me." Turning, he signaled a servant carrying a tray. "Monsieur, over here." The servant approached, offering various liquors.

Elizabeth declined with an annoyed shake of her head while Reagan selected a dark wine. Beauregard chose a snifter of brandy. Swirling the liquid, he closed his eyes and inhaled deeply. "Intoxicating!"

"I thought you had no interest in elections, Beau. I'm rather surprised you're here," Reagan said.

"Oh, I received an invitation from Mr. Bruester as I took my constitution past the saloon," he said.

"In the middle of town?" Reagan looked askance.

Beau nodded. "Oui. As I was saying, I was taking my morning walk when Mr. Bruester spied me from afar. He said my presence would be much appreciated at the Mayor's home since we are all such good friends now. I think to myself, mais oui! I can meet all my friends and see also who wins the elections."

"George was at the saloon, that's true," Reagan said. "But none of the businesses were open." He looked perplexed. "Except of course, the one place always open..."

"De Sot!" Beauregard cast Reagan a piercing look. "I correct you, my friend. Perhaps, while walking I became a little...lost. Otherwise, I wouldn't have been so close."

"I'm sure that was the case, Mr. Barrington," Elizabeth said, looking past Beau's shoulder. She brightened suddenly. "There's someone I wanted to introduce to Reagan, so if you'd pardon us?"

"Miss Elizabeth." Looking apologetic, a young maid came toward them. "There's more carriages arriving, Miss Elizabeth. Your father told me to let you know so you could greet the guests."

Elizabeth pressed together her palms, forcing the irritation from her voice. "It seems duty calls," she said. "Please, enjoy yourselves, gentlemen." She then nodded to Reagan. "I'll make those introductions later."

As Elizabeth turned away, Beauregard stepped close. "Outré, why can't you be more discreet!"

Reagan regarded him with an upraised brow. "I wasn't the one who blurted out that you took your morning exercise past the saloon, which just so happens is next to the brothel!"

"Oui, but if you would've kept your mouth shut, Miss Elizabeth would not be at this moment putting two and two together. I will now be her jack-a-nape! The butt of her jokes."

"Which reminds me," Reagan said, frowning. "Why do you intrude every time I'm in the company of a woman? Don't you have enough diversions to keep you satisfied?"

"Why? *Why*? I can't believe you ask me that!" He threw up a hand. "I do you a favor, cher ami. I see Elizabeth make Doux Yeux at you."

"I'm afraid my French doesn't cover that expression," Reagan snapped.

Beauregard pointed two fingers at his own eyes. "She makes tender glances at you, Monsieur. I think to rescue you from la femme."

"You, rescue me? In truth, it is *I* who should be rescuing all the fair damsels from such a rogue as you."

Beauregard set aside his snifter, considering the pleasure of unsheathing a rapier sharp retort. He was denied his bit of fun however, for across the room Katherine had sensed Reagan's agitation and decided to interject some motherly interference.

Feeling a gentle touch, Beauregard turned. "Madam Burnsfield, it is good you come. I am about to settle a disputation."

"Oh? What has my son done this time?" She looked pointedly at Reagan. "Because if he doesn't behave himself, I'll make sure his bedroom stays as cold as an icebox while he's home. It's the least I can do, since I can no longer spank him."

Beau's pique immediately dissolved. Katherine had shown him too much kindness to cause her distress. "Tis nothing, Mademoiselle, but a misunderstanding between two morons that haven't the sense to quit while their tongues are ahead."

"I had hoped to avoid this, but it seems Reagan's behavior requires an explanation," she said, sighing.

"As you can see, Reagan's not been himself lately. I'm afraid he's not well."

Reagan looked mildly amused, but remained silent while Beau tapped a finger against his mouth.

"I suppose," he said, squinting one eye. "Reagan's been under some stress with the new mill."

Katherine's eyes twinkled. "If you want the truth, he's even mentioned spooks and fairies and forest sprites."

Beau stared, open-mouthed. "He did?" He turned toward Reagan. "Sacrebleu," he whispered. "I had no idea!"

Reagan gave his mother a pained expression. "Is this really necessary?"

"But Reagan, I don't want Beau thinking this is how you normally act."

The Frenchman shook his head sorrowfully. "You're a very sick man, cher ami. Why didn't you tell me?"

Reagan set aside his wine. "Because, my dear mother is fabricating the whole thing to punish me. And, she's going to recant her story, aren't you, Mother?"

Katherine pulled a handkerchief from her pocket and daubed her eyes. "The doctors have assured me-"

"Doctors?" Beau's eyebrows shot up.

"There are no doctors," Reagan snorted, crossing his arms. "Look, I'm sorry Beau. I've been rude, and perhaps jumped to the wrong conclusions. I know you'd never deliberately trample upon my relationships. There," he said, barely containing his ire. "Is that satisfactory, Mother?"

Katherine touched Beau's shoulder. "Could you leave us a moment? I'd like to have a private word with my son."

"But of course!" He cupped her hand in both of his. "And rest assured Madame, your secret is safe with moi." Beau clasped a brotherly hand on Reagan's shoulder before making his way toward a group gathered around Camilla Muelder.

Katherine held her tongue until Reagan gave her his full attention. "I realize your responsibilities can be difficult," she said. "What I don't understand, is taking your frustrations out on those closest to you. It's not like you, and recently it's become a habit."

"You're right," Reagan said, sighing. "I'm sorry. I'll apologize again to Beau. He's always been your favorite." He patted her hand reassuringly. "Let's find Father before he misses you." He led her past several groups until they found Thomas conversing with the Mayor and Judge Ambrose McCleary.

"There you are!" Thomas smiled as he placed his arm around Katherine's waist. "Judge, this is my wife, Katherine. Katherine, this is Judge McCleary, the most feared Justice in the court."

McCleary laughed heartily while taking her hand. "It's a pleasure to meet you. Don't let it get around that I don't actually eat children for breakfast, though. It might strengthen a few weak knees that come before me." He gestured with his hand. "And this must be Reagan. There's no mistaking the resemblance, I'm afraid."

Reagan extended his hand, feeling surprising strength in the magistrate's grip. "Guilty as charged," he quipped. Polite laughter rippled through the group as conversation returned to the prevailing topic.

"So, which delegates will cast the Ohio vote, Republican or Democrat?" McCleary posed the question to Reagan. "Your father seems rather reluctant to venture a guess."

"We won't get official word of who wins the Presidency for a day or two," interjected Mayor Hampton. "But once we know which party takes Ohio, we'll surely know who'll be in the White House."

Reagan grinned. "I agree with the mayor. Whoever takes the Northern vote will also win Ohio."

"Ha! You're just as disinclined to comment as Thomas," the judge huffed in good humor. "What is it about businessmen that keeps them from expressing their views?"

Thomas smiled. "Well, for one thing, we sell lumber to members of both parties."

Casually scanning the room, Reagan spied Derrick Banning. Handsomely dressed as usual, Derrick was in conversation with Lorelda Hargrove, who for once seemed comfortable being away from Camilla's side. With any luck, she would keep Derrick occupied long enough for him to locate George. Excusing himself, Reagan found the banker with a plate in his hand, looking over the appetizers. As George turned, he nearly collided with Reagan.

"Reagan my boy," he said. "It's only you. I nearly spilled my food and this is the only supper I get."

"Surely you didn't spend the entire day extending invitations, did you?"

"Naw," he said. "It's just that when Emily discovered I accepted the Mayor's invitation, she decided we wouldn't have time for a proper meal." He popped a morsel into his mouth. "Besides, she wasn't too happy I consented to a few drinks along the way. But I didn't tell her the half of it." He grinned before thumping his chest. "I had a lot more than just a few!" Leaning close, George shut one eye. "Let me give you some advice about women. Don't ever let them have the upper hand. If you do," he said, shaking his head, "they never give it back." He peered at Reagan suddenly. "Didn't you have a question? It seems you were, uh, going to ask something..." He scratched his head. "You know, at the saloon."

"I did have a request," Reagan began. "Perhaps, it should wait for another time. With all your uh, drinks, I'm afraid you might forget our conversation."

"Nonsense!" He waved his hand before devouring another tidbit. "I'm perfectly capable of making a decision. And, if it's about courting my daughter, then yes, you may," said George with a sudden hiccup.

"Just like that?" Reagan asked. "No questions about my intentions?"

George wrapped a fatherly arm around Reagan. "If I had to stop and question every young man that asked to court my daughter, I'd not be free to do anything else."

Reagan looked dismayed. "That many?"

"It's mostly been invitations to family dinners. So far, Amanda doesn't seem to have a favorite, though Emily seems to approve of just about all of them."

"But, I have more than a passing interest," Reagan said. "I think it's important I express my intentions."

"All right. All right." George sighed and withdrew his arm, giving his best impression of interest.

"First of all, I want you to know my intentions are honorable." Now that the moment had arrived, Reagan found it surprisingly difficult. He cleared his throat before continuing. "However, since my frequent and prolonged absences put me at a disadvantage, I'd like permission to accompany Amanda without a chaperone, if one cannot be arranged on such short notice."

"Oh." George blinked. "That one's going to be difficult with Emily. You understand, she has rules about such things."

"And so she should," agreed Reagan, thinking of Derrick. "Whenever possible, I'll seek proper measures when escorting Amanda."

George nodded, though his attention was drawn to the hors d'oeuvres on his plate. "Yes, the proper measures," he repeated.

"Then, if I have your consent...?" Reagan held his breath, as George seemed to ponder his request.

After selecting a plump tart, George lifted his gaze, grinning. "I'll probably live to regret this decision too." He chuckled as he took a bite of the confection. "But, yes Reagan, you have my consent."

chapter 18

A LONE FIGURE leaned against a tree as sounds of whimpering came from a clutched bundle wrapped in several layers of cloth. The figure repositioned the bundle and began humming while far away; a mournful baying filled the night air. As the howling mounted, the hidden one pressed forward, moving from wooded darkness to shadows of buildings on the outskirts of town. The moon emerged from dark clouds, exposing the figure while it stopped often as if counting houses. At last, the figure found a wrought-iron gate and as the latch closed behind her, she climbed the steps, rapping twice before retreating against the wall.

From within, a slow tapping could be heard. The sound grew, mingling with her beating heart before the portal swung open and a whispered voice bid the stranger come in.

Settled near the parlor fire and with their needlepoint forgotten, Amanda and Gabriella chatted contentedly while time slipped away. From an early age Amanda delighted in visiting the gabled manor, having fond memories of times spent in upper chambers when a younger Gabriella still climbed the stairs with amazing agility. Built before Gabriella was born, the stately manor had been lovingly maintained by the spinster ever since its purchase.

"It's getting late, my dear," Gabriella said. "My bones feel winter approaching and my bed is calling me thither." Reaching over, she patted Amanda's hand. "It's been good having you visit. We shan't let so much time pass before you come again."

Amanda kissed Gabriella's cheek. "I've missed times we spent together. I must've been terribly shy to have grown up with so few friends."

"Nonsense. You were just overwhelmed by your mother's directives. 'Do this! Don't do that!' How could you make friends with so many restrictions? I never forgave George being too weak to stop it. I prayed it wouldn't destroy the joy you radiated as a babe," she said. "Thankfully, my prayers were answered."

Amanda looked away. "Mother says her instructions are only for my own good."

"Not by my recollection," Gabriella said. "But for now, I'll hold my tongue." She sighed as she reached for her cane. "Your mother's actions stem from a deeper hurt. You're coming to an age where if needed, I'll reveal the source of that pain."

"I'm sure you'll tell me when you're ready," Amanda said as she kissed her cheek again. "Good night, Aunt Ella."

Lighting two candles, Amanda handed a flickering taper to Gabriella before blowing out the lamp. Together they climbed the stairs and were nearly at the top when an unexpected knock halted them.

"Who could it be, this time of night?" Amanda looked toward the foyer, missing Gabriella's worried glance.

"It could be a neighbor needing assistance," she said, turning around. "Or, someone who's lost and needs directions."

Amanda grasped Gabriella's arm. "Surely, you aren't going to answer that."

"My dear, I'm an old woman who's long fended for herself." She took a step down before motioning with her cane. "Go to bed. I'll be up shortly."

Amanda bit her lip as she debated whether or not to obey. After taking three more steps, Gabriella turned to glare at her. "Amanda, if I have trouble, I'll call Ben. I don't believe he's retired for the evening. Now, do as I say and go upstairs."

Ben was Gabriella's driver and handy man. Though well into manhood, being unmarried made him available at any hour.

"All right," she said. She paused at the landing to find Gabriella still watching her and reluctantly went to her room.

Grateful Ben had earlier laid a fire, Amanda sat near the hearth to listen for the familiar tapping of Gabriella's cane. She waited, not realizing her lids had fluttered closed until a chiming clock startled her awake.

Amanda opened her door, straining to hear a sound. "Aunt Ella, are you there?" Hearing only silence, she went to Gabriella's bedroom. She found a crackling fire and tidy bed, but no Aunt Ella. Taking a lamp, she descended the stairs.

After sweeping the entranceway she entered the parlor, but the room was empty. Fear began gnawing her insides and if not for the complete silence, she never would've heard the low murmur of voices. She followed the sound through the dining room to the kitchen, pushing open the door.

Amanda froze as she saw a dark-skinned girl sitting near the stove. The girl wore a tattered dress while a bandana covered her head. Wide-eyed, she snatched a bundle from her knees and looked at Gabriella. "She gonna tell? Ah cain't go back! Ah jus' cain't!"

"Oh no, child, it's all right," Gabriella said, laying a hand on her shoulder. "This is my niece, Amanda. She just wasn't expecting *visitors* this late."

Gabriella's voice shook as she gave Amanda a guarded glance. "I think you'd better have a seat. I've something to tell you." Once seated, she faced Amanda. "This may come as a shock, but I'm an abolitionist and have been most of my life. As you can see, I also help slaves escape to freedom."

Amanda spied an open jar of balm and evidence of a recently eaten meal. "Sh-she's a fugitive?"

"I'm afraid so. I wasn't expecting anyone tonight, but one never knows when duty calls."

A sudden wailing erupted from the bundle the girl held. She began rocking, crooning in a soft, sing-song voice. Opening the blankets, she uncovered a baby. Amanda's eyes widened as the girl loosened her garb while guiding the infant's rooting mouth.

"They wuz gonna sell mah baby," she said, shaking her head. "Ah wuz promised Ah could keep mah chile. But I heard mastah say he had t' sell th' boy, cuz crops wuz bad this year."

Gabriella's voice shook as she bent near the girl. "It's going to be all right. You're safe now." Dipping a cloth in a pan of water, she gently washed the girl's face.

"This is why I'm against slavery. It breaks my heart the way these people are treated." Using her cane, Gabriella made her way around the table. "I sent Ben to ready the wagon. It's too dangerous here since the hunters are using bloodhounds. The rest in Nell's party have been captured, and it won't be long before they discover she's missing."

Amanda shuddered, recalling her own encounter with bounty hunters. "What can I do?"

"I have clothes in a trunk that'll protect Nell against the cold. Why don't you hold the babe so she can change?"

"Of course," she said.

Nell rose and placed the baby into Amanda's lap. "His name's Isaiah, which means th' Lord saves. Ah believe th' Lord's gonna save mah chile."

"Hello, little one," Amanda said, brushing a fingertip across his nose. "You're having quite an adventure." He smiled, grabbing buttons on her dress as the women left the kitchen.

Soon, Gabriella returned. Sitting in a chair, she rested against her cane. "The poor girl is near exhausted. How she managed to find her way here is beyond me." She looked at Amanda sternly. "I'm sure you have many questions my dear, but now isn't the time to satisfy them. We haven't much time. Ben's trick of brushing her tracks will only slow the hunters, not put them off entirely. As soon as he returns, we must take Nell to a safe haven."

"Where will you go?"

"That my dear, is none of your business," she said, not unkindly. "You mustn't know if lives are to be saved."

Amanda nodded as Isaiah tugged a captured latch of hair. "What did Nell mean when she said she was promised her child wouldn't be sold?"

"Her master forced her to become his mistress when she turned fourteen. Promising not to sell the babe was a way to keep her from fleeing, as many do when faced with being separated from children."

"How despicable!" Amanda's voice shook as she looked at Isaiah. "Why, he was going to sell his own son!"

"Though vile, it's not uncommon." Gabriella said. "It seems he treated her well, allowing few duties while she carried his child. But once she discovered the truth, she fled with others already set to go." Her eyes softened at Amanda's obvious distress. "Hopefully, you can understand why I've chosen to be an abolitionist. I pray you won't betray me while Nell is in my care."

"I would never betray you," Amanda vowed. "I'll keep your secret, I promise."

"Thank you, my child," Gabriella said. "You can't know how comforted I am and blessed by your bravery."

Wearing new clothes, Nell returned with a clean blanket and yellow coverlet. Peeling rags from Isaiah, she wrapped the coverlet around his body before securing the blanket.

A light knock on the back door preceded Ben's entry into the kitchen. He appeared to have dressed rather hastily as his stylish bowler looked out of place with his workman's garb. "We've got to leave if we're to make our destination."

As Nell shrugged into her coat, Gabriella spoke. "Amanda, be a dear and get my wraps from the hallway closet. My legs are no longer nimble, and I'm afraid we're short on time."

"Surely, you can't mean to go with them," Amanda gasped. "There's no need, with Ben along."

Gabriella thumped her cane. "Do as I bid! I haven't time to argue!"

With a sob, Amanda rushed to gather her aunt's things. "At least, let me go with you," she begged while assisting with Gabriella's wraps.

"Absolutely not. If we were caught, you'd be arrested. However," she said, indicating the pantry, "you could get leftover muffins from dinner. Wrap them in a cloth."

Nell scooped Isaiah into her arms while Amanda gave Ben the bundled food. She only had time to kiss Gabriella's cheek before the servant hurried the women outside.

From the door, Amanda could see the outline of a horse harnessed to an open buckboard. She watched Ben place Nell and her baby inside before lifting Gabriella to the seat. Climbing up, he gathered the reins and after snapping them, sped away.

A shiver ran along Amanda's spine when she heard a faint baying of hounds. The howling rose and fell but never ceased, and spurred by fear Amanda ran through the house. She halted by a window where she detected a light bobbing through the woods at the edge of town. As she followed the lantern's path, she realized Ben was heading toward the same road where she and Reagan had encountered bounty hunters. If they continued toward the river, they'd be trapped! Not only would Nell be caught, Ben and Aunt Ella would surely be arrested.

In near panic, Amanda wheeled from the window to grab her coat before dashing out the door. She ran to the barn and once inside, lit the lantern kept near the door. Though she did her best to saddle Ben's horse, it shifted toward her as she mounted. Amanda left the barn at a fast cantor, praying she'd intercept the buckboard before the bounty hunters could overtake them.

chapter 19

REAGAN'S IMPATIENCE TO be gone from the Hampton party took root the moment he got permission to court Amanda. Soon after, he claimed he needed to step outside for a gentlemanly smoke. With many guests milling around both inside and out, he hoped it would be awhile before anyone realized he had taken his horse and left.

Reagan rode the short distance to Gabriella's home. As he entered the yard, he noticed a light burning in the rear of the house and thinking the women awake, bounded up the steps and sounded the knocker. After a lengthy pause and when no movement could be detected, Reagan knocked again, only louder. As he waited, a persistent sound drew his attention and he realized it sounded like the far off echo of baying hounds.

Just as he turned to listen, a horse galloped from the area of the barn and out the open gate. White, flapping petticoats declared the rider a woman. There were only two ladies in the house, and that most certainly was *not* Gabriella!

Reagan ran to his horse and mounted. Wheeling around, he followed the clattering hoof beats. Unsure of the rider's identity, he decided to follow to see if it was Amanda and why she left alone on a mysterious journey.

Amanda reached the crossroad that led to the river before halting. She blew on her fingers while peering ahead. In the bright moonlight she could see the wagon round a bend. But, just as she feared, the firebrands had grown closer and terrible din, louder.

"If you get me to that yonder wagon," she said, stroking her horse, "you'll get an extra ration of oats, I promise."

Suddenly, a prickling ran up Amanda's spine as she heard behind her, a horses' snort. Kicking her own horse, she rounded the turn, expecting to be nearing the buckboard. But when she saw the empty road she circled, searching the shadows. "Aunt Ella!" she cried. "Where are you?" As she neared a patch of trees, a figure rushed toward her, grabbing her reins.

"Amanda? What are you doing?"

"Thank God I found you!" she said, recognizing Ben's voice.

"What's wrong? We told you not to come."

"I *had* to!" she said. "I heard dogs then saw lights in the woods, heading this way."

Ben cursed before hurrying away. Bringing the wagon from its hiding place, he climbed up. Amanda could see Aunt Ella and Nell were now huddled together in the rear of the wagon.

"Go home," he said. "If anyone comes to the house, you know nothing, is that clear?"

"But, what if I'm stopped before I get there?"

"Were you followed?" he asked sharply.

"I'm not sure. I thought I heard someone behind me."

"She'll be caught!" Gabriella's voice rose. "We can't send her back."

"Then, she'll have to come with us," Ben said. "We'll take Old Trail road. It's no longer used."

"How can we?" asked Gabriella. "The bridge is rotted."

"We'll tie Amanda's horse to ours and pray we get across," he said, slapping the reins. "If we must, we'll ford the creek. It's shallow this time of year." He turned the wagon toward trees and through a weed-filled expanse that narrowed to a footpath. Traveling a short distance, he set the brake and hopped down. He then reached into the wagon, snatching Nell's head wrap before running out of sight.

He returned a few minutes later. "I dusted the ground with her scarf. After tying a rock to it, I threw it beyond this trace. Hopefully, it'll throw off the dogs."

"Where are we going?" Amanda asked.

"To a safe haven," he answered, slapping the reins.

The wagon's progress slowed as wheels became tangled with underbrush. After a laborious half mile,

Ben brought the buckboard to a halt. "Looks like we'll have to walk."

Climbing down, he held Nell's bundle until she alighted. Placing the babe in her arms, he then lifted Gabriella and set her on her feet. "I'll take the wagon across. If it's safe, you can follow. But, stay near the walls, the floor should be stronger there."

While Amanda dismounted, Ben made a harness with a coil of rope, fastening both horses together. He affected makeshift blindfolds by tying rags around their eyes. Then, using soothing tones, he led them into the interior of the covered bridge.

Facing the horses, Ben walked backwards, pulling the traces. Boards creaked as they moved and the horses became agitated. "Easy boys," he murmured. "Easy."

Above the trusses, an unexpected flutter of wings swooped near and a swarm of bats engulfed the wagon. Darting rapidly past in a squeaking, chirping cloud, the horses shied from the swift passage then reared, pulling Ben from his feet. It was then that the sound of baying hounds began to echo inside the narrow bridge.

Ben was nearly trampled as the frightened animals now rushed forward, splintering floorboards that fell to the water below. He clung to their necks, barely keeping his feet above churning hooves until halfway across, the bridge shifted with a terrible groan.

Suddenly a plank broke, jamming a rear wheel. The jarring impact and forceful halt further panicked the horses and rearing up, their hooves clawed near

Ben's face. As whinnies rent the air, he abandoned all attempts to be quiet.

"Go around!" he yelled. "Get across the creek!"

Amanda also heard the snarling hounds and with sick realization, knew they hadn't escaped. She immediately began pulling Gabriella toward the embankment as Nell held out her baby.

"Oh Lord! Save mah chile! Them dog's will kill mah baby! Please-" she sobbed, "-please don' let them kill mah baby!"

Terror gripped Amanda as she propelled both women forward after hearing thrashing sounds of dogs being released. But, without her cane, Gabriella could do little more than a swift hobble. When pounding hooves came crashing down the trail and a dark form vaulted directly in front of her, Amanda screamed.

"Amanda! What the hell are you doing?"

Amanda nearly fainted when she recognized Reagan's voice. "Help us! They're nearly upon us!"

Without further words, Reagan scooped Gabriella up and ran toward the creek as Nell snatched at the mount's reins. As the horse shied backwards, Amanda grabbed Nell. "Come on!"

With a wail, Nell gave up trying to catch the horse and together they ran among steeply banked trees until nearing water. Suddenly, Nell slipped. She caught herself, but the movement roused the baby and he began to squirm.

"Manda," she gasped. "Take Isaiah. I need t' catch mah breath." She handed him over, watching

Amanda wade the knee-high water before climbing back up the bank.

Nell knew what she needed to do. She began to run. As she ran, she felt a renewed strength surging through her limbs and in her heart settled a calming peace. She no longer heard the baying of hounds or her own labored breath. With a mother's love, the young slave never felt more free.

Her lips began moving as two forms burst from the woods, streaking toward her. "Dear Lord," she prayed. "Dear Lord, mah Father in heaven...hallow be yo' name..."

Flickering torches cast the forest with an ominous glow and still she ran on, struggling to remember words her mother had taught her. "...Fergive mah sins, as Ah fergive them that hurt me...save mah son, Lord, so he can be free..."

As if in a dream, the images before her slowed. She felt oddly detached as two shapes with evil eyes lunged at her.

Nell screamed as the ground rose up suddenly. In great surprise, she found herself sprawled beneath a pair of froth-mouthed beasts. With bared teeth, they prevented her from rising.

Writhing in the dirt, she thought to calm the dogs to keep them from attacking. "Good doggie," she whispered before the largest dog sank his teeth into her.

chapter 20

REAGAN SLOSHED THROUGH icy water with Gabriella in his arms. After cresting the bank he set her down before racing into the bridge.

"What's wrong? Why aren't you coming?"

"The wagon's stuck!" Ben yelled. "Get behind and push!"

Squeezing past the wagon, Reagan ran a hand along the buckboard until reaching the trapped wheel. He gripped two spokes and bracing his chest, lifted with all his might. After harrowing seconds where the floor groaned beneath him, he felt a loosening of the pinioned wheel.

"Pull!" he grunted.

While Ben tugged, the horses strained against their collars, eager to flee the hellish tunnel. With a loud crack, the buckboard broke free and surged forward. As the wagon gained momentum, a deafening rumble filled the bridge. Ben kept his feet in front of the shifting floorboards while Reagan clung to the wagon, his boots skimming the floor until the buckboard rattled onto solid ground. Barely had they stopped when Ben lifted his mistress into the wagon and Amanda placed the babe in her arms. Just as they looked around expecting Nell to be nearby, an ear-piercing scream rent the air.

"It's Nell!" Gabriella cried.

Terror congealed in Amanda's heart as she dashed toward the creek. "Hurry! She's staving them to save Isaiah!"

"Amanda wait!" Reagan plunged after her, grabbing a gun he had earlier tucked into his waist. Together they crossed the creek, soon coming to a grisly scene that nearly caused Amanda to retch.

Two enormous canines had clamped into Nell's bloodied form and were dragging her toward several men emerging the woods. The dogs growled at their approach but continued with their mission.

"Amanda, don't move," Reagan ordered. Raising his pistol, he squeezed the trigger.

The report sounded like a cannon in the still night air and as one hound fell, men near the woods scattered, extinguishing lanterns and lowering torches.

The remaining dog snarled but remained clamped onto Nell's arm as he wrenched her lifeless body another few inches. Reagan followed. Cocking the gun, he fired again. As the bullet found its mark, the animal crumpled.

Reagan wasted no time picking Nell up and together with Amanda rushed across the creek and reaching the wagon, gently laid her near Gabriella.

"Go *now!*" he urged, pushing Amanda. "I'll hold them off as long as I can." Outraged shouts could be heard as Ben yanked off the horses' blindfolds and jumped into the wagon.

"She can't come. You must take her with you," Gabriella said, covering Nell with her cloak.

"Aunt Ella..."

"Nay!" Gabriella insisted. "If we're apprehended, it'll be my burden alone." She laid Isaiah across Nell's body before turning to Reagan. "Get Amanda home safely. Ben! Let's go."

As the wagon disappeared from sight, a sudden clattering of hooves sounded inside the bridge. Reagan thrust Amanda behind him before approaching the structure and when no one emerged, he entered and soon led out his own horse.

"The gunshots must've scared him across the bridge," Reagan said while mounting. "We've got to hurry." Reaching down, he pulled Amanda up behind him. As she slid on, her dress dripped icy rivulets on the horses' flanks causing Reagan to lose several moments while the animal pranced about. Then, in a display of sheer strength, he sent his horse plunging toward the creek the same time the bounty hunters penetrated the bridge. They swarmed out the opposite side, their torches illuminating the creek bed as well as the fleeing couple.

Angry shouts rang from the trackers as Reagan's horse left the water and lunged up the opposite ridge. Amanda clung tightly but with the jolting stride she lost her grip and fell backwards, landing with a thud before tumbling down the embankment.

Reagan brought his horse around, spotting her white petticoats as she rolled to a stop. Leaping off his horse, he plunged after her, heedless of branches that tore his clothing.

Though disoriented, Amanda struggled to her knees, her vision blurring as lanterns bobbed closer from the opposite bank, multiplying before her eyes. When a figure loomed above her, Amanda screamed.

"Come on!" Reagan cried. He scooped her up and threaded his way through trees. He had almost made it up the embankment when he heard triumphant shouts.

"There they are!"

"Git 'em. Their gittin' away!"

As trackers crested the bank, Reagan set Amanda on her feet and together they ran toward his horse. But they approached too quickly and when Reagan tried grabbing the reins, his horse shied before bolting. Left with no form of escape, Reagan stepped forward shielding Amanda from more than a dozen swarming men. Though he didn't pull it out, light from the torches revealed the gun tucked in his waist.

"Hey boss," a familiar voice sounded. "It's them people we saw two fortnight ago." He snickered as he approached. "They seem as anxious to see us as the last time." Grinning wickedly, he handed off his torch and reached for Amanda, not seeing Reagan's fist until it crashed into his jaw, knocking him to the ground.

"Hey Ted," taunted a lanky comrade. "That feller really gave you the deuce! You gonna kiss that girl or just lay there, mooning at how purty she is?"

Their laughter ceased when Jebediah shouldered his way into the light. After kicking Ted who scrambled to his feet, the giant turned to Reagan. "Seems we meet again," he rasped. "Mighty suspicious yu being here every time we come to fetch runaways." Crossing his arms, he dropped his gaze to the bloody splotches on Reagan's clothing. "Where's the slave girl and her brat?"

"We were alone. When the dogs attacked, I shot them to defend myself and the lady."

"Yer lyin'," Jeb said. "The dogs had the bitch! We all heard it. And, Ah don't care if you *are* friends with the sheriff, yer gonna pay fer obstructing the law. Besides losing mah bounty, you killed mah best bloodhounds." He paused, seeing if his words sparked any fear. "Unless of course, yer to suddenly recall where the girl is. Then, Ah might go easy on yu and only charge the cost of mah dogs."

Amanda lifted her chin. "You're despicable! If-if there *had* been a girl with a babe, they'd both be dead by now."

"Guess we'll never know now, will we missy, seeing how we ain't got nobody here but yu and mah dead dogs."

"Let me git the truth out of her," Ted offered. "Of course, you'd have to peel her off'n that feller first."

"Shut up, Ted. We ain't gonna hurt th' laidy. Ah know she's gonna come around. Why else would she be out here?"

"I admit, it doesn't look good finding us so far from town," Reagan said. "But the truth is, we stole away together and must've been caught in the wake of whomever you were tracking. We had no idea we were being followed until your dogs were upon us. Let Amanda go home and I'll go to the sheriff's office where you can question me at length."

"You think I believe yu rode all this way just to bed the girl?" Jeb said. "Well, Ah don't! If yu won't tell me the truth, perhaps this girl's folks can jiggle it from yu." Evidenced by the fear on Amanda's face, Jeb believed he had found leverage. "Betcha they'd want to know why their girlie's so far from town, in the dead of night." He chortled as he pushed his way through the men. "Git his horse and put them on it. Mind now, they don't git away."

"What about his gun?" asked Ted. "We ain't gonna let him keep it, are we?"

Jeb pondered the question as he eyed Reagan's protective stance. "Let him keep it. It'll keep you boys from gittin' too friendly. We'll let the sheriff deal with his pig-shooter."

As bid, Reagan's horse was brought back and after lifting Amanda into the saddle, he hoisted himself behind her. A procession of men on foot and horseback entered the woods followed by a mule strapped with dead hounds.

Sometime during the ride back, Amanda leaned against Reagan's chest. She didn't notice when her eyes closed or when he opened his coat, sharing his warmth. But, snuggled against him and encompassed by his arms, she fell into deep, exhausted sleep.

chapter 21

SHERIFF HADLEY WAKENED to loud banging on his door. He dressed hurriedly when told Jebediah Johnson had placed two prisoners in jail. Strapping on his gun, he wondered what mischief the tracker had stirred this time.

The sheriff's curiosity turned to anger when he stepped inside the jailhouse. Reagan and a girl stood against a wall while half a dozen trackers sat crowding the stove. A giant-sized man filled the sheriff's chair, balancing a rifle across his lap.

Fury darkened Jim's face when he recognized Amanda, the daughter of George and Emily Bruester. "What's going on?"

"We got us a couple lawbreakers," Jeb drawled. "They were transporting runaways an' even kilt mah prize dogs, so we's gonna hafta press charges."

"We'll see who'll be pressing charges," Jim said, noting dried blood on Reagan's shirt. Then lifting Amanda's chin, he examined her face. "Are you hurt?"

"Just tired," she said.

Thrusting out his foot, Jim kicked Ted's chair, spilling him onto the floor. "Here," he said, setting it before Amanda. "These men don't know their manners."

"Thank you," she said, sitting down.

"Jim, this whole affair can be explained," Reagan said. "I ask you to let Miss Bruester return to her aunt's house where she was spending the night. It furthers no one's cause to keep her here. Of course, I'll stay as long as necessary to answer questions you or these men have."

"No!" Jeb said, slamming down his fist. "He's too anxious to git the filly out of here. I say neither leaves until Ah know where they spirited off the runaway." Leaning back, Jeb eyed Amanda. "Ah say she knows something. Ah told them if they confessed the whereabouts of the slave, Ah'd drop all charges. Excepting of course, the cost of mah hounds he shot to death."

Jim looked at Reagan who confirmed the last statement with a nod. "The dogs were about to attack. As I stated before, I was defending myself and the lady."

Jim turned to the deputy stationed at the door. "Go fetch George Bruester. He needs to know where his daughter is. As for you, Reagan, I guess you're old enough to take care of your own business. Unless of course, you want me to send for Thomas."

"There's no need. You know me well enough to know I'm no abolitionist. We were simply caught by these ruffians who refuse to believe the truth."

"Huh!" Jeb snorted. "He tried to say he took the missy miles from town to flip her skirt in the dead of winter."

Amanda remained silent, though her face turned crimson. That accusation was preferable to the truth. And although she wondered about her aunt's safety, she felt thankful Gabriella hadn't disclosed their destination. Now, no matter how forcefully they questioned her, Amanda couldn't reveal that which she didn't know.

"We seen evidence of a wagon, and heard more'n one horse," Jeb said, pressing his case. "But found nuthin' but mah dead dogs and these two running like they got something to hide."

Jim looked up sharply. "*Evidence* of a wagon? You don't have it in your possession?"

Jeb rose to tower over the sheriff. "Ah don't *need* possession to prosecute these criminals. Mah eyes and ears is proof enuff!" He pointed at Amanda. "Yu think she'd traipse through the woods just to git bedded by this here stud? Ah say they got caught while the others got away."

"Maybe your word is good enough in the South, Mr. Johnson. But in Ohio, you need evidence to prosecute a man," Jim said.

Jebediah pointed a finger at Reagan's shirt. "Whut do yu call that? Do yu think he'd git within fifty feet of mah hounds and not git chewed up? There's nary a mark on him. Ah say he picked the girl up and got her away."

"Rest assured Mr. Johnson, whatever happened will be thoroughly investigated. I know the law regarding fugitive slaves. You don't have to tell me how to do my job." At the sound of raised voices, two jailers emerged from the back room and stood behind the sheriff.

Jebediah glared at Amanda. "This one's got the answers Ah want. Separate her from the gent, and she'd spill the beans fer sher!"

Amanda looked in anguish from the sheriff to Reagan. "There's nothing to admit except we got caught while slipping away privately."

As whooping and whistling erupted from around the stove, the sheriff nodded toward the door. "I think it's time you boys leave."

For once Jebediah seemed in agreement with the lawman. "Go git some shut eye," he ordered, "cuz Ah may be awhile."

As the trackers filed out, Jeb turned to Amanda. "Ah'm thinking yu being a laidy and all, yu wouldn't want yur name in the papers."

"Now, wait a minute," Jim interrupted. "I won't allow you to make threats."

"Ah can do whatever it takes to git the truth," Jeb said. "But, if she cooperates, Ah'd go easy on her. All Ah want is the runaway and her whelp."

Amanda's chin quivered as she returned the giant's stare. "I've already told you. I met Reagan at my aunt's house and we left, alone."

"Jim, this is ridiculous." Reagan said. "We did nothing wrong but take a ride in the country without a chaperone. Surely, you won't ruin Amanda's reputation for a foolish act I persuaded her to do." He looked squarely into Jebediah's hostile eyes. "This man is trying to blame us for his failing to capture a runaway and stupidly allowing his dogs to attack innocent people. If he wants to prosecute someone, let me bear the responsibility."

"Calm down, Reagan," Jim said, sighing. Reaching for a coffee pot on the stove, he poured a cup then handed it to Amanda. "I know it's after midnight, but you look like you need some." He filled another cup and gave it to Reagan. "You might as well have a seat. This'll take awhile."

"Thanks, but I prefer standing."

The sheriff turned to Jeb. "Want some?"

The bounty hunter snorted. Then pulling a flask from beneath his pelt, he twisted off the cap and took several swigs.

After pouring coffee for himself, the sheriff sat behind his desk, pulling papers from a drawer. "I'll take each of your statements, starting with you, Miss Bruester."

"Yer not gonna question them together, are yu?" Jeb said, looking astounded. "Hell! He'll just repeat whut she says. Why don't you git proof in that old bridge? Yu can see where a wagon got stuck before we ketched them trying to escape. They could have someone there now, spoiling the evidence!"

"All right, Mr. Johnson. I planned to do that later today. But, if you wish to go now, one of my men will accompany you to examine the area. After all, we don't want someone planting evidence either. Ed, please provide Mr. Johnson with a fresh mount. It'll be light soon so take notes on what you observe, and if you recover any items, bring them to me."

Jeb looked suspicious. "Yu ain't gonna let them go whilst Ah'm gone, are ya?"

"Not before I take their statements and determine the probability of their guilt. If you recover evidence proving these two were transporting slaves, I can always fetch them back."

"Whut about their accomplices?" Jeb insisted stubbornly. "They wuzn't alone, ya know."

"As improbable as your story is, Mr. Johnson, I'm going to investigate this completely. I'll send a deputy to speak with Gabriella Bruester as soon as light breaks. Since I can personally vouch for both Amanda and Reagan's parents being at Sam Hampton's last night, it won't be necessary to question their whereabouts."

"Ah'm warning yu just the same," Jeb said. "Ah won't leave until Ah git the slave."

As the door slammed behind the bounty hunter, Jim shook his head. "I've a feeling we haven't seen the last of Mr. Johnson." Then picking up his pencil, he looked at Amanda.

"Could you please start at the beginning?"

chapter 22

It was five a.m. by the time Sheriff Hadley finished questioning Amanda and then took additional notes while Reagan gave his account of events involving Jebediah. Both stuck to their story that they had been out for a ride when they encountered bounty hunters. Reagan revealed he had already obtained George's permission to escort Amanda without a chaperone, therefore proving their story.

Amanda remained silent at Reagan's admission, wondering if that too was a fabrication or an unexpected bit of luck. She determined she would question him about it later when a sharp rapping at the door interrupted their session.

"I guess that's all I needed," Jim said, putting down his pencil. At his nod, the deputy opened the door allowing Emily to burst in, followed by a much slower, bleary-eyed George.

Shocked at her daughter's appearance, Emily hurried over, burying Amanda in her bosom. "Oh, my baby!"

"I'm so sorry," Amanda said, dissolving into tears. "This is all my fault."

Emily took a handkerchief and daubed Amanda's cheeks while examining her. "Don't cry. Are you hurt?"

"No Mama," she said. "Just embarrassed at my foolishness."

Emily turned to glare hatefully at Reagan whose crossed arms concealed much of his stained shirt. "You vile man!" she spat. "What possessed you to bring this shame upon my daughter? Do you hate me so much you'd use an innocent child to ply your vengeance?"

"Emily!" George touched her shoulder. "Please calm down. Amanda's not hurt. Let's handle this without undue discord."

"I will *not* calm down!" Emily pointed an accusing finger at Reagan. "This-this *Burnsfield* has likely destroyed our daughter's chances of a suitable marriage! Not only that, he's somehow entangled her in transporting fugitive slaves! The deputy said-"

Amanda stood, taking her mother's hand. "No, mama. Twas nothing other than we took a ride by ourselves. I can vouch we weren't involved with anything illegal." She hoped her eyes wouldn't belie the truth that her intent had only been to warn Aunt Ella. That she and Reagan had gotten trapped by bounty hunters was unfortunate, but a blessing for those in the escaping buckboard.

"I'm the one at fault, Mrs. Bruester, and I apologize," Reagan said. "I got permission from George to escort Amanda without a chaperone, and in my poor judgment decided to use the privilege that night."

"Surely not!" Emily challenged as she turned wrathful eyes to her husband. "Amanda's father would *never* give such permission, would you, George?"

George sank into a chair before looking into his wife's furious face. "I-I seem to recall such a conversation." His hands shook as he accepted a cup of coffee the sheriff offered. "I gave Reagan permission to court Amanda without escort, because..." he strained at the tendrils of his memory, "...because..."

"Because of my lengthy absences," Reagan finished as he suddenly recognized the gift handed him. "I didn't intend to jeopardize her reputation," he said, looking at Amanda's shocked expression. "But, I'll fully bear the consequences of my actions. And, if needed I will affiance myself immediately."

"W-what?" Emily found it difficult to perceive the meaning of his words. As a dawning recognition spread, she placed a hand over her heart. "Oh, no! Not that!"

Now that the idea had struck, Reagan pursued it with enthusiasm. "I'd consider it an honor to marry Amanda. Once we made the announcement, the rumors should go away."

Amanda felt a sudden weakness that had nothing to do with her recent adventure. Without taking her eyes off Reagan, she sat down. Though grateful he hadn't exposed Gabriella's secret, she nevertheless, couldn't have imagined anything as momentous as a marriage proposal.

Jim broke the sudden silence. "Be that as it may, we have more pressing matters to discuss, namely one

Jebediah Johnson who claims these two were out last night breaking fugitive slave laws." Having gained everyone's attention, he continued. "We should get this resolved without delay. I've sent word to Judge McCleary asking him to have a hearing later this afternoon. I must advise however, that Reagan and Amanda discuss nothing between them until after the hearing."

"Don't worry," Emily huffed. "He'll see Amanda over my dead body."

George stood as his wife draped Amanda's coat over her shoulders. "Now dear, let's not get carried away."

Emily directed Amanda toward the door, stopping in front of the sheriff. "Jim, I trust this news won't leave your office. I don't want my daughter tied to any scandal no matter how small."

"I won't mention a word, Mrs. Bruester, but I can't keep Jebediah or his men from spreading tales." He rose and opened the door, smiling tightly. "Perhaps, with the elections just yesterday, the journalists will be at the telegraph office and miss this bit of excitement."

Emily nodded. "Let's hope so. We'll be waiting in the carriage." After they left, Reagan unfolded his arms and poured himself more coffee.

"Good Lord," George gasped, spying the stains. "What did you do?"

"Stopped two hounds, bent on mauling whatever they could lay hold of," he answered.

George's face turned ashen as he stared at the ruined shirt. "Thank you," he said. "Thank you for protecting Amanda."

"One more thing," Jim said. "Be at Judge McCleary's chambers by four this afternoon. I'll have my report as well as any evidence we find. Be prepared for lots of questions. And expect Jeb to be indelicate. It appears to be his style."

"We'll be there. But, I'm afraid this will devastate my family," George said, his shoulders slumping. "I know I've not always done right by my little girl. But, from now on, I will." Straightening his back, he opened the door before looking at Reagan. "If necessary, I'll consider your offer."

After George left, Jim folded his arms and chuckled. "Reagan, am I to understand you just proposed? Last I knew, you were just one of many vying for Amanda's hand. I bet they never thought to drag her across the countryside, take on dangerous bounty hunters, and *then* ask for her hand in marriage."

"Under the circumstances it was the honorable thing to do."

"Yet, we still have Jebediah and his filthy cohorts to deal with," Jim said, placing Reagan's gun in a drawer. "I can't give this back until after the hearing. And, if I were you, I'd shave before you see the judge. He dislikes unkempt witnesses."

Reagan nodded. "I'll do that. I can pick my gun up later."

After leaving the sheriff's office and all the way home Reagan thought about his newfound advantage.

Without any trickery and a little luck, he could soon secure the means to pay his creditors.

Entering the house, it was evident to Reagan everyone was still asleep. He quietly entered his room and stepped into the adjoining chamber that held a washstand and tub. After stripping to his waist, he filled the basin and soaped his torso, scrubbing vigorously. Dumping the water, he refilled the bowl and shaved off his remaining beard. Lastly, he removed the rest of his clothes, crawled into bed and immediately fell asleep.

What seemed like only moments later, the door burst open. Katherine stood over him, clutching his soiled shirt. "Reagan! Have you been hurt?"

Reagan stretched while sitting up. "Good morning, mother," he said, yawning.

"What's the meaning of this?" she demanded. "I nearly fainted when Lela brought me these bloody clothes."

"I'm sorry you were frightened, but I'm not hurt."

If it's not yours, whose blood is it?"

A movement by the doorway halted Reagan. "Is there anything you need, Mrs. Burnsfield?" Unable to enter unless bid; the maid peered curiously into the room.

"No thank you, Lela. Everything's all right." Without further explanation she went and shut the door before returning. "Tell me. Are you in some kind of trouble?"

"Perhaps, just a little." Reagan kept his voice low as he outlined his encounter with bounty hunters, carefully omitting any reference to Gabriella or her charges.

Katherine's eyes grew wide. "Reagan! How could you do such a thing?" She felt queasy looking at the splotches on the once immaculate shirt. "Do you realize you both could've been killed?"

"I've been so informed by just about everybody," he said. "After the hearing, I'm hoping to persuade Amanda's parents to let me rectify my mistake."

"How do you propose to do that?"

"Mother, do you remember that peach gown you've wanted to wear for a special occasion?"

"What does a dress have to do with this situation?" When Reagan began humming a tune, she recognized the melody and Katherine's mouth opened. "Surely, you aren't suggesting *marrying* that poor girl!"

"Getting married would stop any rumors. Besides, you've been after me for years to settle down." He clasped hands behind his head, looking askance at his mother's expression. "What? Don't you approve my choice of wife?"

Of course I approve of Amanda," she said. "She's all I'd hoped for in a daughter. What I don't understand is your cavalier attitude toward marriage. You just don't choose a wife hastily, as if you're picking which socks to wear." She paced the carpet, forgetting the shirt in her hand. "What about the accusations? I know it's ridiculous, but..." She stopped abruptly, her eyes widening. "Wait! You recently asked me about escaping slaves. Reagan, have you become involved with emancipators? I mean, can those bounty hunters prove anything?"

Reagan debated telling his mother the truth. He decided that though she'd be sympathetic to Gabriella's beliefs, now wasn't the time to reveal secrets.

"Absolutely not. There's nothing to prove, save we found ourselves in the path of slave hunters. I asked those questions because Amanda and I had an earlier encounter with bounty hunters, and my curiosity was aroused."

"What encounter?" Katherine became alarmed once again. "Reagan, you never mentioned this before."

"Because it wasn't worth mentioning. We were coming back from a ride by the river and we chanced upon bounty hunters capturing slaves. The leader was suspicious, but I convinced him we were innocent bystanders."

"I see," she said, sighing. "Should I send for your father? He's at the mill."

"That won't be necessary," he said while reaching for his robe. After donning the garment, Reagan opened his wardrobe and shuffled its contents. "What exactly does one wear to a judge's chambers?"

"Anything but what you wore last night," she said, tossing his shirt to the floor.

chapter 23

REAGAN ARRIVED AT the courthouse before his appointed time and was ushered into a small room by Sheriff Hadley. "The Judge will hear Jebediah's account before questioning Amanda, then you," Jim said. "You might as well have a seat until you're called."

"Have the Bruester's arrived?"

"They came nearly an hour ago. As you can imagine, Emily was quite agitated and George seems to be taking the brunt of it. If he could deny being at Sam Hampton's last night, I think he'd confess to the whole matter himself."

"There's enough blame to go around," Reagan said, removing his hat. "I hope to have this difficulty settled by the end of the day."

Jim nodded. "I'll let the Judge know you're here. He'll send for you when it's your turn to be questioned."

Nearly an hour elapsed before a deputy summoned Reagan. Jebediah as well as the Bruesters were seated in the Judge's chambers while the sheriff stood against a wall. Judge McCleary, looking somber and garbed in a black robe, sat behind his desk. "Come in, come in," he said as the deputy shut the door. "Have a seat. This is an informal hearing."

"Well, lookee there," Jeb sneered. "The scofflaw shaved his face to look less the criminal he really is."

Reagan ignored Jeb as his eyes met Amanda's. Sitting between her parents, she looked nervous but not as frightened as when they had been taken to the jailhouse.

Judge McCleary waited until Reagan took a seat, and then clearing his throat, spoke. "Jebediah Johnson, a bonded bounty hunter from the state of Virginia, claims he was in pursuit of a slave girl and her babe when he encountered a man and a woman allegedly aiding in said slaves' escape." Ambrose paused at Emily's intake of breath before continuing. "Mr. Johnson claims he followed fresh wagon tracks, catching the wagon as it got stuck in a bridge on Old Trail Road. Believing he'd found said slaves, Jebediah loosed a pair of valuable bloodhounds. Am I correct so far, sir?"

"So far," Jeb growled.

"Mr. Johnson believes he then heard the screams of the slave girl he was tracking, followed by two gun shots that sent him and his men scattering for fear of their lives. Minutes later, he claims he came upon his hounds and found them shot dead. Immediately afterward, he witnessed Reagan Burnsfield fleeing with Amanda Bruester."

"Mr. Johnson alleges that Reagan and Amanda deliberately interfered with the apprehension of his client's property and so took them into custody. He now wants to press charges against both parties."

With prosecution likely, Amanda feared the truth would now spill from Reagan's lips. But he seemed unconcerned by the accusations. Not so with Emily, who appeared visibly upset.

"Your honor," she said, desperation tingeing her voice. "Amanda had nothing to do with this. She's a mere child!"

Jeb grinned. Standing up, he flared his pelt, arms akimbo. "According to the law, yer filly's just as guilty as this feller here," he bellowed.

"She's innocent, I say!" Emily said, turning to her husband. "George, do something!"

"Mr. Johnson!" McCleary said, looking over his spectacles. "Sit down. This isn't an inquest. You can't intimidate the Bruester's." The judge waited until Jeb returned to his seat. "You may now present evidence that proves these two were breaking the law and I'll decide if it's enough to support your claims."

Jeb leaned over outspread knees. "First of all, mah dogs wuz trained to only go after whut scent Ah puts them on, and they were hot on that bitch's trail. Ah heard them catch something real good. The screaming wuzn't just fear, it wuz pain, pure and simple. Now this gent claims he shot mah dogs cuz they wuz fixing to attack his laidy. That's a lie. The man wuz covered in blood, yet, there wuz nary a mark on him. Ah say he shot mah dogs and then carried the slave somewhere whilst she wuz bleeding all over him." Jebediah pointed an accusing finger at Reagan. "Just ask him. The sheriff seen the blood, too."

"What about it, Jim?" Ambrose looked at the sheriff. "Did Mr. Burnsfield have an excessive amount of blood covering his person?"

"Seemed a mite overlarge," Jim said, taking a toothpick from his pocket and sticking it between his teeth. "But then again, Reagan claims he got bloody from the hounds. Maybe he tried resuscitating one of them and hugged the beast too tight."

Judge McCleary seemed to struggle to maintain his stern demeanor. He frowned at Reagan. "Can you explain yourself? How did you manage to get so bloody?"

Reagan remained silent as he considered the query. He knew the judge had already questioned Amanda and would listen carefully to his story. Despite McCleary's acquaintance with his family, he didn't doubt the judge would be diligent in his duties. "I remember checking whether the dogs were dead or merely wounded, your honor," Reagan began. "It was dark and I can't recall the exact circumstance of how I stained my shirt, except I may have shot one of the dogs close to his heart. Perhaps, the hound bled out as I leaned over him. Other than that, I have no answer."

Jeb stood up, flexing his hands. "That's impossible, Ah say. Twas too cold fer them dogs to bleed so from a single shot. Besides, he broke the law when he interfered with my method of catching runaways."

Reagan's eyes hardened at Jebediah's words and his body tensed like a steel coil. Having contained his dislike for the bounty hunter, he now welcomed the opportunity to demonstrate his own brand of justice. But, as Reagan's hand curled into a fist, Judge McCleary rose and leaned over his desk.

"Mr. Johnson! If you can't control yourself, I'll conduct this inquiry without you. Now, the story Mr. Burnsfield professes is not unlike the testimony Miss Bruester gave earlier." McCleary resumed his seat before looking at the sheriff. "Did you instruct the witnesses to have no further contact with each other?"

"I can assure you," Emily asserted before Jim could respond. "Amanda hasn't spoken with Reagan since we took her from the sheriff's office."

"Whut fer?" Jeb snorted. "They wuz sitting next to one another the first time they gave their lies."

Ambrose gave Jeb a pained look. "Mr. Johnson, the court takes into consideration all evidence, not just testimony. If you'll allow me to continue without interrupting, I'll be able reach a decision. Now, the court is satisfied with the witness's rendition of facts. If not probable, it's at least possible. What else do you have Mr. Johnson?"

Unnoticed until now, Jeb pointed to a knotted blue cloth on the desk. "Me and the deputy found that dirty rag just past the turn off the wagon took. It had been tossed down the road, to distract mah dogs. They weren't fooled none, though."

Amanda dropped her eyes, her heart quickening as she recalled Ben using the scarf to divert Nell's scent.

McCleary picked up the scarf with a large stone tied inside and directed his question to Reagan. "Did you throw this?"

"No, your honor," Reagan said. "In fact, I've never seen it before."

Jebediah's chin jutted toward Amanda. "Whut about her? She's got guilt written all over her face."

Ambrose looked incredulous. "Good Lord, sir. According to the sheriff's report the deputy found this scarf about forty feet past the road to the bridge. Are you implying this young woman could throw a rock that far?"

"Mah gut tells me she knows about it," he growled.

"No your honor," Amanda said. "I didn't throw anything."

"Of course you didn't!" the Judge said, dropping the stone. "Do you have any evidence, sir, linking this scarf to these two witnesses?" Fixing his eyes on Jebediah, McCleary waited, already knowing the answer.

"Just that they were at the bridge where mah dogs tracked the girl. He admits he shot mah dogs. He wuz covered in blood, and they wuz running away." Jeb paused to glare at Reagan. "How else can you explain this wuz the *second* time we seen the gent and his filly whilst fetching runaways?"

"Second time?" Emily said, looking aghast.

"Yer daughter ain't so innocent now, is she?" Jeb said. "Yu should've seen how fer she wuz unwrapped, too. Gives a feller notions about her virtue—"

Just as Reagan stood up, George launched himself from his chair and punched the giant's face with all his might. Emily gasped as Jim threw himself between the two while grabbing for his holster. He found the act unnecessary for Jebediah only rubbed his jaw, amused at George's show of manliness.

Ambrose stood, vigorously beating his gavel. "Order! Order I say! There'll be order in my chambers!" Flinging the gavel, Judge McCleary pointed a finger at Jebediah. "If you cannot contain yourself Mr. Johnson, I'll end this inquiry here and now."

Jeb held up his hands in contrition. "Mah apologies, yer Honor. Ah sometimes fergit mesself."

The Judge waited while everyone resumed their seats. George, though visibly provoked, sat a little taller while Emily sank further in her chair, quietly weeping.

McCleary thumbed through several notes. "What of the wagon, Mr. Johnson? Did you recover any evidence in the wagon?"

"Didn't git the wagon," Jeb said. "We found a break in the floor where it got stuck in the bridge. But it got away."

"Do you mean to say you have no wagon?"

"Ah have eye witnesses!" Jeb ground out. "All Ah want is the slave and her brat. If yu can git the gent to hand them over, Ah'll drop all charges."

Emily stopped sniffling and looked at Jeb. "You'd drop all charges?"

"Except of course, the cost of mah dogs," he said. "After that, Ah'd fergit yer girlie wuz even there."

At Emily's hopeful glance, Reagan shrugged his shoulders. "As I said before, I have no information that would be of help to Mr. Johnson." He then looked toward Jeb. "If you have further accusations, I suggest you say so now."

The Judge slammed down his hand. "*I'll* decide the questions here. Now, let's get to the crux of the matter." He turned to Jebediah. "Do you have a warrant for either Mr. Burnsfield or Miss Bruester?"

"Ah don't need one as long as Ah keep the peace while doing mah job. Everyone knows that," Jeb said. "And Ah kept the peace."

"Mr. Johnson, you don't have a wagon and you don't have a slave. You don't even have the babe you claim was there." Ambrose folded his arms, staring. "You sir, have wasted these good people's time and sorely tempted my patience. Furthermore, this court will be sympathetic to either party if they decide to prosecute you for false imprisonment."

"Ah'd have yer evidence if yu'd search where they came from last night. The sheriff didn't find Dame Bruester at home. Ah say the biddy's in on it too."

McCleary sighed. "Mr. Johnson, as you should well know, the Constitution asserts no authority in unreasonable search and seizure. You sir, have tried to circumvent the law. Until you show proof that withstands the scrutiny of this court, you shan't harass either party again. Is that clear?"

Jebediah couldn't believe his ears. "So, yer believing their lies about courting, miles from town, in the damned middle of winter?"

"It's not what I believe, Mr. Johnson, it's what you can prove. And you haven't proven otherwise."

Judge McCleary then stood and gave a final rap of his gavel. “This investigation is hereby concluded. You are all free to go.”

chapter 24

RELIEF FLOODED EMILY'S countenance at Judge McCleary's words. Believing this ordeal over, she tried gathering her wits. Not since her father had rejected Thomas as a suitable husband had Emily felt so aggrieved. Back then, her ego had been sorely bruised when Thomas withdrew his courtship. At first, she insisted he ask again but he refused, claiming no amount of wealth would be enough for her blue-blooded sire.

Thus, the shock of his betrayal pierced her heart; planting a root so deep it choked all reason. In Emily's imaginings, Thomas should've fought for her. Instead, he abandoned her to marry another. Because she never stopped loving him, she never lost hope. She chose to believe his marriage would fail and invited him to lavish balls where she richly displayed her charms. But Thomas seemed only to have eyes for his honey-blond wife and not until Reagan was born would she concede failure.

Deeply embittered, Emily had thrown herself at the son of the oldest and wealthiest family in Cantonsville. Timorous and somewhat awkward, George proved easily manipulated. With her father's encouragement, Emily accepted George's proposal later that year.

Over time, Emily had been able to conceal her animosity toward Thomas and his son. But now, with this latest turn of events, no one would fault her if she refused Reagan further contact with her daughter.

Emily's thoughts returned to the present when the Judge stood up. Not waiting for George, she took Amanda's arm and approached the door where Jim promptly opened it.

"Good day, Mrs. Bruester. Amanda," he said as they left.

"Ah cain't believe it," Jeb said. "Is that it? Ah got no recourse?"

McCleary looked annoyed. "For one thing, if you ever enter my chambers again, I'll expect you to make yourself presentable. A bath and clean set of clothes goes a long way toward civilized discourse."

The sound of George clearing his throat caused everyone to turn. Reaching inside his coat, he withdrew a billfold and began thumbing currency. "Mr. Johnson, I understand you lost two dogs. What would you consider fair payment for the hounds?"

Jebediah wet his lips. "Well, they wuz special bred, ya know."

"I'm sure they were," George said, holding out several bills. "Included is a bit more to make amends for your lost time." He smiled as Jeb seized the cash.

"Will you need anything else before returning to Virginia?"

"Ah cain't rightly say," he said, stuffing money in his pocket.

"I see. If you need supplies, let the sheriff know and I'll be happy to furnish the remainder."

"Mah boys need a few days rest, fer sher," Jeb said. "Ah'll be fixing mah next move after Ah wire mah client to see if he still wants me to pursue his wench."

As Hadley opened the door for Jebediah to leave, the bounty hunter sneered. "In the mean time, if Ah find proof of th' gent's guilt, Ah'll be back. Mah client still ain't got his property."

Elizabeth Hampton happened to be passing the courthouse in the mayor's landau when Emily and Amanda emerged. The hurried steps of the women caught her eye and as she gazed out the window she recognized the Bruesters in the pool of a streetlamp. She became even more intrigued when Emily lowered a veil over her face before being assisted into a carriage.

Elizabeth rapped on the wall until the driver opened a small aperture and inquired of her wishes. As he turned the carriage around, she settled into her seat, smiling smugly. She would soon know the reason for the odd behavior. Being the mayor's daughter certainly had its advantages among the talkative clerks at city hall.

Later that evening, Elizabeth left a dinner party where Camilla Muelder had been among the guests. With calculated nonchalance, she had whispered to Camilla the reason for Amanda's visit to the judges' chambers, repeating the account told by a clerk. She enjoyed seeing the astounded expression on Camilla's face that turned into an excited interrogation of all she knew. Emboldened by her own importance, Elizabeth embellished the story, implanting her own rationale to suggest Amanda had lured Reagan into a tryst that backfired with their arrest. Elizabeth little doubted that before the week was out, Amanda's reputation would be so damaged that no one would desire the girl, including Reagan Burnsfield.

On the ride home she decided to throw her own dinner party. Having the gathering next week would give her time to fan the gossip. She smiled, realizing there was no greater satisfaction than plucking a morsel from the lips of another.

chapter 25

For the hundredth time, Gabriella glanced at the mantel clock as she waited in the Bruester's parlor. Following their escape from the bridge, Ben had driven to a farmhouse where fellow abolitionists took Nell in to nurse her wounds. Yet, despite their efforts, the girl succumbed to her injuries. Sorely grieved, Gabriella instructed they bury Nell while she and Ben took Isaiah to a wet nurse in the next county. Later, he would be transported to the Canadian border with others who would raise him as their own. Lacking sleep and exhausted with worry, Gabriella then hurried home.

She found the house empty and after a quick search realized Amanda had never returned. After changing clothes, Ben drove her to the Bruester's where she was told Amanda and her parents had yet to return from an appointment. So, she waited.

As afternoon aged into evening a servant came to announce the family had arrived. Gabriella rose, wincing at the arthritis that sometimes plagued her after being out all night. She was halfway across the carpet before Amanda burst through the door, running to her side.

"Aunt Ella!" she gasped. "I'm so relieved to see you."

Gabriella touched her cheek. "Are you all right, child?"

"Yes," she whispered. "How's Nell?"

Gabriella's eyes grew moist. "Once Nell's babe had been delivered into safe hands she passed away."

"And the baby?"

"Safe for the moment," she whispered as George and Emily reached the parlor.

"Look Papa, I told you Aunt Ella would come when she found me gone from my room. See?" Amanda looped her arm around Gabriella and led her to the nearest chair. "She's here, just like I said. It was all my fault because I'd left without her knowledge or permission." Amanda furnished details, all the while plumping a pillow for Gabriella to lean against. "She retired early, while I stayed in the parlor. When Reagan came to visit, she didn't know we went for a ride by ourselves. After all, Papa had given his permission."

Emily frowned as she watched Amanda fuss over Gabriella. If not for Gabriella's insistence on a visit from her niece, this never would have happened. Sitting heavily on the sofa, Emily bared her displeasure. "She couldn't have been too concerned. She didn't check on you until this afternoon. You could've been dead for hours before anyone knew you were missing."

"Mama!" gasped Amanda. "You can't mean that."

"No, no, it's all right," Gabriella said. "Emily's right. I left early this morning to visit a friend and didn't wish to disturb Amanda. I simply left without checking on her. When I returned home and found her missing, I hurried here as fast as I could." Gabriella patted Amanda's hand. "Although Wills informed me she was with you, I felt I should stay until you returned."

George smiled while putting an arm around his daughter. "Despite bad judgment on everyone's part, Amanda has returned to us whole." He then sat beside Emily, spying leftover scones on a platter. "You know, it's past mealtime. Why don't we have supper served here? I think it would be cozy to have a quiet evening amongst ourselves."

"In the parlor?" Emily said. "What would the servant's think?"

"It would be lovely," Gabriella said. "I could use a bit of fresh tea myself."

"I'll have Wills prepare something," Amanda said, rising. A short time later she returned with the servant bearing trays filled with meats, cheeses, fruit and tea.

As the meal progressed, Emily's countenance softened and her words turned gentle. When she laughed with George over a trivial remark, Gabriella felt she was witnessing a different Emily than the one she had become accustomed to. Long after Amanda retired, the threesome shared a rare moment of companionship not unlike the times surrounding Amanda's birth. Later, Gabriella would wonder if it was only at times like these the old Emily emerged to tame her sour temper.

chapter 26

Bad news travels fast. Damning news is equally swift when borne on wings of malicious tongues. By weeks' end, the account of Amanda and Reagan's arrest grew less accurate and more salacious until it little resembled the truth. Invitations ceased and the requests Emily extended were declined with the same excuses she had often used when sending regrets.

Finding her afternoons empty, Emily soothed her pride with shopping at boutiques and jewelry stores. Clerks, who normally fell all over themselves at her approach, now lapsed into unusual silences, tittering unkindly at her departure. It wasn't until acquaintances pretended not to see her that even shopping became unbearable. She wondered if they snubbed her, how would they treat her daughter? And more importantly, what would this do to Amanda's future?

Though frustrated, there remained in Emily a small, hidden cavity of tenderness. From this, she withdrew shards of patient restraint, vowing to turn this calamity around and provide a marriage she believed best for her daughter. Not from the heart, where a heart could be broken, but calculated to bequeath a better inheritance than the funds in Amanda's dowry. The first maneuver toward that end was to reassert Amanda's place above scandal.

Without telling Amanda every invitation had been declined, Emily declared the family needed a few days rest. They'd postpone all activities until after the Sabbath services where she hoped others would be on their best behavior. She would begin repairing Amanda's reputation there.

❧

Amanda's insides felt knotted as she rode with her parents to church. Glancing at her hands, she wondered if she'd ever wear a wedding band. And if so, would she be allowed to grace anyone's parlor, save her own? Forlornness settled on her heart. She decided if she must be disgraced, she'd rather be thought wicked than have Gabriella exposed as a lawbreaker.

Soon, the carriage entered the churchyard and as it came to a stop Amanda spotted the Burnsfields entering church. She lost courage at the thought of facing Reagan's family. *"What must they think of me?"* she wondered, stepping from the carriage.

An excited buzz erupted in the sanctuary when the Burnsfields entered their pew. Amid chords of prefatory music many turned to look, but quickly turned away when finding either Thomas or Reagan returning their stare.

"Psst!" whispered a woman elbowing her companion. "Did ya see the way he looked at me?" She peeked around her bonnet before gawking at Reagan. "Bold as can be, he is. Betcha I could have him too, if I wanted."

"Shhh!" her companion said. "He might hear ya, and think ye a harlot. And you in the house of the Lord! Have ye no shame?"

"Ain't no shame in wanting a man like that."

"Ye're a no good woman, Molly Carnes. After what he was supposed to have done, what would ye be wanting with the man, anyway?" She shook her head. "Ain't he the one that got caught with some high falutin' girl and thrown in jail by her folks?"

Molly leaned close, lowering her voice. "His name's Reagan Burnsfield. One of the saloon gals told me he was arrested for hiding a slave and her baby. But the babe was his, and he used the rich girl as a ruse to git his lover away."

"Ye're mad! And what are ye doing around those strumpets anyway? I told ye they'd bring ye to ruin."

"Just cuz the owner said I didn't have the right voice for his shows, don't mean I ain't pretty. He said he's got another job where I'd get paid more'n I make cleaning sheets and what not." She turned for one more look. "But, if I was to catch the eye of a rich man, then I wouldn't have to work no more."

The glare of others finally hushed Molly and she picked up a hymnal. She decided to introduce herself. If the gent could get a wench with child, then surely he'd fancy a vigorous woman ready to bear his children. By his looks, he would want a willing and lusty maid.

The church had filled to capacity by the time the Bruesters walked inside. "Good morning," Emily said, nodding and smiling. "Hello...nice to see you..."

Amanda observed a wave of turning heads and a hush that fell at their passage. If not for the weighty timbre of the first hymn, she would've heard every footfall on the tiled floor. Dropping her gaze, she missed Reagan's glance as well as the concerned empathy radiating from Katherine's face.

By the time the Bruester's settled in a front pew, Reagan knew he needed to speak to George. The tale of their unfortunate mishap had traveled faster than he thought possible and according to Beau, the rumors had turned unsavory.

It seemed an eternity before the service ended and when it did, Reagan expected the Bruester's to pass by on their way out. But with so many people thronging the aisles, it appeared they were heading for a side door.

"What's the matter with these people?" Thomas muttered, stepping outside his pew. Grasping Katherine's arm, he succeeded in getting both she and Amy into the aisle before the crowd moved them along. "We'll wait in the foyer," he called to Reagan who began exiting the other side.

Reagan had just rounded the corridor when a plainly dressed woman blocked his path. She then dropped her handkerchief. Though it became obvious she released it on purpose, she made no attempt to retrieve it. There seemed no way to step around her without abandoning his manners.

"Allow me," he said, snatching it up and placing it in her hands.

"Why, thank you very kindly," she said. "I don't believe I've had the pleasure of yer acquaintance. My name is...." Molly's heart quickened, for she didn't realize how devastatingly handsome he'd be up close. But the amber flecked eyes weren't on her. They were scanning the front of church.

"If you'll excuse me," he said, turning away. "I have pressing matters to attend." He strode up the aisle, leaving Molly with her mouth agape.

"Ye could have him, hah!" snorted her friend as she approached. "What did I tell ya?" She shook her finger under Molly's nose. "A fine gentleman ain't having anything to do with the likes of us! Why, we look like paupers compared to him."

Molly grabbed the girl's wrist and squeezed cruelly. "Shut up! The gent had pressing business, is all. He told me so."

"Let go!" the girl said, yanking back her arm. "I no longer want ye as a friend, Molly. Ye'll bring me to ruin too!"

As the woman fled, Molly took a good look at her own dress. "There'll be no more washing dirty sheets for me," she vowed. "I'll take that new job and get me some fine clothes and a hat. Then, I'll be a right pretty girl any man would fancy." Leaving church, Molly didn't care if her dress became soiled for she intended to throw it out the moment she reached the saloon.

Though Reagan had been delayed only moments, it was enough for the Bruesters to reach their coach. From across the churchyard he saw their driver set the barouche in motion. Disappointed, he reentered the narthex to find his family talking with the Barringtons.

"Ah, there you are," Beauregard said as Reagan drew near. "Were you successful in catching Le miel?"

"Sorry to say, my clumsy feet are not nimble like yours," he said before turning to Beau's mother. "Bon jour, ma mere petite. You are looking well."

"Good morning, Monsieur Reagan." Though small in stature, Yvette Barrington won notice with her vivacious manner and sharp wit. By the glint in her eyes, today would be no different. "I understand you were a naughty man," she clucked, tapping him with a closed parasol. "I hear many things, Monsieur Reagan. If you're to be respected, perhaps you should be like the Parisians." She then tossed her head while snapping fingers. "Learn to be a better sneak!"

Reagan laughed. "You're right, of course," he said. "I could learn much from your son."

"Yvette! For once, take a hold of your tongue." Charles Barrington spoke up, hoping none would take offense. His own wealth had come late in life and he often felt uncomfortable with those he considered his betters.

"Bah!" Yvette tapped the floor with her parasol. "I simply jest to lighten the mood. I love Reagan like my own Beauregard, you-you English stick in the mud."

"Mrs. Barrington, you simply must come to our house next week for tea," Katherine said. "Reagan's been neglectful for not introducing us before now."

"Please, Madame, call me Yvette," she said. "Beau spoke of inviting your family to sample Chef Énrie's fine cooking. But he never did say when I should extend our hospitality." She gave Beauregard an accusing stare. "If we've always worshiped at the same church, my son's also been remiss in not introducing us before now."

"But ma mère, we usually attend the late service."

Katherine laid a hand on Beau's arm. "We've enjoyed Beau's company for many years. Despite the delay, I'm sure we'll take pleasure in your acquaintance as well."

"We look forward to that time," Mr. Barrington said. "Beau, would you please bring around the carriage?"

"Yes, Papa," he said, bringing Amy's fingers to his lips. "Au revoir demoiselle." Then gathering Katherine's hands in both of his, he clicked his heels and bowed. "Madame Burnsfield."

chapter 27

GEORGE SETTLED IN his seat and removed his hat as the barouche moved. "Well, that was certainly one of Pastor Fuller's better sermons, don't you think, dear?"

"Don't be ridiculous, George!" Tossing her purse, Emily glared at her husband. "I didn't hear a word the pastor said. Besides, how could I concentrate with all those people staring at us?"

"Well, the pastor spoke of the-ah-difficulty of forgiveness and the music seemed especially inspiring." His eyebrows lifted hopefully. "I mean, I particularly enjoyed the final hymns...."

Emily's eyes turned stormy. "It seems everyone knows what befell Amanda and blames *her*, not that damnable Reagan!" She shook a finger at the drawn curtains. "Did you see Harriet Reckewig? She drew back when I spoke to her. The nerve of that woman! Why, she was never invited to Matilda Harper's spring ball until *I* brought her. And Clara Farrington had no social life until I recommended her for Ladies Aid. How dare she snub my wishes of good morning!"

Attending church had been worse than Emily imagined. Her friends had been slow to greet her while others clearly shunned Amanda. *Damn Reagan! Damn the day he was born!* "Something must be done," she burst out. "I cannot tolerate our daughter being made a laughing stock!"

"I think you've said enough," George said, inclining his head toward Amanda whose lips quivered. "We should discuss this later, after tea."

"Well," Emily said more gently. "We could invite Derrick to join us for dinner. It's been several days since his departure and I'm sure he'd enjoy a visit."

"No Mama, please. I don't want company yet," Amanda pleaded.

"But dear, he's more family than guest. Don't you agree, George? In fact, that's just what this day needs. I'll send an invitation as soon as we get home. We'll have a nice dinner and then enjoy music in the parlor."

"Now Emily," George warned. "If Amanda isn't up to company, she's not up to company. Is that clear?"

The strain of the day's ordeal had worn on Emily and her face began to crumble. "I'm just trying to make things better," she said through sudden tears. "We're being treated like pariahs in our own church. We must do something..."

"It's all right," Amanda said. "Derrick can come over. I've changed my mind. It's better than sitting at home feeling sorry for myself."

"See George? It'll be good for us," Emily said, smiling. "By next week, this'll all be forgotten."

"Are you sure you want a visitor so soon?" George asked. "It's fine with me if you wait til after the Festival of Plenty before taking callers."

"Mother's right," Amanda said. "Perhaps having Derrick over will cheer us up."

❧

The following week Emily called attention to a lone envelope that arrived as they lingered over breakfast. "Didn't I tell you these rumors would come to nothing? You've received an invitation from Camilla Muelder to dine with her and a few of her friends Wednesday evening."

"You'll accept of course," she declared when Amanda looked uneasily at the mailer. "It's obvious not everyone has lost good sense. The Bruesters cannot be dismissed." She tapped her finger on the table. "Your father's too important a man."

"Isn't that the same evening Sam Hampton's daughter is entertaining?" George said from behind his newspaper.

"What of it?" Emily said, huffing. "Camilla's family has more distinction than Sam's. Once he's out of office, who'll ever go to an ex-Mayor's ball?"

George folded his paper. "My dear, with all that's happened, the least of our worries is whether or not Amanda is invited to the most important dinner of the evening."

"Poppycock! We've not received nor would we have accepted Elizabeth's invitation. I know the friendship between the Hamptons and the Burnsfields. Most likely, Reagan will be attending and that means Amanda will not!"

"I see," he said. "So, we'll be forever avoiding the Burnsfields. Do you know how ridiculous that sounds, how impossible that'll be?"

"Not so ridiculous, nor impossible," Emily retorted. "Have you forgotten what Reagan has done to our daughter?"

"Forgotten? How could I forget?" George slammed down his hand in a rare display of anger. "That young man, despite what you think of him, saved Amanda from certain death. And I for one will be eternally grateful." Emily gasped as he rose to lean over the table. "And, if you say one more derogatory remark about Reagan or his family, I'll...I'll...personally take away your credit from shops. And I mean all of them!"

Emily covered her mouth.

"Do you really think, my dear, the bank would cover your accounts without my consent?"

"George..."

"I've known for years your taste for extravagance and I've not minded nor begrudged you anything. But this I will not tolerate. Is that clear, *Mrs. Bruester*?"

Emily nodded; astounded he had been aware of items she charged under the guise of household expenses. This, on top of the many gifts he had given her, caused Emily to feel remorse. "I'm sorry, George. I'll do whatever you say."

After an awkward silence, he resumed his seat, pretending not to notice Amanda's shocked expression. "Very well. Amanda, you may accept or decline Camilla's request. It's your decision."

"It's all right, Papa. I'll go."

"Very well," George repeated before picking up his paper. "By the way, Emily, you may as well pick up that gown at the dressmakers. It's been paid for."

"Yes George. I'll send for it this afternoon." She handed the invitation to her daughter, smiling tightly. "Since you've given your consent, you must send an acceptance at once. Wills will make sure it's delivered on time."

Amanda excused herself, quaking at the thought of spending time with those who were aware of her embarrassing situation. As painful as it was, she knew further delay would only give weight to the many rumors.

chapter 28

BURROWING INTO HIS collar, a man squatted among weeds while staring at Gabriella's house and barn. For the second time in two weeks he witnessed an elderly woman being dropped off in a carriage, followed by a wagon driven by her handy man. Both times, Ben placed the wagon in the barn before entering the house with nary a parcel in his hands.

After another hour, the hidden one heard a horse approaching before a voice whispered. "Ted! Where are ya?"

"Over here, ya big lummox. I'm freezing my arse." Ted rubbed his posterior as a man drew near. Suddenly, he wrinkled his nose. "Jeez Willie, you smell like rose water."

Willie grinned. "Maggie got some new gal and wanted me to break her in, good and proper." Pushing up his hat, he exposed freshly washed hair. "I took a bath cuz I didn't want t' scare her off a'fore we got started."

"A new girl, huh? Whu'd she look like?"

"Kind of freckly over her face," he said, gesturing. "Dark hair, bound up in some silly thing on top of her head."

"Pretty?" Ted asked hopefully.

Willie chuckled. "Not too bad with face paint and all. But ain't nuthing I'd take home t' maw."

Ted frowned suspiciously. "I wuz there last night and didn't see no new gal. How'd you git her first?"

"I heard about her and told Maggie I should be first cuz I wuz gentle with women. Besides, I paid more'n I had to."

"You, gentle?" Ted jeered.

"Sure! I can be as gentle as a lamb if'n I want to," Willie said, winking. "She wuz scared at first til she had some wine. Then she got bolder sitting on my lap as I taught her a thing or two about kissing."

"I bet you kiss like a mule!" Ted scoffed. "Probably learned how to kiss off'n that mule you call a horse."

"Yeah, but I wuz doing the kissing, not you," Willie pointed out.

Ted licked his lips. "Then what?"

"She acted real shy, pretending like she didn't know what she's supposed t' do. So's I played along, saying the more I got t' look at, the more she got paid." Willie smirked at his cleverness. "She seemed okay with that til I got her on the bed. Well, once I got started, she tried slowing me down." His chest expanded proudly. "But I told her the best way is quick and hard, so she gits it over with, real fast."

"Did she like it?"

"Oh, she cried a little," Willie said. "But afterwards, she asked me if that's what all men wanted. I said sure, if they're real men. After that, she drank more wine." He shook his head. "The bitch didn't even know she wuz supposed t' leave. So I got her for another go round a'fore I came here."

As if waking from a dream, Ted pulled the reins from Willie's hand. Climbing up, he turned the horse around. "So, what's her name?"

"Ain't you gonna report to Jeb first?"

"Course I am," he said, backing up until abreast of Willie. "I just want t' know her name!"

"You best wait t' ask fer that one," he offered. "She's a mite tuckered."

"Willie, so help me, if'n you don't tell me her name—"

"Aww, I wuz just funning ya. Her name is Molly. Molly Carnes."

Ted kicked the horse, taking off.

"Be sure t' take a bath!" Willie hollered. "You smell worse'n Jeb's bear pelts!"

chapter 29

On Wednesday and at the requested time, Amanda arrived at Fay and Emory Muelder's home. Large stone pots dotted the porch where, she guessed, flowers had graced the entrance throughout summer. Once inside, a manservant took her wraps and a maid led her to the parlor.

"Amanda dear, do come in," Camilla called gaily. Stepping around a table laden with tea and pastries, she put her arm around her newest guest. "Of course, you've already met Leroy and Beauregard," she said as three men rose to greet her.

"Hello, Amanda," Leroy said, nodding coolly. Initially shocked when rumors of Amanda and Reagan first surfaced, Leroy thought he now couldn't pursue a tainted woman. But as he was reminded of her beauty, it occurred to him his generosity might gain her gratitude. And her wealth, he thought, offering a smile.

"Bonjour, demoiselle." Leaning over, Beau kissed her fingers. "How are you this evening?"

"Very well, thank you."

Camilla next indicated the man beside Beauregard. "I don't believe you've been introduced to Anson Rutledge. Anson, this is Amanda Bruester, daughter of George and Emily Bruester."

"I feel as if I already know you," Anson said. Taking her hand, a thick wave of hair bounced above one eye. "Leroy's blubbered all summer about dancing with a beautiful girl named Amanda. I have to admit, he didn't exaggerate."

"Anson," Leroy said. "One doesn't reveal words spoken between friends." He turned apologetic eyes to Amanda. "However callous it sounds, I can assure you my rendition of our time together was most proper."

"Of course it was," Camilla said, smiling sweetly. She then turned Amanda toward a seated young woman. "This is my cousin, Marietta Stowe. She's visiting from Virginia until after the New Year."

"It's a pleasure," Amanda said, noting the girl neither rose nor extended her hand. "I hope your stay has been agreeable so far."

"Nice to meet you," Marietta said before directing her smile to Beau. "And yes, it's been *very* agreeable. Everyone here is so pleasant Ah've determined Ah must come more often."

Camilla laughed rigidly. "Why *dear,* you visit nearly every year. Cantonsville hasn't changed that much."

"But, this time, Ah've met the most enchanting people. If Southern gentlemen were this interesting, Ah never would've ventured past Richmond," she purred demurely.

"Merci beaucoup," Beauregard said before glancing around. "But you must agree, it is the French who give the best of affections, oui?"

"Let's hope my cousin doesn't leave Cantonsville knowing the answer to that," Camilla said, flashing Marietta a warning glance. Touching Amanda's elbow, she indicated the sofa. "Let's all get acquainted, shall we?"

While Anson and Beauregard took their former seats, Leroy installed himself next to Amanda. "Before you came, Marietta was just saying how much she admired the city's shade trees. I was about to mention that it was the Bruester Bank who proposed the beautification project." As Camilla poured tea, he boldly touched Amanda's hand while turning to Marietta. "As founders of the bank, my father and Amanda's determined Cantonsville should emulate the eastern provinces. They insisted on planting the trees you so rightly admire."

"How splendidly progressive," Marietta said, nibbling a confection. "Did y'all help in planting?"

Leroy looked aghast. "Certainly *not.* My dear, Spelding's never dirty their hands. We provide wherewithal, not muscle and sweat."

"Don't get your nose out of joint, old boy," Anson said. "Besides, to my recollection, it was Mrs. Spelding who insisted on shade trees. Your old man thought it was a terrible waste of money."

A flush crept up Leroy's neck. And, although Amanda had been aware of his stretching the truth, she felt sympathy for his exposure.

"I believe when Papa mentioned it, he indicated it was a joint effort," she said, laying a hand on Leroy's sleeve. "Perhaps, Mr. Spelding felt resistant at first, but it seems I recall both our fathers became enthusiastic supporters before the project was completed."

Leroy smiled gratefully. "Yes, that's what I meant. I simply avoided the trivialities of the matter."

"Oh dear," Marietta pouted, looking from Anson to Leroy. "Ah didn't mean for y'all to have words. It doesn't matter how the trees came about. Ah simply wished to compliment y'all on such a comely city."

"Don't fret," Anson said. "It's a lesson well learned if we all heeded your genteel manner."

"You're very kind, sir," she said, batting green eyes. "Any time you wish to observe our southern ways, y'all are welcome to visit Richmond. You'll find our people take life more leisurely. Up here, y'all are quite ambitious."

Camilla silently fumed, aware of Marietta's need for attention. "Beauregard," she broke in. "I understand you've spent a great deal of time both above and below the Mason Dixon. How do you find the comparison?"

"Indeed," he said, raising dark brows. "There are many differences but to which only a few can be recounted. If I may, I'll speak only on where my expertise lies."

Amanda looked amused, but everyone else became interested. "For instance," he said, standing to move behind Marietta's chair. "Demoiselle Marietta is an example of the finest the South has to offer." He indicated her loose curls, falling thickly past her shoulders. "An array like this isn't customary here because it could cause a man to go mad with desire. Only a southern lady could display her charms with such poise and remain above scandal."

Marietta fairly swooned as Beauregard lifted her hand while gazing into her eyes. "By her very nature, she keeps passion in check. But a man of discernment sees how deeply they run." Turning over her hand, he kissed her palm. Marietta's mouth fell open and as he stepped away, she put her hand to a cheek.

None spoke as Beau stepped behind Camilla's chair. Looking first to Anson then Leroy, he touched her shoulder. "Gentlemen, as you may've already observed, women of the North desire self determination. This is also true of our hostess. When a man wants a bit of fire, a woman like Camilla won't leave him wanting. She possesses an angel's voice and a soul as mysterious as the ancients. But, if he isn't careful he'll be ensnared by her gentilesse."

Camilla patted his hand, looking to see her cousin's expression. "He's lying of course," she said. "But I like to hear it just the same."

"Non, mademoiselle," Beau said, feigning shock. "None can deny your beauty. With this complexion and flaxen hair, can any say they've known anyone else with such rare coloring?" As the men nodded in agreement, Camilla had the good sense to blush. But everyone quieted as Beau's gaze turned to Amanda.

"Oh no," she pleaded in sudden embarrassment. "It isn't necessary to speak further. You've quite covered the differences between both ends of the country."

"But ma chéri," Beau said as he knelt before her. "You are the rarest of blossoms."

"Only the most common flower, I'm afraid. I know how often you bandy about the phrase."

"But now I tell the truth," he said, lifting her chin. "When a man wants loyalty and a place to find his rest, this is the woman he seeks. She possesses beauty, no one can deny. Yet, there's something else..." Furrowing his brow, he tapped his lip with a finger. "Oui." He seemed struck by a sudden thought. "There's no guile in her eyes."

"My, my," Marietta pouted prettily. "You can see all that?" She had tired of the game. Once attention was focused elsewhere, it all became a terrible bore. "Her eyes just look blue to me." She twittered at her own joke, but found herself alone in its enjoyment.

Camilla deftly kicked her cousin, unseen by the fullness of their touching skirts. "Not *now*, dear," she murmured low.

Unable to scream, Marietta reached over and secretly pinched Camilla's arm. "You little witch," she whispered. "You promised we'd have fun."

Camilla looked around but all eyes were on the Frenchman. So she kicked Marietta again.

"Il ne parle pas au roi qui veut," Beau quoted as he released Amanda's chin. "Only the eagle can gaze at the sun."

"Excuse me, Miss Camilla," the maid said, entering the parlor. "Dinner is served."

chapter 30

By the time everyone took seats around the table, Amanda decided she had worried needlessly about accepting Camilla's invitation. Emily had been right and she had the Muelders to thank for being the first to receive her since her capture.

At Camilla's insistence, wineglasses were replenished and all had their fill before the first course ended. "Amanda darling," she said as she blotted her mouth. "Now that we've all become friends, you must tell us a little more about yourself."

Amanda's throat tightened when Camilla's eyes flitted to Marietta before settling upon her. "For instance, you simply must settle a little argument between me and my cousin."

"Oh?" She glanced nervously toward Beau, but his focus was on Camilla.

"I'm sure there's nothing to it, but being so scandalous, I just knew you'd want to clear it up. I told Marietta just yesterday that a lady like yourself could never be the person everyone is talking about."

A flutter began in Amanda's stomach as Camilla leaned forward, her eyes rounded. "We heard there was a girl caught in the woods, her dress all torn and dirty—by who knows what—with none other than Reagan Burnsfield." She looked at her cousin who now stared at Amanda with rapt attention. "A man with a known reputation," she said. "I knew it couldn't be you, as it's been suggested, but perhaps a girl that resembles you. Reagan and the girl were supposedly caught by bounty hunters on the trail of slaves, of all things! Why, what kind of trash would do such a thing?"

Amanda felt as though the floor had been yanked from beneath her but refused to swallow her up. Initially turning red, she paled and grew sick as Camilla's eyes became slits. "Can you tell us why anyone would have such notions about you?"

"I-I-" Amanda couldn't speak as her mind searched for explanations. Anson's jaw dropped and Leroy appeared pained as he was once again reminded of his own doubts.

"Camilla," Beauregard spoke softly though his eyes grew hard. "I fear I should remind you that this conversation has become indelicate, even for your table. I must insist Amanda not dignify your questions with an answer."

"Why not? I'm only allowing the poor girl to pluck herself from the disgrace laid at her feet. Everyone would like to know the truth. I'm sure, given the chance, she'd be happy to deny the accusations of being a tramp! Wouldn't you, Amanda?"

Marietta tittered unkindly then coughed into her napkin. "Excuse me," she murmured.

Amanda felt the full force of Camilla's betrayal. She looked around the table as everyone waited expectantly. With meticulous precision, she folded her napkin before laying it on her plate. "What stories you've listened to, I can only imagine. I've also heard the accounts though they're greatly distorted. In truth, I *was* the one apprehended with Reagan by those renegades. It's easy to see now what a foolish decision it was to ride alone with a suitor." Amanda almost faltered, but steadied her voice. "My impulsiveness has cost me much. Though I can't repair my reputation, I can assure you it's a case of mistaken identity as far as those bounty hunters are concerned."

Beauregard noticed the slight quiver beginning in Amanda's voice and rose suddenly. "Demoiselle," he said, holding out his arm. "Allow me the pleasure of escorting you home."

"Is that necessary?" Marietta blurted. "I mean," she corrected herself, "you've not finished your dinner."

"As a gentleman, and a friend, I insist," he said as Amanda reached for his sleeve.

"Oh dear!" Camilla appeared contrite. "I only meant to clear her name. I didn't think..." She looked at Leroy. "Perhaps, you can convince Amanda of my sincerity."

"How so?" he said, clearly annoyed.

"I thought Amanda would *want* to set the record straight. There are so many stories going around, I just knew she'd want to explain herself."

"There's nothing more to explain. And though it distresses me to part company, I pray you'll forgive us if we take our leave," Beau said, assisting Amanda to her feet.

"Must he leave too?" Marietta glared at her cousin as Beau and Amanda left the room. "Surely, Miss Bruester can depart as alone as she came, can't she?"

"Oh, shut up, Marietta!" Camilla allowed a pained expression to cross her face while stabbing her food with a fork. "Sometimes I can't believe the foolishness that comes out of your mouth!"

Marietta stared at her cousin in utter astonishment before regaining her composure. Turning to Anson, she smiled sweetly. "Tell me sir, how deep does the snow get up here? Can one actually get home-bound for days on end?"

Finding the closet that held their wraps, Beau placed Amanda's cloak around her shoulders. "It's all right, ma petite. I had a notion all wouldn't go well this evening."

Amanda swallowed as tears filled her eyes. "Will it always be this way? I'm sure you've heard the stories, too."

"Non, chéri," he assured while putting on his coat. "I don't believe Reagan will allow such talk to go on." The manservant opening the door went to do Beau's bidding of sending around their carriages.

"But what can he do? It's not his fault, nor his problem. I'm afraid it's one of my own doing."

"Don't be so sad, my little friend," he said, tucking a hanky into her hands. "I know Reagan, and it's not like him to let those he cares about suffer."

"Unless he can turn back the clock, I'm afraid there's little he can do." She sighed, wiping away her tears. "The worst of it is the shame I've brought on everyone."

"Don't cry," he said as both carriages came into view. It may seem hopeless, but I give you my word. Soon, you'll be yesterday's news, all but forgotten.

Beauregard aided Amanda into her conveyance and signaled his driver to follow before climbing in and taking the opposite seat. Striking a match, he lit a lamp then arranged a blanket over her lap. "There," he said, surveying his handiwork. "You should stay warm."

"I'm sorry I spoiled your evening."

"Don't berate yourself, demoiselle. It wasn't you that ruined my appetite."

"But I ruined the party by leaving, despite what happened." Amanda shook her head. "Camilla was so sweet, at first..."

"Non!" Beau sat up, indignant. "Le miel est doux mais l' abeille pique!"

"Beau," she said, smiling. "You know I don't speak French. Pray, what did you say?"

"Honey is sweet, but bees sting." He let his head drop against the cushion. "Be careful of that one, ma petite. Camilla is more wasp than honey bee."

Amanda felt grateful Beau afforded her what privacy he could in the nearness of the carriage. She needed to brace herself for the explanation her parents would surely demand at her early return.

When the carriage slowed to turn into the Bruester lane, Beau leaned forward. "Feeling better, chéri?"

"Much better, thank you." Amanda held out the hanky. "I shouldn't need this anymore."

"Keep it, just in case," he said. As he assisted her from the carriage, Amanda prayed her parents had retired early. But when Wills opened the door she saw them emerging from the parlor.

"Amanda," Emily said, approaching. "You're home early. Have you taken ill?"

"No, but..." Amanda paused as tears brightened her eyes.

Sensing it had gone badly for her daughter, Emily quickly dismissed the servant. "That'll be all, Wills."

"Very good, madam," he said, accepting Amanda's coat.

Taking Amanda's arm, Emily led everyone to the parlor. A fire, burning low, still gave warmth to furniture littered with Emily's tapestry and George's book lying open.

"Have a seat, Beau," George said as Emily sat with Amanda on the sofa.

"Merci," he said, unbuttoning his coat.

"What happened?" Emily wanted to know.

"The evening started out lovely," Amanda began. "I met Camilla's cousin from Richmond as well as a friend of Leroy's..."

"Leroy was there? Surely, he was civil, wasn't he?" Emily broke in.

"Yes, he was very nice to me. It wasn't until dinner when Camilla said since we were friends, maybe I could answer a few questions...that had to do with..." Unable to finish, Amanda began to sob and covered her face.

"How dare she!" Emily said. "What did you say?"

"I told demoiselle not to dignify the question with an answer," Beau interjected. "But with the grace of a true lady, Amanda spoke with candor."

Emily remained silent, for once having nothing to say. No one knew more than she, how difficult it would be to repair broken respect. She looked at George as he sank into a chair.

Taking this moment to stand, Beau vowed to himself he wouldn't sleep until he spoke to Reagan. "It's time for me to go," he said. Turning to George, he extended his hand. "Monsieur Bruester, with your permission?"

"Thank you for bringing Amanda home. It was very generous of you."

"Bah! Twas nothing. I consider it an honor. Remember my words, demoiselle," he said to Amanda. "Tomorrow will be a better day."

Once outside, Beau turned up his collar. After giving the driver instructions, he looked at his watch before climbing inside the landau. He had just enough time to speak privately with Reagan before the Hampton guests departed. Despite his misgivings, Beauregard believed not only would Reagan do the honorable thing, but he would also see the wisdom in marrying such a rare flower as Amanda.

chapter 31

Ben helped Gabriella into the general store where she purchased items for the planned Thanksgiving meal with George and his family. While he carried out supplies, two men on horseback reined in a few yards away. Later, when Ben halted the carriage at the dressmaker's, the same men pretended to find the display of weaponry in the gunsmith's shop to be of exceeding interest. However, they lost their curiosity the moment Ben slapped the reins to take his mistress to her next destination.

Sunrays dappled the sidewalk as Ben aided Gabriella through the arched doors of St. Mary's church. Though not majestic like churches built in recent times, Gabriella felt at home and could think more clearly in the small, quiet sanctuary.

Ben stationed himself in a pew while Gabriella approached a candle-lined alcove. There, she lit the taper of a dark red votive before kneeling.

Crossing herself, she clasped her hands then bowed her head as she recalled her unease of the last few days. With increasing certainty she felt unseen eyes watching her. She often noticed through her windows the passage of miscreants at all hours of the day. Greatly alarmed, she had halted her underground activities until she could know the bounty hunters had given up on capturing Nell.

The creaking door broke the quiet as two men entered and took an empty pew. Removing their hats, they stared toward Gabriella as she knelt by the alcove.

Fear gripped Gabriella's heart as she glanced at the strangers for they bore a striking resemblance to those patrolling her home. Rising from the rail, her cane tapped an urgent tempo as she hobbled toward Ben who promptly took her arm and assisted her outside. He pretended not to notice the men exiting the church while he guided the horses into the street, not stopping until arriving home.

While Ben set the brake, the pair on horseback rode past the property where trees and overgrown weeds filled an empty lot. Placing the step, he opened the carriage door.

"It seems we're being followed," he said as Gabriella stepped down.

"I know," she said. "I've already sent messages to our contacts not to send any more visitors. I can't jeopardize the rest of the route. We can however, keep giving to the Negro settlement. There's no crime in helping the emancipated." After climbing the steps, she patted his hand. "After you unload the packages, return to the store and pick up those blankets we purchased. Once they're added to the clothing we gathered, we should have a nice donation to take to our friends."

Gabriella then went inside. She removed her bonnet, feeling a measure of satisfaction no one could stop her donations to the Negro settlement. It was secretly understood the provisions would be shared with any runaways that mingled for a time with their freed brethren.

chapter 32

A CAMPFIRE BURNED near a shanty by the river. Above the flames, twisting fingers of smoke rose toward a sky filled with scudding clouds. From out of the darkness, a voice called. "Ho there! Is a stranger welcome?"

The woman stirring a pot over the fire peered into the shadows. "Who's there? Is yu friendly?"

"Course, Ah friendly," called the voice.

At the sound of scraping leaves, the woman's eyes grew wide. Presently, a man wearing a tattered coat emerged, swinging his arms oddly and dragging his left leg. "A hungry man's always friendly," he said, removing his hat. Sniffing loudly, he looked at the simmering stew. "If it's allowable, can a poor travelin' man have a bit of that fine cooking?"

The woman hesitated for her husband wasn't home and she hadn't seen this one in the settlement before. Wary of strangers, Eliza knew runaways often found their way to communities like these on their journey north.

"Where you headed?" she asked.

"Ah heered there's a safe house in town where Ah kin git a ride," he said, tottering unsteadily.

"Oh, sit down," she said, pointing to a nearby stump. She filled a bowl and handed it to him before dipping water from a bucket.

Bolting down the meal, he wiped his mouth on a sleeve before drinking the water. "Thank you kindly. Ah ain't had nuthin' to eat all day."

Eliza felt pity for the stranger as she watched him massage his leg. She noticed his light colored fingers. Sitting on a stool, she spoke her mind. "You ain't very dark for a southerner. Do yu have family around here?"

"Ah's got no family left," he said, sniffing. "They's all gone. Kilt whilst tryin' to escape, or, sold down the river." Wiping away tears, he managed to go on. "So, Ah decided it wuz time for old Whipper to git hisself up north where Ah kin be a free man before Ah git sold agin."

Eliza's heart melted. "Perhaps, my husband can help find who yer lookin' for."

Whipper smiled gratefully. "Yu's surely an angel ma'am. Ah nearly got catched a ways back before Ah wuz told about a woman that takes in such as mesself, and gits them on. If yer husband kin show me the way, Ah..." Whipper looked up in alarm at the sound of a wagon approaching.

"It's all right," Eliza said, rising. "It's just my man." Whipper watched as she hurried away. Nervously, he turned his hat over and over while listening to voices speaking in urgent tones. As he stared into the dark, a large figure suddenly loomed over him. Whipper stood abruptly, then looked into the eyes of a towering, broad shouldered man.

"Who are you and where do you come from?" the man demanded.

"Mah names Whipper, and Ah-Ah-Ah's from South Carolina, off a place owned by Mistah James Burr..."

"Ain't never heard of him. Why are you here?"

Whipper's eyes fell on Eliza as she returned to the fire. "Yer missus kindly shared some vittles and let me rest a spell."

"Reuben! Cain't yu see he's near exhausted?" She pushed past her husband. "Now yu just sit back down. Yer leg appears to be paining yu." Eliza found a large rock and set it near Whipper. "Here, use this to prop up yer lame leg."

Whipper eased himself back onto the stump. "As Ah wuz saying, Ah heered of a place where Ah kin git a ride. Mebbee yu kin tell me how to git there, though Ah cain't say if mah leg'll hold up much longer."

"Where'd you hear that?"

Whipper scratched his chin. "Ah think it wuz a boy named Billy, by the river, several miles back."

"Tall and skinny, with a straw hat and patches on his knees?"

"Legs skinny as toothpicks!" Whipper said, bobbing his head. "Told me to follow the river til Ah git to the Negro settlement. Then Ah wuz to inquire about a laidy that'll git me on to a safe place."

"That halfwit will flap his jaws at anybody," Reuben said, sighing. "I told that boy to let his elders do the talkin' when it comes to strangers."

"Ah ain't told no one," Whipper assured. "Ah followed the river just like he said. He seemed an honest chile, not meaning no wrong." Whipper watched as Eliza ladled stew for her husband.

"Still, he's got a child's mind in a man's body. I told his daddy not to bring him when he visits. It'll bring nuthin' but trouble." As Reuben hunkered down to eat, Eliza poured from a coffee pot and handed him the cup.

Whipper looked from one to the other. "Yu mean there *is* such a woman?" His voice rose in excitement while kneading his thigh. "Yu kin take me there?"

Reuben spoke between mouthfuls. "I have clothes and blankets to unload first. Eliza," he said turning, "because of Miss Bruester, our babies are gonna sleep warm tonight."

Her face split into a grin. "Bless that woman. She's always bringing relief to families living here." Jumping up, she headed into the darkness.

Reuben chuckled as he chewed a piece of meat. "She'll wake our neighbors and have that wagon unloaded quick as lightening. Nuthin' gets wasted with Eliza, not even time."

Whipper rubbed his threadbare coat. "Sure is cold up here. Never knowed a man could live in such raw weather."

"Ain't nuthin' yet," Reuben said as he swallowed the last of his supper. "Gits colder come winter. And, where you're headed, you'll likely freeze your britches right off."

"Ah surely do appreciate what yer doing fer old Whipper. If not fer yu, Ah'd still be cold an' hungry."

Reuben grabbed a stick from the fire and left, soon returning with a bundle. He tossed it into Whipper's lap.

"Whut's this?"

"What's it look like? It's a coat, compliments of Miss Bruester."

Whipper stood and quickly doffed his ragged frock before donning the newer garment. "Ah do thank you kindly," he said. "Seems to fit well."

"Think nothing of it," Reuben said. "You wait here while I see how Eliza's doing."

Once alone, a jabbing pain forced Whipper to step urgently around the fire while dragging his bad leg. He stopped often and massaged his shrunken thigh in an attempt to ease his hurt. When Rueben returned, he found Whipper still pacing.

"It's time to go. Should I bring the wagon closer?"

"Nah," he said while putting on his hat. "Ah's got to keep moving to limber up me gimp leg." As he stepped around Reuben, he began his odd, arm-swinging motion, merging into the darkness with Reuben close behind. The snort of horses guided Whipper and he deftly scaled the buckboard by climbing the spokes of a wheel.

Reuben climbed into the drivers seat and settled his massive body. "Best you git underneath the straw in case we run into strangers. And don't make noise."

Whipper burrowed into the silage near the front of the wagon. Twisting in his seat, Reuben smoothed the obvious bump, then picked up the reins and slapped the horse with a hearty "Hee-ah!"

For nearly an hour Whipper felt nothing but the wagon's motion as it traveled over hard ground. Without anything to brace against, it hadn't taken long for him to sink through the straw. Once the weight of his body became pressed against floorboards, his thigh began throbbing. Whipper thrust a palm under his knee but after a while, even that couldn't relieve his discomfort. In desperation, he bunched up his coattail and stuffed it beneath his leg.

"Be still!" Reuben growled as he again rearranged the bedding. Whipper stopped moving, mostly because the trapped cloth relieved the pressure from his cramped position. When the horse slowed, he perceived the wheels were no longer on the road, but rolling over grass. Soon, the wagon stopped.

Whipper raised himself enough to peek over the rim. He could see Reuben tie a cloth over the horses' face before leading it through a dismantled split rail fence. The moonlight revealed the outline of a large barn and a house marked by a gabled roof. As Reuben reassembled the fence, Whipper lay down and pulled back the straw. The wagon advanced a short distance before he heard a creaking door and smells of a barn assailed his nostrils.

"Can Ah git up now?" he implored. "Mah leg's all stiff."

"Not yet," Reuben said as he fumbled for a lantern kept under the seat. Striking a match, he lit the wick, turning the taper low. "I got to find out if it's safe, first."

After climbing down, he leaned against the wagon and looked inside. "You got to stay put." He reached down and smoothed the straw. "And quit your twitchin'! You keep uncovering yourself." Leaving the lantern on the seat, Reuben left the barn, squeezing his bulk through a side door.

In the silence that followed, Whipper cautiously stretched his leg. But instead of easing the cramp, his muscles went into a sudden spasm. Muffling a scream, he clambered from the wagon before madly kneading his thigh until the pain subsided. When he leaned against the horse, it snorted uneasily.

"Easy, boy," Whipper soothed, looking around. Suddenly, he noted several bales of straw as well as two stalls occupied by other horses.

Whipper's interest perked. Where there were horses, there were liniments and such to doctor injured animals. Oftentimes, flasks of alcohol were stored with medicines. Limping toward a workbench, Whipper found a narrow-necked crock. He sniffed the opening but was disappointed at the lack of a familiar odor. He next felt along a shelf, but found only cobwebs long undisturbed. Retracing his steps, he retrieved Reuben's lantern. Lifting it high, he searched first above the workbench, then below, spying a small shuttered cabinet near the floor.

Placing the lantern on a nearby bale, Whipper grasped a knob and tugged. The door opened, revealing various bottles and tins. Ignoring the ones with horse pictures, Whipper removed each cap to sniff the contents. The third bottle emitted the familiar odor of rye whiskey. He sat beside the lantern and tipped his head, swallowing the liquid in great gulps.

The whiskey burned his throat but Whipper didn't stop until he emptied the bottle. Soon, the fire that warmed his innards spread to his legs. Tossing the flask, he continued testing other bottles as the alcohol numbed his thinking and he forgot about being quiet.

"Damn!" he muttered. "There ain't no more!" Like a child who can't believe he'd received all his presents, Whipper kept revisiting bottles, sniffing hopefully. Spying a vial in a dark corner, he gleefully tugged at the stopper, but it resisted his efforts. Unable to keep hold of the barely protruding plug, Whipper turned the vial sideways and brought it to his mouth. He bit the cork and pulled with all his might. With a sudden pop, it released, spilling the contents onto his coat as well as straw at his feet.

He sniffed deeply. "Shit! It's ether!" He threw the vial, smashing it to bits while muttering about his sorry state and scarcity of liquor. He kicked the cabinet door causing it to bang shelves and rattle bottles. Suddenly, the door facing the house was thrown open and a man with a bowler hat entered. It wasn't Reuben.

A wave of nausea washed over Whipper as cloying vapors of ether clouded his mind. He fumbled with the lantern, his fingers feeling thick and useless as he tried snuffing the flame. Instead, he knocked the lantern to the floor with a loud crash of splintering glass.

An unfriendly voice called out, "Who's there?"

Whipper looked stupidly at the fire spreading around his feet. As if in a dream, he reached out and touched the flames. The searing heat had the effect of a hot firebrand torching his brain and it occurred to him if he didn't escape, he would burn to death.

As he scrambled toward the shadows, he accidentally pushed the bale into the fire, causing it to ignite. Whipper pressed against a wall and groped around obstacles while the man ripped off his coat and rushed toward the spreading blaze. He first slapped at loose straw, but the motion sent burning strands flying in every direction. When that failed, Ben tried stomping out the flames. Yet he couldn't keep apace with the engulfing fire and he once again beat at it with his coat. As the fire intensified, so did Ben's efforts. He'd put one fire out; only to accelerate another by the breeze he created from his coat.

Reuben's horse, still hitched to the wagon, shied from noise Ben made as his garment hit the floor. When the stench of burning fodder filled the barn, the penned horses began snorting and banging fearfully against stalls.

It wasn't until the barn began glowing from multiple fires that Whipper grasped what he had done. Petrified, he stumbled forward, gasping as smoke threatened another surge of bile in his throat. The weight of his coat made him feel as if he were neck deep in water. Ripping it off, he cast it to the floor before detecting fresh air from the open doorway. In great relief he hobbled through it. Then, with his odd, arm-swinging motion he limped out into the night.

chapter 33

WHEN REUBEN LEFT the barn he felt sure Whipper would stay out of sight. He knew fugitive slaves were well aware of the need to stay hidden. So he hadn't been in hurry when he skirted the yard to reach the back door of the house.

Nearing the porch, he heard voices outside and hurriedly crouched behind some shrubs. Reuben couldn't make out their words. But by careful listening, he determined the voices came from the road in front of the house. Fearing renegade bands that snatched Negroes to sell to Southern buyers, he hunkered down, pulling himself into a ball.

A lamp shone through a window, beckoning him to approach. Yet Reuben knew if he could hear voices, they might also hear him knock at the door. Though he was a free man with his papers always tucked in his pocket, his actions would be viewed suspiciously. If caught, he could claim no good reason for being at the back door of an elderly white woman this late at night.

The echo of approaching hoof beats matched the uneasy cadence of Reuben's heart and he shrank further into the bushes. Barely had the clatter subsided when the back door opened and a man emerged. Reuben held his breath while the man struck a match and lit a cigar. Just as he determined the man to be Gabriella's driver, Ben stepped off the porch and headed toward the barn.

"Ben!" Reuben whispered. "Ben!" As the moon suddenly lit the barnyard, Reuben quieted. He felt it best to wait until the moon retreated behind clouds, then hurry to the barn and explain the wagon's presence.

Ben approached the barn, his mind on the events of earlier that day. Having witnessed his mistress being followed, in all probability by Jebediah's men, Ben had learned from Gabriella of her suspicions of being watched.

Upon reaching the barn, Ben paused when he heard sounds of breaking glass. The hairs on his neck stood up as he imagined bounty hunters ransacking the property, searching for evidence. Another bang sounded and Ben steeled himself, bursting through the door. A dim light illuminated the area beside the horse pens, but little else.

As he neared the stalls, a crash sounded before the barn plunged into darkness. "Who's there?" Ben called. Running forward, he caught a glimpse of a man against flickering light. To his horror, he realized fire was eating a partially burned bale of hay.

A pungent odor hit his nostrils as he tore off his coat and beat at the flames. But, rather than smothering the blaze, he only seemed to be making it worse. He tried stomping and more beating but realized his efforts were futile when the fire spread to several areas.

Throwing down his coat, Ben whirled before running toward the main doors. Rounding the stalls, he skidded to prevent running into a buckboard wagon. "What the hell—?"

"Mistah Ben! Mistah Ben! What's happening?"

Ben recognized the voice as the man he had delivered supplies to that day. "Reuben! There's a fire! Open the doors so we can get the animals out!" Ben felt along the wagon til he reached the hitched horse then began pushing the animal backward.

Reuben rushed to open the barn doors as Ben backed the wagon out. Once it was safely away, Ben grabbed the kerchief from the animal's face and dashed back inside while Reuben tarried long enough to feel around the straw. Fear squeezed his heart as he realized Whipper wasn't in the wagon. If the cripple had hidden in the barn, he might not escape. Spurred by a sense of responsibility, Reuben ran back inside where night breezes flooded the barn, spreading flames to nearby feedbags.

Ben had opened a stall and was twisting the kerchief around the horses' halter when a glowing ember landed on its muzzle. The frightened animal reared, pulling Ben off his feet and slammed him against a wall. The punishing blow knocked Ben senseless and as he fell, the horse backed out of the enclosure and raced out the door.

Reuben barely missed being trampled as the horse galloped into the barnyard. "Mistah Ben! Where are you?" he called.

Seeing a movement, he rushed into the stall finding Ben sprawled on the floor. "Are you hurt?" Without waiting for an answer, Reuben scooped Ben into his arms then straightened with a powerful contraction of his back. Turning sideways, Reuben elbowed his way out of the stall, half trotting, and half running until he reached the back porch.

As he gained the steps, the door flew open. Gabriella stood in her wrapper, holding a candle. She gasped as she saw a large figure looming toward her.

"It's me-Reuben," he panted, "with Ben. He's hurt!" Reuben burst into the kitchen and dropped Ben onto a nearby chair. "Ben got squished by a horse!" he said in a rush. "And, the barn's afire! I've got to go back!" Reuben ran out, his breath coming in great gasps as he plunged into the barn now eerily lit by flames. In his absence, the fire had formed an upward draft, climbing timbers that supported the haymow. The horse still confined in a stall shrieked as sparks showered it from above.

"Whipper!" he yelled. "Whipper, come out! You's gonna die in here!" As smoke billowed around him, Reuben's eyes began watering and his lungs burned. He heard nothing but the crackle of fire and the frenzied screams of the remaining horse. Unable to stand its cries any longer, he rushed to open its stall.

As the horse bolted through the doors, Reuben searched places a man might hide. He checked inside Gabriella's carriage and behind a row of water barrels before feeling around a tack room. When the heat became unbearable, Reuben covered his face and ran out the door straight into the arms of several men. Many on horseback were still coming from the road and into the barnyard.

"Ho there! Lookee what we caught!" snickered one. "We got us a troublemaker, fer sher!"

"Whooee! He's a big'un!" exclaimed another. "Betcha this'n will fetch us a pretty penny, eh boys?"

Reuben's lungs protested the sharply cold air after the singeing heat, and he began to cough. "I-I's a free man!" he sputtered. "I ain't no troublemaker! I wuz helping Mistah Ben git the horses—"

"Stealing horses, no doubt," scoffed the one who appeared in charge. "Ain't knowed no darkie that'll do honest labor lest he's stood over by a white man with a whip."

"Hey Charlie, ya think Jeb'll want to keep him? Or, can we have some fun since he started the fire?" The men murmured agreeably as he continued. "We ain't done nothing but spy on the old biddy fer weeks."

"Shut up, Willie," Charlie said. "Yu know better'n that. Jeb will want to talk to him a'fore yu'uns do anything. I already sent our scout to go fetch him."

"Aw, Charlie, I'm not talking 'bout killing the feller, just having some fun is all."

Charlie crossed his arms. "Willie, yu ain't nuthing but a no-account moron! Our orders are to bring any and all information to Jeb immediately, not after yu torment the poor bastard. Once we git rid of this feller we can see if those saloon gals are ready fer a good time."

"Hey Charlie," another spoke up. "Ain't we gonna do something 'bout that fire?"

"Naw," he said, clamping on a cigar. "We ain't paid to save the old lady's barn. It's whut she deserves fer letting nigra's come and go as they please. Let her git her own friggin' fire brigade."

Striking a match, Charlie puffed on the stub before laying a hand on his gun. "Now mind yu," he said, pointing at Reuben. "If yu's to try running from us, we'll be obliged to shoot yer black ass. Yu understand?"

Reuben managed a weak "Yes Suh!" as his hands were lashed with twine. The men then mounted their horses, forcing Reuben to walk behind.

Flames had broken through the barn's roof when a horse-drawn wagon bearing a water tank raced into the barnyard. Men clinging to the sides jumped down and began unwinding a hose connected to a hand pump engine. Ignoring the bounty hunters, several men unhitched the horses and led them a safe distance away while others formed a bucket brigade. Working the pump and passing buckets, none of the firefighters noticed the large black man being led away.

chapter 34

SHERIFF HADLEY STOOD outside his office and watched an unnatural glow in the sky. After the sudden departure of the fire wagon, he had sent Deputy Welch to investigate, hoping the blaze was nothing more than the act of a careless citizen.

Just then, a group of riders thundered past. Most of them halted in front of the saloon while a few approached the boardwalk where he stood. As they reined in their mounts, Jim counted four riders and a fifth that stayed purposefully behind.

"Evening, Sheriff," the leader said.

Recognizing the graveled voice, Jim didn't doubt the bounty hunter knew something about the unfolding events. "Evening, Jeb," he said, leaning against a post. "What brings you out tonight?"

"We-ell, fer one, Ah got the proof yu need to recoup my client's property."

The sheriff looked unconcerned. "Oh?"

Dismounting, Jeb approached the boardwalk. "Is that all yu got to say? Ah just said Ah got proof, and yu just stand there?"

"I'm just wondering what's on fire, and who started it."

"Ah didn't start no damn fire, that's fer sher. But yu'll be pleased to know, Ah caught the culprit fer yu." Jeb signaled with his arm. "Bring him on up, boys."

As the riders parted, the one who had remained behind came forward. Sheriff Hadley quickly descended the steps when he saw a large black man cruelly roped. "Good Lord!" he raged, withdrawing a pocketknife and slicing cords. "This is Reuben Kincaid! He's a free man!"

"Ain't free no more," Charlie snickered, looping the rope around his arm. "We caught him running out of th' barn whilst it was burning."

"Reuben's no criminal. I'll vouch it wasn't him who started it," the sheriff said, cutting away the twine. "Whose barn is on fire?"

"It were th' old woman that lives on th' edge of town, all by herself," Charlie supplied.

Jim looked alarmed. "Gabriella Bruester? Is she all right?"

"No need to git riled," said Jeb. "We saw the old laidy tending her driver. Appears he got hurt fighting the fire."

"What the hell were you doing there?"

"Gitting the evidence Ah need to satisfy the good judge!" Jeb snarled. "Y'all seem to fergit Ah got the right to seize runaways by whatever means necessary."

"But you keep fetching the wrong people," Jim said. "Reuben isn't a runaway and neither were Reagan or Amanda."

Jeb grinned. "Ah got more'n that, now. Ah got a witness proving yer townsfolk are nuthin' but law-breakers. And all Ah'm asking is fer yu to do whut Ah cain't do mesself."

Hadley stared at the giant. Having sworn to uphold all laws and not just the ones he liked, obliged him to hear Jeb out. "You sure pick the most unhandy times to demand legal process. I don't suppose you'd consider delaying this until after the Thanksgiving celebration?"

"Nope. By then, Ah'll be heading home to collect my bounty." Reaching under his pelt, he withdrew a tobacco plug and bit into it. "When faced with jail, the guilty c'n git helpful, real quick."

"We'll see who'll end up in jail," Jim promised while taking Reuben's arm. He sniffed suddenly. "Reuben, are you burned? Should I send for Doc Turner?"

"No thanks, I'm Okay."

Jeb snorted as he chewed his quid. "Huh! Ah cain't believe the way yu-uns molly coddle them that ain't no better than stupid, filthy mules!" He spat a stream of tobacco that splattered Reuben's boots. "It's no wonder nigra's want to lickity-split up North. Next thing yu know, they'll be putting on airs like they wuz our equals or something."

"Of course, that would imply you were above the Negro race, Mr. Johnson. An assumption not proven by any act on your part."

Jeb's lip curled. "That's the trouble with y'all. Yu think yer better'n us just cuz yu outlawed slavery! Yu'uns quote the Bible with one hand whilst stealing property with the other. Yu tell me sheriff, how's one worse than the other?"

"I'm not here to argue the morality of slavery. Right now, I want this over with so we can all go home. If you present your witness within the hour, I'll hear your evidence and then determine if it's worth bothering Judge McCleary." As the sheriff pushed Reuben up the steps, a deputy emerged from the jailhouse.

"Done," Jeb said as he mounted his horse. "And me'bbe this'll be the last time we lay eyes on one another."

Once the riders departed, Hadley spoke to his deputy. "Ed, see what's taking Joe so long. He's at Miss Bruester's place." He opened the jailhouse door, allowing Reuben to enter. "And, fetch Doc Turner in case anyone's injured."

"Sure thing," Ed said.

Once inside, Reuben sat in a chair while the sheriff grabbed a wet rag from the back room. "Here, this should help."

"Thanks," Reuben said, holding the cloth against his eyes.

"Is there anything else I can do?"

"I'd be obliged if you sent a message to my wife Eliza that I'm all right. Tell her while I'm detained, she's to go to Purvis, our neighbor, if she needs anything."

The sheriff nodded as he pulled paper and a pencil from his desk. "I'm ready for your version of what happened tonight. Take as much time as you need."

Afterward, having settled Reuben in a cell, Jim waited at his desk, wondering what trickery the giant was up to this time.

chapter 35

AFTER APPLYING A cold compress to Ben's head, Gabriella insisted he drink a mixture of water and aspirin powder. She then opened the back door and watched as firemen passed buckets while others pumped water into a hose aimed toward the burning building. Yet, despite their efforts, it was apparent the barn would be a total loss. Soon after, the firemen gathered their equipment and retreated a safe distance.

"Well, Ben, I guess we can forget about that coat of paint the barn needed," she said, closing the door. "We can at least be thankful you and Reuben saved the animals."

"Re-Reuben?" Ben sat straighter as images of being picked off the floor drifted like vapor through his mind. "Oh, Reuben...he was here because..." He searched for an answer, coming up blank. "I can't remember," he said as another, smaller form floated before his eyes. "But, I think I saw—"

Gabriella canted her head. "Where *is* Reuben?" She opened the door and peered out. "Do you suppose he left without telling us why he was here?"

Ben shook his head. "That's not like him. He would've let us know he was all right."

"Good heavens! Do you think he's trapped in the barn?"

"I'll go see," Ben said, rising. "I feel better now."

As Gabriella opened the door wider, a man entered while removing his hat. "Excuse me, ma'am. I'm Deputy Welch. Sheriff Hadley sent me to see what happened and report if anything's amiss."

Gabriella spoke hurriedly. "There's a man missing, a friend. He rescued my driver from the barn but we haven't seen him since."

"What's his name?"

"Reuben Kincaid," Ben said as he grabbed a spare coat and headed out the door with Joe close behind . "We'd given him a wagonload of donations to take to the Negro settlement. He must've been returning the wagon even though we told him to keep it until tomorrow."

Standing in the doorway, Gabriella witnessed flames break through the barn's roof and she slowly closed the door. The loss of the barn meant nothing. Yet, combined with Nell's death, it broke the barrier of her pent up emotions and she bowed her head and wept.

Ben and deputy Welch approached the fire wagon and asked the gathered men if anyone had seen a large black man.

"I ain't seen no black feller, though I did see a group of white fellers leaving when we first got here," volunteered one while storing a bucket. "I heard the captain found a man's coat before it got hotter than Hades and we had to skedaddle!"

"Where's the captain?"

Looking around, the young man pointed his finger. "Here he comes now. He's the one with the cap on his head."

After Deputy Welch spoke to the captain, the man approached the fire wagon and pulled out a man's woolen coat. "Is this what you're looking for?" he asked.

Ben looked closely at the garment. By its size, he could tell it never would've fit Reuben. "I'd like to keep this, if it's all right with you," he said as a peculiar odor emanated upward, stirring memories of a medicine cabinet and broken bottles.

The captain shrugged. "It's your barn. I don't see any reason why you can't."

Ben laid the coat over his arm, turning to Joe. "I remember a man inside the barn just as it caught fire. I didn't get a good look at him, but I believe this is his coat."

"And it wasn't this-Reuben?"

"No, this man was much smaller. I caught him rummaging through the barn. That's when the fire started. I tried putting it out, but couldn't. That's when Reuben came and helped with the horses. When I got knocked senseless, Reuben carried me to the house."

"Do you have any idea who this other man could've been?"

“I think it’s one of Jebediah Johnson’s men. They’ve been following Miss Bruester for weeks.”

“This doesn’t seem like an accident,” the deputy said. “I’ll need to take that coat to the sheriff.” Ben handed it over as he continued, “Since you’re a witness, you’ll need to give the sheriff an accounting of what happened.” At Ben’s nod, Deputy Welch spoke to the captain again before riding off with the coat slung over his saddle.

Ben then hurried through the kitchen door. “I think we better get to Sheriff Hadley’s office,” he told Gabriella. “Reuben may be in some trouble.”

“Yes, I believe you’re right,” she said. “Tell me, did we lose the carriage?”

“I’m sorry. They weren’t able to save it.”

“No matter, our neighbor’s the Thompson’s, will allow us the use of theirs.”

As Ben turned to go, they heard a rapping against the kitchen door.

Gabriella fumbled with the ties of her wrapper. “My goodness, who else could it be?”

“Doc...” Ben’s voice rose in surprise as he opened the door. “What are you doing here?” As he stepped back, Doctor Artemus Turner entered with his medical bag.

“I was sent by Sheriff Hadley to see if you or any firemen needed tending.” Setting his bag on the table, he removed his coat. “I came as soon as I could.”

“There’s your patient,” Gabriella said, indicating Ben. “He has a head injury.”

“Please have a seat. I’d like to examine you.”

"Is this really necessary?" asked Ben. "I feel fine."

"I want to be assured you're not hurt," Gabriella encouraged. "We've had enough sorrow for one night."

Ben sat down, flinching as the doctor felt his head. "Ouch! That hurts!"

"Hold still," Artemus commanded. "It appears you have a good-sized lump."

"Yes, I *kno-ow*! I got slammed against the wall by a fifteen hundred pound animal!"

Taking a candle out of his bag, the doctor lit the wick and proceeded to move it back and forth in front of Ben's eyes. "Good, your pupils are responding. Now follow this," he said, holding up one finger. Swinging the digit in different directions, he watched as Ben's eyes tracked the path of his finger. "How does your head feel?"

"Fine until you started messing with it. Can I go now?"

"He doesn't seem to have a concussion," Turner said. "But, to be on the safe side, I'd like to do a thorough examination in my office tomorrow afternoon."

"Of course," said Gabriella. "I'll see to it." Ben rolled his eyes but remained silent as the doctor put on his coat.

"Is there anything else I can do for you, Miss Bruester? A sedative to help you sleep, perhaps?"

"Oh, no," she said. "I'm afraid I have too much to do."

Ben opened the door. "If you'll excuse me, I'll go fetch Thompson's carriage."

The doctor looked surprised. "Surely you're not going out at this late hour?"

Gabriella forced a smile. "I'm afraid I must. But thanks for coming to examine Ben. He was a little confused at first. However, he now seems to be his old self."

"Very well. I'll take account of the men outside. There may be some burns that need attention."

After Artemus left, Gabriella hurried to get dressed. Much time had passed since Reuben disappeared and she felt something was amiss.

chapter 36

JUST AS HADLEY requested, Jebediah returned to the jailhouse with Ted and Willy. All three sat in front of the sheriff as he leaned against his desk, taking notes. He raised a hand. "Slow down, Jeb. Before you go further, I need to hear the story from your men. I just can't take your word for it."

"Why not?" he growled. "Yu's accepting the word of that nigra yu got locked in that cell of yurs!"

"I only recorded the account he gave about himself," Jim said. "And I can only accept direct testimony from your men. Understand?"

Jeb swiveled his shaggy head. "Well boys," he barked. "Give the sheriff whut he wants! Ah ain't got all night."

"We-ell," Ted began. "We wuz watching the old lady's house. Surveying, see, to see if she wuz doing anything illegal." He nervously cleared his throat. He never knew if their activities were legal or not, and didn't care as long as he got paid. He swallowed hard. "Anyhow, when she-the old lady I mean-"

"Miss Bruester," Hadley corrected. "You'll refer to her as Miss Bruester from now on."

Ted licked his lips as the sheriff began scribbling. "As I said, we followed Miss Bruester and seen that she'd bought lots of blankets and winter coats..."

"So far, you've not told me anything Miss Bruester's done that's illegal." Jim tapped his pencil against the pad. "Keep going."

Ted nodded. "We decided to watch at night, since Miss Bruester twice come home without us seeing her leave a'tall." He glanced toward Jeb, wondering if he was supposed to reveal that bit of information. "So, we wuz only doing our job when we catched the black feller running out of the barn that wuz on fire."

"Why would you take a freeman into custody if you're only looking for runaway's?" asked the sheriff. "Why waste everyone's time over an unfortunate accident?"

Jeb smirked. "B'cause that Nigra wuz transportin' a runaway when we caught him, that's why!"

"He was what?"

"He was breaking the law! We snagged the one he wuz taking directly to the Bruester house!"

Sheriff Hadley stared at Jebediah. "Do you mean to tell me, you have a slave who claims Reuben took him to Miss Bruester's to help him escape?"

Willy snickered. "Grabbed his skinny ass whilst he was trotting past our camp—"

"Shut up!" Jeb flung a fist into Willie's chest. "Cain't yu see we's conducting business?" Willy quieted, but grinned at Ted while Jeb continued. "Not only do we have the little cripple, he'll even testify he was taken directly to the Bruester place after admitting he was fleeing his master!"

"How do I know you aren't making this up?" Jim asked. "So far, you haven't produced anyone."

"Ah'll do better'n that," Jeb boasted. "But first, don't yu want to question yer prisoner? Or, did he already confess to his crimes?"

"I think it's time we get to the bottom of this," Jim said. "I'll bring Reuben out for questioning while you get your prisoner. I'm anxious to speak with this escapee."

"Of course!" Jeb nodded his agreement. "Ted, go fetch the little whippersnapper!"

Jeb's laughter still echoed as the sheriff entered the cell where Reuben slept. "It's time, Reuben," he said, touching his shoulder.

Reuben sat up and rubbed swollen eyes. "Is it morning?"

"It's several hours before daylight, if that's what you mean," the sheriff said. "I need you come out to my office and tell your story again."

Reuben shielded his eyes from the lamplight as he entered the room. "Have a seat," Jim said. "I'd like you to retell the events as you explained it to me. Start with the arrival of Miss Bruester's wagon to your home."

Reuben took a deep breath. "Miss Bruester, she's always bringin' provisions to the settlement, especially around winter-time. Actually, it was Ben that brought the wagon to the dry goods store where I was working.

I guess he'd seen me earlier that day, and decided to go there, rather than all the way to the river. He told me I didn't have to return the wagon til morning."

"What was in the wagon?"

"Blankets, clothes and vittles. Miss Bruester's a good woman."

"So why did you return the wagon tonight rather than tomorrow morning, like Ben suggested?"

"I didn't want to be seen at Miss Bruester's whilst she was gone. Y'see, Ben said they were going to her brothers house the next day. I was afraid if someone saw me there when no one else was about, it'd raise suspicions. I was trying to avoid problems, but it seems I got troubles anyhow."

Jeb leaned forward. "An' whut kind of cargo did ya have under the straw? Seems yu fergot to tell the sheriff 'bout that!"

Reuben thought quickly. If Whipper had been captured, how much had the runaway revealed? He tried recalling if he had mentioned Gabriella's name. Not knowing what to say, Reuben stared silently at the bounty hunter.

"Whut's a'matter? Ain't yu gonna tell the sheriff who wuz in the wagon? Seems the old boy ain't so talkative now, is he?"

The sheriff recognized uncertainty in Reuben's face. "Is there something you need to tell me?" he asked.

Reuben shook his head. "Don't know nuthin' 'bout that. Anyone could've sneaked into the wagon whilst I wasn't looking."

"Just like someone snuck into the barn and set it afire!" Jeb scoffed, rising to his feet. "Ah suppose that's just a coincidence, too!"

"I didn't set no barn on fire! Me and Ben, we saved the horses, is all."

Jeb leaned over Reuben. "Then why'd yu go back into the barn after the animals wuz out?" At his continued silence, Jeb chuckled. "Mayhap, yu wuz lookin' fer a runaway to keep his hide from frying. Mighty noble of yu, considering the old boy couldn't wait to tell us who took him to Miss Bruester's." Jeb looked triumphantly at the sheriff. "He ain't so innocent now, is he?"

"We still have the matter of you producing this runaway," Hadley said. "My report isn't complete until I question everyone."

The clatter of feet accompanied by a step-scraping noise sounded on the boardwalk moments before the door burst open and a thin mulatto was pushed inside. He stood trembling, looking from one to another until his eyes rested on Reuben. Ted shut the door before sitting down, leaving the cripple in the middle of the room.

"Sheriff, Ah'd like yu to meet Whipper." Folding his arms, Jeb raised his chin. "Whipper here will tell yu everything from the minute he met Reuben til he come running round the bend, where mah boys wuz camped out."

Hadley eyed the mulatto. "How can I be sure you haven't promised him his freedom if he says what you want?"

"B'cause, Ah cain't promise him somethin' he's already got."

Reuben, who had been staring at the floor, looked sharply at Whipper whose expression suddenly changed.

"Ah's a free man, just like yu," he cackled. "Ah work fer Jeb whenever he needs an *inside* man!"

Jeb slapped his thigh as his chortle turned into a full-blown belly laugh. "Always gits 'em, eh Whipper?" At Whipper's gleeful nod, Jeb pulled out his flask. "Here, yu deserve this."

Whipper eagerly drank the contents, reveling in the warmth that dulled his aching leg. When reporting to Jeb, he had carefully omitted his part in the barn's demise, instead inferring the barn caught fire because of Reuben's carelessness with the lantern.

Though only a hireling, Whipper feared the giant. Due to his need for liquor, he was never far from Jebediah's bidding, readily accepting whatever whiskey the bounty hunter offered. In his more generous moods, Jeb even provided women for the mulatto's pleasure. But what he needed most was the steady employment only a man such as Jebediah was willing to give.

Sheriff Hadley looked from Jebediah to Whipper. "It seems you have use for Negroes after all, Mr. Johnson. You gave the impression you thought they weren't any better than mules."

"Whipper here is only half Nigra," Jeb said, dropping a hand on the mulatto's shoulder. "Ah can overlook the dirty blood in him, cuz that's the part that gits him places, me and mah boys cain't. He's ratted out more Nigra lovers than Ah can count, ain't ya, Whip?"

Resentment showed in Whipper's eyes as they traveled over Reuben's muscular form. "Yassuh! Ain't no man Whipper cain't fool!"

For most of his life, Whipper had known only hate. Hate for the master who had cruelly crippled him and then freed him, deeming him too worthless to feed. Reduced to fighting for scraps among mongrels, he had grown to resent even slaves, for at least they were fed and clothed. Finding solace in the sediment of abandoned liquor bottles, Whipper had learned to enjoy dulled senses. By the time he reached manhood, his malice encompassed all humanity and he became easily recruited to betray even those who treated him kindly.

A knock sounded and Sheriff Hadley opened the door. "Miss Bruester!" he said. "What are you doing here?"

Gabriella tapped her cane impatiently. "Well, Jim, are you going to let me in or keep me standing in the cold?" Backing up, the sheriff allowed her to enter, followed closely by Ben.

"Just as I thought." Gabriella's gaze fell on Reuben before giving full attention to Jebediah. "I had a notion you were behind this. Amanda told me all about you. What kind of skullduggery are you brewing now?"

"Mebbee Ah should be asking the same thing," Jeb said. "Only this time, yu won't be able to hide behind the skirts of that fine niece of yurn's." He nodded at Whipper who had retreated toward the stove. "This time, Ah got the ace up mah sleeve."

chapter 37

Emily Bruester sat at her desk, staring at the sealed envelope. Unknown to George or Amanda, the missive had remained unopened for a week as she spent sleepless nights searching for any alternative other than what she knew to be scripted inside. The bold handwriting belonged to none other than Reagan Burnsfield, posted the day after Camilla's dinner party.

A cold fury swept over Emily as she picked up the envelope and placed it among the mail that just arrived. Taking the tray, she proceeded to enter the downstairs study where George sat reading the paper.

"The post has arrived," she said, slamming down the tray.

"What's the matter, dear? With tomorrow's holiday, I'll have plenty of time to look over the mail."

"No, you won't. Gabriella will spend the entire day and keep you from attending your affairs."

George winced at the unquiet way Emily departed. He lifted a few pieces to scan their marks of origin and smiled when found Reagan's letter. Ripping open the envelope he read swiftly and then more slowly read the letter again.

Ever since the night of the elections, Amanda had become the target of crude and malicious gossip. It now appeared Reagan was trying to remedy the situation with a formal request for Amanda's hand.

George gazed at the ceiling, wondering if this was the only avenue left. A proper marriage despite the controversy would put an end to the talk. George bit his lip as he fretted if this was the right thing to do. The last thing he wanted was to bind his daughter to a man she may never love. Yet, if it turned out well, Amanda could regain the respect and honor she deserved.

Wills entered, carrying a tray. "Your coffee, sir."

"Thank you, Wills. Would you please send for Amanda and Mrs. Bruester? We've something to discuss. Afterward, I'll have a letter to be delivered to the Burnsfield home."

"Very good, sir," he said before leaving.

George drew up three chairs and waited until the women came and took seats. He then sat beside them, taking Amanda's hand. "The reason I've called you is because I received a letter from Reagan Burnsfield. He's asking for your hand in marriage. It seems that everything your mother and I have done to stop the stories have failed. Reagan too, realizes the tales have only gotten worse and wishes to correct his part in the scandal with this proposal." As the color rose in Amanda's cheeks, he spoke gently. "Under the circumstances, I believe it's something to consider. But,

I need to know if you've any feelings for the man. I mean, before any of this occurred, would you have considered him for a husband?"

"Wait! There are other possibilities," Emily blurted. "There's Leroy Spelding to consider. I know he's interested in Amanda. Why, you should've seen him at her coming out ball..."

"I don't think so, mother," Amanda said. "If he were, I'm sure that changed at Camilla's party."

"You don't know that," Emily said. "He's probably waiting til this blows over to extend an invitation."

George held up his hand. "I'm afraid not. Ezra informed me only this week, his son's been invited to the Muelder's for the Festival of Thanks. He let me know, rather loudly I might add, that he believes Leroy and Camilla to be a good match."

Emily looked taken aback, but recovered quickly. "Why does it have to be Reagan? You only have to look at Derrick to know the man desires Amanda! Surely his family has as much prestige as Reagan's."

Amanda's stomach lurched as she realized to protect Gabriella, she couldn't refuse Reagan. Ever since he first offered to marry her, Amanda wondered if he had spoken rashly. With this formal request, she assumed his sense of duty was stronger than his desire to love her. But either way, once he became her husband, he'd be obligated to keep her secret.

"Mother, it's all right," she began.

"I believe Derrick to be a *better* match," Emily insisted. "We could contact his family and invite them here." George took his wife's arm, but she only yanked it from his grasp. "Why not? What's wrong with Derrick?"

"Nothing that I know of," he said. "Except that he left two days ago on personal business and said he wouldn't be back for some weeks."

Emily gasped. "Why didn't you tell me? We could've spoken forthrightly to him!"

"Because, I only received Reagan's letter today. Had I known even two days ago, we could've discussed this with him. Now it's too late. Derrick didn't leave an address where he could be reached and I need to give Reagan an answer. He's requested a wedding before Christmas due to work obligations. It's not in Amanda's best interest to turn Reagan down only to discover no other offers would be forthcoming."

"Oh no!" Emily said, covering her face. "What've I done?"

"Please, don't blame yourself," Amanda said, laying a hand on Emily's shoulder. "You weren't the one who acted foolishly. Besides, I knew someday I'd marry."

Emily felt defeated, realizing that waiting to hand over Reagan's letter had ruined her lifelong ambition. Her voice shook as she wiped her eyes. "Your father asked if you've considered Reagan-for-a-a-husband. I guess we'll now need to know."

All her life, Amanda had envisioned her marriage as a time of joy and happiness, not one that would be coldly calculated. Yet, to protect Gabriella, she didn't hesitate. "I accept his proposal," she said.

George nodded, much relieved. "That settles it. We'll announce your engagement the day after Thanksgiving. And with your permission, Amanda, we'll invite Reagan to dinner. I'll send a note at once."

Later, in her chambers, Amanda sat at her vanity preparing to receive their guest. It remained a mystery to her why Reagan was willing to go to such lengths to protect her and Gabriella. And although she preferred him to the other choices, she felt ill prepared to marry a man she barely knew.

A knock at the door preceded Gertrude's entrance. "Yer guest has arrived," she said, placing clean linens in a drawer. "And a right fine specimen he is."

Amanda frowned in the mirror. "Does *everyone* have an opinion? What would you know of the gentlemen callers I've had?"

"I've had my eye on that one since the night of your ball," Gertrude said, picking up a brush and running it through Amanda's hair. "He's a sight better'n that Mr. Banning."

"I suppose," Amanda said. "However, Mother was rather hopeful about Derrick."

"Harrumph. All the more reason to not like the gent," Gertrude said, forming an elegant twist before fastening pins in Amanda's hair. "Ain't no man worth his salt that your momma ever liked. Excepting, Mr. Bruester, of course."

"Now Gertie, what've I said about that briar-like tongue of yours?"

"Nobody's here but me and yu, little missy. Since when haven't I spoken my mind?"

"Never, I guess," Amanda said, sighing. She turned her head to inspect Gertrude's handiwork. "It looks wonderful."

Gertrude touched Amanda's shoulder. "Pay no mind to what others are saying," she said. "I got a good feeling about this gent."

"It's all right, really. I believe this to be the best choice for all concerned."

As Amanda rose, Gertrude removed a silk poplin gown from the wardrobe and laid it on the bed. "Yer papa's in the study with yer soon-to-be. As soon as they're done talking, dinner will be served."

"Thank you Gertie. Mother and I will wait in the parlor. You may go," she said, brushing aside the maids hands. "I can fasten the buttons myself."

After Gertrude left, Amanda put on the gown, rhapsodically described by her dressmaker as Ashes of Roses. She looked in the mirror as she fastened her favorite brooch. *Don't kid yourself,* she thought. *Reagan is only marrying you out of obligation. He can't possibly love you.* Amanda raised her chin. What had to be done would be done. Steeling her nerves, she gathered her skirts and descended the stairs.

In the study, George poured two drinks from a sideboard. "I keep sherry for times I need to think clearly," he said, handing a glass to Reagan. "I spoke with Amanda after receiving your letter and she's consented to be betrothed. Yet, due to the delicate nature of the situation, I must know if this had been your intent all along. I wouldn't want Amanda's heart broken by a rash decision."

"If it'd put your mind at ease, I've considered marriage to Amanda since the night of her ball," Reagan said. "And though I lament the circumstances surrounding my proposal, I certainly don't regret the offer."

"I see," George said. "That was my concern. Since you never had a chance to formally court Amanda, besides that one night—I couldn't determine your sincerity." He then offered his hand. "Well, it looks as if we're going to have a wedding."

After finishing their drinks, Reagan touched his pocket. "I brought a gift for Amanda. May I present it this evening?"

"Of course. No need for ceremony here."

"I've *one* formality I'd like to discuss," Reagan said. "As I must soon leave for camp, I wanted to make arrangements for Amanda's dowry before the first of the year."

"That shouldn't be a problem," George said, holding open a box of cigars. After taking one for himself, he lit both cigars. "Since Amanda's birth, I've set aside funds for her security. Also, her grandparents established accounts that are exclusively hers. Should you decide to build a home, there'll be more than enough funds to do so."

"I'll look into that soon," Reagan said. "Right now, getting the new mill up and running is taking all my attention."

"How is that coming along?"

"A few bumps in the road, but thanks to the business loan you provided, come spring we'll be back on track."

"That's good to hear," George said. "You say you're returning to camp? Isn't that unusual this time of year?"

"What's odd is my returning home at all. If not for the elections, I'd still be in New York."

"And, we wouldn't be having this conversation," George said, smiling. "Only the future will determine if any of us have made wise decisions." He tamped his cigar. "Let's go find the women and get better acquainted, shall we?"

As the men entered the parlor, Emily barely glanced from her needlework. "Good evening, ladies," George said. "As you can see, our guest has arrived."

Reagan took Amanda's fingers, his gaze sweeping her with more than mere admiration. "Good evening, Amanda." He then extended his hand to Emily. "Madam Bruester. How good of you to receive me."

"Won't you have a seat?" Emily managed a grimacing smile. "This is all rather sudden and we have much to discuss."

Later that night, long after others were asleep, Emily wondered at Reagan's unshakable composure despite her lack of enthusiasm throughout dinner. Nothing, it seemed, could sway his decision on having a December wedding even after she offered reasons to extend the engagement. It wasn't until every subtle objection had been countered that Emily finally admitted defeat. Reagan would be Amanda's husband.

At George's insistence, the couple finally had a few moments' privacy in the parlor. That was when Reagan gifted Amanda with a magnificent diamond and ruby ring.

Emily's last thought before falling sleep, was that she very much hated Reagan Burnsfield.

chapter 38

"PLEASE, MISS BRUESTER, have a seat," the sheriff said, bringing near his chair. Pulling aside her skirts and despite the ache in her back, Gabriella sat with a straight spine. Ben remained standing, his scowl a warning that all but Jeb took seriously.

Sheriff Hadley resumed his place while pulling a pencil from behind his ear. "This is what we have so far," he said, tapping his notebook. "As a fact, Miss Bruester made a donation of clothes and supplies, which she gave to Reuben to dispense among his people." He looked toward Gabriella as she loosened the ties of her bonnet. "Is that correct, ma'am?"

"It is, most assuredly. Reuben's been a trusted friend for many years."

"Sorry for all the trouble, Miss Bruester," Reuben said. "I didn't mean for this to happen."

"It's all right. I'm confident this'll be cleared up. It's shameful you were even entangled in this mess." She glared at Jebediah. "It's obvious the man has no soul, and would do anything, including lying, to obtain what he wants."

"Ah ain't the one doing the lying," Jeb said. As Ben stepped forward, he snorted derisively. "If yu's fixin' to tangle with old Jeb, yu'd fer sher, git the little end of the horn!"

"There'll be none of that," Hadley warned. "I'm just about tired enough to call this off until we've all had a good night's sleep."

"Oh hell. Just git on with it," Jeb said. "Ah want to git some sleep, too."

"Reuben stated he was returning the wagon to Miss Bruester's residence when the fire broke out," the sheriff said. "And this is where the accounts no longer agree." He tapped the air with his pencil. "Now, Mr. Johnson claims Reuben transported a runaway to Miss Bruester's for the purpose of aiding said person in an escape." The sheriff looked at Jebediah. "Is that correct?"

"Damn straight!" Jeb growled. "Ah got mah witness." He jerked his thumb in Whipper's direction. "Which should be good 'nuff fer the judge!"

Gabriella looked from Reuben to Whipper, trying to piece together the truth. "It seems to me," she offered, "that it's come down to one man's word against another. And as much as I hate calling someone a liar, I trust Reuben over anyone who's a man hunter." She allowed her eyes to settle on the sheriff in innocent repose. "Don't you agree, Jim?"

"It seems ma'am, it's more than that." Lifting a bundle from the desk, he shook out the material, revealing a man's woolen coat. "Could this be one of the garments you purchased today and gave to Reuben?"

Gabriella could feel the confidence draining from her face. Free from rips or patches, the coat was obviously new. As the sheriff held it for her inspection, a faint odor wafted upward.

Gabriella pretended to examine the material. "Well, I-I suppose it's-possible-but I fear all men's coats look the same to me," she finished weakly. "Why?"

"Deputy Welch obtained it from the fire brigade who found it just inside your barn. This is the coat Whipper claims Reuben gave him just before he was brought to your home. It looks too small to fit either Reuben or Ben, the two men we know were there."

"Oh. I see," Gabriella said.

"Ah cocked his hat, a'right!" Whipper cackled. "Dumbest bootlicker Ah ever laid eyes on! He done th' deed an' deserves everythin' he's gittin'."

Reuben closed his eyes. He could no longer look at the man. Crippled or not, he believed he just witnessed the lowest form of betrayal.

Jebediah pointed at Whipper. "There's mah proof! Now Ah want the old biddy to tell me where she hid the slave girl. And since it's the holiday," he said, puffing out his chest, "mebbee Ah'll fergit about prosecuting the guilty parties. Now, mind yu, that's only if Ah git the wench Ah come after in the first place."

Gabriella could feel her panic rising. That the bounty hunter could no longer harm Nell held little comfort for the babe was still hidden nearby. How could she choose between the child and Reuben? As she fumbled with her bonnet, a hand squeezed her shoulder.

"Sheriff," Ben spoke suddenly. "Would it interest you to know who started the fire?"

"What do you mean?" he asked, missing the shocked look that crossed Whipper's face.

"It wuz the darky we caught comin' from the barn whilst it wuz burning!" Jebediah said, interrupting.

"Reuben wasn't in the barn when it caught fire," Ben said, pointing to the coat. "Whoever it was, he broke into the medicine chest in search of something."

"Are you saying it was Whipper who started the fire?" Jim asked. "But, why?"

"I was wondering the same thing, until I had a chance to watch him," Ben said. "A man with a chronic pain might look for something to numb his discomfort."

"No, Ah never!" Whipper shook his head as his hand madly kneaded his thigh. "It were him!" he shrieked, pointing at Reuben. "He left th' lantern a'crooked on a bale and it tipped over!" Whipper swung his gaze toward Jeb. "Honest, boss, just like Ah said!"

Ben nodded toward Whipper as flashes of memory formed with more clarity. "I believe I startled him, and that's when the lantern got knocked over. One of the bottles was ether, which we keep to sedate horses when doctoring wounds. If he claims that's his coat, I believe you'll still be able to smell the ether."

Sheriff Hadley put his nose to the cloth, inhaling deeply. "You're right. I couldn't figure out what that odor was."

Ted reached over and cuffed Whipper. "So, that's why yu wuz acting so corned. Yu wuz a'sniffin' ether."

Willie, not wanting to miss any fun, kicked the mulatto who fell to his knees. "We figured yu wuz a'wobbly just cuz yer so plug-ugly."

If Whipper's mind had been clearer, he would've continued denying his guilt. But the liquor befuddled his mind. Groveling, he raised his arms. "Ah's sorry, laidy, Ah wuzn't trying t' hurt nobody! Ah didn't mean t' ketch th' barn afire! Ah just needed sompin' to help mah leg!"

Enraged, a guttural sound emitted from Jebediah's throat as he vaulted from his chair, grabbing Whipper's collar. "Yu worthless guttersnipe!" he growled, shaking him. "Ah could kill yu fer this!"

Whipper covered his face as he screamed in a high-pitched, child-like voice. "Ah's sor-rry!! Ah's sor-rry!!"

The room seemed to explode as the sheriff yelled, drawing deputies from the back room. As they grabbed Jebediah, Ben flung his arms around Gabriella, dragging her away, chair and all. Reuben squeezed between the deputies to grip Whipper's shoulders, peeling the cripple away while Ted and Willy sat shocked anyone would dare put hands on the infuriated giant.

"Enough!" Jebediah roared, shaking himself loose. "So, the pickaninnie started the fire! So whut!"

"Sit down, Mr. Johnson," Jim said, touching his gun. "Or so help me, I'll put you under arrest and keep you locked up until after the first of the year."

Jeb eyes burned as he righted his chair and settled in it. "This don't change a thing. Ah don't care if the half-breed burned the whole damned town. Ah still say the laidy hid the runaways and Ah ain't leaving without them."

Jim took Whipper from Reuben. "I think you need to lay down," he said, taking him back and placing him in a cell.

After returning, the sheriff stared at his notes. He tapped the paper causing all, including Gabriella, to hold their breath.

"Well folks," he said. "This is as much about money as it is the law. As I see it, you Jebediah, are here to recoup your client's property."

"Yu betcha," he said, nodding eagerly. "A young slave girlie is worth a lot of money. The bitch proved she could breed, that's fer sher!"

Sniggering, Willy spoke up. "Th' master himself had at her, Ah hear tell."

Gabriella drew in a sharp breath, covering her mouth.

"That's it!" the sheriff said. "I insist you two leave."

Ted and Willie looked toward Jebediah. "Git!" the bounty hunter said. "Yu boys git some sleep. Ah'll be along shortly."

Soon after they left, the door flew back open. George burst in, his eyes falling on Gabriella. "Thank

God you're all right! I got word your barn was on fire, but couldn't find you at home. You're neighbors told me you'd come here."

"I'm fine, George," Gabriella said.

"What happened?"

"That's why we're all here," Jim said. "We have allegations and charges to sort through."

George's eyes hardened as he looked at Jebediah. "Who's making the charges?"

"Mr. Johnson is alleging Gabriella is involved with illegal transportation of slaves-"

"What?!" George sputtered. "Why, that's preposterous! Gabriella is no more involved with the Underground Railroad than I am!" He turned toward the bounty hunter. "First you slander my daughter and now you're preying on a helpless woman." He shook his finger. "How dare you!"

Jeb shrugged. "Cain't help it if'n yer family are nuthin' but lawbreakers."

"What are the charges?"

Reading his notes, Jim outlined the details of the evening, including the evidence of the coat as well as Ben's recollection of the fire, ending with Whipper's admission.

George stood aghast as he stared at his sister. "I don't know what to say..."

"Oh, grow up George," she chided. "You've led a sheltered life. Sheriff, what's to happen next?"

Jim stuck his pencil behind his ear. "Well, ma'am, as I was saying before. This isn't just about law, it's about money as well."

"Yeah, yeah, we already covered that," Jeb spat. "Let's git to the part where Ah git the girl."

Jim ignored Jebediah as he looked directly at Gabriella. "It seems ma'am, that we no longer have one felonious act, but two."

Gabriella steeled herself. "What's the other charge?"

Sheriff Hadley smiled. "Malicious destruction of property."

It took George only a split second to understand. "The barn!" he nearly shouted.

"Whut?" Jeb looked confused.

"Of course! Why didn't I think of that?" George turned excitably to Gabriella. "The barn's a total loss. This Whipper has already admitted his guilt. As he was acting as an agent for Mr. Johnson, *he's* liable for the barn as well as its contents!"

"Now, hold on," Jeb snarled. "Whut d'ya mean Ah'm responsible?" He pointed a finger at Reuben. "If it weren't fer him, none of this would've happened."

"Reuben didn't start the fire," Ben said. "Whipper did."

"Your client can certainly press charges against Miss Bruester for the loss of his property. That's his right," the sheriff said. "But, Miss Bruester also has the right to press charges against you for the loss of her barn."

"And I would," Gabriella said. "Most vigorously!"

Jeb shook his head. "Ah don't b'lieve it."

"Well, Mr. Johnson, it comes down to money," Hadley said. "Will your client's property be worth pursuing in light of the action Miss Bruester could press against you?"

For once, Jeb was speechless. He stared at the sheriff who had thwarted him at every turn yet still fulfilled the letter of the law.

"Well, Ah'll be damned!" Jebediah breathed. "Ah cain't b'lieve Ah've been bested by a woman no bigger'n a mite!"

"Does this mean you're going to drop all charges against Miss Bruester?"

"Hell and damnation!" Jeb said, scowling. "That's exactly whut it means."

"Then this meeting is over," the sheriff said. "You are all free to go."

chapter 39

FOLLOWING THE CONCLUSION of the jailhouse meeting, Reuben left, accompanied by Deputy Welch while Ben went to ready the carriage. George stood near the door gazing at his sister, recalling times when for no apparent reason, Gabriella would change or cancel plans. Dismissing the behavior as oddities of an aging spinster, he now realized what a fool he had been.

Unsure what to do, Jeb tarried in his seat while the sheriff finished writing his report. He stared at his boot tips pondering what story he could tell to keep his client from reclaiming his fee. Raising his gaze to the cane in Gabriella's hands, he noticed her fingers shaking. A grudging admiration caused him to wonder what kind of woman would risk her final years trafficking fugitives. He also wondered what the hell happened to his quarry.

"D'ya suppose that girlie ever made it to her destination?" Jebediah asked.

Gabriella studied his face warily before speaking. "I'm sure I wouldn't know."

"Ah mean, if yu wuz a betting woman, whut would be the odds of her makin' it to Canada?"

"If I were a *guessing* woman," Gabriella said, "I'd have to believe no one could live after what you claim your hounds were capable of doing."

"Ah see." Jeb appeared long in digesting that possibility. It hadn't occurred to him the hounds could've fatally mauled the girl before help arrived. He rubbed his eyes, feeling fatigued. "Ah suppose yu reckon the babe, too?"

"My prayers would be that all children grow up free, as God intended them to be," Gabriella said. "I pray no differently for that child."

"D'ya suppose those prayers will be answered?" Jeb prodded.

Gabriella paused, mindful of her words. "If there's a God in heaven," she said, turning back around. "They will be."

Ben entered the jail. "The carriage is ready, ma'am."

As Gabriella stood, George aided his sister with her coat. "Will you still be attending Emily's dinner tonight?"

She patted her brother's hand as Ben took her arm. "I wouldn't dream of missing it. Besides, I promised Amanda." She then turned to the sheriff. "Give my regards to your wife."

Sheriff Hadley grinned as they departed. "Sure thing, Miss Bruester. You take care, now."

"Now ain't that sweet!" Jeb said, rolling his eyes.

"There's no call for antagonism, Mr. Johnson. We've already settled our differences. So, why are you still here?"

"Ah suppose Ah need to git mah half breed out of yer jail." Jeb said, rising. "He ain't no good to anybody but me."

"Are you sure? You were awfully rough on him tonight."

"Oh hell! Ah ain't gonna kill the little bastard!"

"You've admitted he's a free man. I can't compel him to go with you."

"Ask him!" Jeb challenged. "And if he don't wanna come, fine! But Ah guarantee no one's gonna be as good to him as Ah am, and he knows it!"

As George buttoned his coat, he cleared his throat. "So," he said, wrapping a scarf around his neck, "are you going back to Virginia?"

"Suppose so." Jeb scrutinized the banker. "Why?"

George held out his business card. "I think I can offer you a better solution than the last time we spoke. Be at the bank in one hour. Someone will be there to let you in."

"Hell," Jeb huffed peevishly as he looked at the card. "If that don't pile on the agony. Ah ain't never gonna git any sleep."

After his meeting with George, a bank officer and a lawyer, Jeb stepped outside just as the sun began lighting the sky. Tucked in his pocket was a signed contract for the purchase of one female slave called

Nell, and her male offspring named Isaiah. In return for the payment, Jeb swore to never make contact with George Bruester or his family again.

George had been thorough. In the expanse of one hour, he had roused the family attorney and had him finishing the finer points of their hastily drawn agreement by the time Jeb arrived. George drafted a bank cheque for the sum of $2,500, payable to Jeb's client. Upon cashing the cheque, a certificate of freedom would be issued for Nell and her child. If Jeb broke any terms of the agreement, George would pursue a warrant for his arrest and sue him for triple damages for Gabriella's barn.

Jeb smiled as he guided his horse through the street. He too, received a cheque. It could only be cashed if he were successful in convincing his client to accept the deal. Of that, he was certain. In a settlement against a neighbor, Nell's owner had purchased her for a pittance. Besides, Jeb smirked to himself, there were always other slaves to take her place.

He had done well. Not only had he recovered his client's investment, he also acquired a hefty sum for himself. With that thought in mind, Jebediah hitched his horse outside the saloon and went in.

As he mounted the stairs, a disheveled woman garbed in a robe, descended. She didn't see him until she reached the stairwell, but reading the hunger in his eyes, she pulled back. "I'm not a'workin' right now," she said.

She tried retreating, but with swift steps Jeb overtook her and throwing her over his shoulder, entered the room she just left.

It wasn't until late afternoon Jeb descended the stairs. Spying several of his men, he grinned broadly. "Howdy, boys."

"Whew-ee!" Ted said. "Where's your bearskin? Yu look like yu just plucked th' hen."

Jeb reached out and smacked Ted's shoulder. "Course Ah did, yu ninny."

"Jeez, boss, whut yu so wraithy for?"

"Ain't," Jeb said as he straddled a chair. "Well, boys. Looks like we're heading home today."

chapter 40

IF EMILY HAD ever before arranged elaborate plans on such short notice, she couldn't recall. With barely a fortnight to organize a wedding, she began a flurry of activities.

Without time to order Venetian tulle for Amanda's gown, seamstresses were commissioned to replace the tatting from Emily's own wedding dress while others fashioned a veil and matching slippers. Daily, Amanda modeled the gown so it could be basted before being stitched for the next day's fitting.

At the dressmaker's recommendation, Emily was also fitted with a magnificent dress of deep burgundy silk. Softly draped and short waisted, the gown could be easily finished while the hat maker created a headdress with black and burgundy feathers.

Emily often abandoned the dinner table in favor of overseeing the staff airing linens, unpacking fine china and polishing silver. The same day she supervised decorating the ballroom, she procured services of a minister and musicians. Tirelessly going over her lists, Emily found solace in the consuming nature of the task.

Once invitations were sent, Amanda accepted well-wishers and curious alike who flocked to the mansion. And though she appeared poised, had any found themselves alone with her, she might have been plied with meddlesome questions. But no matter the time or day of week, Aunt Ella was at her side guarding conversation.

❧

The wedding day broke as wet and cold as Emily's heart, as her ambitions of gifting Amanda with a fitting marriage died. Though her bitterness knew no bounds, she would portray nothing amiss, knowing there would be time enough for airing displeasure at her daughter's forced pledging.

On the other side of town, the Burnsfields were enjoying breakfast. Thomas refilled his coffee cup while Amy stifled a yawn.

"Aren't you nervous?" she asked Reagan.

"No ma'am," he teased, giving her ear an affectionate yank.

"But, it's your wedding day," she said. "You're supposed to be excitable. You know, jumpy and fidgety-like."

"I do believe, little sister, you have the wrong party. I understand it's the woman who experiences those things on her wedding day."

"But, you should at least feel anxious," she persisted. "It's common knowledge all parties are prone to fevers." She looked toward her father. "Daddy, weren't you nervous on your wedding day?"

Thomas chuckled. "Nervous wouldn't describe how I felt. I was so distracted, I forgot the wedding ring."

"You didn't," Amy said. "What happened?"

"I sent someone back to get it, but was too scared to let anyone know."

"Then what?"

"Then the ceremony starts," he continued. "And I'm terrified the minister's going to ask for the ring."

"By the look on his face, I thought he was about to faint," Katherine said, smiling in remembrance. "Why, I'd have to say your father was turning a frightful shade of green."

"And then?"

"So my friend returns, running down the aisle, yelling 'Wait! Wait!'"

Amy's eyes grew round. "How dreadful! I'd have perished from embarrassment."

"Of course, your mother handled the whole thing beautifully. She never once mentioned it afterward."

"I was too mortified," Katherine said. "The men folk had the good graces to leave me out of the ribbing they gave your father. He didn't hear the end of it for weeks."

"Reagan, what would you do if someone tried to stop your wedding? Would you engage him in a duel?"

Reagan grinned. "Why would you think that someone would be a *man*?"

"Reagan!" Katherine nearly choked. "There'll be none of that talk."

Amy looked confused. "But why *wouldn't* it be a man?" Then as a dawning expression crossed her face, she smiled knowingly. "Oh, I see."

Reagan chuckled as he folded his napkin. "If you'll excuse me, mother, I believe it's time to get ready."

"We should all get going," she said, rising, "so we can be at the Bruester's before eleven o'clock."

❧

Tightly sealed barouches began arriving at the Bruester manse while servants swarmed the grounds escorting guests inside. As George greeted each caller, wraps were whisked away and guests were left to mingle between parlor and ballroom.

When the Burnsfields arrived, murmurs quickened among those mingling inside the halls, causing Elizabeth to turn. Tarrying just inside the parlor, she spied Reagan as he doffed his coat, revealing a Vandyke brown tuxedo. Searching for signs that this was a reluctant groom, she felt a stab of jealousy that Amanda, not she would be exchanging vows with the flawlessly attired lumberman. She watched him shake George's hand before he exited a side door.

As everyone moved to the parlor to occupy chairs set up for the occasion, Elizabeth found herself seated between her father and Ezra Spelding. With no confidant nearby with whom to share an opinion, she sat fuming in silence.

After the Burnsfields were settled in the front row, Elizabeth observed Emily on the opposite side of the makeshift aisle sitting next to Gabriella. Emily's gown revealed her recently slimmer appearance and Elizabeth peevishly hoped Emily had lost as much sleep as she had apparently lost in appetite.

As latecomers filled remaining seats, a bespeckled minister entered, followed closely by Reagan. Taking his place in front, the clergyman nodded and the organ began playing.

Sharp intakes of breath could be heard when Amanda's magnificently layered dress filled the doorway while entering on her father's arm. Clasping white roses, she appeared to float in a cloud of ivory while orange blossoms attached to the headpiece contrasted vividly against her dark, upswept hair. As they passed each row, all eyes were drawn to Amanda's snug fitting bodice as if looking for a darker reason for the hasty nuptials. If any were disappointed, they kept it prudently to themselves.

Reagan gazed in wonder at the vision coming toward him. Never had Amanda appeared more beautiful and despite his casual approach to matrimony, his spirit soared knowing she would soon be his wife.

When George placed her hand in his, Amanda beheld the obvious pleasure in Reagan's eyes. Time seemed to stop as she appraised his demeanor, praying that he would someday feel more than duty toward her. When they faced the minister, she felt him gently squeeze her hand.

The minister smiled before opening his hymnal, giving a short discourse on the vows of marriage and ending long before she could calm her thumping heart. She heard Reagan's voice as if from a distance before obediently repeating her vows.

As Reagan slipped the ring on her finger, a single tear slipped from the corner of Emily's eye. With the barest of movements, she flicked the wetness from her cheek.

Closing his prayer book, the minister saluted the groom. "Reagan, you may now kiss the bride."

Not since the night by the river had Amanda been kissed by Reagan. In the hurried planning of the nuptials, she had forgotten she would be called to partake in this public display of affection. She turned stiffly. Anticipating his touch, her heart beat wildly as she tipped her chin and when Reagan drew near, her eyes fluttered shut. His lips had barely touched hers when all at once Reagan ended the embrace.

With his arm around Amanda, he turned around, smiling broadly. The couple became surrounded as guests lined up and Emily took her place next to Amanda.

"Quite extraordinary, Emily," Constance Spelding said as she studied a vase of flowers through her lorgnette. "How did you obtain such a splendid array?" Despite her husband's business partnership with George, when rumors of Amanda's arrest circulated, she quickly forbade Leroy from pressing his intended courtship. She even insisted Ezra let it be known their son had other interests, namely Camilla Muelder.

Emily smiled tightly, recalling that particular treachery. "Why, I threatened the manager of the conservatoire, my dear. It's doubtful anyone will find as much as a sprig between now and next summer." She lowered her voice. "So, I wouldn't advise a spring wedding without first checking to see if blossoms are available."

Constance nearly dropped her eyeglass. "But-we're not planning a-"

"I'm so pleased to hear that Leroy and Camilla are much the couple now," Emily said.

"Of course, one doesn't always know about these things," Constance stammered. "Leroy has yet to make his choice." After offering best wishes to the newly married couple as well as the Burnsfields, Constance disappeared into the crowd.

"Ah, my friend!" Beauregard approached, pumping Reagan's hand while simultaneously slapping his back. "You do something quite foolish, eh?"

"Not quite so foolish, I think," Reagan said.

"Grosse tête, peu de sens," Beau said, winking. He then turned his attention to the bride. "Ma petite," he said, bringing her hand to his lips. "Ouch! What is this?"

"How could you not see her ring?"

"It is too big. How can I pretend demoiselle is not married, if she must carry around such a boulder as this?" Lifting her hand, he gave closer inspection. "Magnifique!" He raised an eyebrow. "You amaze me, mon ami. This ring is much too superb, coming from a lumberman."

"It should be no surprise since it came from someone who has a big head but little sense, as you so kindly put it," said Reagan.

Beau smiled. "Ah, your French does not fail you."

"It never does. Remember, I can read your soiled little mind," Reagan said, pulling Amanda close.

Beauregard sighed deeply. "It is always so, Madame Burnsfield. I am just a misunderstood Monsieur who only wishes to be a friend." He shook his head. "See how your husband abuses me?"

Amanda smiled. "You'll always be my friend, Beauregard. Just as Reagan is, so will I be."

"Merci." He bowed his head. "I shall forever be at your service." Eyes sparkling, he took a prudent step back. "And, if your husband were to undergo an untimely demise, my desire would be to give you my utmost and *personal* condolences."

As Beauregard retreated toward the punch bowl, Reagan tightened his arm around Amanda. "Don't encourage that scoundrel. I can see he's not going to respect the vows we just exchanged."

Amanda had no time to respond before the next guest approached. It would be much later before she dwelt on Reagan's seeming overreaction to the Frenchman's banter. At the moment, it was taking everything she had to portray herself as a happy bride with nothing to worry about.

chapter 41

After the ceremony, guests were ushered to the ballroom where a lavish dinner awaited. A maid relieved Amanda of her bouquet before Reagan escorted her from the parlor and into the hall where Amanda paused to take a breath.

"Don't worry," Reagan said in her ear. "I won't let the wolves devour you."

Amanda looked surprised. "How'd you know?"

"My dear, I haven't been blind to the embarrassment you've suffered. But until you became my wife, I wasn't in a position to protect you."

She smiled. "Thanks. I'm ready to go in now."

"Not yet," he said, taking her down the hall. "I have something for you." Amanda's heart leapt as they entered an empty room, thinking he was about to proclaim affection for her after all. She held her breath until he withdrew a ribboned box from his jacket.

"I couldn't let you join the others without giving you a wedding present," he said, extending the box.

Hiding her disappointment, she lifted the lid. A necklace of diamond-encrusted rubies lay beneath teardrop shaped ruby earrings dangling from diamond solitaires. "This jewelry completes the set of your wedding rings," said Reagan.

Amanda looked astonished. She couldn't imagine being gifted with such magnificent jewels when no words of love had been spoken between them. "Oh, Reagan. They're beautiful!"

Sweeping aside her veil, he draped the necklace around her neck and joined the clasp. When his fingers accidentally brushed her skin, a quivering shiver followed its wake until they rested at the base of her throat. Amanda stood immobile, her heart quickening as he slowly ran a knuckle from her collarbone to her shoulder before she felt his eyes staring at the soft swell of her breasts.

Throughout the wedding, Reagan had kept tight rein on his imagination, not dwelling on pleasures to come. But now that they were alone, he couldn't resist drawing closer. Lowering his head, his mouth becoming a firebrand, scattering pinpricks of pleasure as he traced his lips over hers.

Startled, and not knowing how far he intended to satisfy his impulses, Amanda stepped back. She went to a mirror and with shaking fingers inserted the earrings.

"Thank you," she said, making a show of admiring the jewelry. "They're the most beautiful things I've ever seen."

"They're not nearly as beautiful as you," Reagan said, stepping behind to plant a kiss on her neck. " And though I'd like to tarry longer, we should return to our guests."

When they entered the ballroom the jewels were noticed immediately. Reagan found himself standing outside the circle of admirers as those anxious to look closer drew near.

From across the room, Elizabeth spied that he was momentarily alone and quickly approached. "Congratulations, Mr. Burnsfield," she said, twisting the reticule on her wrist. "You've set Cantonsville on its ear with the suddenness of your nuptials."

"Thank you," he said, smiling. "And yes, I believe more than a few have been taken aback."

As the group around Amanda increased, Elizabeth stepped nearer to Reagan. She felt her composure slipping as she stared at his handsome face. "So, how does it feel to be a-a married man?"

"Exceedingly well. Although, it's still new to me."

"I assume you'll be spending more time in Cantonsville now that you have a wife," she said, nearly choking. Secretly, she hoped he couldn't wait to get away from the conniving chit. Many whispered it had been Mr. Bruester who insisted Reagan do right by his daughter. Elizabeth had been quick to agree.

"Unfortunately, not in the immediate future. There's much at the lumber camp that requires my attention."

"But, isn't Amanda expecting a honeymoon?"

"We've not had time to discuss it," he said, watching Amanda over Elizabeth's shoulder. "Business has been pressing."

Elizabeth felt a surge of confidence. "I understand," she purred, stepping close. "I can only hope Amanda is aware of your importance. Papa says without businessmen, great societies could never flourish. And having hosted many dinner parties, I've come to understand the needs of a powerful man. So, if you ever require such a gathering, I'd be happy to offer my services."

Reagan felt her hand touch his arm. "What? Oh yes—a dinner party." His gaze briefly returned to Elizabeth. "I'd consider it a kindness if you'd remind the Mayor I'm always interested in those involved with lumbering. Now, if you'll excuse me, I should return to Amanda."

"Ladies," he said, making a show of wading through the women. "Make room for the groom!" A burst of giggles erupted while they parted and as he reached Amanda's side, Reagan missed Elizabeth's smile when she turned away.

Under Emily's watchful eye, the buffet stayed replenished and wine glasses filled as festivities continued into evening. Finally, the orchestra began testing instruments and at the conductor's signal, Reagan escorted Amanda to the center of the ballroom. When the music began he drew her into his arms, sweeping the floor in perfect tempo. Passing under the chandelier, Amanda's jewels flashed like crystals of fire and ice that sparkled with every movement.

"Milady," he said. "You have truly beguiled me with your beauty. And by the looks of the unattached men, I'm thinking many now wished *they* had taken you on a scandalous journey."

Amanda warmed under his perusal yet still managed a stern demeanor. "How can you jest after all that's happened? I was nearly ruined, as were you. Tis no laughing matter being caught as we were."

"You're right," Reagan said, quick to dampen his elation. "I shouldn't be trying to make light of what happened. In truth, I had no idea your aunt was involved with...*conducting*."

"Neither did I until that night." Amanda whispered as the music ended. "Tis a shock I'm still recovering from."

With the briefest of intervals, the orchestra commenced the second musical piece, signaling others to join in. As the floor filled with couples, a tap on Reagan's shoulder brought him to an abrupt halt. He looked over his shoulder. "Don't you ever cease your endless prowling?" he said at the grinning Frenchman. "I've barely begun this dance!"

"A faint heart never won a fair lady," Beau fairly sang as several males assembled behind him to form a queue.

With a sigh, Reagan stepped back. "Don't be gone very long," he said sourly. "It seems it's going to be awhile before I can reclaim my wife."

Swept from partner to partner in a relay that rivaled her ball, many were eager to view the bride up close. So it was with gratitude that Amanda found

Thomas Burnsfield her partner when a popular waltz began.

"Hello, my dear," he said, smiling. "How are you holding up, so far?"

"Very well, thank you," she said. "I hope you've been enjoying yourself...I mean...in spite of everything that's happened..." Suddenly nervous, Amanda sputtered into silence, fearing he judged her guilty for his son's forced betrothal.

"It's been an adjustment for everyone," Thomas broke in, "I'm sure this decision wasn't made lightly."

"No, not lightly," she said, thinking of Gabriella.

Thomas noted her troubled brow and wondered if she had noticed Reagan's cavalier attitude toward marriage. Fearing she would become suspicious of her husband's motives, he blurted out what had long been on his mind.

"Amanda, I'm sure you have certain expectations...as any wife should..." he said as her perplexity grew. "Yet, because of the suddenness of your engagement, you've not had time to become familiar with how Reagan conducts himself." Thomas plunged on before changing his mind. "For example, when Reagan is deeply involved in a business endeavor he may seem distracted or inattentive and he's often gone for months at a time. I pray you won't be concerned because it won't be from any lack on your part. It's just his way."

Amanda's heart fell, assuming Thomas's distress was due to his shame over the wedding. How else would a husband act toward an unwanted bride? *Per-*

haps, the honorable thing would've been to reject Reagan's offer of marriage.

"Of course," she answered, blinking back tears. "I'll not entertain the matter further."

A look of intense relief flooded his face the same time someone tapped his shoulder. Distracted by her thoughts, Amanda didn't notice whom her next partner was until roughly seized. Startled, she found herself staring into Derrick Banning's furious eyes.

"How could you?" he said through clenched teeth. "How could you marry the minute I left town?" Not waiting for an answer, he snarled, "Not here. I must speak with you privately." He redirected their steps until nearing the entrance then taking her wrist, led her down the hall and into a vacant room.

Slamming shut the door, his eyes lowered to her jewelry. "If it was diamonds you wanted, my dear, you had only to ask."

"That's not how it was!" she said, aghast. "All I can say is that events occurred which altered my situation...."

Derrick didn't seem to listen as he drew near. "How could you do this when you knew how I felt? I waited patiently for you, giving you time to realize *I* was your best choice. You even had me take residence elsewhere so we could properly court. Was it all a lie, Amanda?"

Amanda worried Derrick wouldn't keep her secret if he knew the real reason she married. If he spilled the truth, Reagan's protective alibi might crumble and Gabriella's freedom would be lost. She decided to lessen Derrick's rage by skirting the truth. "I'm sorry you felt misled, but an unexpected circumstance befell me-"

"Everything is ruined! Ruined, I say!"

Amanda touched his arm. "Please don't be upset. It wasn't anyone's fault. Reagan and I were caught alone near the trail of runaway slaves. We were accused of being criminals and even though we were innocent, Reagan offered marriage as a way to keep me from being ruined. It's true you spoke of marriage first and had we gotten to know each other *sooner*," she said, forcing the lie past her lips, "perhaps it would've turned out differently." She spoke in a rush, struggling to convey sincerity without exposing her nagging dislike for him. "You were a gentleman, of course, and one any woman would be thrilled to have. Yet, because I knew Reagan longer, I-I believed him to be a more comfortable match."

Derrick clasped his hands behind his back, forming them into fists. "I see. So, it was impossible from the first."

"I believe so," Amanda said, feeling relieved. "So, you do understand?"

"Mayhap, if not Reagan, it would've been me?" Letting his words dangle, Derrick watched Amanda closely.

She hesitated to agree, but saw no reason to tell him otherwise. "Very likely..." she said, feeling as if she were stepping around a pitfall.

Derrick's eyes clouded as he forced a smile. "Well, then I suppose it's time I returned you to your husband. I see that I am indeed, too late on all counts." He held out his arm stiffly.

Amanda accepted, not realizing she had in fact planted a seed; one that Derrick would turn over and over in his mind.

He then escorted Amanda to the ballroom. "Enjoy your evening, my dear." As he raised her fingers, Derrick spied Reagan looking at them from across the room. He allowed a smile to cross his face before he leaned forward to suddenly kiss her cheek.

Indignation filled Reagan's eyes as he abruptly headed toward them. Derrick turned. He then left the same way he came, uninvited, and through a side door.

chapter 42

As revelry of the wedding celebration stretched into evening, Reagan longed to be rid of the fanfare. He took Amanda aside when the hall clock chimed nine tones, suggesting it was time to leave. As Amanda went upstairs to change, Katherine quietly gathered her family. It wouldn't do to have an empty house greet the newly married couple.

While Amanda packed her gown and jewelry, she couldn't help but wonder if the evening's gaiety had mocked the integrity of her vows. *Was she truly wed before God if her pledge was spoken under false pretenses?* She determined that despite the circumstances she would try to be a good wife. Perhaps, she would eventually be forgiven for her part in entangling Reagan with her troubles.

Descending the stairs, she found Reagan standing near the bottom step. "I hope this is suitable," she said, smoothing her skirt.

"You look captivating," he said.

"Truly spoken like a husband," she said taking his arm.

"In this case, madam, it's most assuredly true. Now, let's find your parents and bid them goodnight."

"Must you leave?" Emily asked, setting down her wine glass on the parlor table. "Amanda may wish to bid her guests goodbye."

"No, dear," George said. "We should see to the task ourselves." He planted a kiss on Amanda's temple. "I bid you good evening, daughter. Or, should I call you Mrs. Burnsfield?"

Amanda wrapped her arms around his neck and gave a quick squeeze. "Oh Papa, what am I to do?" she whispered.

"Why, you're going to make a home for yourself," he said in her ear.

"Thank you, Papa, I will."

She then kissed Emily while Reagan extended his hand to George. "Good night, sir. This has been the most significant day of my life."

George accompanied the couple to the door and waited with them until Wills brought their wraps. Once their carriage was brought around, Reagan assisted Amanda inside before settling on the seat next to her.

As the carriage took off, Amanda sat in silence, all schooling in conversation fleeing as Reagan drew near and draped an arm over her shoulder. Unaccustomed to sitting closely, Amanda tried moving away but found herself trapped against his side. Moments later, her qualms only increased when his thumb found her cheek and stroked it gently. Her ring reminded Amanda she was a married woman, but it couldn't alleviate her feeling like a helpless prey about to be devoured.

"Aren't you going to light the lamp?" she asked.

"No love," he whispered in her ear. "It isn't necessary."

"But-it's too dark." Amanda's heart quickened when she felt him bending toward her. "Reagan, please," she breathed, pulling back. "I'd like the lamp on."

"It's better this way," he said, following her retreat. "You wouldn't want it on. It'd only distress you more." Having curbed his thoughts all evening, Reagan allowed his imagination to follow its own path as he nuzzled her ear before grazing her temple with his lips. "Come here," he whispered, turning her face toward him. Savoring the moment, he hovered above her lips as his breath caressed her face.

Amanda trembled as a budding excitement stirred her emotions and when his mouth finally touched hers, she wondered anew at the sensations coursing through her body. Yet, the pleasure of this game turned alarming when Reagan rested a hand on her thigh. She resisted by brushing it aside.

"Don't pull away, love," he said, boldly reclaiming the spot. "Just relax and let me...get to know you." He waited until she allowed his hand to remain and then lowered his mouth to hers. Under his insistent pressure, her lips parted and she falteringly allowed his tongue to come into contact with hers as his hand crept upward. Just like the night by the river, she marveled at this new and strange activity that left her feeling as if she had consumed a goodly amount of wine. She didn't realize Reagan's hand had slipped past her cloak until he brazenly cupped a breast. Fiery heat flooded her being at the unexpected contact and she gasped as much from embarrassment as the pleasure she felt.

"Please," she breathed, staying his hand. "I beg a moment. I know we're wed good and proper, but I pray you'll wait until we reach your chambers."

Reagan groaned inwardly as he straightened in the seat. "As you wish, my dear," his voice was ragged and tight. "My apologies." Though every fiber in his being urged him on, Reagan sensed he had pushed Amanda to her limits. If he pawed her like a rutting blackguard, he risked frightening her unduly.

Amanda's hands shook as she straightened her cloak. She knew she was being cowardly. Women from the beginning of time had endured the joining of husband and wife. And yet here she was, resisting her husband's touch. Throughout the planning of the wedding, Emily made no mention of Amanda's new role as wife. She had secretly wished her mother had given council of what to expect. Her own embarrassment had kept her from asking and now it was too late. She quaked as she wondered if Reagan would take her brutishly, ravishing her in a heated moment.

As the landau came to a halt, Reagan wasted no time opening the door and lifting Amanda to the ground. He fully intended to whisk her to his chambers without delay. Much to his chagrin, Katherine stood just inside the door.

"Welcome, my dear." She planted a motherly kiss on Amanda's cheek as a servant stood near to take their wraps.

"Thank you, Mrs. Burnsfield."

Katherine turned to Reagan. "Your father's in the study. I believe he wants a word with you."

"Tonight?" He could barely contain his agitation. "Surely, mother, it can wait until morning!" He rested a hand stubbornly on the small of Amanda's back. "Besides, Amanda's unfamiliar with the house and needs to be shown our rooms."

"I'll take Amanda to your chambers," Katherine offered. "And don't smoke one of those foul cheroots you're so fond of."

Exasperated, Reagan threw up a hand before turning toward the study. "I'll make short shrift of whatever he has the audacity to require me this night!"

Katherine chuckled as she led the way upstairs.

"A ruse?" Amanda asked.

"Of course!"

"But, why?"

"The men folk in this family are single minded to a fault. And, I wanted a word alone with you," she said.

"Oh." Amanda's heart leapt, fearing she would now be accused of tarnishing the Burnsfield name. But Katherine said nothing until they reached the top of the staircase.

"This is Amy's room," she said, pointing to the nearest door. "I hope her comings and goings won't unduly disturb you."

"I'm sure it won't," Amanda said, expecting a reprimand at any moment. She suspected that if Katherine were anything like her mother, she would give her criticisms when no one was around to witness them.

Katherine led Amanda along the corridor where several gas sconces lit the hallway. "At the end of the hall are Thomas's and my private quarters, but here," she said, stopping at a door in the middle, "is where you'll share Reagan's chambers." Turning the knob, Katherine went inside. "As you can see, your trunks are at the foot of the bed. They were delivered earlier today."

Inside, a fire crackled behind the grate giving the room comfortable warmth. Amanda counted two chairs near the fireplace where one might relax while reading. An armoire resided against a wall next to a matching dresser. The nightstand next to the bed held a kerosene lamp and beside that was a tray with a glass and decanter.

If Katherine was about to upbraid Amanda she gave no indication as she presented the chambers, including a connecting room with a tub, commode and two bureaus. She opened drawers to show Amanda linens, towels, and various accoutrements. A blush darkened Amanda's cheeks when she saw a newly installed changing partition and turned her attention to a dish of scented soaps. When Amanda drew near a brush and comb set on top of the nearest bureau, Katherine smiled.

"You didn't think I'd forgotten your wedding tribute, did you?" Amanda saw kindness in the elder's eyes and realized Katherine was welcoming her into the family.

"Thank you! You've been most kind, despite... the situation..."

"Oh posh! We were so pleased Reagan finally chose a wife, we couldn't be happier." Putting an arm around Amanda, she led her back into the bedroom. "Now you just put any disagreeable thoughts out of your mind. You're a Burnsfield now. Any unpleasant experiences should be put behind you. What's important is what you do now. Which reminds me," Katherine mused, looking around. "I've something else for you." She walked over and picked up the crystal decanter. After pouring liquid into the tumbler, she pressed it into Amanda's hands. "Here, drink this. Does a world of good for calming nerves."

Amanda took a sip. "No, drink it all," Katherine urged, pressing the glass to her lips. "It's only sherry, but it'll give you fortitude."

Amanda coughed, smiling weakly. "Is it so obvious I'm a coward?"

"We're all cowards at first," Katherine said, taking the glass. "But no matter how frightening tonight may seem, what you'll share, will become a thing to be cherished."

"I suppose," Amanda said, blushing. But, I-I don't know..."

"You may experience pain," Katherine said bluntly. Amanda's eyes widened as Katherine shed her normal mien of propriety. "Many things a woman must bear, involve pain. But it'll be short-lived. You'll soon enjoy the blessings that come with the respect and commitment you extend each other. I promise." She squeezed Amanda's hand reassuringly. "I'll make sure you've time to prepare yourself before Reagan barges in like a mad bull. I told his father if he knows what's best, he'd better keep his son downstairs until I returned."

"I also took the liberty of purchasing a nightgown," Katherine said, indicating the wardrobe. "As your mother had more pressing matters to attend."

"You needn't have. I have several of my own."

Katherine winked as she stepped across the threshold. "Oh, I've a feeling this will be exceedingly more appropriate," she said, closing the door.

Perplexed, Amanda opened the armoire to find a large space had been cleared and in its center hung a translucent shift. Removing it from the hanger, she approached the lamp to get a better view. Under the light, the indigo silk shimmered, reflecting a myriad of silver and gold threading. She ran fingers over the garment, awed by its beauty. As she undressed she folded then placed her clothing in the trunk. She wasted no time lest Reagan find her completely disrobed and donned the gown which opened to her cleavage and ended several inches above her knees.

In the antechamber, Amanda removed her hairpins. Shaking her hair loose, she barely recognized the woman-child gazing back whose curves were softly draped by the shift.

Then climbing into bed, she kept glancing at the sherry until with trembling fingers she filled the tumbler. After draining the glass, she blew out the lamp, leaving only firelight to illuminate the chamber.

A soft tread forewarned Amanda that her husband was approaching, and after a warning knock, entered. A bursting log sent cinders into the air, revealing his missing jacket and loosened tie. A heady euphoria settled over Amanda as the sherry took effect, giving a sense of composure she hadn't felt all night. When Reagan sat beside her, she no longer quaked, but calmly awaited what this night would bring.

chapter 43

After his encounter with Amanda, Derrick left the Bruester manse in a fit of rage. He viciously kicked his horse, sending it into a dangerous run until reaching his hotel.

Once inside his room, Derrick opened a bottle of whiskey. It was he, not that roughneck who should've married the Bruester heir! Leaving for a few weeks had proven disastrous, for the lumberman had worked quickly. Derrick flung himself into a chair as he recalled his string of bad luck. Born the son of an illiterate dockworker, Orville Farnsworth had spent his youth carrying luggage for families of privilege. He had walked among them, but by their indifference it was clear he could never be one of them. Resentful of his meager lifestyle, Orville learned to pilfer valuables from bags he carried, and when theft failed to satisfy his lusts, he learned ciphering to secure positions of trust. To sever himself from his humble beginnings, he changed his name. Overnight, Orville Farnsworth became Derrick Banning.

After embezzling money where he worked as a lowly bank teller, he had fled New York in search of his next mark. Derrick recalled meeting George Bruester while masquerading as an escort for the New York Bank. Besides spending money like it couldn't be exhausted, George also mentioned having a daughter of marriageable age. With any luck, the girl would be unattached. Although Derrick disliked the idea of marriage, the thought of going to prison seemed even worse. He simply must wed the girl. If he were later apprehended for his crimes, a discreet payment and banishment from New York would take care of things nicely.

In Cantonsville, Derrick had easily manipulated his visit into a pursuit for Amanda's hand and when she requested he leave her home to formally court her, he had willingly complied. But once on his own, his funds rapidly dwindled. Forced to look for other sources of income, he daringly stole a bank draft from George's office. Cashing the cheque required opening an account in a different city under his true name Orville Farnsworth. He waited several days before withdrawing the substantial sum. It was following this caper that he had returned to discover the nuptials had already taken place. Though enraged, Amanda had unwittingly presented him with another course of action.

Rising from his chair, Derrick stared into the mirror above the washstand. He ran a hand across his jaw, deciding that side burns and an unclipped beard would go a long way in hiding his identity. He would move into less conspicuous lodgings and once again change his name. Then, Orville thought shrewdly, he would apply for a job at the Burnsfield lumber mill.

chapter 44

DURING THE DAYS leading up to Christmas, Amanda found herself graciously included in family activities. On Christmas Eve when Katherine insisted on going shopping, Amanda found gifts for everyone. For Reagan, she had selected half a dozen embroidered handkerchiefs. Later recalling the jewelry she received from him, she also purchased a gold plated timepiece. As much as Reagan hadn't declared his love, she decided to only have it inscribed with 'Eternally Yours, Amanda'.

A light, powdery snow fell as the Burnsfield women journeyed home, their treasures placed securely in the rear compartment. Tomorrow was Christmas and Amanda felt more at ease than she thought possible, as the family seemed to accept her without reserve. Reagan, though attentive, was always constrained in front of others. It wasn't until behind chamber doors that he displayed an unquenchable desire to possess her. His passions were easily kindled and he took delight in introducing Amanda to the more pleasurable aspects of marriage. She blushed when she thought about her abandonment while in the midst of their love play. Reagan would chuckle at her embarrassment, and snuggling under the quilts, he would bring her to that place of bliss she was learning to relish.

Christmas day proved delightful. She received many wonderful gifts, including two bottles of French perfume Beau had delivered by courier. The Burnsfields declared the gifts they had received from her were just the things they needed. Afterward, they had enjoyed a leisurely breakfast where much laughter was shared.

Later that evening, Reagan and Amanda spent time in the library, she, to finish a book, and he, to read yesterday's paper. Amanda stole glances at the man she had married, admiring his handsome profile and powerfully built frame. Outwardly, Reagan had not shown resentment for snatching her and Aunt Ella from the jaws of the law. Yet, neither had he demonstrated the affection one would expect from a man who wished to be wed. Perhaps, his fondness would grow, she thought, turning back to her book.

Without warning, Reagan broke the silence. "I'll be leaving for camp the day after tomorrow and won't be returning until spring."

Bewildered at his brusque manner, Amanda tried hiding her sudden hurt. "Must you?"

Reagan laid the paper down, frowning. "Yes, Amanda, I must. My foreman has only so much authority. I need to be there."

"Will you be home for visits?" she asked hopefully.

"There are few roads and even fewer towns where I'm going. Travel is dangerous enough in winter and you suggest I trot back and forth just to *visit*?"

"I thought we'd have more time..." She stopped as sudden tears brimmed her eyes. Hiding behind her book, she daubed her cheeks. "I'm sorry. I didn't realize you'd be leaving so soon."

Avoiding Amanda's eyes, Reagan stood to gaze out the window. "I thought it best to say nothing until now. We had enough to deal with these past weeks, but now it's time I go." He had put off his announcement, thinking a short notice would be easier. Instead, he had turned the situation into an exchange of disagreeable words. He didn't understand his lapse in manners and sought relief by pouring a drink. Rather than apologizing, he turned his anger outward. "Damn it, Amanda, lumbering is what I do. You can't expect me to ignore my obligations simply because we are wed."

"I know," she said, her voice cracking. "It was foolish of me to think you'd stay this winter. You never anticipated being...I mean...of course this was unexpected..." Amanda struggled to remain calm but as her control dwindled so did her composure and she soon fled the room.

Reagan started after her but stopped at the door. He couldn't explain his haste in leaving for tomorrow Amanda's dowry would be transferred. Until the documents were signed, he dare not risk exposing his rationale for marrying Amanda. He returned to his chair and picked up the newspaper. Yet, all he could see was the anguish provoked by his retched behavior and that he was the cause of Amanda's unhappiness.

chapter 45

REAGAN RETURNED FROM the Bruester Bank and Trust astounded by the small fortune George had amassed for his daughter. After transferring Amanda's dowry to Reagan's account, George then combined two trusts started by her grandparents into a single account to which Amanda would have sole access. A courier would convey the official documents to her later that week.

In good spirits, Reagan sat in the study arranging invoices to be paid in order of importance. Later that night, he announced to the family he would be leaving the following morning. Though silent, Amanda managed a calm demeanor as Reagan discussed business matters with Thomas. Not until alone in their chambers did she venture conversation.

Propped against the pillows, she watched Reagan fill two satchels with clothing. He had unbuttoned his shirt and it undulated softly as he moved. "Will you be leaving early?" she asked.

"Pretty early, I'm afraid," he said, glancing at her. Ever since his boorish behavior in the library, he expected Amanda to remain aloof, if not icy. Making up with her suddenly seemed more important than packing. Approaching the bed, he leaned against a post. "Will you miss me?"

Already feeling alone in the bed, she nodded.

"I'll miss you, too," he said, sitting beside her. "I'm sorry for my cross words yesterday." He stroked her hair, fascinated by its silkiness. "Truly, there was no cause, and I apologize if I hurt your feelings."

Amanda's lip trembled while tears began spilling down her cheeks. *How could love form in his heart when she was nothing but an intrusion?*

"Come here," he murmured, pulling her against him. He let her use his shoulder as a mop while he rubbed her back and brushed her tears with his shirttail. After awhile, her sniffles ceased and she relaxed in his arms, sighing contentedly.

Amanda didn't pull away when Reagan lifted her and leaned against the headboard, draping her across his lap. Within this cocoon-like embrace, he savored her weight against his groin as well as the lavender scent from her recent bath. "You smell good," he murmured, rubbing his cheek against her hair. "Feel good, too."

Amanda snuggled against his chest, listening to the cadence of his heart. "When you hold me like this, I feel safe," she whispered.

"You *are* safe, you little ninny. So safe, in fact," he said, tilting her chin, "not even Hell's demons would dare breach that yonder door." Gazing into her eyes, Reagan became suddenly awed by his emotions. It was as if her very nearness kindled the urge to protect her and from the depths of that awareness came a need to possess that which was his. His eyes dropped lower and his breath caught when he viewed a peaked crest outlined against her gown. Desire flooded his loins. Dipping his head, he slowly, languidly possessed her mouth, tasting salty tears. To his delight, Amanda didn't resist, but reached upward, encircling his neck with an urgency that belied her earlier coolness. Needing no further incentive, Reagan lifted her and holding her thus, pressed her into the pillows where his body held her trapped.

They stared at each other, neither wanting to break the spell seemingly cast by an unknown sorceress. Reagan brushed hair strands from Amanda's face before cupping her cheek. The first gentle brush against her lips turned into hungry assault as he delved once again into her yielding mouth. With growing passion, he felt the need to discover anew every part of her, taste her lips and touch her skin.

Amanda's breath left her when his searching mouth found a breast through an opening in her gown and eagerly took possession, caressing her with his tongue. From somewhere in the recesses of her mind the thought arose she should refuse him for his callous disregard of her feelings. It wasn't too late. She could end it now. But even as her mind demanded she deny him, her body begged for his touch and she clung to him with an abandon she didn't understand.

Amanda's quickening breath stirred Reagan but he did not rush as he savored each moment of heightened pleasure. His hands found her hips and pressing himself against her, his need grew while his lips traced a path between her soft, heaving mounds.

She became aware that her gown provided no protection as his hand began a slow ascent up her thigh, halting at her womanhood. With his palm, he applied gentle pressure at the same time his mouth claimed a peaked nipple. She gasped as a pulsing sensation began in her lower body and expanded upward until she felt near consumed. With a will of their own, her hands slid over his shoulders and past his ribs, pushing away his shirt. Reagan feverishly shed his clothes before stripping away her shift.

"I get lost in you," he breathed, sweeping her nakedness with his gaze. His mouth became a firebrand burning a path between her breasts and over her belly. When he again latched onto a pliant peak, she arched in unbearable pleasure, her heart beating a frantic rhythm that matched the throbbing in her loins. The pulsing cadence became a raging fire that demanded to be quenched. Breathing raggedly, she lifted her knees while Reagan lowered his hips between her thighs, his blunt hardness entering in one swift motion.

As her warmth surrounded him, he groaned in pleasure, pausing to hold back every sensation that screamed to be fulfilled. Amanda wasn't aware the exact moment he began to move but with his hands cradling her shoulders, he began thrusting with vigor. The fusion of their bodies melded them into one as they moved in quickening tempo, straining toward their common goal. Amanda pulled Reagan's mouth to hers in a primal desire to be completely possessed and in that moment, believed she was wanted, needed by the man she had betrothed her love. There was no barrier to be breached, no uprooting of hope when she lay entwined in his arms. As the budding, blossoming pleasure intensified, Amanda met his passion with a fire of her own, arching, rising to meet him until a bursting of a thousand flickering pulses washed over her. When she cried out, Reagan gripped her tightly; his own crescendo of pleasure engulfing him in what seemed a never-ending convulsion.

Amanda felt Reagan's lips nuzzling her throat before he lifted himself to lie beside her, and in the warm aftermath, Amanda sighed contentedly. Indeed, she felt more than wanted as he kissed her, encompassing her with his arms and nestling behind her.

Sometime during the night, Reagan awoke to feel the press of Amanda's breasts against his side. As she snuggled against him, his ardor was aroused anew. His searching lips awakened her and they made love slowly, knowing it would be the last intimacy they would share for a long time.

When Amanda awakened again, she found herself alone in the bed. Startled, she sat up and looked around. "Reagan?"

"Go back to sleep," he urged from across the darkened room. "I'm getting dressed. It's too early for you to be up."

"But, I want to be with you," she said.

"Let me build a fire first," he said. "Then you can get up."

Reagan stirred ashes in the hearth before stacking wood pieces. He then laid a match, fanning the flames til the room warmed.

"Would you please bring me my wrapper?" Amanda said.

"I'd much rather see you do it," Reagan said, laughing. "I know you're not wearing a stitch." After bringing her robe and slippers, he turned his back in gentlemanly fashion.

Amanda retreated to the bath chamber but soon emerged with her hair brushed and a chemise under her robe. "Would you like to join me for breakfast?" Reagan asked, gathering his gear.

"I don't know. Are you cooking?" Amanda said with a grin.

"Don't worry. Mother usually makes sure something's prepared." After descending the stairs, he set his gear near the front door before entering the dining room. As Reagan assisted Amanda into a chair, the cook entered with a tray and pot of coffee. "Will you be dining as well, madam?"

"No thanks, just coffee." Amanda said, accepting a cup. She tried not to grimace as she took a sip.

"Here, this'll help," said Reagan, retrieving the sugar dish. "It's probably stronger than you're used to."

After finishing his meal, Reagan rubbed his bristled jaw. "I'm regrowing my beard. By spring, you'll scarce recognize me."

"Mayhap, it'll seem as if I've acquired a second husband."

Reagan laughed before standing. "With the memories we created last night, I'll come to you in any form you wish."

"Is it time to go?"

"Just as soon as I take you upstairs and tuck you into bed."

As they climbed the stairs, Amanda felt the weight of their impending separation. "Where exactly is this lumber camp? Is it far away?" she asked. And when he didn't immediately answer, she hastened to add. "Sorry. I-I was just interested."

"That's okay. I can fix that," he said. Upon entering their room, Reagan opened his bureau and withdrew a folded paper. "Here's my map." He opened it to trace a marked line with his finger. "This is the route I'm taking, and there's my destination, the Cattaraugus River in New York."

Amanda inspected the course as it tracked northeast, ending near Lake Erie. "I see," she said refolding it. "That helps."

He thrust the map back into her hands. "You keep it. You might find it interesting to follow. It takes about a week to get there."

"But won't you need it?" she said, setting the map aside.

"No, I've traveled the distance enough times that a map isn't necessary. Now back to bed you go," he said, steering her toward the bed. "It's still too early for a lady to be up."

Amanda giggled as Reagan peeled off her wrapper and tossed her among the quilts. "But, I won't be able to sleep."

"Sure you will. Just lie back and close your eyes."

"All right," she conceded. "But, I want a kiss goodbye."

"Whatever the lady wishes." Leaning over, Reagan gave her a feathery peck. But Amanda impulsively wrapped her arms around him, prolonging the embrace.

"Whoa! If you kiss me like that, I may have to take you with me." He made as if to draw back the covers.

"Indeed!" Amanda said, blushing. "You'd think I displayed a wanton act of lewdness."

Reagan laughed, not at all put out by her boldness. He brushed her cheek. "I'll be back as soon as weather permits."

After he left, all of Amanda's uncertainties came flooding back. Did he truly want her or was he simply duty bound? Drawing Reagan's pillow against her, she drifted to sleep, not awakening until the maid brought water for her bath. Sitting up, she pulled the map from the nightstand to study the markings. She sighed. All her questions would just have to wait. When Reagan returned next spring, the rumors should have faded and Aunt Ella's secrets would finally be safe.

chapter 46

IN THE DAYS following Reagan's departure, Amanda received various invitations to New Year celebrations. About the same time, events occurred around the country that stirred the curiosity, but not much else, of those in Cantonsville. Many felt that reasoned men would find a solution to South Carolina's Ordinance of Secession as well as resignations from the Secretaries of Treasury, State and War. Few believed the country was verging on war but were of the opinion that the new president would put any discontent to rest. Though South Carolina's leaving Congress raised eyebrows, it didn't cause many to rethink their planned festivities. After all, it was so very far away.

Amanda agreed with Thomas that due to somber times, they would forego any festivities. She declined all her own invitations, but promised instead to visit as soon as her husband returned.

With little else to occupy her time, Amanda often studied Reagan's map. She envisioned a forest where snow fell softly, and a cabin nestled far from prying eyes. Her daydreams were filled with promises of love, if she could only share winter with her husband.

Each lonely night reminded her how accustomed she had become to the warmth of Reagan's body. Alone under the quilts, she found that it now took far longer to fall asleep. Often, her dreams were troubled, with visions of Jebediah and his henchmen. She would awaken, her heart aching for the comforting protection of her husband's nearness.

With barely a week gone by since Reagan's departure, Amanda began dreading nights. Between interludes of sleep, an implausible idea sprang to mind. At first she dismissed the fantasy as foolish, yet it constantly plagued her, blossoming like a flower starved for sunshine. Unable to eradicate the notion, she decided to uproot the thought once and for all by proving it couldn't be done. She went into town on the pretense of shopping, waiting until the carriage left before entering the nearest hotel and approaching the desk.

"May I help you?" the clerk asked.

"I wish to enquire if you have any scouts occupying your rooms," Amanda said. "Someone to take a person on a trip."

"Don't you mean the stagecoach?" He indicated a chalkboard with destinations, dates and times written across it. "The circuit runs a few more weeks. After that, it'll depend on the weather."

Amanda shook her head. "No. There aren't any routes where this person's going."

"I see," he said, scratching his head. "Well ma'am, it's possible we might have someone like that. Seeing it's so far into winter, that is."

Amanda's heart beat faster. "Then, would you be so kind as to post an inquiry? Just say a person wishing to travel to New York needs an experienced guide who can follow a map. Please include he'll be well paid."

"May I ask if the scout's for you?"

"No, you may not!" Amanda struggled to keep panic from her voice. If the Burnsfields discovered she was trying to join Reagan, they would put an immediate halt to her plans.

She opened her purse and withdrew a bank note. "This is for your trouble *and* your silence." Amanda pushed the five-dollar bill toward him. "If anyone responds, please inform him I'll return in two days."

Shrugging his shoulders, the clerk decided it wasn't his concern. "I'll post it today," he said, stuffing the bill in his pocket.

Amanda left the same inquiries at two other hotels before making a purchase at the hat shop. The next two days seemed like an eternity. One moment she felt emboldened at the possibility of a guide, the next, she prayed there would be no takers.

Amanda returned to town two days later. There were no respondents at the first two hotels. She entered the last one with little hope until the clerk pointed to where an unkempt man sat hunched over, sleeping. Approaching the bench, she touched his shoulder and instantly two steel-gray eyes snapped open.

"What'cha want?"

The man's face, covered with a beard, appeared so weathered she couldn't tell if he were closer to forty or sixty years old. His clothes lacked a good washing and by his odor, Amanda doubted he bothered to bathe.

"Are you a scout?"

The man sat up, inspecting her closely. "You're the one with the note? Surely, you ain't the one I'm being hired for."

"I can sit a horse," Amanda said. "I'll only need your services for one week. Besides, you'll be well paid."

He crossed his arms. "I don't take women," he stated flatly. "Not in winter, not anytime, but especially not in winter."

"I see," she said. "I assume you don't need five hundred dollars then, either." She hadn't intended on such a sum. In fact, half that amount was what she had thought to offer. But, losing her only chance to be with Reagan emboldened her to raise the amount.

Her hopes grew with the man's silence. "Five hundred dollars. Will you accept?"

"What in hell's tarnation do you need me for? They got stagecoaches for you women folk."

"I wish to be with my husband and where he is, no stagecoach goes."

"Did he send for you?" He snorted as Amanda shook her head. "A man don't send for his wife and you want me to take you to him?"

"It's a surprise. He told me before he left, he wanted me to come."

"Any man that'd leave a smart lookin' woman like you at home must've had good reason. I don't figure he'd be too happy with me doing him a favor he didn't ask for!"

"My husband won't take you to task. Besides, you'd be on your way the minute we stepped into camp."

Cocking up his battered hat, he scowled at Amanda. "Camp? What kind of camp you talkin' about?"

"My husband is a lumberman—"

"Now hold on," he said, sitting straighter. "Taking a female on horseback is one thing, but into the forest is downright stupid."

"One week," Amanda repeated, holding out her map. "Or, should I look for someone else?"

The man mulled it over several moments. The money from his last job was nearly depleted. With malcontents becoming bold below the Mason-Dixon, few were willing to travel where he plied his trade this time of year.

He gave an exasperated sigh, snatching the map. "You cain't wear them," he said, gesturing toward her clothes.

"I have riding outfits," she said. "Will those do?"

"Them ain't warm enough." He eyed her a moment longer before speaking. "You ever pissed in the woods?"

Amanda bit back an outraged reply. If he were trying to shock her, he had surely succeeded.

"Have you slept in an open field with only a fire to warm your backside?" he asked gruffly. "That, my fine filly, is what you're asking from me...paying me for."

Amanda swallowed hard. "Surely there'll be places to stop along the way."

"On the trail, I make the decisions," he said. "We may have to bypass them stops because it's late in the season."

"I can do it," she said, thinking she could endure anything for a week. So, do you accept my offer?"

"If I'm not held accountable for any mishap along the way. I don't understand why you're doing this, but I can git you there." He frowned a warning. "But, if you prove to be a bother, I'll turn around and bring you home, missy. I ain't no babysitter."

"I understand," Amanda said. "If you look at the map, there are towns along the route. If we're near one when we stop, would you object to spending the night in a hotel?"

"Lady, it's your money. If you intend on paying for rooms and a stable for the horses, no, I've no objections." Folding the map, he stuck it inside his vest. "The name's Hogan. Earl Hogan."

"I'm Amanda Burnsfield."

Hogan scratched his chin. "For starters, I'm gonna need about fifty dollars for supplies. You wouldn't know what to git anyway." He watched as she opened her purse and handed him the money. "Good. You came prepared. I trust you got a horse?" At Amanda's nod, he continued. "A regular saddle, ya hear? Not one of them silly sidesaddles. I don't want to be picking your scrawny behind off'n the ground." He folded his arms as he took in your youthful appearance. "Ain't you afraid of being alone with a stranger?"

She looked at him sharply. "Why, Mr. Hogan, do you intend on causing me harm?"

"Nah," he smiled. "For one, you're too spindly to my liking, and two, I never mix business with pleasure. You'll be safe enough with me, missy."

"Then, no, I'm not afraid," she lied.

He laughed loudly. "Well, that just about covers everything. Okay, lady, you got yourself a deal." He pointed to her feet. "Wear heavy socks and boots. Find a man's coat with plenty of padding. And if you're smart, you'd git a hat to stuff that hair into. There are unsavory sorts that might kill a man for a little bit of pleasure. The sooner we head out, the better. Be here at six o'clock, tomorrow morning. That's when I'm leaving, and by God, I don't like to be kept waiting!"

"I'm not sure I can be here that early...I mean... not without having to explain myself..."

"You'd best understand one thing, lady. When I guide, it's my way or no way a'tall. So you just better make up a good enough excuse. Be here or it's off." As she turned to leave, he spoke again. "One pair of saddlebags lady, for your clothes and such." He held up a finger for emphasis. "And real gloves, not them things you women wear."

He shook his head as she departed. He would have his hands full if the girl proved troublesome. But once the task was completed, he'd have enough money to carry him through winter. Looking at the crisp bills, Hogan grinned. This was going to be a good season after all.

chapter 47

AMANDA'S HEART HAMMERED as she crossed the hotel lobby, her mind reeling with all she had to accomplish. She had no idea how she was going to slip away from the Burnsfield home, let alone hitch a horse to a carriage.

As she passed the front desk, she had an idea. "Have you any vacancies?" she asked the clerk.

"Yes, ma'am, we do."

"I'd like a room. I'll return later with my things," she said, signing the register.

Before going home, Amanda stopped at the dry goods store and bought three boy-sized flannel shirts, three heavy pants, a saddlebag and a pair of buckskin gloves. At the counter, she spied a stack of long johns and added a pair to her purchase. When she arrived at the Burnsfield home and with the drivers help, she spirited her packages upstairs.

Digging through Reagan's side of the wardrobe, Amanda found a hat and coat so small, they must have been boyhood possessions. She rummaged his bureau and retrieved woolen socks before filling her saddlebag. Draping the bag over a chair, Amanda stuffed package wrappings in the wardrobe bottom before a knock at the door made her jump.

"Dinner is ready, Mrs. Burnsfield," the maid called.

"Thank you, Lela, I'll be down shortly."

Throughout dinner, she spoke in forced cheerfulness as she addressed the first of many problems. "If you've no objections, I'd like to spend a few days with Aunt Ella. I haven't visited her since before the wedding. We're working on a quilt and I thought I'd bring my sewing basket. I know it's getting late, but I'd like to go over this evening."

"That sounds lovely," Katherine said. "I'm sure you'll both have a good time."

Amanda then turned to Thomas. "I also promised Aunt Ella we'd go shopping. Since she's yet to replace her carriage, I was hoping to borrow the buggy during that time."

"Why, of course," he said. "We'll still have our carriage, if we need to go anywhere."

"Thanks ever so much," she said, overcoming her final obstacle. "I can use my own horse."

Later in her chambers, Amanda dragged a small trunk from the closet. After filling it, she summoned the maid to have it carried to the waiting conveyance. Earlier that day she had withdrawn enough from her account to pay Hogan as well as any unforeseen expenses. Placing the funds in her handbag, she donned her cape and bonnet before going downstairs.

While saying goodbye to the family, Amanda made a show of fetching her sewing basket from the parlor. It was still in her hands when the groom aided her into the buggy. But before he could climb up, she picked up the reins. "Please, don't bother," she said. "I'll take myself."

The lad looked uncertain. "I don't think it's permissible, ma'am. I was told to take you to Miss Bruester's."

"Nonsense! It's not very far," she said. "You go right back to where you were." Slapping the reins, she left before he could stop her.

Amanda arrived at the hotel and approached the desk, asking for her trunk to be taken to her room. She then laid down several bills next to a handwritten note. "I'd like my trunk and buggy stored for three days before returning them to this address. Also, I need awakened by five o'clock tomorrow morning." The clerk nodded as he scooped up the money.

He showed Amanda to her room, lighting the lamp and starting a fire while the stable boy retrieved her trunk.

Once alone, she undressed and placed her feminine clothes in the trunk. It was only when she reached her chemise that she realized she hadn't brought a nightgown. Amanda took from her saddlebags the recently purchased long johns. Before putting them on, she retrieved her scissors and cut her chemise to just below her derrière. Though she regretted ruining the shift, she couldn't bear removing the only softness in her new wardrobe.

Amanda didn't know when she fell asleep, but it seemed only moments before a rap on the door roused her.

"You up, ma'am?" a voice called. "It's five o'clock."

"Yes," Amanda said, fumbling with the lamp's wick. "It's cold!"

"Yes ma'am, it is," agreed the servant. "Breakfast will be ready soon."

Amanda dressed quickly, removing her chemise before donning the boyish garb. After plaiting her hair she gathered her outerwear and saddlebag and went downstairs. As she entered the dining room she heard someone clearing his throat.

Hogan sat at the table holding a cup of coffee. He looked her up and down. "You'll do," he said. "Though, you look like a little girlie."

"At least *I* changed my clothes since yesterday," Amanda said, taking a seat. "And take my hat off at the table."

"Don't recall you paying for manners," Hogan said as a woman set down two large platters of food. "Now, get to it."

"I can't eat all this," Amanda said, staring.

Hogan stabbed a sausage. "It's a long time til noon, missy. You'd best put as much in your belly as you can."

Amanda looked at the cook as the woman poured coffee. "May I have tea instead?"

"Maybe you should have baby milk," Hogan snorted. "You don't appear old enough to stomach real brew."

Rather than irritate Hogan further, Amanda remained silent as she ate. But his look of disgust returned when she pushed back her plate.

"Ain't you going to finish that?"

"I'm done," Amanda said, thinking a week with him was beginning to look like a long, trying time.

Leaning over, he devoured the rest on her plate before wiping his mouth. "C'mon, let's saddle the horses."

Amanda's eyes suddenly grew wide.

"What's the matter, now?"

"I forgot a saddle!"

"Dammit! Git your things and come with me," he said sourly. In the barn, she watched him strap supplies to a packhorse. He then spoke to the stable boy who soon emerged from the tack room with a bridle and saddle. "You owe the kid twenty dollars."

Amanda counted the correct amount as Hogan led her gelding from the stall. "On my trips, every man saddles his own horse," he said. "I'll help you once. From then on, you do it yourself."

Hogan watched how Amanda put on the saddle; much like she had the night she followed Gabriella. Shaking his head, he brought the cinch up several inches while instructing the correct way to ready her mount. Once he was satisfied, he saddled his own horse.

Outside the barn, the three horses stamped their feet. Amanda's hands felt equally uncomfortable despite her gloves but found a solution by unrolling her cuffs and pulling her hands inside.

Early morning shadows had just given way to hazy dawn when they started their journey. Amanda felt a surging excitement as she played the scenario of a happy reunion over and over in her mind. Yet, she grew concerned Reagan's family would worry when they discovered her missing.

She settled on the solution of writing a letter and mailing it in the first town they came upon. In due course it would arrive at the Burnsfields, but by then it would be too late for anyone to stop her. She regretted the deceit she used, but would later beg their forgiveness.

As they traveled, Hogan appeared to have forgotten about her. He occasionally viewed the map but he neither talked nor looked in her direction. By midmorning, Amanda's thought's turned to more pressing needs. She grew miserable, hoping Hogan would stop without prompting, but finally, necessity forced her to speak. "Earl—"

"Hogan," he corrected.

"Hogan," she began again. "Isn't it time we stopped?"

"We'll eat while riding. It gains time."

"But, I...have...to..."

"Well, why didn't you just say so," he said. Reining in, he pointed to a clump of trees. "Over there'll do just fine." With as much dignity as she could, Amanda directed her horse off the road and into the bushes.

By nightfall, Amanda realized Hogan had bypassed the nearest town and any chance for a warm bed. Too tired to protest, she dismounted. Yet, her icy feet refused to cooperate and she stumbled sideways into Hogan.

"Unsaddle your horse, then fetch wood. That'll git your circulation going," he said, pushing her upright.

Amanda hobbled to do her tasks, thankful that he didn't demand she also build a fire. That accomplished, and by the time they consumed burnt beans and vile coffee, Amanda peevishly decided Hogan couldn't cook, either.

After checking the horses and tie lines, he returned with two bedrolls. Amanda followed his lead by unrolling her blanket near the fire but the blanket kept catching her boots, and in agitation she removed them. Her last thoughts before falling asleep was not of Reagan, but how she was going to survive the week with this madman, Earl Hogan.

chapter 48

IF AMANDA BELIEVED traveling by horseback would be a pleasant experience, she soon learned otherwise. By the end of her first day she was cold, sore and exhausted. She couldn't even look forward to mealtime, for Hogan lacked the skills to cook without ruining food.

Amanda had slept with her coat and blanket and in what seemed like minutes felt a boot nudge her. Waking felt painful, and as she rolled over, her breath formed a vaporous column. Dimly, she could see Hogan standing over her.

"Git up," he ordered in a tone she was learning to hate.

She reached for her boots finding they had stiffened during the night. She yanked them on and by the time she returned from the bushes, Hogan had breakfast ready. Afterward, he brought over the horses. Saddling her mount proved easier the second time, although Hogan still had to tighten the cinch.

By midday, Amanda had tired of Hogan's penchant for silence and prompted her horse next to his. "How far have we come?"

He peered at the sun. "About thirty-five miles."

"Today?" Amanda said excitedly.

"From Cantonsville, Mrs. Burnsfield."

"Oh." Though disappointed, she was encouraged by his meager civility. "Then, will we be near Meadville come nightfall? Even a lumpy bed would feel soft after last night." She also envisioned a hot bath and a meal prepared by a competent cook.

Hogan opened the map. "If the weather holds, we'll be passing through about two hours before making camp."

Amanda's face mirrored her disappointment. "Wouldn't it be better...?"

Hogan reined in his horse, forcing Amanda to do the same. "Look, missy," he growled. "I don't intend on gittin' caught in a snow squall with another man's wife! As it is, I'm squeezing every hour before hard winter sets in. So no, we ain't stopping."

"I've a letter to send," Amanda said, quelling her sudden pique. "There are those who need to know I'm visiting my husband. So, you can just spare a few minutes!" Before he could respond, she slapped her horse and galloped ahead.

Hogan felt amused as he watched her braid bounce upon her back. By God, he was starting to like the girlie. She had pluck. In all his fifty years, he had found little use for the female gender. Women were always demanding strict rules of conduct, always trying to change him. This one made requests, but she neither quarreled nor complained to get her way.

Kicking his horse, he galloped ahead then slowed to ride alongside. "Mind you," he said in a warning tone. "Before we git to town, you best hide that mane of yours."

When they neared Meadville, Amanda stuffed her hair into her hat and pulled the brim low. They rode directly to the post office but found it locked and shuttered. Hailing a passerby, Hogan inquired of the unexpected closing. "Once the mail's delivered, the Postmaster goes home for the day," came the hurried response.

"I got a better idea," Hogan said. "C'mon." Grabbing her arm, he crossed the street and entered the nearest building. Amanda found herself inside a telegraph office facing a clerk in a short-billed cap. "The boy wants to send a message," Hogan said, jerking his thumb in her direction. Amanda took a second too long to step forward and found herself being propelled toward the counter. "The brat's a little slow," he tapped his head as he glared at Amanda. "C'mon, let's git this over with, so we can git a move on."

Amanda cleared her throat before speaking; not realizing the lilt in her voice sounded decidedly feminine. "I wish to send a message to Mr. and Mrs. Thomas Burnsfield in Cantonsville, Ohio."

Just then, two men wearing long coats entered. The door banged noisily as one fished through his pockets. He stepped behind Amanda and stood there, chewing on a cigar. Before she could give her message,

Hogan stepped forward and pushed her aside. "Just write 'I'm going to visit...'" he paused, staring at Amanda's surprised face until she provided a name.

"Reagan," she said.

"Write 'I am fine, will return soon,'" Hogan dictated while the clerk scribbled.

As the teller finished, he looked from one to the other. "And who should I say sent the telegraph?"

This posed a problem, for Amanda couldn't give a woman's name in front of all these men. Suddenly, Hogan reached out, pulling the pencil from the clerk. "Show him," he said. Amanda wrote 'A. Burnsfield' on the paper, then handed it back.

"That'll be seventy-five cents," the clerk told Hogan who was clearly in charge.

"Pay the man," he barked.

"It's—it's—" Amanda pointed toward the door. "—in my saddlebag—" Hogan growled under his breath as he reached inside his coat and slammed down the coins. Grabbing Amanda under her arm, he hustled her outside.

"Every time you open your mouth, you give yourself away," he rasped while pushing her toward the horses. "From now on, when we're around others, I'll do the talkin'."

Amanda wanted to cry, but dared not for the two emerged from the telegraph office just as she hoisted herself onto her mount.

One removed the stub of his cigar, his mouth agape. "That ain't no boy," he mumbled to his companion.

The other squinted to get a better view. "Nope," he answered. "My guess, it's a mite purty filly under them men's britches."

"Blackie, why d'ya suppose they's hiding the fact she's a girl?" he asked, sticking the cigar into his mouth.

Blackie rubbed his jaw, watching the riders fill their canteens at a well pump. "Don't know, Fletch," he said. "Appears th' feller ain't too keen on anyone knowing."

"S'pose he's keeping her all to hisself?"

Blackie's eyes gleamed. "Most likely. Th' way I figger, it's downright rude to keep all that young flesh for an old codger like him. That filly ain't never going to appreciate a real man, if'n that's all she's ever known."

Fletch snickered as he watched Hogan and Amanda leave town. "We best git a move on. It's gittin' dark and they'll be setting up for th' night."

As the two men mounted, Blackie imagined the many ways he would pleasure himself on the wench. He knew of an abandoned cabin not far away he could use for brewing mischief.

In the moonlight, the road became a dark ribbon, giving the miscreants an easy path to follow as they scanned the trees looking for a campfire.

Hogan had gotten a bad feeling at the telegraph office. Leaving town, he had glanced back and saw they were being watched. Recognizing blackguards when he saw them, Hogan believed he and Amanda looked like easy pickings and scouted for a secure place to camp.

Toward dusk, he found a well-protected area hidden behind the rise of a hill. After tending the horses he started a fire. Unsheathing his Bowie knife, Hogan cut several pine branches to form a crude mattress before disappearing into the trees. Amanda finished gathering firewood and now sat by the fire. As she waited, she fanned the flames with her hat, not hearing footfalls until they were right behind her.

"Well lookee there," an unfamiliar voice cackled. "Th' boy's a girl after all." Amanda stood and faced two figures outlined in shadows.

"Where's yur old man?" rasped one as he gazed at her parted coat.

Amanda looked around for Hogan. She stepped back, putting the fire between her and the strangers. "What do you want?"

Fletcher came into the light. "We just want to visit a spell." He opened his hands. "See, no weapons. We ain't gonna hurt ya none." While Fletch spoke, Blackie slipped from sight.

"You wait right there," she said to Fletch. "If you fellows need food, we'll share some of ours." As Fletcher's eyes brazenly lowered to her bosom, Amanda panicked. She turned to flee. All at once, Blackie's arms encircled her waist.

Amanda screamed before Fletch ran over and covered her mouth. "Shhh!" he growled. "Be quiet or we'll hurt th' old man!" With his free hand, he fumbled with the buttons on her shirt but Amanda slapped away his fingers. "Hold her," Fletch said, removing his hand so Blackie could clamp her mouth. With both hands free, Fletch succeeded in unbuttoning part of her shirt. Terrified, Amanda squirmed even harder.

"C'mon girlie," Blackie said, laughing. "Fighting ain't gonna do yu no good."

The click of a hammer preceded a loud voice booming from the darkness. "Hello boys! Now, I don't mind sharing vittles, but, ain't you being a mite unsociable?"

The men looked around. "Where is he?" Fletch whispered. "I can't see him."

"I'm afraid you're gonna have to release my client," Hogan's voice snarled. "She didn't pay to get mauled by filthy varmints."

"There's no need to git riled," Fletcher said, reaching under Blackie's coat. He pulled out a gun. "We wuz just gittin' friendly."

Hogan's voice moved in the darkness. "Let her go, boys. I ain't too particular on shooting me a couple rattlesnakes."

"Where is he?" Blackie asked as he gripped his squirming captive.

"Shut yur pan!" Fletcher hissed. "We need to git out'a this light." As they dragged her toward the shadows, Amanda's terror increased. Fuelled by desperation, she ceased tugging at Blackie's hand and instead bit with all her might. Blackie screamed before yanking away his palm. Wasting no time, Amanda lifted her booted foot and stomped hard on Blackie's instep. Drawing a yowl, then a muffled 'oomph' when her elbow punched his midsection, Blackie doubled over, releasing her. Amanda stumbled away just as the sound of a gun exploded.

Fletcher shrieked. Dropping the pistol, he clutched his hand and fell to his knees. "You son of a bitch!" he said, panting. "You shot me!"

Hogan stepped into firelight. "Drop your weapons," he ordered. Soon there were three guns lying on the ground as Blackie tossed his revolver and fished another out of Fletcher's pocket.

"You'd better find something to wrap that wound," Hogan said. "Or, your partner's gonna bleed to death."

Blackie hurriedly wound a kerchief around the Fletcher's hand while Amanda rushed to get behind Hogan. In the flickering light, she couldn't tell whether the man still possessed all five fingers.

"Now, if you're a God-fearing man, you can git this scoundrel to a doctor. Though, it won't cost me a lick of sleep if he dies. I could've kilt you right off. But, I felt sorry for you since there's only two of you against just one of me."

Blackie nodded, his eyes focused on the barrel of Hogan's shotgun. After lifting Fletch up, they hastened away, their curses drifting through the darkness.

Amanda suddenly felt weak and would've collapsed if Hogan hadn't caught her. Leaning against his chest, she began sobbing.

"What'cha crying for *now*?" Hogan sighed. Fumbling for a hanky, he stuffed it in her fingers while patting her back. After several moments she quieted, allowing him to help her to the pine-bough mattress.

"Listen. It's time to git some sleep, but keep your boots on," Hogan said, tossing her a blanket. "It feels like it's gonna turn cold."

"Where are you going?"

"Back to my post where I can keep an eye on you." He kicked snow over the bloodstains before gathering the dropped guns. "You never know if those wastrels will be stupid enough to come back."

"Hogan?"

He paused, looking back at her.

"Thank you."

Without answering, he entered the woods and disappeared from sight.

Sometime during the night a light snow began to fall. Dropping temperatures turned the swirling snowflakes into tiny, glass-like shards that coated the earth with a hard crust. Amanda burrowed under her blanket, unaware of the storm silently imprisoning camp with rime.

Blissfully, in her dreams she had reached the cabin and even now lay snug within Reagan's warm embrace.

chapter 49

HOGAN HAD WATCHED over camp, snatching bits of sleep while propped in the crotch of a tree. Toward dawn, the sound of snapping branches drew his attention. His gaze passed over the burned-down fire, stopping where Amanda lay sleeping. With a start, he saw her body quivering like a cowering mongrel, her blanket covered in ice. Using his shotgun as a balance he half ran, half slid to her side. The blanket crackled as he yanked it away and turning her over found her face alarmingly pale.

"Mrs. Burnsfield!" He tossed his rifle and shook her. "Amanda, roll out!" Instead of opening her eyes, Amanda only mumbled slurred words before curling into a ball. Hogan's voice rose apace with his fear and twisting her arm around his neck, he lifted her, setting her on unsteady feet. "Dammit girl, wake up."

Amanda's legs crumpled and she would've fallen had Hogan not caught her against him. "You got to wake up, girlie," he said. "C'mon, now."

Rubbing her back briskly, he continued to support her until she lifted her head from his shoulder. "That's a girl," he said. Keeping a wide stance, Hogan set Amanda again on her feet. Though she wavered and her eyes remained closed, she could stand. Hogan gripped her waist and taking small steps, stomped through the ice while she hobbled stiffly beside him.

Amanda soon became aware someone was holding her, urging her awake. Yet, it took several times around the campfire before she lifted her eyelids. The images she saw confused her and when she tried speaking, no words came. Turning her head, she was surprised to see concern in Hogan's eyes. "Wha-?"

"Don't talk yet," he said. He sat her down and wrapped her in his sheepskin coat. Breaking ice off sticks of wood, he soon had a fire. The aroma of strong coffee wafted to Amanda's nose just before Hogan shoved a cup to her lips. She grimaced but sipped the brew while Hogan made soup from a can of beans.

As she ate, Hogan packed provisions then fed the animals. He saddled the horses, all the while cursing himself for taking this job. He should've known he'd have to play nursemaid to the girl. His best bet now was to deliver the twit into the arms of her husband and be rid of her. By the time he brought Amanda her horse the sun had crested the eastern sky.

She stood, holding out his coat. "Thanks. I'm better now."

"You sure? You were kind of foggy for awhile."

"I-I think so," she said, limping to her horse. "My head feels clearer."

Hogan stood close as she footed the stirrup. He wasn't surprised when she hadn't the strength to mount and without asking permission, hoisted her up.

As they rode, he kept a constant eye on her. It was one thing to take a spoiled brat on a journey, quite another to have a nice girl mauled by scoundrels and then nearly froze to death. Damned if she didn't get to him too. She never complained when he knew damn well she was cold and miserable.

"We'll be hitting McKean in a couple hours," he said, breaking the silence. "We can stop for a hot meal if you'd like." He glanced at Amanda. "Wipe that grin off your face. This don't change a thing. I'm still in charge, you hear?"

Once they entered McKean, Hogan headed for the first hotel in sight. He surprised Amanda by putting down his own coin for meals and a bath. Carrying her saddlebags, Amanda followed the matron to a small but immaculate bathing chamber where cabinets held towels as well as an assortment of soaps, tonics and skin creams.

Once the tub had been filled, Amanda added scented crystals before undressing then sinking into hot water. The heat relaxed her aching muscles and even her feet, which had pained her all day, felt free from the throbbing discomfort. Closing her eyes, she imagined her reunion with Reagan and giggled as she pictured first his shock and then delight at her arrival.

It was a much-refreshed Amanda that descended the stairs in a clean set of clothes, her damp hair re-braided. The dining room was empty save for Hogan.

He had long since finished his meal, but stayed to keep an eye on his client.

Amanda took a seat and when the waitress brought her food, finished everything on her plate. The tea was a refreshing contrast to the strong brew Hogan usually prepared. Though Amanda could feel fatigue creeping over her, she stood up. “If you’re ready, so am I.”

“I gave the horses extra rations,” he said. “If they don’t get some rest, they’ll turn sour.” He pointed a thumb over his shoulder. “I paid for a couple of rooms while you were soaking in...” he sniffed loudly, “...rose water. The clerk’s got your key.” Amanda grinned but said nothing as she turned away. Hogan called after her. “If you need anything, just pound on my door across the hall. I’ll be there, strait away.”

“Damn women!” he muttered after she left. “Always knowing when I ain’t telling the truth. It’s a good thing I never married.”

The next morning, Amanda was awakened by a loud knock on her door. “You up, girl?” Hogan’s voice rasped. “We need to git going.”

“I’m coming,” she called, rubbing her eyes. After getting dressed, she stopped at the open door of the bathing room to comb her hair and use scented hand cream. By the time she joined Hogan in the dining room, except for wearing men’s clothing, she felt almost womanly.

Amanda noted Hogan wore clean clothes and his face appeared freshly washed. She knew better than to mention it, but the scout had obviously bathed.

After their meal, a clerk provided a lantern for the walk to the stable. Amanda thought she had been doing a good job saddling her horse until Hogan checked the cinch. "This here horse, he's got you fooled," he admonished in a fatherly tone. "See, he don't like being saddled tight. So he puffs out his belly until your done. When he lets out his breath, the saddle is nice and loose." He lifted his knee hard, bringing it into sharp contact with the horse's ribs. As it grunted, the gelding released its breath and Hogan tightened the cinch.

Amanda's jaw dropped. "Why, you little traitor!" she said, poking her horse. "I thought we were partners."

"Ain't no man or beast, that won't turn a situation to his advantage if a fool will let him," he said while fastening her saddlebag. "My advice is to be wary of others trifling with you. You're young, but you don't gotta be stupid." Turning away, he strapped supplies to the packhorse, leaving her to wonder at his words.

After leaving the barn, Hogan surprised Amanda by tossing her a pair of mittens. She tried thanking him but he ignored her. In other ways he began granting comforts along the trail. Additionally, they always seemed to be near a town at nightfall with Hogan insisting they stay at a hotel or boarding house.

In the primitive town of Stockton, Amanda put on her last change of clean clothes. She didn't care that she wouldn't be in her best finery to greet Reagan. His smile would be enough.

When she entered the dining room she handed Hogan his fee. "You've done it," she said. "I might as well pay you now."

"Now hold on, girlie. We ain't there yet. You sure you want to pay me before the job's done?"

"Oh, Hogan, I'm not letting your temper ruin my day."

"Huh!" he snorted, stuffing the bills into his pocket. "It ain't a day too soon."

"Are you saying you're not glad I hired you?"

"I've regretted every step," he growled. You're a burden I'm happy to be rid of."

"Oh, you!" She swatted his arm. "You've been nothing but irritable, ill-tempered, annoying..."

Hogan grinned. "That's because only a fool argues with a skunk, a mule or a woman. Now, let's go. We're wasting time."

Later, as they saddled their mounts, Amanda secured the cinch to its proper tightness. Though she still swam in her overlarge coat, she no longer felt lost in it. Indeed, a new assuredness had taken hold. It was a budding poise, unknown even to her.

But Hogan knew. He knew by the way she sat her horse and the way she held the reins. He realized she was the type of woman he would've been happy to marry had he been fortunate enough to find one. He sighed. The sooner he had her delivered to her husband, the better.

By late afternoon and miles into a timberland, heavy snowflakes began to fall. As shadows darkened the forest, they came upon some tracks.

"Men on foot, and two horses dragging a tree," said Hogan. He turned his horse to follow the new path. "These ain't but an hour old."

chapter 50

Reagan had just left his cabin to go to the cook's shack when he saw two riders approaching. He knew one of two things. They were either passing through and needed a place to bunk, or they were drifters hoping to find work. As the riders approached, he noticed an older man leading a packhorse while a lad brought up the rear. "Hello," he called. "What can I do for you?"

"Looking for a Mr. Burnsfield," the bearded man said.

"Speaking," he replied.

"I have something to deliver to you." With that, the man turned his horse back to the forest. Passing the boy, he tipped his hat before slapping the rump of the lad's gelding.

Mystified, Reagan took a step closer, watching as the boy drew near. The brim of his hat protected his eyes while the drawn up collar hid most of the face.

Amanda's voice stuck in her throat when she saw Reagan standing there. When it became obvious he didn't recognize her, she dismounted, and calling his name, stumbled forward. She was almost upon him before he realized the boy was really a girl.

"Amanda?" he said, yanking off her hat. "Is that you? What are you *doing* here?"

"I-I-" Although she had planned her words carefully, Amanda was struck dumb at his distraught look.

"Has something happened?" he said, grabbing her arms. "Has there been an accident?"

"No! No, nothing's wrong! I only came because... because...I wanted to be with you!" she blurted.

"*What*?"

"I-I wanted to be here...with you...I-I thought you wanted me here...."

"Are you mad?" Reagan shook her with talon-like force. "You little fool! You could've been hurt!"

Amanda couldn't believe her ears. He was angry with her. No not angry, he was furious! With a cry, she broke his grip. "Reagan, stop it! Stop it!" Her tears tumbled as fast as her words, drenching her cheeks. "I couldn't stand being alone all winter...without you... I deceived everyone...dressed like this..." she said, throwing open her hands, "...I nearly froze, just to get here..." Unable to go on, she covered her face and began to weep. Before leaving Cantonsville, Reagan seemed eager to share her company. But now he acted as if she were the last person he wanted to see.

Hearing voices, Danny came from the cook's shack. "Anything wrong, boss?"

Reagan pointed at Amanda's horse. "See that nag? Bed it down!" He picked up Amanda's hat, then taking her by the arm, half-lifted, half-dragged her to his cabin. Thrusting her inside, he threw the hat before slamming the door.

"Explain yourself," he said, putting his arms akimbo.

Amanda wiped her eyes, too ashamed to look up. "I must've misunderstood. I thought you'd be happy to see me. You said you wanted to take me with you..."

"I didn't mean that literally!" Reagan said, pushing her toward the stove. "This job keeps me too busy. What were you thinking?"

"I thought we needed time together," she said, sniffing.

"I'm never here except at night," he snapped. "And when I am, it's to work at my desk or sleep. This is no tea party, madam. There's no time for pleasantries."

"I see," she said, mopping her face with a sleeve. "I didn't realize...."

"Who brought you?"

"Hogan."

"Who the hell is Hogan?"

"The man I hired to bring me."

"You what? Never mind! Why did my father agree to this?"

Amanda's chin rose. "I told you. I didn't tell him or anyone. He thought I was visiting Aunt Ella." In the sudden silence, she gazed around. The room seemed smaller than she imagined.

Reagan set a chair before her. "Sit," he commanded. As she sat down, he unbuttoned his coat. "You were a fool to travel this time of year and a bigger fool to come here. We have no conveniences for a lady. One way or the other, you're going home."

"But Reagan, I'll stay out of your way."

"I will *not* have my wife in a lumber camp. Your presence would distract the men."

Amanda rubbed her eyes, already dreading the return trip. "But, I came all this way...."

"Amanda, it's impossible. I couldn't be with you all the time. I'd hate for someone to get hurt because your presence caused him to do something stupid."

Amanda nodded. Her eyelids felt heavy as the stove's warmth enveloped her. "Then, I guess I'll be ready to go come morning," she said, her shoulders hunching.

"You look exhausted," he said, motioning toward the bed. "Get some sleep. We'll talk tomorrow."

Obediently she rose and fumbled with her buttons. With an exasperated sigh, Reagan pushed away her hands and unbuttoned the coat himself. "Good Lord, this is my old coat," he said, draping it over a chair.

Amanda appeared to have forgotten his presence as she removed her shirt, exposing the top half of her long johns. She next tried pulling off her boots but tugged uselessly while hopping on one foot.

"Come here," Reagan said, pulling her toward the bed. Sitting her down, he removed her boots and peeled her socks before reaching inside her waistband to unbutton then strip off her pants. After a yawn and a stretch, Amanda lay on the quilts and promptly fell asleep.

Reagan stared as she slept. Consumed with work, he had almost eliminated her from his mind. Now here she was to remind him that just a few scant weeks ago he had delighted in exploring her every curve. Bending down, Amanda's clean scent struck him when he lifted her to pull back the covers. He enjoyed a few moments with her nestled against his chest before easing her under the covers. After dimming the lamp he headed for the door, catching his foot on Amanda's hat. He smiled when he recognized his boyhood possession and hung it on a peg before leaving.

Danny was only mildly surprised to see Reagan enter the bunkhouse. As they sat away from others, Reagan explained Amanda's presence. "I'm sending her back tomorrow and since I need to stay, I want you to take her home. You know the boys better than anyone. Pick two men trustworthy enough to serve as guards. Your wages will be paid even if the weather makes it impossible for your return."

"Sure, boss," said Danny. "I'll make my decision by morning."

Reagan looked around. "I guess I'm going to be needing a bunk."

Danny chuckled as he pointed to an empty bed. "Later on tonight, you'll get to hear why I say the boys saw logs even when they sleep."

After the lights went out and throughout the night, snow fell. It grew heavier and thicker with each passing hour. Toward midnight, a north wind began blowing and as it grew strong, it whistled through chinked logs and between buildings forming pyres of snow that crested and troughed like a rigid sea. The gusts intensified and both man and beast burrowed deeper into bed, hiding from the mournful sound. By the time the North Star descended the wind had weakened, leaving the camp entombed in a silent, frozen vice.

The cook and her helper were the first to rise. With lanterns held high they struggled through drifts until reaching the cook's shack. Once inside, Hattie took massive frying pans off the wall while Theo lit the stove. Soon the sound of sizzling bacon mingled with Hattie's curses as she ladled batter and brewed the first of many pots of coffee.

By four o'clock, the cook'ee left to awaken the teamsters who would in turn feed and ready the animals. When the weather turned foul, the oxen would remain unharnessed until the boss confirmed a workday. It wasn't until Theo blew the breakfast horn at quarter til five that the storm showed signs of ending.

Reagan emerged from the bunkhouse and from his upraised lantern saw a camp nearly buried in snow. He softly swore as he waded through hip deep drifts before entering the cabin. Amanda stirred but didn't awaken as he scraped ashes from the stove and started a fire. After adjusting the vents, he approached his sleeping wife. The fact that she couldn't go back, didn't anger him as much as he expected.

He touched her shoulder while placing her clothes beside her. "Breakfast is coming. You'll want to be dressed when it arrives." As she arose he couldn't help but watch, ogling her like a schoolboy while she put on her clothes. It occurred to him much could be gained from her coming, after all.

"You know, you'd cause a scandal back home if anyone saw you dressed like that," Reagan said, feeling the stirrings of desire. "I hope you kept your coat on while traipsing about the countryside."

"I did," she said quickly. "Most everyone just thought I was a boy." Reagan missed the catch in her voice as Amanda ran fingers through her hair before braiding its length.

Finding the washbasin, she poured water into the bowl. "Am I to leave right away?"

Reagan crossed his arms as he glanced toward the window. "No."

"Oh?" she said, splashing her face before finding a towel. "Then, could I be shown around camp before I go?"

"Perhaps, but not today."

"Truly?" she said, turning around. "You'll not send me back right away?"

"It seems we had quite a snowstorm last night. So, it looks like you're stuck for awhile."

"Thank you!"

"Don't thank me," Reagan said, amused at her obvious delight. "If I had anything to do with it, you'd be halfway home by now. But, since you're here, you might as well know where things are." He pointed around the room. "Over by the door is a barrel I keep filled with snow. The heat from the stove melts it and provides whatever water I need. My desk is usually filled with ledgers and important papers. I ask that you leave them alone."

"Of course, there's the bed and table, which you've used. But against the other wall I have a chest which stores most of my clothes and some books you might find useful to pass the time." Amanda took note of the small trunk as well as a mirror lying on the table. "And, I have a pan hanging above it," he continued. "It's much more pleasant to wash with hot water."

Amanda suddenly frowned. "But where do you keep the chamber pot?"

Reagan chuckled. "My dear, lumbermen don't use chamber pots."

She looked perplexed. "But, where...?"

"We use outhouses, madam. Outside."

Her eyes grew wide. "You mean, I have to..." she said, pointing toward the door.

"Uh-hmm," he nodded.

"Where the other men...?" Amanda said, nearly choking.

"You'll be relieved to know I have a personal privy behind the cabin. I'll show you where it is," he said plucking up her coat.

"Are you the only one who uses it?"

"Indeed, I am, until now." Opening the door, he handed her the lantern before lifting her in his arms. After carrying her over the drifts to the rear of the cabin, he scooped snow away from the privy.

Once the door was loosened, he swept an arm wide. "Milady, thy throne!"

chapter 51

AMANDA GAZED THROUGH the window as the rising sun revealed the magnitude and beauty of the storm's wrath. The sunlight had evaporated the bluish pall, turning the wintry expanse into a dazzling radiance of thousands of sparkling diamonds. Fir trees were freshly draped in ivory mantles, their tops frozen in majestic poses. Bunkhouses appeared to squat in snowdrifts that in some places were five or more feet high. The normal workday was suspended so the men could shovel paths between buildings, stable, and cook's shack. Even Reagan took a turn with the shovel by clearing a narrow path to the privy out back.

When the outside activities ceased to hold her attention, Amanda inspected the books lining Reagan's trunk. She marveled at the variety of subjects and settled on a book of poetry, alternating her time between reading and stoking the fire.

Reagan entered the cabin hours later with a rush of cold air. His cheeks were ruddy, yet his eyes radiated warmth when he saw Amanda curled on the bed. "I see you found my stash," he said, chuckling.

"Have you finished shoveling?"

"Not quite," he said, straddling a nearby chair. "We still have to cut another access into the forest."

"How will you do that?"

"We'll use oxen first. Then widen the path they form by running an empty skid loader through the snow."

"What's a skid loader?"

"It's a sleigh-like vehicle with runners instead of wheels. We use them to transport logs," Reagan said. As his eyes wandered over her boyish garb, he imagined how easy it would be to undress her with no pantaloons or corset to get in the way.

"So when will I be able to see the camp?" Amanda asked, closing her book.

Reagan tore his mind from where it had been wandering. "We can go right now. The men are having their noon meal."

Outside, Amanda burrowed into her coat while Reagan pointed toward various buildings. "The blacksmith's shop is the first in a line of buildings that run east, turn, and then swing back to form a rough U-shape. The buildings facing each other are the men's bunkhouses. Under no circumstances are you to go near them. The small sheds in front are where the men keep their tools." He then led Amanda down one of the shoveled walkways crisscrossing the yard. "Over there is the cook's shanty. It's the largest so it can hold everyone at once. I'll take you there when the men are finished eating."

"That looks like a stable," Amanda said as they neared the next structure.

"You're right. We keep eight teams of oxen, mules and horses. And one recently arrived city nag," he added with a smile. "That small building at the end is the saw-filer's shack. With weather like today the men will be sharpening and repairing their tools."

She stared at the rude structures. "It's hard to imagine living like this. How can anyone stand it?"

"My men are willing to work in these conditions to provide for families, my dear. Not everyone can be like your Mr. Banning who looks like he's never dirtied his hands."

"And yet you do," Amanda observed. "Your hands aren't soft like his."

"That's the difference between me and your guest. I'm not ashamed of sweat," Reagan said, grabbing her arm. "But for now, let's get back to the cabin. You're nose is red. Hattie's the closest we have to a doctor and you wouldn't like her medicine."

Lumbermen began emerging from the cook's shanty just as Reagan opened the cabin door. "I'll see that your meal is sent over," he said, putting her inside. "I need to get back to work."

"Won't you be joining me?"

"Not today, there's too much to do." After closing the door he approached the men. "Okay boys, get your shovels." He then turned to the bull driver. "Fritz!

Yoke up the Ayrshires. We need the big fellas to break these drifts."

"Sure, boss!" As Fritz headed for the stables, Reagan formed the men into teams, clearing the area for the massive bulls. Nearly two tons of muscle and brawn emerged from the barn, guided by the curses and goad stick of the bull whacker. "Hump, you, Buck! Move!" Fritz roared. Straining and grunting, the bulls pawed for traction as their shoulders broke into the nearest snow bank. Under Fritz's guidance they made steady progress and by late afternoon had reached the forest's edge. After returning to the stable for a much-deserved rest, a fresh team of oxen was hitched to a skid loader to widen the Ayrshires path.

At dusk, the cook'ee rang the triangle bringing a swarm of men. Kerosene lamps kept the shanty lit while the loggers elbowed their way onto benches. Hattie slapped meat onto platters as fast as Theo could carry them. Stew and beans soon followed, passed from hand to hand down tables. Theo refilled pitchers of milk before bringing fresh pies that were quickly devoured. Known to make twenty or more pies a day, Hattie brought many a logger back just for her flavorful fare. When not fetching food, Theo filled a rack with kindling that supplied stoves for heating as well as cooking.

Once the men had left and as promised, Reagan brought Amanda to the cook's shack. Their boots sounded against the floor as they approached a woman rolling dough on a knife-scarred table. A lad wearing an apron stood beside her, washing dishes.

"You busy, Hattie?"

"Jus' makin' biscuits for tomorrow," she cackled before turning around.

"I have someone here I'd like you to meet," Reagan said. "This is my wife, Amanda, who took it upon herself to come here, unannounced. It looks like she's going to be here awhile."

"'Lo," Hattie said, wiping her hands. "The boss told me 'bout you this mornin'. And a fine young, purty thing she is, Mister Reagan."

"Hattie keeps the boys well fed and in line. In fact," he said, grinning, "I think the men are more afraid of Hattie than they are of me."

"Damn right they are," she said. "No shanty boy ever got the best of Hattie! If'n he thought otherwise, he soon found hisself marked with one of my fryin' pans!"

Amanda could only stare while Reagan appeared amused by Hattie's words. "Her helper is Theodore," he said, nodding toward the lad whose ears had turned bright red. "He does whatever needs done in the way of fetching, mopping, cutting wood and whatever else Hattie sets him to do."

Theo barely glanced up. "Pleased t' meet ya," he squeaked.

Hattie waved in his direction. "Don't mind him. That boy ain't said ten words since he's been here." Picking up her rolling pin, she resumed working the dough. "I best git back to work. I got lot's to do. Mrs. Burnsfield is welcome to come whenever she wants," she said over her shoulder. “But probably the best time is when the boys are in the woods.”

“That’s the *only* time you’ll see Mrs. Burnsfield,” Reagan said. “I’ve instructed Amanda to stay in the cabin when the men are about. During the week however, I’ll let her come over while we’re working.”

Amanda felt as if she were a child being redressed and was relieved when they returned to the cabin. “So, you mean to tell me I won’t have any company all day?” she asked.

“You’ll have Hattie,” he said, hanging his coat beside hers. “I thought I just said that, not five minutes ago.” Seeing Amanda’s cross face, he folded his arms and calmly awaited the brewing storm. It came in a flurry of words.

“I can’t imagine having a semblance of a conversation with that woman. She’s crude, and dirty, and... and...” she searched for a fitting pejorative, “...indelicate, to say the least!”

Reagan shrugged, not at all moved by her outburst. “Hattie is Hattie.”

“Why can’t I just be with you? I won’t be in the way, I promise.” Unused to hearing herself whine, Amanda scowled at the mewling quality of her voice. This wasn’t the romantic winter she had envisioned when she left Cantonsville.

“I told you. That’s out of the question. I can’t have you traipsing about in little-boy britches around a bunch of love-starved men.” He was quickly losing his patience. If he could barely contain his desires, how could he expect his men to act any better? “You’ll stay in camp, in my cabin, unless I bid you otherwise. Is that clear?"

"Then, what *can* I do?"

"That, my dear, is what you should've thought of before you came." He resisted the urge to shake his finger under her nose, though he was sorely tempted. She was acting like a child, and deserved to be treated like one. Yet, he was having very unchild-like thoughts at the moment.

Removing the pan from the wall, he dipped it in the water barrel before setting it on the stove. Then hanging a mirror, he spent the next several minutes lathering his face and shaving. Afterward, he stripped to his waist before filling the washbasin with heated water.

Amanda had picked up a book and plopped on the bed, clearly annoyed. "I'd appreciate it if you'd make sure there's enough kindling for the stove," she spoke without looking up. "Before you leave, that is."

When he didn't answer, she glanced up to see him towering over her. "There's plenty of wood for tonight," he said. "And, if *we* run out, I'll get more from the woodpile." He sat on the bed and took her book. Raising an eyebrow, he waited for her protest but she only got up to take his place at the washbasin.

"Then, I'll take your word for it there's enough wood." Unwinding her braid, she looked over her shoulder. "Do you have a shirt I could sleep in?"

Reagan realized this wasn't going to be as easy as he thought. Annoyed as she was, she probably wouldn't be receptive to his overtures. After giving her a flannel shirt, he sat back on the bed and boldly stared. He'd be damned if he was going to deny himself the pleasure of watching his wife undress.

If Amanda thought that presenting her back would somehow deny him, she was mistaken. He watched with growing anticipation as she unbuttoned her shirt and set it aside. Removing her boots, she kicked them away before squirming out of her britches. Reagan devoured the sight of her, recalling it hadn't been so long ago that he'd satisfied his desires with eager regularity. Now, he hesitated for fear of rejection. He watched her unbutton her long johns and from the reflection in the mirror, saw breasts emerge between the openings of her garment. His breath caught as he silently willed the cloth to fall. As the garment descended, it caught on her flanks, exposing the beginning roundness of her backside. He became fascinated by the tiny indentation centered above her hips, reminding him of his pleasure lingering there during love play. As his lust grew, he cursed himself for stupidly setting rules before establishing their nightly routine. He now faced an irate wife who wasn't sympathetic to his plight.

Unaware of Reagan's torment, Amanda picked up the flannel and with one arm covering her bosom, slid it on. She left open the shirt while removing her socks, briefly exposing her perfectly curved bosom. Then, hopping from one foot to the other, she peeled off her leggings, causing her breasts to bounce. Reagan nearly strangled and his lungs wouldn't expand until mercifully, she buttoned the shirt. Even covered, Reagan could still visualize every delightful part of her. He resisted the urge to seize her, hoping he could persuade her to share his bed. As yet, Amanda had no idea what she was doing for she hadn't once looked in his direction.

It wasn't until she began running fingers through her hair that Reagan could no longer curb his impulses. The sight of her with arms upraised and her hair falling down her back caused lustful cravings that demanded to be appeased. He sprang up and drew her against his chest.

"Come here, you little minx," he breathed near her mouth.

Startled, Amanda stared into his eyes, seeing clearly his intent. She resolved to resist, but faltered when he slid his hands past her hips in a slow caress. With his clean, fresh scent filling her nostrils, Amanda's heart beat rapidly and every nerve quickened.

"What are you doing?"

"Kissing you goodnight," he murmured before lowering his mouth.

She thought she possessed a stronger will but it seemed to give way as his tongue found hers. Amanda felt caught in a whirlwind, rendered helpless by sudden cravings and it wasn't until his hands trailed upward that her mind protested his trespass. Why should she grant him the pleasures of her body when he so easily disregarded her feelings?

Pushing a hand between them, she pulled back. "I'm not in the mood to kiss you goodnight," she breathed shakily. "You can leave now. I need my rest."

"Then I suggest we go to bed so we can *rest*," Reagan said. "I'm feeling rather tired, myself." With a grin, he grabbed her shirttail, lifting upward.

"Quit that!" She slapped his fingers, but he only caught her hand before reaching for her buttons. "Why should I swoon at your feet when you'll otherwise have nothing to do with me?"

"Because," he whispered, brushing her cheek with his lips. "I want you."

Trapped in his arms, Amanda avoided his mouth but he nuzzled her ear, sending shivers in every direction. She lifted her shoulder, breaking contact, but suddenly found lips pressed against hers while a hand rose to brazenly capture her breast. Amanda gasped at the scalding pleasure when, through the cloth, he teased a peaking crest.

"Woman," Reagan whispered, "I think I will have you *now*." Slipping an arm beneath her, he lifted her up and, before she knew it, had pushed aside the quilts and lowered her to the bed.

"Wait," she said, placing a hand against his chest. "If I'm not sharing your days, you shan't spend your nights with me."

"Oh, but my dear," he said, capturing her hand and pressing it against his lips. "That's when I *want* to be with you."

Amanda squirmed beneath him. "How dare you ignore me all day, then use me at night!"

"How dare you come to me and then forbid me to love you," Reagan said while capturing her hands. "You being here, drives me mad for want of you."

Amanda wriggled but it only worked against her as her shirt shifted upward. Seeing his advantage, Reagan stroked a bare leg before running his hand beneath the cloth. With slow deliberation he unbuttoned her shirt until her softness lay bare to his eager gaze. "Stop that!" she demanded.

Ignoring her command he lowered his head. Amanda gasped when his mouth made contact, setting her afire with a myriad of sensations. "Stop..." she whispered. But he kept on, and under his persistent assault, a fervor built within her until she stopped resisting. Reagan removed his trousers before ensnaring her body. Then, twining his fingers into her hair, he reclaimed her lips while moving against her with gentle, teasing strokes. Amanda was vaguely aware of his murmurings as he kissed her eyes, lips and throat. She forgot about everything as she lifted herself upward to accept him fully. As they moved, she found herself once again carried to heights she never dreamed possible. For that brief span of time, she was wanted, needed by Reagan, and all was right with the world.

Later, he slept with one arm slung around her waist. With her back to his chest, Amanda listened to his breathing. Her mind drifted over the past months and how circumstances had spiraled out of control until she found herself married to a man she little understood. *Do I really know you*, she wondered, drawing his hand against her cheek. *Will I ever come to know you?*

chapter 52

By the end of her second day at the lumber camp, all of Amanda's fantasies were undone. Reagan made firm his habit of leaving before sunrise and returning after dark where his evenings were spent at his desk. Though she had Reagan's attention at night, this certainly wasn't the romantic interlude she expected and soon felt greatly disappointed.

A few days later, Amanda stood at the mirror working tangles from her hair when she heard a knock. She opened the door to see Theo standing there.

"I'm to get the dishes, ma'am."

"They're on the desk," she said, missing Theo's curious glance as she returned to the mirror and her tangles.

In the cook's shack, Theo scrubbed dishes. By the time he finished, he had an idea.

He searched through the woodpile and after finding a suitable chunk, sat down and pulled out his pocketknife. He whittled for an hour, forming a crude comb with widely spaced teeth. Theo then slipped the comb into a pocket before going to the stables. Sifting through implements, he found a never-used bristle brush and soaked it in water while he sanded the comb smooth. After rounding the points until the teeth were no longer sharp he took a small chisel and carved scrollwork into the wooden grip. He knew it was time to ready the sleigh, but first dried the brush then ran to Reagan's cabin and knocked.

When Amanda opened the door, he held out the brush and comb. "You might...could...use these..." He placed them in her hand the same time Hattie emerged from the cook's shack.

"Boy! Where in hell's tarnation are you?"

Amanda looked in surprise as Theodore tore across the yard and disappeared into the barn. She had often regretted not packing her brush or comb, and though these were neither shiny nor finely crafted, looked to work just the same.

Amanda forgot about obtaining her meal. She closed the door and went to the mirror to unwind her braid. Taking the comb, she began with the bottom strands and worked upward until it slid easily through her hair. She next used the brush, savoring its feel until she heard a commotion outside. Through the window she could see Hattie and Theodore leaving in a sleigh laden with provisions.

"There goes lunch," she muttered. "And now, I'm all alone with nothing to do." After taking turns staring out the window and feeding the stove, she rummaged through Reagan's trunk and pulled out a book. A few hours later, she grew bored and began cleaning the cabin. But, Reagan's penchant for neatness didn't give her much to do save wetting a rag to wipe away cobwebs. By the time she heard the sleigh return, she had changed her mind about never visiting the cook.

Hattie and Theo had made several trips indoors by the time Amanda approached the cookhouse. "Well, don't just stand there," Hattie said, pointing to the sleigh. "Grab those dishes!"

Amanda scraped off the pan and followed Theo inside as Hattie disappeared into a back room, emerging with a large ham. She began slicing off chunks while hollering over her shoulder. "Theo! You got that sleigh unloaded?"

"Yes'm."

"Git that horse bedded! We's late gittin' dinner on!"

Amanda set down her pan while Theo scurried outside. She stared at Hattie's back, wondering if the woman ever conversed in a civilized manner. "Seems your entire day is spent preparing food," she ventured.

"All I got is this half-witted boy," Hattie said, her knife thumping the board. "Ain't had no decent help since a'fore Jed grow'd up and became a logger hisself."

"Jed?"

"Jed was my last boy a'fore this'n and two others. Scrawny as chickens, they all been, since Jed. This'n don't do nuthin' lest he's told, and then drops half whut he fetches."

Amanda approached while Hattie tossed a log into the stove. "Is...is there anything left of what you took to the men?"

"Some biscuits and cold coffee is all." She turned to give Amanda a hard stare. "You c'n have them, but from now on, you eat when it's time or not a'tall. I won't have my routine upset more'n it is a'ready."

"I will," she said, grabbing a biscuit. Finding a stool, Amanda watched the cook as she bustled about. Theodore returned and began washing dishes while Hattie placed lumps of dough into the oven before stirring simmering vegetables. As aromas filled the kitchen, Hattie filled several platters, bidding Theo to set them at intervals on the tables.

"Theo!" she barked. "It's time to milk ol' Betsy! She's prob'ly near to bustin'!" As he grabbed a bucket, Hattie looked to where Amanda occupied a corner. "And you girl, you best git to the cabin. The boys'll be back a'fore long."

After being in the warm cookhouse, the cabin seemed unusually cold and Amanda realized the fire had gone out. She went to the woodpile as several wagons emerged from the forest. She grabbed a few pieces before going inside, hearing Reagan's voice as he gave his horse to a teamster before entering the cabin.

"You let the fire die?"

Amanda knelt before the stove, her hands full of kindling. "I-I went to see Hattie this afternoon and forgot about it."

"I thought you couldn't have a semblance of a conversation with her," he said, hanging up his coat.

"I guess I didn't really mean it," she said, scooping cinders into a bucket. "It's just that this hasn't turned out like I imagined."

"Of course it didn't, you ninny." Reagan hunkered down and took over the task. He then formed a rick in the stove while Amanda handed him pieces of wood. "So, what do you think of Hattie?"

"I'm not sure. We didn't talk much."

"She may be a bit gruff but you'll soon appreciate her talents. Not everyone can keep order while feeding two-dozen roughnecks. With Hattie, I don't worry about undercooked food or coffee tasting like shoe polish." Striking a match, he lit the kindling. "She keeps the men happy. Happy loggers run this operation. So, I guess you could say our success rides on the bellies of our men." He closed the stove and adjusted the vent before helping Amanda to her feet.

"She does all that?"

"And more. She runs a tight ship and she never complains."

"What's that supposed to mean?"

"Nothing," Reagan said. "Here, hand me your coat."

"Not yet. It's still cold. But look what Theodore brought me," she said, positioning her treasures until they lay just so.

"They look nice," he said, drawing near behind her. "So, besides fixing your hair, what did you do all day?"

"Oh, I straightened up a little. Read some, too."

"Perhaps Sunday, when the boys have a day off, I can take you to the work site," Reagan said, slipping his arms around her waist. "You won't see the operation in action, but it'll be the next best thing."

She smiled over her shoulder. "Truly? You'd take me?"

"As long as weather permits, then yes, I promise," he said, pressing a kiss against her temple.

"I seem to remember another pledge made, but never fulfilled," she said, smiling.

Reagan searched his memory while Amanda pointed her finger at him in the mirror. Raising her thumb, she wrapped her remaining fingers back, simulating a gun. Suddenly, Reagan recalled when they were first accosted by bounty hunters and his offer to show her the use of a pistol. "Oh that," he said, giving a playful squeeze. "Since you're now my wife, you shouldn't have need of that particular talent."

"But what of the times we're apart?" she asked. "It's obvious we'll be seeing little of each other during winter."

Reagan felt the air warming and unfastened Amanda's coat. "Oh, I don't know," he said, turning her around. "Maybe, it's time to promote Danny. Then I could stay at home and pursue the full time job of defending your honor."

"But, how am I to protect myself against you?"

Reagan lowered his lips near hers. "Why, my dear, there *is* no safeguard against me." All day, he had thought of their passionate lovemaking. So heated were his imaginings, it was as if last night's coupling hadn't occurred. His need to possess her became a hunger that refused to be satisfied. As he moved over her lips in eager anticipation, a loud knock startled Amanda, causing her to break away.

Reagan threw open the door, viewing an obviously embarrassed Danny. "What is it?"

"The Koshak brothers are at it again."

With a frustrated sigh, Reagan shrugged on his coat. "What are they doing this time?"

As they hurried away the men passed Theodore laden with a tray. The boy knocked and then waited for Amanda to open the door.

"Hello, Theo," she said, stepping back. "Please set that on the bed. I also want to thank you for the brush and comb."

"T'weren't nuthin'. I seen ya needed 'em, that's all."

"Well, I really appreciate it. It'll make a world of difference while I'm here," she said, smiling. "So, tell me, where'd you learn to carve?"

Theo looked down, his face flushing. "Used to do such for my ma. She had purty hair, like you. But, it was red, 'stead of dark."

"It was a thoughtful gift," Amanda said. "And since we're on the subject of comfort, do you suppose there's another chair somewhere? With two of us occupying the cabin, it'd be more comfortable if one didn't have to sit on the bed all the time."

"Sometimes Danny brings in a chair when he goes over maps with Mr. Burnsfield," Theodore said. "I know where it's kept. I could also bring an old washtub. Turned upside down, it'd make a good table."

"That'd be lovely. But only when you have time. I don't want you getting into trouble on my account."

"Mebbee tomorrow I c'n fetch 'em for you," he said. "Right now I need to call the men to supper, so I gotta go."

Amanda had uncovered the food by the time Reagan reentered the cabin. "Did you get the problem fixed?" she asked, handing him a plate.

"Theo's signal took care of the situation," he said, sitting on the bed. "Nobody fights after the bell rings."

"I can see why," Amanda said. "This food is delicious. I could eat it everyday."

Reagan stabbed a chunk of meat and began slicing. "Don't worry, you will. Come spring, you'll not want to look at another flap-jack or fried beef again."

"I see you're still eating," she said sipping from a glass of water.

He took his time perusing her form before meeting her eyes. "When a man is hungry, he eats."

Amused, Amanda arched a brow. "But, you can't say it matters not what you have to choose from. I mean, would you look at simple fare as eagerly as a sumptuous meal?" By the look on her face, Amanda expected his next response to be a tribute to her charms. After all, he had showered her with amorous attentions from the moment they wed.

"If there's food to be had, milady, I'll consume it. On the occasion it turns out to be a delectable morsel, then all the better."

Amanda frowned. "I think you jest," she goaded, her chin rising. "I don't believe anyone cares so little about his...stomach. The food's merit should be as important as how it's presented."

"Should someone starve while waiting for the perfect meal?" he asked, grinning. "I think not."

"So, you're saying a man isn't particular, even if it displeases his palette? I thought men of breeding were more discerning."

"Then you don't know much about men, madam. He'll accept whatever's set before him until something more savory comes along."

Amanda felt stung. Once again she felt foolish to think Reagan had ever considered her first choice. Yet her pride refused to admit what her heart conceded. There might come a time Reagan would choose another. "Then I would doubt the worth of the man more than the cook," she said, her eyes clouding. "Either that, or I've badly misjudged your gender."

"Well, my dear, that may be true of most men," Reagan said as he reached out and caressed her cheek. "But you needn't worry. For indeed, the cook's a master chef, and I a bondservant who awaits the sweet sampling."

Disarmed at his touch, Amanda held her breath. But he seemed to drop the matter and they finished their meal in peace. Afterward, Reagan set water to heat before placing the empty dishes outside. He then sat at his desk making notes in a ledger while Amanda resumed reading her book.

When the water began simmering, he poured it into the washbasin, adding cool water from the pitcher. He then stripped to his waist and washed. After dumping the water outside, Reagan removed his boots and stretched out beside Amanda. At first he rested an arm on her hip as he snuggled against her backside. It wasn't long before Amanda felt his hand move from hip to shoulder, then slowing to caress her cheek. "It's time for bed," he murmured, taking her book.

"Says who? Cook or bondservant?" she asked. His hands were already unbuttoning her shirt when Amanda rolled away. "Kitchen's closed, I say!"

Yet, despite pretending to fend against his advances, she soon gave in and allowed his lips to claim hers. Matching passion with passion, she quickly went to that place where doubts no longer existed and Reagan's love was certain.

chapter 53

THE MORNING DAWNED cold, but a clear sky promised a full workday for the men. After breakfast, Amanda spent time with a needle and thread mending one of Reagan's shirts. Later on, Theodore brought the promised chair and half-barrel with handles cut near the top. She instructed he set it upside-down near the bed but as she moved about the cabin, Amanda found its placement a hindrance. She decided to store it against the wall. Grasping a handle near the floorboards, she tried dragging it but found her leverage poor.

Amanda rested while studying the situation. Maybe by overturning the barrel she could better control the unwieldy thing. Gathering her strength, Amanda wrested the barrel onto its side then pushed with the momentum until it settled upright.

She peered inside at encrusted filth and immediately gagged on odors that emanated upward. "Ugh!" Covering her nose, Amanda grabbed her buckskin gloves then hurried outside, scooping snow into a bucket. She dumped rime into the barrel and scrubbed its insides while balancing precariously on the rim. After discarding the slush behind the privy, she next heated water laced with soap and rinsed the barrel from top to bottom. Perspiration covered Amanda's face by the time she finished mopping out the water. As she wiped her brow, she noticed the outside of the tub had remained dry. No leaks!

Suddenly, Amanda envisioned the barrel filled with hot water, and she, up to her neck in warmth. The thought of obtaining a real bath gave her courage to bring her request to Hattie.

"Best you just heat up a little snow and wash in a basin," Hattie cackled as she stirred a stew pot. "This here goulash is the closest thing yer gonna git to a large kettle of water."

"A half-barrel was brought to the cabin for a table," Amanda said, careful to omit Theo's name. "Turned upright, it would make a useful tub."

"Look, missy," Hattie said. "I don't care if'n you is the boss's wife. I ain't got time to heat water all day, just so's you c'n sit in it!" She banged her spoon as she dumped carrots into the stew.

"I didn't mean for you to do it," Amanda said. "I'll gladly do it myself. Besides, I need to wash my clothes. I happen to know the *men* wash their clothes. So, there should be some means to do so."

"Clothes washin' day is Sunday. Always been, and always will be." Hattie eyed Amanda up and down. "Your clothes look plenty clean to me, but the wash kettle's in the equipment shed." She then turned her back. "Theo!" she hollered. "Fetch me some wood!"

Setting aside his broom, Theodore snatched his coat and trotted outdoors. Amanda followed. But once outside, she hesitated.

She was forbidden to go near the bunkhouses. Yet, that was the most likely place for the kettle. Glancing toward the sun, she guessed there were three hours before nightfall. After a moment's indecision, she approached the nearest shed. Tools and saws lined the walls, but nothing inside resembled a kettle. Amanda crossed the yard and opened the door of the next shed. It too, lacked the desired items. She became nervous about being so far from the cabin but her need for a bath overrode her fears and she approached the third shed. Swinging open the door, she spied a wash kettle alongside a tripod and a tin of soap. She removed the tripod and soap and then with a twisting motion, dragged the kettle out. After only moving it a couple feet, tears brimmed her eyes for the cabin seemed too far to drag it.

The sound of crunching snow told her someone was approaching and she quickly wiped her eyes. Amanda turned to see Theodore lift the kettle by its handle and head toward the cabin. She grabbed the tripod and soap and then hurried to catch up. Despite his size, Theodore was surprisingly strong. His shoulders and back had developed a sinewy toughness from hours of chopping wood.

"Thank you," she breathed as he took the tripod from her hands. "But, I don't want to cause you trouble."

"Hattie don't own me," he said while hoisting the cauldron onto the hook. "As long as my work gits done, I do what I want." After clearing a spot, he started a fire from the cabin's wood supply. Meanwhile, Amanda filled the kettle by making several trips from the water barrel. She then found a snow bank and made an equal number of trips back, refilling the barrel.

Theo went back to the shed and returned with a wooden lid. "Just keep the fire going," he instructed. "It's gonna take awhile for it to git hot."

After he left, Amanda went inside and set a pot of water on the stove. When it became hot she poured it into the tub before adding cool water from the pitcher. She scrubbed her clothes with soap, wringing and draping them on chairs before checking on the kettle outside. Seeing percolating bubbles, Amanda made several trips inside with bucketfuls of hot water. On the last trip, she kicked out the fire. After setting out towels she undressed and climbed in, sighing as she lowered herself to the bottom. Though she couldn't stretch out, it was enough to sit in water with only her knees peeking out. She raised her arms in childish glee, laughing as droplets splashed her face and throat. After soaking for nearly an hour, she dug into the mushy soap and lathered her body. She then spent a great deal of time sudsing and rinsing her hair before wrapping it in a towel.

Amanda wasn't ready to end her unexpected luxury and closing her eyes, rested against the rim. She didn't notice the fire in the stove dwindling until a sudden, cold blast of air startled her from her slumber.

Sitting upright, she covered her bosom until she saw Reagan in the doorway, looking surprised.

"For God's sake, close the door," she said, shivering. "And bring me another towel." Amanda stood as he hastened to do her bidding. She quickly wrapped the towel about her, but not before Reagan got an eyeful of glistening, goose-fleshed limbs.

"How'd you obtain a bath, milady?" he asked, helping her from the tub before turning to the stove.

Amanda dried herself off before donning a flannel shirt. "I just did, with lots of help from Theodore."

"I wondered why the kettle was outside. I assumed you decided to wash your clothes." He closed the stove, viewing her wet garments. "I guess I was half right, anyway," he said, leaning against the barrel to peer inside. "If I'd have known what you were about, I would've come back sooner and joined you."

"As if there would've been enough room," she scoffed.

"Oh, there's plenty of room." Reagan spoke with such assuredness, Amanda turned to inspect the barrel herself.

"I don't see how." She tried to imagine them both fitting in the bottom. Though large in capacity, Amanda was sure it wasn't spacious enough for them both. She raised quizzical eyes to her husband, and saw the humor in his look.

"Why, you'd be sitting on my lap," he smirked, holding his arms to demonstrate her legs straddling his torso.

The image was so vivid that Amanda was momentarily speechless. "Oh you!" she said, throwing her towel. "Your lecherous mind roams where no gentleman would go."

Reagan laughed as he lit the lamp before stretching out on the bed. He was amazed at the great contentment he felt when nightly, he returned to his cabin. His eyes followed Amanda as she pulled a chair near the stove and began working tangles from her hair. He watched with growing fascination as she combed her hair until the strands dried. Then sweeping her tresses over her shoulder, she brushed her hair with long, even strokes.

"Reagan?"

"Hmm?"

Amanda set the brush in her lap. "Hattie seemed upset when I asked about having a bath. She didn't know I wanted to do it myself. Well, as I said earlier, Theodore helped me and I'm afraid after today, she'll not allow him to."

"You can't expect Hattie to give up her help every time you wish to bathe, madam."

"I know," she said, sighing. "But what can I do? I can't lift the kettle to its hook, and I'm terrible at starting a fire."

"Tell you what," he said. "You let me know the mornings you wish to bathe, and I'll set the kettle and start a fire. That way, it'll be ready a lot sooner. How does that sound?"

Amanda's face lit with pleasure and she rose to kiss his cheek. "Thank you!"

Reagan grinned, catching her arm. “I think this deserves a better kiss than that.” When Amanda obligingly leaned near, he pulled her onto his chest and rolled over, trapping her beneath him. With deliberate slowness, he repaid the kiss. As her fragrance snared his imagination, Reagan ignored the clanging triangle that announced supper was ready.

chapter 54

As the camp's activity stretched on in unending similarity, Amanda's routine became equally monotonous. She would rise for breakfast, get dressed, stoke the fire and after the men left, seek Hattie's company. At first she would sit on a corner stool while Hattie told stories of rugged lumbermen. According to Hattie, the strapping Scandinavians were used to working in harsh conditions and preferred saws over axes. The colorfully dressed French-Canadians and cheerful Swedes contrasted with Germans whose sour dispositions caused many a brawl over games of smear. She told about a few city men who tried lumbering but had a hard time dealing with tricks and jibes of others. "They wuz always bein' sent for left-handed hammers, shore lines and ricochets," Hattie cackled over her shoulder. "All except this big old Injun. The boys were afraid of him. Claimed he could cast spells from an amulet he wore."

As the days passed and Amanda's stool moved closer to the stove, she found herself involved with kitchen duties. At first, it was to fetch this or that item from across the room. Then it was to stir batter while Hattie took pies from the oven. Once, when Theo needed to fetch more kindling, Hattie directed Amanda to pick up his knife and finish slicing potatoes. She complied, evoking a few 'devil damns' from Hattie who got spattered after the vegetables were scraped into boiling water. By degrees, Amanda went from washing and slicing vegetables to mixing ingredients from any of Hattie's many recipes. Finally, it seemed natural to walk in and without prompting, make a batch of biscuits. As always, Hattie banished Amanda from the shanty before the men returned.

One day, Amanda was occupying her stool while Hattie made pancakes. "Theo. Go fetch the eggs, lest the chicken's try hatching them."

Theodore obediently slipped out the door as Hattie tossed Amanda a dirty towel. "Put this in that yonder pile," she said, pointing to the floor. "They git boiled on wash day. Which reminds me 'bout the time the boss fetched a kettle from another camp and got chased by some ornery timber wolves."

"Wolves?" Amanda gasped.

"All by hisself, he was," Hattie said. She scooped bacon from a skillet before ladling in fresh batter. "The boys talked 'bout it for months, on account of how lucky he was to not git eaten by the critters."

"What happened?"

"Like I said, Mr. Burnsfield went to fetch us another kettle. Seems the boys had more dirty clothes than they could boil on washday. And whooey! Them boys sure know how to smell up a bunkhouse! Mr.

Burnsfield hitched a couple horses to the sleigh and crossed a frozen lake. Well, he made it to the camp just fine, but the trouble started on the way back."

"Mr. Burnsfield thought he heard wolves howling, and sure enough when he looked, they wuz a'comin' out of the woods. He later told us the kettle wuz so heavy it was slowin' him down. So he tied down the reins, grabbed an axe and tossed that kettle onto the ice before jumping off with it."

Hattie stopped her story as Theo returned with a brimming basket. "Boy! Come git these flapjacks!"

As Theo scurried to set filled platters on tables she continued her story. "Once him and the kettle dropped off'n the sleigh, those horses skedaddled like nuthin' you ever seen! When the horses got back to camp with their eyes as big as saucers and no boss, the men went lookin'." Amanda inwardly groaned as Hattie paused again to remove muffins from the oven.

"So, tell me what happened!"

"I'm gittin' there, missy, I'm gittin' there," she said, chuckling. "It seems once the wolves found they couldn't keep up with the sleigh, they went back to see what fell off. Mr. Burnsfield crawled underneath that kettle, just a'fore those varmints got there. They started digging in the ice, but the boss, he just chopped them paws when they got too close. Blood wuz runnin' all over the place, I heard."

Hattie grinned at Amanda's suddenly pale face. "Despite gittin' their toes clipped, them wolves didn't stop till our boys got there. By the time they lifted the kettle off poor Mr. Burnsfield, he was nearly out of air!"

"Enough!" Amanda said, reaching for her coat. "If I hear another word I'm going to be sick."

"But there's at least two hours of daylight left," Hattie said.

Amanda buttoned her coat. "The wind's kicking up, and I should check our stove. It's hard to keep the cabin warm when it gets windy."

Upon reaching the cabin, Amanda saw the fire had indeed burned out. She tried relighting it, but the draft from the flue kept dousing matches. She imagined Reagan's displeasure at finding a cold cabin and looking around, her eyes stopped at his desk. Of course! She could light some paper to start a fire. Hadn't she seen Reagan do that very thing? She recalled he'd been careful to select paper he no longer needed, twisting them into tight spirals before placing them beneath kindling. Searching cubbyholes, she found invoices and supply lists but no useless scrap with which to start a fire.

Opening a drawer, Amanda withdrew several sheaths folded together. The dates at the top indicated Reagan penned them last summer and her hopes grew that this forgotten stack was no longer needed. Scanning the sheets, she found it was a list of expenses for the new mill as well as accounts and revenues from which Reagan could draw. Yet, even with her untrained eye, Amanda could see his bank accounts fell short of the expenses. Just as she was about to refold the papers, a note at the bottom of the last page caught her eye.

She saw her name. Perplexed, Amanda took a closer look. In his usual neat handwriting, Reagan had written 'Amanda's dowry' with a question mark where an amount should've gone. She rechecked the dates, seeing it had been recorded early August of last year.

How could that be? How could Reagan have anticipated her dowry before the bounty hunters captured them? Her hands trembled as she stared at the paper. When the news of their capture got out, she'd assumed Reagan's proposal had come from his sense of duty. But now it appeared he had wanted to marry her for financial gain.

Tears blurred her vision. "No," she murmured. "Oh, no!"

The past weeks had been some of the happiest she had known. Despite his anger at her arrival, Reagan seemed to enjoy their shared meals as well as the long, cold nights. But now, it seemed a cruel joke. Reagan had never cared about saving her reputation. He had simply used the situation to barter his bachelorhood for money.

Amanda didn't know how long she stared at the papers, but when she stood, they scattered from her fingers. She opened the door, looking from the cook's shack to the stables before heading to the barn.

She hadn't laid eyes on her horse since her arrival, but she easily picked her gelding from the few horses not being used at the work site. She thought quickly while saddling him. Staying was impossible.

She felt she could make it home with the aid of her map, but where was home? Amanda rested her head against the saddle as she considered her options. She worried the Burnsfield's wouldn't believe her if Reagan denied the truth. If she returned to her parents' home, she'd shame them by breaching her marriage contract. Amanda lifted her head. Perhaps Aunt Ella would take her in.

She wiped away her tears, resolving Reagan wasn't worth her grief. Yet, the ache in her heart decried that notion. By his actions, he seemed to have protected her at every turn. He denied her involvement with Gabriella's activities and even convinced the judge the bounty hunters were wrong. He'd also shown tender regard of her person when she, a frightened virgin, faced the unknowns of the marriage bed. And yet nothing could dispute the fact that Reagan had anticipated receiving her dowry before Jebediah captured them. There could be no other explanation. Reagan had used her.

Amanda stiffened her back and led her horse outside. Suddenly, a gust of wind ripped the door from her fingers, slamming it against the wall. The horse pranced skittishly but Amanda hung on. She kept both hands gripped around the reins and made her way to the cabin, tying him to a post. Hurrying inside, she felt an urgency to leave as she stuffed her saddlebag, unaware she was being watched.

Hattie happened to glance out the window as Amanda left the barn with her horse. She watched in growing alarm as the girl emerged from the cabin minutes later and attached a bag to the saddle before heading into the forest. Feeling something was awry, Hattie sent Theo to get Mr. Burnsfield. For the first time ever, the cook ceased all activities as she stared out the window and waited.

It was nearly an hour before Reagan's horse burst from the woods with Theodore trailing behind. He galloped to the cabin and rushed inside. Picking up the scattered papers, it wasn't until he looked them over a second time that Reagan realized he had forgotten to burn the incriminating tabulations. He ran outside, nearly colliding with Hattie. "Which way did she go?" he yelled.

Hattie pointed westward as the wind blew away her words. Reagan cursed while jumping on his horse. "When Danny returns, send him after me!"

Hattie held onto her hat as she hustled back to the shanty. There was much to be done, the least of which was feeding the men. Much trouble was brewing. Hattie could feel it in her bones.

chapter 55

AMANDA FOLLOWED THE trail used to transport logs to skidways. She recalled Reagan describing how logs were stacked into piles like way stations along sleigh roads. The piles were eventually loaded onto sleds and hauled over iced roads to what he called rollways. Rollways were where logs would be stacked on riverbanks to await spring thaw. As she passed skidway after skidway, Amanda was struck by the irony that because of her dowry, these mighty pines had fallen.

A steady dusting of ice crystals caused her to wrap her face with a scarf. She could do nothing however, about the prickles that pelted her horse. When he began skittering sideways, she was forced to pay more attention to keeping her seat than staying on the trail. It wasn't until the trees closed in around her that Amanda realized she had somehow veered from the road. Struggling against a panic that threatened to overwhelm her, she turned her mount around. It wasn't fair; she thought darkly, that she must fight the elements as well as her horse.

Without warning, a huge **cr-ra-ack** exploded overhead as a branch, heavy with ice, fell directly in front of them. Despite her commands with her knees and reins, the gelding reared then bucked with all its might. Amanda felt herself being tossed through the air before hitting the ground in a plume of snow. She lay motionless, gasping for breath until the painful weight on her chest receded and she rolled onto her knees. Her hat lay a short distance away and Amanda reached for it, wincing as snow showered her neck while putting it on. All the while her horse stood, eying her suspiciously.

Although hurting from the fall, Amanda got up and held out her hand. "Here boy," she said. "It's all right." The horse snorted at her quivery voice and pranced away when she moved toward him. "Come on, boy," she said, taking another step. "We need each other." Yet, despite her soft pleadings, the horse turned and plunged into the darkening forest.

Amanda sobbed as she fell to her knees. Her life had become meaningless. She had hoped a true marriage could emerge even from troubled beginnings, but now her faith lay as frozen as the snow around her. A soft snow began to fall, sticking to her lashes like thistledown. Amanda curled in a crevice of a tree. Even as her mind warned her to find her way back, her heart repelled the idea and she shouted at the trees, "I'd rather die first!"

Reagan found Amanda's tracks as soon as he entered the forest. Yet, despite the trail being free of obstacles, it appeared her mount had skittered all over the road. He knew that a confined horse would make an unsafe mount and feared Amanda might be lost.

He swore, first at himself for leaving evidence for her to happen upon, then at Amanda for finding it. Fate had dealt him a royal flush in providing a reason to marry, and now his hand had been cruelly exposed. He would now have to explain his actions while at the same time, assuage her feelings.

From Reagan's experience, young women thought marriage to be all romance with no obstacles to conquer. The best way to approach the situation, he rationalized, would be to impress upon his aggrieved wife that their troth was bound by contract. Along with that pledge came obligations and commitments. With the passage of time, he expected Amanda to see the necessity of their union. For despite his ruse in obtaining her hand, Amanda still needed protection from her accusers on both sides of the law.

To his chagrin, the hoof prints he had followed left the road. Reagan urged his steed to a brisker pace just as a powdery snow began to fall.

When the moon rose above the treetops, he came upon an area that seemed recently trampled. A large branch darkening the ground gave credence to his suspicions that something startled Amanda's horse. If not for the tan coat contrasting against a dark trunk, Reagan might've missed the figure hunched against a tree. His heart lurched, for when he approached, Amanda didn't move. Dismounting, he knelt beside her and turned her face. "Amanda," he said and when her eyes remained closed, he shook her. "Amanda! Wake up!"

"Go away," she mumbled, her head lolling against him.

Reagan wasted no time with useless words, but lifted her into his arms. He positioned her in the saddle, and then holding her steady, mounted behind her. Gripping her tightly, he gave a savage kick, sending his steed racing toward camp.

Amanda struggled to unravel what seemed like conflicting bits of reality. She felt she was moving and she could hear the distant pound of hoof beats. Had she somehow recaptured her horse and was now fleeing through the darkness? Her body felt strangely upright, but bands of steel encompassed her. And, there was something else. She furrowed her brows, trying to interpret the rasping sound near her ears. She opened her eyes to visions of dancing branches and a moon that vibrated in a black sky. Unable to discern reality, Amanda drifted into a downward spiral from which she could not escape.

She became locked in a savage nightmare. A cacophony of voices tortured her with accusations of naïveté in the face of her betrayal. Visions of Elizabeth and Camilla whispering behind fans, taunted her. She imagined Beauregard gazing at her sadly while Reagan grinned lecherously nearby. The voice of Hogan drifted to her in stern reproval..."ain't no man nor beast that won't try to turn a situation to his advantage if'n a fool will let 'em..." Amanda felt herself drowning in a pool of disgrace as she turned away from the blinding light of an overhead chandelier.

As Reagan neared camp, the trail became illuminated with lanterns, held high. The men holding beacons cheered as they detected the returning horse burdened with two riders. Soon after, Danny emerged from the woods, leading Amanda's horse behind his own.

Reagan approached the cabin and quickly dismounted as Danny neared. "The palfrey dumped the little fool," he said.

I'll take the horses," Danny said as Reagan gathered Amanda in his arms.

Reagan then kicked the cabin door wide before yelling over his shoulder, "Fetch Hattie!"

A fire had been laid in his absence and its warmth greeted him as he laid Amanda on the bed. Removing her hat and scarf, he became alarmed by her pale skin and bluish lips. He had just removed her boots when Hattie arrived with a tray, followed by Theo, whose arms were filled with quilts.

Pushing Reagan aside, she laid a hand on Amanda's brow. "Put the quilts on a chair Theo, and git to bed. You need to git up in a few hours and start breakfast without me."

"She gonna be a'right?"

"Pray, Theo," she said. "That's all I c'n say."

After Theo left, Hattie unbuttoned Amanda's coat. "Let's git this girl warm," she said. "Take off your coat and finish this while I heat them quilts a mite."

Reagan took over the task of undressing Amanda before putting one of his heavy shirts on her. Meanwhile, Hattie dragged a chair next to the stove and draped a quilt over it. “Every few minutes I want you to turn this here blanket so it’s heated on both sides.” Returning to Amanda’s side, she gently prodded the girls’ bruises. “No broken bones, thank God,” she said before feeling Amanda’s pulse. “C’mon, girlie, it’s too slow. You’ve got to help me.”

Lifting a foot, Hattie rubbed vigorously. Her brow moistened while she worked from limb to limb, massaging her skin. “How’s that quilt a’comin’?” she snapped.

Reagan placed a blanket over Amanda while Hattie took the time to remove her coat. “Git another started,” she instructed, “and put that pot I brought, on the stove.”

She fussed over Amanda for another half-hour before noting the girls’ returning color and normal breathing. Feeling relief, the cook went to stir the contents of the pan. “This soup’s for your wife. But the rest,” she nodded toward the tray, “is for you. I’ll watch over your missy, whilst you eat. Ain’t no sense in me having to fret over both of you tonight.”

Reagan stoked the fire before going to his desk. He could imagine Amanda’s shock when she discovered he had used her dowry to keep his lumber business running. Now that she knew, he’d most likely lost her trust.

Hattie succeeded in getting a few spoonfuls of soup between Amanda’s lips before turning her attention to the pile of wet garments. She clucked while spreading them near the stove. "Cain't figure why your wife would just up and skedaddle," she said, looking askance. "Cuz when she left my kitchen, she wuz just fine."

Reagan didn't answer, but instead picked up several papers from his desk and tossed them into the stove.

Hattie watched with interest. "Well now, I bet whatever upset your missus is no more'n a pile of ashes! I don't reckon that's gonna fix your problem. She done seen what was on them."

Reagan stared at Hattie's defiant stance. "Thank you Hattie, for those words of wisdom. I can take over now."

"You best fix what's between the two of you," she warned. "It's a long time a'fore winter breaks, and you c'n take your missy home." Putting on her coat, she headed for the door. "Amanda's a good girl, not prone to airs. Remember, a good woman's worth more'n all the riches in the world," she said, yanking open the door. "The Good Book says so. And any man that don't think so, is a fool!" Glaring over her shoulder, she slammed the door behind her.

Hattie's words stung Reagan. True, he hadn't been honest in his pursuit of Amanda's hand, nor were his motives entirely honorable. Yet, fate had prohibited almost any other outcome. Now that same fate had shifted, giving him no slack and no way to maneuver the facts. Amanda knew the truth and within a few hours her accusing eyes would proclaim how his deceit had ensnared her.

Sitting by the bed, he thought of all the reasons he could use when his wife awakened and questioned him. He practiced one excuse after another, yet they rang hollow even to his own ears. The more he reasoned his position, the more contemptible he looked. Realizing there *was* no excuse, Reagan's defenses rose to the fore. He decided he wouldn't try to justify his actions. What was done was done. Amanda was his wife, and his wife she would stay.

Reagan dozed fitfully until the call to breakfast sounded. He left the cabin and instructed Danny to take the crews out without him. Not wanting a repeat of yesterday, he needed to be here when Amanda awakened.

Reagan returned with a pot of coffee. Opening his ledgers, he consumed half the pot's contents before bringing his books up to date. While putting away the ledger, he noticed he'd somehow torn his cuff. He found a thread and needle and sewed the tear without bothering to remove his shirt. As he stitched, he recalled another time when Amanda had sewn a rip on one of his flannels. Although she basted the tear with cross-stitch precision, it had come apart within hours. Not wanting her to be embarrassed, Reagan had hidden the shirt in the bottom of his trunk. He smiled at the memory and lost in that thought didn't hear Amanda stir.

Amanda's first perception was feeling the warmth of several blankets. When she opened her eyes, she saw Reagan at his desk, snipping a thread from his cuff. Confused why he wasn't out working when sunlight showed through the window, her memory suddenly returned and she felt a stab of pain. She must've made a sound for Reagan was soon beside her, halting her attempt to rise.

"You're staying in bed," he said quietly.

Amanda shoved away his hand. "Get away from me," she said, pushing herself upright. Her look of loathing gave way as a wave of nausea washed over her. When she began to gag, Reagan grabbed the washbasin and held it beneath her chin while she retched putrid liquid. When her sickness subsided, he fetched her a cloth before emptying the bowl outside.

Hattie came in with a tray, followed soon after by Reagan.

"Brought your lunch," she informed Amanda cheerily. "Hot from the oven."

"I don't want it," Amanda said, looking away.

Hattie set the tray near the bed. "I brought tea and biscuits. Your favorite kind."

"I'm not hungry, and I have a headache."

"But child, you gotta eat." Hattie looked at Reagan who shrugged while replacing the washbowl.

"She got sick."

Hattie felt Amanda's forehead. "Ain't got no fever," she said. "The headache comes from being out in the cold too long." She then turned to Reagan. "Now, I don't know what happened yesterday, but if this girl don't eat, she's gonna git sicker. Her body got froze and needs nourishment. You'uns can figure it out cuz I got work to do." With those words, Hattie stomped from the room.

Reagan placed the tray on Amanda's lap and then stood back; giving her the space she obviously wanted. But she only stared at the food as tears formed in her eyes.

"I'm sorry that you had to find out that way," he spoke softly, his heart tugging at her wretched misery.

"Sorry?" Amanda choked as she gazed at him. "I believe sorry is the last thing you'd be. Now, I know why you couldn't wait to marry me."

Reagan tried to speak but her anger tumbled forth in a raging flood. "What a fool I've been! All this time I believed you were protecting Aunt Ella. But no, you only wanted my dowry to build this camp—the mill. How you must've laughed at my stupidity! You took advantage of my circumstance, you betrayed me, my family—"

Reagan knelt down, looking into Amanda's eyes. "Despite what you believe, the situation was real, your trouble genuine. Gabriella was guilty of breaking the law. She could've been prosecuted and sent to prison. You were with her that night and would've been found guilty as well. This marriage helped both of us," he said, laying his hand on hers.

Amanda felt as if her heart had been savaged. He didn't apologize. An apology would've at least expressed sorrow for her pain. Neither did he ask forgiveness, for that would've admitted wrongdoing. Instead, she heard only an argument that rationalized his bartering of her innocence to further his fortune.

Her pain congealed into a lump that wouldn't be softened by matter-of-fact words. Her heart demanded more tender regard. "I hate you!" she said, wiping away her tears. "I was nothing but a plaything that came with my dowry! I..."-she struggled to inflict as much pain as she was feeling- "...I will never again be a wife to you!"

She stared in triumph as it dawned on her what avenue of revenge she could take. "I'll never bear you children. You shan't ever touch me again."

Reagan's face clouded at her refusal to accept his attempted contrition. Had he considered the shock of her painful discovery, he might've overlooked her anger. But all he could see was her refuting the soundness of his reasoning. By marrying Amanda, he'd not only silenced rumors that would've destroyed her, he'd also thwarted Jebediah's attempt to prove Gabriella's guilt.

He stood, clasping his hands behind his back. "Listen Amanda, despite what you think, this can be fixed. I've already made plans to repay the funds—"

"Fixed!" Amanda shrieked. "How can you fix a fraudulent marriage? There's only one thing to do and that's to expose you as the charlatan you are!"

"You don't have to threaten me, my love," he said with restrained anger. "I didn't *force* you to the altar. Though, when it suited you to take my name, you didn't act outraged at *my* disadvantage. You didn't protest my efforts to keep Gabriella from being arrested and said nothing when I became your alibi when Jeb caught us. Neither did you refuse my offer of marriage though you knew rumors of your defilement were false and made me appear as a rake. As you can see, we both had something to gain. So, my dear, don't portray yourself as innocent," he said, ignoring her furious look. "There's only one thing I demand. As my wife, you'll not dishonor either of our families by airing our private affairs. I've had enough of gossips picking at my bones." Though Reagan voiced no threat, Amanda felt the warning in his tone. For the first time, she felt she was seeing his iron core nature. "There won't be a repeat of yesterday, either. I didn't ask for you to come, but since you're here, I'll say when you leave." As they stared at each other, Reagan noticed her trembling hands. "Please eat," he said. "I don't wish for you to be ill."

She picked up her fork, gaining a small measure of privacy as Reagan retreated to his desk. Yet, despite her hunger, she could only swallow a few morsels. Setting the tray aside, she gained Reagan's attention.

"I-I have to get up," she said.

"You need rest. You should stay in bed."

Amanda's cheeks reddened. "I...nature calls..." she sputtered.

The effort of dressing and visiting the privy exhausted Amanda, and once she was back inside she knew she couldn't leave. It wouldn't be until she returned to Cantonsville that she could decide how to free herself from Reagan's entangling threads of betrayal.

chapter 56

THOMAS SAT IN the library reading *The Cantonsville Daily*. Though he scanned headlines that heralded the inauguration of Abraham Lincoln, his mind kept drifting over events that occurred between the election and the President's oath of office. After South Carolina shook the country with its Ordinance of Secession, it started a wave that surged through the South like a billowing flood. On the heels of Amanda's departure, Mississippi left the Union on January ninth. Florida and Alabama followed suit on the eleventh, Georgia on the nineteenth, and Louisiana on the twenty-sixth. In February, Texas voted for secession to take effect in March. Southern states began seizing Federal forts and arsenals. In the midst of this upheaval, the reins of power passed from the willing hands of Buchanan into the more dubious grip of Lincoln. Thomas was now reading the president's inaugural speech, reprinted in the *Daily*.

"In YOUR hands, my fellow countrymen, and not MINE, is the momentous issue of civil war. The government will not assail YOU. You can have no conflict, without being yourselves the aggressors. YOU can have no oath registered in Heaven to destroy the government while I shall have the most solemn one to preserve, protect, and defend it..."

The wily fox! How clever to proclaim to be the aggrieved party instead of the one laying groundwork for battle. Thomas sighed. Either that, or Lincoln was an ignorant fool, as yet unaware of the government's involvement in war preparations. It's the innocent who suffer, he thought sadly. Those with principles end up broken, while the corrupt bend pliantly with the storms of change. Thomas rubbed his brow as if to relieve a dull pain that kept itself just under the surface of his skin. The events of the last few months seemed to haunt him. If his providing lumber for the government resulted in war, men like Lincoln would be dangled as scapegoats. It's men like us, he thought darkly, who put Lincoln there.

Thomas found solace in a glass of brandy he poured from the sideboard. Unable to share his ruminations with anyone now that Reagan was absent, he felt more alone than ever. But, Reagan would soon be returning and a log-jammed river would keep his mind occupied.

He stared into his snifter as he recalled the telegraph Amanda sent while supposedly visiting Gabriella. Katherine had burst into his office, her hands shaking as she handed the missive to her husband. He'd immediately sent men to find her and bring her back. But due to severe weather, they had returned empty handed. Next, he had the unpleasant task of informing the Bruesters. When Emily stared at him with pain-hardened eyes, he felt he had caused her suffering. After promising he'd keep them informed, Thomas left. It was only afterward that it had struck him how thin Emily had become.

Thomas drained his brandy as he returned his attention to the paper. More now than ever, war seemed to be the only means by which the country could resolve the question of slavery. He'd never been one to withhold his opinion and yet he remained quiet while others appealed for restraint. If he, like some, urged for peace, he felt himself a hypocrite. On the other hand, if he sided with those who demanded war in order to preserve the Union, he'd be sacrificing his pragmatism for profit. His very silence thundered in his ears. Nothing! Nothing! He said nothing. Thomas sighed again and then laughed at his own melancholy. He retired early. Sleep had become his last vestige of relief and he sought it with increasing regularity as a way to escape despair.

chapter 57

BY LATE MARCH, nature had thrust out tender leaves in the forest while flinging wildflowers among trees and around creek beds. Reagan's horse devoured a patch of new grass as he and Danny inspected rollways lining riverbanks. Recent rains brought the river to the right pitch and before long Reagan would give orders for key logs to be pulled. Then, with a deafening roar, logs would spill into water while riverhogs, having switched from shoepacs to corked boots, would stand with pike poles and peaveys at the ready.

"This year, you'll be in charge of booming the logs," Reagan said. He had once again allowed his beard to grow, and looked more the lumberman than ever.

"Sure, boss," he replied.

"How're the wanigans coming along?"

"All three will be done before week's end." With their raised decks and crude shacks, the wanigan was kitchen, dining room and sometimes sleeping quarters for the men. Chained together, they floated behind the boom while the drive was on.

"Good. I'll inform the boys that you're running the river drive since I'm taking Amanda home."

Danny nodded. He knew a wanigan was no place for a woman among female-starved riverhogs. Many changes had occurred since Amanda's flight into the forest. No longer were the stables left unattended during work hours. Reagan once again dined in the cook's shanty and most surprising of all, he had taken up residence in one of the bunkhouses.

As they headed back to camp, Reagan's thoughts drifted over the last few weeks. After Amanda banished him from her bed, he had angrily withdrawn himself entirely. Now it was Theodore who saw that her water barrel was kept full and a fire burned in the stove. Reagan had foolishly believed that by removing himself he could dismiss her from his mind. But instead, his self-imposed exile only served to punish him. He tossed nightly on his bed despite it being no softer than the one Amanda inhabited. Just knowing she lay alone in his cabin caused him to display a surly temper and foul mood.

When the two reached camp, Reagan turned his horse towards the cabin and knocked briefly before stepping inside. Startled, Amanda clutched a washcloth over her bosom, sopping her chemise. Her surprise turned to displeasure when she saw it was Reagan. For many days she had dwelt on his pitiful explanation of his foul deed. Yet, with no way to vent her feelings, her outrage had continued to simmer.

"Now look what you've done," she said, reaching for a towel. "I'm all wet!"

The view of her breasts, visible through the wet material, caused him to have a sudden and fervent burst of desire. She was unaware of his heated gaze as she wiped droplets from her legs. When she bent lower, the edge of her shortened chemise rose, nearly exposing her bottom. Reagan felt as if a knife suddenly twisted his insides. Stirred to take her in his arms, he stepped forward, hoping her anger had cooled enough to approach her in a husbandly way.

"I came to tell you when we'd be leaving," he said in a suddenly thick voice.

"Don't come near me," she said, wrapping the towel about her. "Stay right there."

His gaze raked her form. "So, this is how you want it to be? Always pricking with your thorny barbs?"

"Yes!"

In truth, Amanda ached to hear him speak words of contrition or at the very least, ask for her forgiveness. It wasn't her nature to treat others with malice. But Reagan remained silent, and so she steeled her heart.

Under his watchful regard, she threw off her towel and put on her pants, stuffing her chemise inside. Donning a shirt, her fingers then flew over buttons.

"Perhaps you should also put on your boots," Reagan snorted. "So it'd be more difficult to remove those little-boy britches."

Amanda ignored his comments as she picked up her brush. "When will we be leaving?" she asked, facing the mirror.

Reagan finally clamped down his amorous thoughts and straddled the nearest chair. "In a day or two, once I'm satisfied everything's ready."

Watching Amanda, he was reminded how much he missed her companionship. He felt with time her ire would soften, for despite her frosty manner Reagan didn't believe her a shrew. Indeed, until she discovered his secret, she had displayed a sweetness of spirit that soothed like a balm. Being deprived of it had brought him no small amount of discontent.

"Will I..." she said as she stopped brushing, "...be going back to your house...?" Amanda held her breath. With so many unanswered questions, she didn't know if Reagan felt compelled to allow her to live with him. The few situations she'd heard of came to mind, of a marriage grown cold and a husband and wife occupying different homes.

"Of course," Reagan said, frowning. "Where else would you go? Until we make a home for ourselves, we'll stay with my parents. Where, in fact, you should've stayed in the first place."

"Where I would've been a good little wife, never knowing how you defrauded my parents?" she needled. "Where your lies would've continued until you had no more use for me?" She clutched the brush tightly. "Where would I have gone after that?"

Reagan stared at Amanda, his lips tightening in anger. "You think I would discard you? Perhaps I'd also throw our children into the streets no better than orphans. Suddenly, I'm a fiendish ogre that destroyed your otherwise fairy-tale life. An existence so promising that had we not wed, you'd have every male still vying for your hand." Reagan rose and advanced until he towered over Amanda. "I can tell you madam, after what happened, *no one* was asking for your hand in marriage."

Amanda turned with blazing eyes. "How dare you! Do you think I preferred a loveless marriage to the possibility of finding happiness elsewhere? Don't think yourself so noble, sir, that you did me any favors! We are wed, simply and true, because I knew no other way to protect Aunt Ella from being arrested and charged with breaking the law by that snake, Jebediah. Under those circumstances, I accepted your proposal, as my parents advised me. But had they waited just a short time longer, they would've discovered that not everyone believed the rumors. I could've married another."

"You'd have married another after we were caught together? I'm afraid that would've caused another scandal all by itself." Reagan crossed his arms and lifted a brow. "Your Mister Banning, if that's who you're alluding to, was seeking the same prize as I. In actuality, I believe the man was after more than the purse strings to your dowry. He seemed intent on burrowing into your father's firm like a tick on a mongrel. I say the man was up to no good, and you are well rid of him."

"And you're so pure, you can judge another? You sir, have the audacity to tell me one kind of blackguard is better than another? I think not!" She faced the mirror and vigorously stroked her hair. "If I live a hundred years, I'll never know a man more calculating or dishonorable!"

Reagan released a pent-up sigh. "I'll not argue the depth of my worth since you judge it so poorly. However, I've no wish to burden others with our problems and as a matter of respect, we should keep this to ourselves."

Putting on his hat, he headed for the door. "Whatever you're taking home should be packed by tomorrow morning. If you have need of anything, I'll send Theo over."

Giving Amanda a few moments to air any requests and receiving none, Reagan shut the door behind him.

chapter 58

REAGAN PLANNED FOR the trip home, beginning with having Amanda's horse exercised for a week prior to their leaving. He mapped a route suitable for staying in a hotel each night and packed minimal food and clothing. Once they reached Jamestown, he would see if the stagecoaches were running. If so, they would take the stagecoach the rest of the way home.

The sun was just beginning to lighten the sky when Amanda emerged from the cabin with her tightly packed saddlebag. Though Reagan had saddled her horse, she checked the cinch before mounting. She had plaited her hair in a single braid and looked very much like the lad Reagan thought her to be when she first entered camp.

After a few hours of travel, the sun warmed enough for Amanda to remove her coat. If she had gotten herself with child, it wasn't apparent to Reagan's probing eyes as she tied her coat to the back of her saddle. If anything, he thought, Amanda looked more slender than the day of her ball.

They reached the Stockton hotel shortly before sunset. Reagan carried their saddlebags into the lobby, placing them on the counter. "I'd like these to be taken to our room," he informed the clerk while signing the ledger. "I also want a hot bath drawn for the lady."

"Will you be dining with us tonight?" the clerk asked. "They're serving a fine pot roast with potatoes and gravy. There's also mincemeat pie that should be cooling by the time dinner is served."

"Not at the moment," Reagan said as he pocketed the key handed him. "We've other things to take care of."

"Why not?" Amanda said. "We've been riding all day. I-I'm..." she looked sheepishly at the clerk, "... ready to eat," she finished lamely. Amanda had forgotten she'd earlier unbuttoned her collar and the clerk's gaze now fell to that opening. He drew up his frame to its uppermost height, hoping to impress her.

"I beg your pardon, sir, but the young lady seems to be in some distress. Surely your business could wait until after you've dined?" He eyed Amanda brazenly, as it crossed his mind the girl would be so thankful, she might agree to a rendezvous behind the barn.

"That lady you are staring at is my *wife*!" Reagan's lips curled as he recognized hunger in the clerk's eyes. "If you don't take your eyes off her, you'll find that bony head of yours ground into the carpet!"

Choking, the clerk's eyes widened and his Adam's apple bobbed. Judging by their clothes, he had taken them to be poor relatives traveling together.

"Now, are you going to get that bath ready, or not?"

"Y-yes sir!" he stammered, scooping up the saddlebags and hurrying toward the stairs.

Grasping Amanda's arm, Reagan headed toward the door. "Come on," he growled.

"Where are we going?"

"To get you some decent clothes!"

An hour later, the proprietor of Clancy's Dry Good's handed several packages into Reagan's hands before locking up for the night. He couldn't wait to get home and tell his wife about the plainly dressed man who had purchased a man's suit as well as the most expensive woman's riding outfit he carried. Not only the outfit, but also fine leather boots and several accoutrements necessary for a lady. He cackled to think how he had convinced the man that two hats, not one, would be advantageous for a traveling woman. If by chance her hat became ruined in a sudden rain, she wouldn't be forced to wear the spoiled headgear.

Amanda hadn't expected generosity from Reagan and found it difficult to remain aloof when he provided for her needs so well. Though she felt he had played her false, her thoughts remained conflicted as they approached the boardwalk near the hotel. Eagerly, she crossed the threshold as the smell of food assailed her nostrils. Because he stood there with all those packages and because she couldn't keep silent forever, Amanda spoke up. "If it's acceptable, I'd very much like to eat."

Reagan looked at Amanda's clothing, recalling the clerk's impertinence. "I wish you would've used Clancy's changing rooms like I suggested. Those boy clothes need to be thrown out."

"I told you," Amanda said firmly. "I need to bathe first."

"I'll have our meal sent to our room so you won't have to wait," he said, turning toward the lobby. The clerk from before was nowhere to be seen, so Reagan spoke to the woman behind the counter.

"Of course, Mr. Burnsfield, I'll have a tray sent up with a full selection from our menu. And madam," she said to Amanda, "your bath's waiting. I took the liberty of putting your bags in the suite reserved for our special guests."

"I don't believe I reserved a suite," Reagan said. "We simply had a room."

"That's true," the woman said. "But, I have to make atonement for my *former* employee's boorish behavior. I was in the kitchen when I heard angry voices. By the time I walked through the dining room, I heard the last of your conversation and witnessed your departure. I can assure you, we may be a small establishment, but we don't treat our guests that way."

Reagan smiled. "In that case, we'd be delighted to take your offer."

"If you'd give me the key you now have, I'll exchange it for the new one," she said, laying down a key. "I'm sure you'll find it to your liking."

Reagan and Amanda followed the owner up two flights of stairs and down the hall. The matron opened the door and stepped inside. "The suite has two bedchambers, with a bathing room in between," she said opening a side door. "Here, we have a bath prepared as well as items for the gentleman."

Steam rose from a porcelain tub flanked by a commode holding a washbasin, shaving mug, razor and strop. A full-length mirror filled the space in the opposite corner while a dresser with the first drawer pulled open, showed towels and washcloths. On top was a basket filled with perfumed soaps, awaiting use.

Bustling through the narrow space between the tub and washstand, the owner opened the far door. "This room is usually used for guests who have children. It's every bit as spacious as the other, but 'twill be up to you whether or not you have use for it," she said, smiling. "Your meal will be up shortly. If you have need of anything, please don't hesitate to ring." She reentered the first bedroom and indicated a cord hanging near the bed. "That's attached to a bell in the kitchen. When you pull the cord, a maid will answer your call."

"Thank you," Reagan said. "You've been very kind. If we travel this way again, we'll be sure to reserve this suite."

The proprietress's eyes twinkled. "Perhaps, you'd also like to recommend our establishment to others, Mr. Burnsfield." It hadn't escaped her notice that the name written in her ledger happened to be the same person who had purchased a large tract of land along the Cattaraugus River. Having gained sole proprietorship since the death of Mr. Bonham, Kate Bonham had a nose for information that pertained to her business.

"Indeed, I will," he vowed. After escorting her to the door, Reagan placed their packages on the bed.

The lure of a bath proved too much a temptation and Amanda removed her boots. After finding a small dish of hairpins, she forgot about shutting the bath chamber door as she pinned her hair. She then removed her clothes with all the haste of one in need of a hot soak.

Reagan found it impossible to ignore Amanda as he hung new clothes in the wardrobe. He took a great deal of time placing them on hangers, for it afforded him a clear view of his wife's naked back as she sank into the tub.

Wanting a better view, he entered the bath chamber and pretending to ignore her, splashed water in the mug before applying the brush to his face.

"Must you do that *now?*" she asked.

"My dear, I need cleanliness as much as you," he said, meeting her gaze in the mirror. "Though I too, long for a hot bath, I'm content to wait until after you've finished."

"Then at least turn so you can't watch," she compromised.

Seeming not to care, Reagan turned til his view of her was blocked. When Amanda could no longer see his reflection, she assumed he couldn't view her while she bathed. She didn't realize that he had turned just enough so that he could now see her in the full-length mirror.

Unaware of his hungry gaze, she reached for a washcloth from the dresser, pressing her breast against the tub until it nearly spilled over the rim. The alluring sight caused Reagan's hand to suddenly tremble and he accidentally nicked himself with the razor. Suppressing a curse, he dragged his eyes from her to survey the damage while she tore open a soap wrapper. Inhaling its scent, Amanda wasted little time lathering the cloth, washing her face and neck until bubbles dripped from her arms. Bending to rinse, she didn't see him wipe blood from his razor and when she daubed her eyes with a towel, he appeared to be concentrating on shaving. She barely noted his presence as Reagan's hand made a steady journey from jaw to washbowl and she remained blissfully unaware she was being watched as she sudsed her leg while extending it above the tub. The lamplight cast her skin in a dewy glow when she got on her knees, soaping her belly as well as other areas concealed by water. With his eyes constantly viewing her nakedness, Reagan suffered additional cuts with the razor, and if Amanda had been listening, she would've heard his muted grunts.

A few tendrils escaped their pins and as she lifted her arms to fix her hair, her breasts played an enticing game of peek-a-boo with the suds. Reagan's mind filled with other, erotic images of their sharing a bath when a knock at the door interrupted his reverie. Splashing water on his face, he viewed his wounds before exiting the bathroom and shutting the door.

He crossed the bedchamber and opened the door to the hallway. A young woman wearing a cap and apron held a tray. "Evening, sir," she said. As Reagan stepped back, she entered and set the tray on a table near the window, pulling a wine bottle from her pocket. "Compliments from Mrs. Bonham," she said, arranging two place settings.

After she left, Reagan returned to the bathing chamber to see Amanda wrapping herself in a towel. She stared at his many, small mutilations. "Good heavens, what did you do?"

"The blade was dull!" he said as he began to disrobe.

Dismissing his surly tone, Amanda went into the bedroom. She heard him splashing in the tub while she donned a new nightgown. Then finding her comb, she returned to the bath chamber and stood where Reagan had earlier shaved. She turned her back and after removing her hairpins, began combing her hair. It wasn't until she heard the sound of Reagan hoisting himself from the water that she saw his reflection in the full-length mirror. To her horror, she saw every inch of him as he reached for a towel and her lowered gaze found the reason for his sour mood. After draping the towel about his middle, Reagan looked to see Amanda gaping. He grinned, knowing she had discovered his secret voyeurism.

"You jackanapes! You were spying on me the whole time!" she said, as he stepped from the tub. "I asked for a little privacy and you deliberately ogled me while I bathed unawares."

He shrugged as he pulled the towel from his waist and dried himself. "I never promised not to look at you, *wife*, just as I haven't forbid you to look at me." He gave her a lecherous look while running the towel over his chest as if daring her to gaze at his exposed member.

"You—you should have sliced your throat," she sputtered before storming from the room. As she left, she didn't know that the bedroom lamp revealed her shapely form through her nightgown or why Reagan suddenly laughed.

Amanda sat at the table and lifted the lid of the chafing dish as mingling aromas wafted toward her nose. She was nigh starving, and didn't care if Reagan was ready to join her or not. She filled her plate, determined to show that nothing had changed between them. He was still a cad and her silence would attest to her loathing of him.

Reagan had donned clean trousers and nothing else before joining his wife at the table. As he filled his plate, Amanda tried to ignore his presence and though she hated herself for it, she had to admit her husband had a near flawless physique. His arms and shoulders had become even more sculpted these past weeks, though his belly remained taut. Despite her intentions, she found herself drawn by his magnetism and kept averting her eyes to look at anything but his wide, bare chest.

"Wine?" Reagan forced her attention as he held the bottle over her empty glass. Amanda would've preferred water, but as none seemed available, she nodded, thinking a few sips wouldn't unduly affect her.

After eating his fill, Reagan continued to drink and twice refilled his glass while waiting for Amanda to finish. He had always appreciated that she wasn't a woman who gabbed incessantly, yet this constant cold shoulder was wearing on his temper. "How'd you fare on your first day in the saddle?" he ventured as he refilled her glass.

"Fine," she said, taking a sip.

Reagan found it difficult to keep from devouring her form beneath the thin batiste and forced his gaze upward. "Sore anywhere?"

"A little, maybe," Amanda said politely. "It's been awhile since I've ridden."

"If there's anything I can do to help," he let the offer hang a moment, one eyebrow raised hopefully. "A massage would do wonders for your aching muscles."

Amanda gazed at him warily as she daubed her lips. "No, thank you," she said, pushing back her plate. "I prefer to remain sore rather than suffer your hands upon my person."

Reagan grew incensed that she thwarted his every attempt to regain her good graces. He had never encountered a woman he couldn't charm, and struggled to believe his overtures could be so easily dismissed. Scowling, he emptied his wineglass before setting the tray with the remains of supper in the hall.

Keeping the bottle of wine, Reagan closed the door. Perhaps he could yet persuade Amanda to share his bed. How long, after all, could she keep up this portrayal of aggrieved wife?

As he returned to his chair, Reagan winced, moving his shoulder as if it suddenly pained him. "I seem to have developed a knot," he said, responding to her questioning eyes.

Amanda watched in quiet amusement as Reagan stretched and then rotated his arm. It served him right, she thought. After everything he'd put her through, he deserved a cramp or two. He struggled for some moments, appearing to be woefully inept at easing the pain before he spoke. "Madam, I appear to be in some distress. If you'd be most kind, I'd appreciate your help."

If not for his recent purchases, Amanda would've had no qualms refusing. However, the favor seemed small considering that at this moment she was wearing a fine muslin gown. She moved behind his chair and placed her fingers on his shoulder. At first, she applied light pressure, kneading the area much like dough from Hattie's bread recipe.

"Right there," he breathed. It'd been weeks since he felt her touch, and he basked in having her hands on his skin.

When Amanda drew closer, her hair accidentally brushed against his back, eliciting a sudden rise in gooseflesh. She hurried to finish, lest she awaken more than a shiver. "There," she chirped as she gave a final rub, "that should do it." Suddenly, she found herself pinned against his chair as a hand reached around to firmly grasp a buttock. Shocked at the unexpected assault and the pleasurable response it elicited, she yanked his hand from her. "I see you keep showing your churlish proclivities," she snarled, stepping away.

Reagan rose from his chair, his face darkening with both anger and unappeased passion. He had hoped to seduce his wife and end their estrangement, but at every turn she reasserted the barrier between them. He had only been able to endure the past weeks by working to exhaustion. But seeing her in various states of undress, forced him to deal with his whetted appetite moment by moment. "Keep your claws sheathed, madam!" he growled, amazed that even now, with his own fury ignited, he still wanted her. "I shan't breach your chastity tonight!" Reagan grabbed the wine bottle and stomped through the bath chamber to the other room.

For some reason, the slamming of his door caused Amanda to feel let down. Despite the certainty of her convictions, a small part of her protested the banishment of her husband.

Amanda placed a trembling hand on her forehead. *What was wrong with her?* Wasn't she the aggrieved party, the one Reagan practiced his deception on? Why should she feel guilt now that the truth had been revealed? The wine was affecting her judgment, she reasoned. Things would look clearer in the morning.

Turning down the oil lamp, she drew back the covers and climbed into bed. It seemed to take forever before sleep stole over her, and the last things she recalled were muted sounds of Reagan pacing the floor, not unlike that of a tormented animal.

chapter 59

TRAPPED IN THE tentacles of sleep, a small, persistent noise disturbed Amanda. A clawing, creaking sound permeated her dreams, filling her with unease. When a nearly noiseless shuffling crossed the floor, she opened her eyes to see moonlight stretched between her bed and bathing chamber. Yet, the door as well as the wardrobe remained hidden in shadows. Just when she believed she had dreamt the mysterious noise, she heard a muted footfall. Sudden terror congealed in her throat as she realized someone had entered the room and was even now, rifling through the wardrobe.

A thief! Should she call out and hope to scare away the burglar? Or should she flee? A muffled thump revealed the intruder had found a saddlebag and would now have his back to the room.

After a moment's hesitation, she flung back her quilt and vaulted from the bed, sprinting toward the bath chamber. As she passed the table, she grabbed a chair, flinging it behind her. Amanda heard swift footfalls before a muffled crash indicated the intruder had tripped. Still, he managed to grasp the back of her nightgown, halting her flight.

Terrified, Amanda swung her arm trying to knock away his hand and when that didn't work, she turned and kicked him. He grunted, yet tenaciously held on while twisting her captured foot. She fell, landing on her stomach with enough force to knock her breath away and lay gasping as the prowler twined his fingers in her gown, pulling her toward him. Squirming onto her back, she struck him with her fists, but he finally gained a stronger hold and subdued her hands with one of his. As she sucked air into her lungs, the apparition clamped his fingers over her mouth.

"Shut up!" he hissed. Rising to his feet, he pulled her with him. "No one can hear you!" Amanda's mind raced. He believed her alone. Either, he didn't realize there was an adjoining room, or he didn't know it was occupied. As he yanked her toward the bed, she struggled to free her mouth.

Suddenly, she remembered a similar situation and using both hands, pressed the man's palm into her mouth and bit with all her might. Despite his obvious pain, the robber held on, cuffing her face. "Do that again, you little witch," he snarled, squeezing her harder, "and I'll knock ye senseless!"

In desperation, Amanda reached back and clawed at him with her nails. Forced to shield his eyes, the attacker loosened his hold and Amanda wriggled free, running into the bath chamber and sidestepping where she knew the tub to be. Just as she reached Reagan's bedroom, he wrenched open the door. She rushed inside as the thief stumbled and tripped headfirst into the tub, causing a large splash.

"What the hell—?" Reagan's lamp shone dimly through the doorway, revealing a pair of legs protruding from the tub. Reaching in, he hauled the unconscious man from the bath water and dropped him onto the floor. "Who's this?"

"I think he was robbing us," she said, returning. "I tried to run but he caught me."

Reagan lifted her chin and viewed her swollen lip. "The bastard *struck* you?"

"I didn't feel it," she said, surprised at his concern. "It happened so fast, I was more shocked than anything."

"Bring over my lamp and we'll see who we've got." When she returned, he reached down and turned the man over. Several scratches marked his face. "Good Lord, woman, did you do that?"

"I-I was trying to get away," she said while Reagan held the lamp to the man's face.

"Why, it looks like our friend, the clerk."

"The clerk? Why would he rob us?"

"I don't know. You stay here," he ordered, setting the lamp down. "I'll take him into the other room and summon help."

Amanda felt immensely relieved when Reagan dragged the unconscious man into the next room. She heard him strike a match and surmised he'd pulled the cord, because it wasn't long before there was a knock at the door. She hurried to her room. "Wait! I need to put something on," she said. Walking around the crumpled man, Amanda took one of Reagan's shirts from the wardrobe and put it over her gown. "I'm ready now."

A maid stood outside the door holding a candle. "You rang, sir?"

"We have an uninvited guest," Reagan said. Widening the door, he revealed the man sprawled on the floor. "Kindly inform your mistress as well as the sheriff."

The girls' eyes widened when she saw the clerk, bereft of his senses. "Right away, sir! I'll get Mrs. Bonham immediately!" Lifting the hem of her skirt, the girl hurried down the hall as Reagan shut the door.

When the clerk began to stir, Reagan took a glass from the table and went into the bath chamber. "Let's see if we can get some answers," he said returning with tub water and dumping it on the man's face.

Sputtering, the man winced as he touched his bruised forehead before opening his eyes. He looked shocked when he recognized Amanda standing beside Reagan. "W-what happened?" he mumbled, staring at the blood on his fingers.

"You were in the process of robbing us," Reagan said, pulling the man to his feet. He kicked the overturned chair upright before shoving the clerk into it. "The law's on its way, so you better speak up. What do you have to say for yourself?"

Before the man could answer, there was a loud knock; then the door burst open and Mrs. Bonham rushed inside, followed by the scullery maid. It was apparent by her twisted belt and crooked nightcap that she'd hastily donned her wrapper. Spying the recently fired clerk, Mrs. Bonham's eyes turned stormy.

"What's the meaning of this?" she demanded and when the clerk's expression remained belligerent, she seemed further angered. "Tell me, I say! How did you manage to enter these rooms?"

"It was easy, you stupid bitch! For months I've outsmarted you." He paused, touching where his face had been raked before he glared at Amanda. "If not for her, you'd have been none the wiser!"

Mrs. Bonham took a step closer. "Are you going to answer me, or should I let the sheriff get the information? Tell me how you entered these rooms without a key!"

"Why, I stole the keys and had copies made. You never noticed when they were missing," he smirked, looking at his fingers as if they were instruments of skill. "Any time I saw a suite had been let, I knew the occupants were wealthy, and therefore worth pilfering any trinkets left about. By their lack of alarm, they never missed the baubles anyway." His face grew contemptuous as he glared at Reagan now bereft of his beard. "So! You're a man of means, after all. The rich! They make their money off the backs of working folk." His chin rose as he pressed a palm against his wound. "It's only fair we take back a little of what's rightfully ours."

"It's usually the lazy who find themselves wanting," Reagan said. "Those who work hard are capable of improving their lot."

"Oh, and you don't love money, either," the clerk spat.

"I don't steal from others to get it," he said, missing Amanda's sudden look.

The clerk snorted, but lowered his gaze under Reagan's stare. At that moment a man barged into the room, a pair of pistols strapped to his hips. "Sheriff Ritter," Mrs. Bonham said. "I'm so relieved you're here." She pointed to her former employee, "It seems we have a burglar in our midst. If you'd be so kind as to search his pockets, I'd like to make a formal complaint."

chapter 60

PRESIDENT LINCOLN HAD barely begun his term when he was informed of the desperate situation at Fort Sumter. The small garrison had been denied provisions and correspondence by South Carolina ever since the breakup of the former President's cabinet. Taking advantage of the situation, authorities of the rebel state planted batteries on James Island, Morris Island and Cummings Point. In every spot where guns could be brought to bear, earthworks were erected. Built on an island at the mouth of Charleston Harbor, the fort hadn't been designed to withstand bombardment from fortifications it was meant to work alongside. With guns pointed from all directions, Major Anderson and his men became isolated from the rest of the country.

President Lincoln insisted that these men could not be left to starve. He notified the governor of South Carolina that provisions would be sent to the garrison, peaceably, if possible, if necessary, by force.

When three vessels of war, three transports and three steamers sailed from New York and Norfolk, the commander of the Confederate forces demanded Major Anderson surrender and evacuate the fort. General Beauregard knew that Anderson was ignorant of the coming aid, and hoped the garrison's state of semi-starvation would force the surrender.

He was wrong.

❧

The shocking news that Fort Sumter had been fired upon, reached Cantonsville the same day Reagan and Amanda arrived by stagecoach. Amanda couldn't help but stare at throngs of people clogging the boardwalks. Excited citizens maneuvered around the stagecoach while men with knapsacks and muskets gathered at the post office. At Reagan's query to a passerby, he was informed that volunteers for the Union Army were assembling. It seemed much had occurred during their absence.

Despite the press of people, Reagan was able to procure a rented buggy and after securing their luggage, headed home.

A chorus rose throughout the household as soon as they turned in the drive and by the time they reached the stoop, the family stood waiting to greet them. Thomas shook Reagan's hand and Katherine hugged Amanda while Amy plied both with questions.

Watching Amanda closely, Thomas noted that something about her bespoke painful awareness and with sudden insight, perceived that she knew. It was the way she held herself and avoided his eyes that told him his fears had come to pass.

"It's started, hasn't it?" Reagan said, interrupting Thomas's thoughts.

"The news came this morning. The South has struck," he said, keeping his voice low. "I've closed the mills for today." As the women whisked Amanda into the parlor for refreshments, the men retreated into the study.

chapter 61

GREEN EYES GLINTED beneath the brim of a hat that looked to have seen grander times. With his work closed for one day, the bewhiskered man loitered near the saloon, scrutinizing passersby. By mid-morning, he was beginning to lose interest until his eye caught a bold flash of color. A harlot, wearing a low cut red frock, sashayed toward him along the boardwalk. Her equally red parasol was held at a jaunty angle to keep the sun from darkening the freckles that smattered her nose. Men whistled as she walked past, but she only grinned and kept up her promenade until reaching the saloon. She then looked back over her shoulder.

"Well boys, she said, placing a hand on an outthrust hip. "Since the mills are closed, the saloon's decided if you join the ladies inside, the first drink's on the house!"

Her words were greeted with whoops and hollers as men jostled each other to be first inside. The woman stood close enough for the green-eyed man to notice the scent of her cheap perfume. As he leaned against a post, his eyes roamed her body, lingering where her breasts seemed ready to spill from her bodice. It had been a long time since he'd allowed himself hard liquor and a strumpet. Ever wary of divulging secrets when strong drink clouded his mind, he felt the sudden need to relieve his cravings. When the harlot tried entering the saloon, he reached out and grabbed her arm.

"Hold off, Mister," she snapped, eying his clothes. "There're plenty of girls inside that'll satisfy yer needs. I only socialize with gentleman callers."

"Your name's Molly, isn't it?"

"How d'ya know me?" she asked. "We haven't met."

The man reached down to finger a velvet necklace around her throat. "I gave this to you, before Christmas, when you were newly employed." He smiled, allowing his fingers to brush her skin while tucking the pendant into her bodice. "Don't you remember?"

"Orville?" Molly's eyes widened as she tried connecting the crudely garbed man with the dapper gentleman she knew as Orville Farnsworth. "Is—is that you?"

After the rough treatment from the bounty hunters, Molly had been swept off her feet by a handsome stranger who introduced himself as Orville Farnsworth. Though well bred and attentive, once in the privacy of her room, the aristocrat proved to be just as rough as the others. Molly had learned to tolerate the discomfort with benumbing effects of cheap wine. "Where've you been? I-I thought you had left town," she stammered.

"I've been busy." Derrick Banning transformed into Orville Farnsworth released his grip and guided Molly into the saloon. "I'm going to be around for awhile, but I don't wish to be recognized. That's why I look this way," he said, indicating his clothes.

"Are you a spy?" Molly whispered as they took a seat in a corner.

"Yes," Derrick murmured. "I'm an informant for the government. Nobody must know I'm in town."

chapter 62

ELIZABETH HAMPTON HAD spent many weeks planning her strategy by the time Reagan returned from camp. Recalling his words about his interest with anyone involved with the lumber trade, she formed an idea. She suggested to her father that his influence would spread if he formed an alliance between Ohio and the war effort. She devised a scheme that included inviting her father's cousin, Bertram Hayes, who worked for the Secretary of War, for a visit. If Bertram could turn the eyes of the government to industries in Cantonsville, her father, being the mayor, would gain an incredible boost of power.

Her influence would increase as well, she thought. Reagan would surely be grateful once he realized how beneficial her intercession could be. Elizabeth spent many hours fantasizing how she, not Amanda, should've been Reagan's wife. After all, she was the one who knew how to make connections in circles of power. Hadn't Reagan, on the day of his wedding hinted that he could further his business contacts with her help?

Elizabeth penned her invitation with a brief description of its purpose, then scrolled Reagan's name and address on the envelope. Pinning on her hat, she looked in the mirror and smoothed her collar. "I'm off to post a letter, Daddy!" she called. "I'll be back in a little while." Before he could answer, she was out the door.

chapter 63

Reagan awakened to the sound of someone calling his name. Squinting through the morning light, he could just make out his mother standing in the doorway.

"Reagan, is that you?" Clearly confused why her son slept in the guest room, Katherine stepped inside. She noticed that his shirt appeared to be the same one he had worn the day before. Also, his vest and jacket were thrown over a chair. "Were you ill last night?" she asked.

Reagan swung his legs over the mattress. "No. I went to the mill last night. It was late when I returned. I sometimes sleep here so Amanda's not disturbed by my late hours."

Katherine sat in a wing chair and folded her hands. She wasn't oblivious to the changes in her son's behavior. "Is-is there something amiss, Reagan?" she asked.

"No, Ma," Reagan cut in, running a hand through his hair. "I'll wash and shave, then be down for some coffee." He peeled off his shirt then turned to the washstand.

Katherine looked at her son, recalling when a much younger Reagan had begged to shave like his father. Thomas had laughed as he allowed the boy to cover his cheeks with soapsuds before handing him a dull butter knife. She remembered how Reagan's back had been boyishly narrow. Now, a strongly muscled man stood before her performing the routine matter of shaving. She felt apprehension because he seemed nonchalant about the developing estrangement between himself and Amanda. She had long ago ceased to be a confidant when it came to her son's private life and it pained her to see his troubles increasing.

"I just came upstairs to tell you breakfast is almost ready." Katherine rose, forcing a cheerful tone. "And don't bother with straightening up," she said indicating the disheveled bed. "I'll send Sarah to tidy the room later."

chapter 64

THOMAS BURNSFIELD PAID little attention to the whine of circular saws as he sat in his office and finished his daily report. He glanced at his watch, noting it was almost quitting time when Reagan entered and handed him a neatly written roster. "Here's the list of new hires," he said. "The accountant will need to add them to the payroll by Saturday."

Thomas ignored the paper. "Your mother's informed me you're using one of the guest rooms. Is there something awry between you and Amanda?" He braced himself, already sure of the answer.

Reagan stood by the window, avoiding his father's eyes. "Oh, a minor inconvenience in the scope of things," he said. "Amanda happened upon a damning bit of paperwork while tidying my desk." He shrugged as he thrust his hands into pockets. "Nothing that I hadn't expected eventually."

Thomas sighed. "I'm sorry to hear that. I'd hoped that misfortune could somehow be avoided."

"Contrary to what you think, father, I still don't consider my marriage a failure. It's allowed us to expand our business," he said, pointing to the list of new employees. "These men have jobs, their children will be fed, and their wives can purchase a new bonnet by month's end. Merchants will sell more wares and banks will loan the additional revenues to new clients. Over all, I'd say it was a very good deal."

"I wasn't thinking of the profits," Thomas replied with a frown, "but of the losses..."

"Look, father, I can't go back and undo what I've done," Reagan said. "Besides, I'd do it all over again. Somebody was going to marry Amanda. It may as well be someone who'd know what to do with all that money."

"You could at least try to mend the harm you've caused by behaving like a husband," Thomas reasoned. "There's much a man can do to woo back his wife. For starters, don't cause the servants to gossip with your taking up residence in another bedroom. It won't take long for that kind of thing to get beyond our walls. That's only going to add to Amanda's shame."

"I'm only doing that—"

"I heard that cockamamie tale you told your mother!" Thomas said, growing impatient. "Despite what Amanda knows, you need to be a man and try to make amends. For God's sake, Reagan, she's going to be the mother of your children someday. You cannot treat her like a pariah! I won't have it!"

Reagan's brow darkened as his father's words struck a nerve. He knew only too well that his bedroom had become a torture chamber of his own making. If he couldn't absent himself from Amanda's presence, he'd grow mad with lust for her. "I have my reasons," he said, crossing his arms.

"Then Reagan, at least make sure you're home at a decent hour. It's becoming painful to see Amanda sitting beside an empty chair every night at dinner."

Having grown surlier by the moment, Reagan turned away from his father and reached for the door.

"Where are you going?" Thomas asked. "I'm not finished yet."

"I'm going to get a suite at the Rochester Hotel," he growled over his shoulder. "Where I'll stay until my parents quit meddling in my affairs."

Reagan paused outside of Thomas's office and pulled an envelope from his pocket. He had intended to give Thomas the invitation from Mayor Hampton to have dinner with the mayor's cousin, Bertram Hayes. But when the conversation had taken an unexpected turn, Reagan had quickly forgotten about the invitation. Still furious at his parents' prying, he decided he could handle dinner on his own.

A bearded mill worker watched with interest as Reagan paused outside Thomas's office. Flexing hands sore from unaccustomed work, the man continued to watch until Reagan left the mill. Though he detested the sawdust and unrelenting shriek of saws, the man mostly detested Reagan.

Vowing revenge upon the one who had thwarted his plans, Derrick had plotted his next course of action. He'd had no trouble getting a job at the old lumber mill. Once he became familiar with the place, he returned one night to break into Thomas's office to steal anything of value. He broke open the safe where he found contracts from the United States Government as well as letters from suppliers demanding payment for past due receipts.

The dates of the contracts intrigued Derrick, because they were signed just before construction of the new mill. That was about the time Reagan had begun courting Amanda.

That wily bastard! he thought. *He's doing business with money that should've been mine.* Derrick felt murderous rage that he didn't realize Reagan's plan sooner. He could've warned George. Well, he might have been bested, but he wouldn't stay defeated. Derrick took a few contracts and placed them in his pocket before returning to his hotel. At first, he thought to present his evidence to George, but that wouldn't be enough to financially ruin the lumberman.

He decided to wait for the opportune moment to pay Reagan a visit. It would be the first of many visits that would prove profitable enough for him to return to a grander lifestyle. Then, when he tired of the game, he'd still turn over to George the evidence of Reagan's treachery. At the very least, it would ruin his sham of a marriage. Only then, would Derrick feel as if he'd repaid Reagan for his trickery in marrying Amanda.

chapter 65

WITH HER RETURN to Cantonsville, Amanda had been invited to many afternoon teas. What first seemed a respite from her troubles turned sour as conversations invariably centered on her daring journey. She learned to respond to inquiries with a curtness that soon dissuaded their curiosity. Though it didn't keep people from wondering, few dared gossip about the unladylike behavior since as some pointed out, she merely acted like any foolish bride missing her spouse. But darker rumors also circulated. A hint of marital discontent percolated as servants passed the goings-on between Reagan and Amanda to friends and family, who then passed them to others.

Yet, even a marriage gone awry couldn't hold the attention above news splashed across the front pages of daily papers. By early May, every parlor was filled with talk of the Confederate Congress declaring war on the United States. As more states left the Union by issuing letters of marque and reprisal, troops were amassed on both sides and skirmishes broke out.

Amanda found shopping a good way to ignore the headlines and together with Amy, wandered the boardwalks. For hours they enjoyed perusing merchandise as each found things to buy.

One morning as Amy went inside the dry goods store to look for stationary, Amanda stopped at an outdoor table to sift through wares. She didn't notice the man coming near until his hand ensnared her wrist. Amanda turned in indignation, but was abruptly startled as she recognized the emerald eyes.

"Derrick!"

"Good morning, my dear," his gaze swept her form. "Enjoying the fresh air?"

"I thought you'd gone home," Amanda said. "I mean, Papa hadn't mentioned that you were still in town."

"That's quite understandable, seeing as I've not called on your father in some time," he said, rubbing his fingers across his jaw. When he spied Amanda, he had rushed back to his room and hastily shaved. He hoped his razor hadn't resulted in a telltale rash.

"So, how've you been?" Amanda asked politely.

"I've been busy with many projects." He stepped closer, eager to change the subject. "But, pray tell my dear, it doesn't appear as if marital bliss has found a place in your heart. Is something amiss? Perhaps I could be of some assistance."

Amanda dropped her eyes as she turned over a spice box, pretending to inspect its finish. "Tis nothing. Perhaps I've overtaxed my energy this morning."

"You're as beautiful as ever," he crooned near her ear. "But even I know when you're troubled." He lifted her fingers, pressing them to his lips. "You can confide in me, Amanda," he insisted. "Surely, you can speak freely to a friend."

Amanda searched his face. *Could he be aware of her circumstances?* She remembered Derrick's dislike of Reagan even before the horrifying incident with the bounty hunters. She recalled his visit at her wedding and how disturbed he'd been to find the vows already spoken. Though she never considered him a confidante, she fought the urge to unburden herself.

"I fear I was simply ill-prepared for changes in my life," she said, forcing a laugh. "I had notions of an easy transition, but it's taking me a little more time to adjust." Amanda became alarmed at his suddenly fervid look. "Is something wrong?" she asked.

"Fear not, Amanda," he said, reclaiming her hand. "I know what you've suffered and I want to help. There are ways to make Reagan pay for what he's done."

"What've you heard?" she gasped.

"It's not what I've heard, Amanda, but what I know." He turned over her hand, caressing her skin. "I know Reagan married you for his gain," he said, staring into her eyes. "I must see you in private. Meet me next week under the willows, where we first met."

Shaken by Derrick's words, Amanda could only wonder at how he had come by this information. Over his shoulder she saw Amy approaching with several packages in her arms. "I must go," she said, trying to brush past him.

"Promise you'll meet me," he pressed, refusing to release her hand.

"I promise!" she hissed. "Now please, I must go."

Derrick stared after the women, his mind churning with cunning ways he could use the situation to his advantage.

chapter 66

REAGAN WENT ALONE to the dinner Mayor Hampton hosted for his cousin, Bertram Hayes. Still annoyed with his father for needling him about Amanda, he never told Thomas of the meeting. During dinner, Reagan informed Hayes that a quantity of lumber had already been supplied at the Government's request and suggested he was now ready to double his quota. Bertram promised the offer would be forwarded to Simon Cameron, the Secretary of War, and should more lumber be needed, a contract would be forthcoming.

The mayor fairly preened throughout the meal as he poured wine, nodding jovially when Bertram reminded him to keep their talks confidential. His cheeks became flushed as he considered what deals were taking place at his very own table. At the conclusion of the evening, he had insisted that any correspondence be sent to his home to ensure privacy for all parties. Secretly, he didn't want to lose his significance in bringing about the possible arrangement. If the Burnsfield's had to go through him, surely they'd show gratitude in ways he had yet to consider.

It was one week later that Sam sent a message to Reagan inviting him for after-dinner cordials. He had received a letter from Bertram. In his message, the Mayor expressed his intent to share with Reagan the contents of Bertram's letter.

The day of the appointed meeting stretched endlessly for Elizabeth. She had managed to wheedle the information from her father the moment she noticed his excitement while reading the mail. She was especially eager herself, because the rumors of Reagan and Amanda's estrangement hadn't escaped her ears. She had heard it whispered that the couple no longer shared a bedroom and Reagan spent his evenings at the Rochester Hotel. So she secretly went to the hotel and bribed a chambermaid to pilfer a duplicate key.

The key, hidden in her bosom was a reminder of her plan and fortified with that knowledge, she decided that tonight she would offer herself to the lumberman.

Elizabeth studied her reflection in the mirror. She had arranged her hair over one shoulder to direct Reagan's attention to her daringly exposed bosom. The man would have to be a eunuch to overlook such a promising sight. For her final weapon, she opened a bottle of rose scent and liberally sprinkled her skin.

Soon after, she stationed herself at the top of the stairs to await his arrival. She didn't have long to wait. A quick rapping at the door sent shivers of anticipation up her spine and when a servant entered the hallway, Elizabeth began descending the stairs.

"Good evening, Mr. Burnsfield," the maid said. "Please come in. Mr. Hampton is waiting in the study." As Reagan stepped inside he noticed a movement on the stairway and looking up, saw Elizabeth draw near.

"Why, Reagan," she said. "Are you coming to see Papa? If I had known, I could've changed my plans. As you can see, I'm going out." Elizabeth deliberately delayed in wrapping herself in a lacy shawl, allowing a long glimpse of her bosom.

Reagan averted his eyes but not before a rush of arousal stirred his senses. It had been months since he and Amanda had truly been man and wife, and it took no small effort to ignore Elizabeth's charms. "I'm only here for a short time, my dear," he said. "So there's no need to trouble yourself." He smiled politely, offering his arm. "Although, it'd be an honor if you'd escort me as far as the study."

"Why, of course I'll escort you," she said before glancing at the maid. "You're excused Tilly. I'll make sure Mr. Burnsfield gets safely to Papa." She took small, slow steps as she headed down the hall. "Now tell me, what are you two up to? First, you have dinner with cousin Bertram, and now you're back no doubt to discuss business with my father." She tilted her head sideways. "Seems to me, you've realized much can be gained through Papa and his contacts."

"I'm always grateful for those who are on the same side of business as I," Reagan said, patting her hand.

"Would it surprise you to know that *I* was the one who suggested we bring cousin Bertram to meet you?"

"You? Why, my dear, I had no idea you could be so clever! I'm at a loss as what to say."

Elizabeth basked in his attention and gave his arm a gentle squeeze. "There are many things about me you've yet to learn," she purred. "Someday, if it pleases me, I'll reveal them to you."

She left Reagan wondering at her words as she stopped at the study. "Here we are," she said, rapping on the door. "Let's see if Papa's here." She gave him a saucy look. "If not, dare I wait with you until he returns?"

Before he could answer, the mayor opened the door. "Reagan, my boy, do come in. Elizabeth," Sam appeared surprised. "I thought you were going out this evening."

"I am, Papa," she said, stepping inside with Reagan. "But first, allow me to get you some refreshments." After reaching the sideboard, she rejoined the men with a bottle of port and two glasses on a tray. As Reagan sampled his drink, she gazed at his lips, envisioning them pressed against hers in a heated embrace. The hint of desire she imagined in his look made her even more confident her strategy would be successful.

She then turned to Sam, still preoccupied at his desk with finding Bertram's letter. "Papa, I'll be late this evening. Camilla asked if I could stay after dinner to help plan her birthday party."

"What? Oh, yes-yes. That's quite all right, dear," he said as he fumbled through the papers. "Ah, here it is!" Turning, he couldn't wait to dismiss his daughter. "You have a good time."

She stepped forward to plant a kiss on her father's cheek. "Now, don't wait up for me. You know how cranky you get when you don't get enough sleep."

"I know. Now, hurry along, child," he said. "I promise I shan't wait up."

"Good, for I've no idea when I might return. You know how Camilla can go on and on." She stopped, as if a thought just struck her. "Why, if it gets too late, Papa, I might just spend the night and come home in the morning." She looked at her father with innocent eyes. "Would that be permissible?"

"Of course!" Sam was becoming exasperated by her delay in leaving. "Whatever you wish." He gestured toward the door. "You mustn't keep the Muelder's waiting."

Elizabeth looked at Reagan. "I pray your evening will be as enjoyable as mine," she said, touching where the key lay hidden. "Until we meet again."

After closing the door, Elizabeth stood reviewing her plans. She'd boldly lied about dining with Camilla because the two families barely knew each other and it'd be unlikely that Sam would discover her deception. If she knew anything about her father, he'd keep Reagan well beyond the time necessary to disclose the contents of Bertram's letter. It'd give her ample time to drive the buggy to the alley next to the Rochester Hotel where she would wait until Reagan returned. She'd learned of the servant's entrance from the maid at the hotel and would later take advantage of that discreet access.

chapter 67

IT SEEMED TO Reagan that Sam Hampton couldn't make a succinct comment if his life depended on it. Like all politicians, he waxed eloquent and with much verbosity upon his importance in improving Cantonsville since taking office. Reagan allowed the prattle to go on while refilling his glass in an effort to be patient. The sweet liquor soothed his nerves already jangled from his encounter with Elizabeth and her provocative display. As he glanced at the mantle clock, he noted the hour of ten approaching. With a sigh, he realized he'd be spending another night at the hotel. He had promised Katherine he wouldn't come home at an ungodly hour. He would have to use his suite to avoid another unpleasant quarrel.

The bottle of port had long been consumed by the time Reagan learned he had obtained another contract from the government. The mayor beamed as he shook Reagan's hand before giving him the papers Bertram had sent. With much patting on his back, Sam escorted him to the door.

Reagan cursed himself for his overindulgence as he climbed into his buggy. Though annoyed with the mayor, it was only part of the reason he had numbed his mind with liquor. Elizabeth's tantalizing display had rekindled a battle he waged daily. Ever since Amanda forswore his husbandly rights, he'd become like a man starved, always seeking but never finding ease. Whenever she prepared a bath, he became no better than an ogling lecher while lust tore at his gut strings. And no matter how agreeable he tried to be, as soon as the water was poured, she'd lock the door against his possible intrusion.

Reagan found himself watching for a softening resolve as she played the role of wife, greeting guests or conversing pleasantly at dinner. But, if by themselves in the parlor, Amanda's soft demeanor dissolved into that of a harpish shrew, pricking his endurance. Yet, it was the nights Reagan found most torturous. The moment they were behind closed doors, Amanda would become guarded, avoiding him as a mouse avoids a cat. Rather than converse, she'd find small tasks to fill her time such as reading books or writing a letter. And when she rose for bed, he found himself staring as she took down her hair and unbuttoned her dress. As always, she would step behind the screen, depriving him the pleasure of her naked body. When she finally lay down on the bed's outer edge, it took every ounce of will to keep from taking her in his arms and ravaging her with white, hot desire. As a gentleman, he couldn't impose his demands while she spurned his advances. Instead, he went to the Rochester to drink himself into a stupor. At least then, he could subject his will over his rebellious body.

Once inside his suite, Reagan shrugged out of his coat. Unbuttoning his shirt, he splashed whiskey into a glass and downed it quickly. He looked around the room thinking he would gladly trade it for the cabin, if he could but regain his wife's love. Even the liquor couldn't quell his longing to hold her in his arms, touch her, and love her. After stripping off his clothes, he poured another draught. If it took all night, he would banish the demons that plagued him.

After awhile, the deliverance Reagan sought stole over him, and with only a sheet covering his nakedness, he fell into a deep sleep. Though mastering his body, Reagan couldn't control the visions that frequented his dreams. Images formed of Amanda entwined in his arms as they spun amid music and light. They were happy. No damning perplexities stood between them. The scent of her perfume rose to tantalize his senses.

"Reagan..." she smiled at him impishly, "Reagan...I'm here..."

"Of course you are," he grinned. "I've been waiting for you." Her hand rose to caress his face and he turned to kiss her palm. "My love," he breathed, "where've you been?"

"I must know if you want me..." she whispered.

"I've always wanted you. From the first moment I saw you," Reagan assured. "I can't live without you." He was determined she wouldn't vanish again. Yet, without warning, the music stopped and the lights grew dim. They stood uncertainly, looking at each other.

"Do you really want me?" she asked, pulling away.

"Don't go," Reagan begged as she slipped from his fingers. Reaching out, he seized her and her arms returned to envelop him in a passionate embrace. "Stay with me, please..." Reagan beseeched as warm lips caressed his, "...I need you..."

The heady scent of roses filled his nostrils as Reagan held her against him and her soft breasts instilled a ravenous appetite that had been too long suppressed. Covering her with kisses, his hands sought the secret places he knew so well and when he finally possessed her, her nails raked his back in equal passion. With mounting fervor, she arched her back while meeting him thrust for thrust in a frantic race for fulfillment. As her hands cupped his buttocks, Reagan buried his face in her neck, clinging to her until he received complete and blessed relief.

"Amanda..." he held her tenderly as he heard soft whimpering. "Amanda, please don't cry. I love you... I'm sorry if I've hurt you..." he wanted to kiss away the hurt of her finding the damning notes, "...I don't want us to ever be apart again..."

He thought he heard a faraway, sharp intake of breath. Despite his intentions to comfort her, a drug-like stupor stole over Reagan and he slumbered.

chapter 68

Reagan was thrust awake by hammer-like poundings that pierced his skull. He pressed a pillow to his ears hoping the racket would go away and leave him to his misery. Within seconds, the sound of a door slamming against a wall brought him to his senses. If it hadn't, the bellowing would have as Thomas entered the room like a snorting bull.

"What in God's name are you doing?" his father shouted, tearing the pillow from Reagan's hands. "You didn't come home last night and this morning, you didn't show up at the mill! Get your *arse* out of bed and get back to the business of being a man!"

Reagan flinched, feeling his head was being rent from his shoulders. "Please," he croaked. "I'll do whatever you ask, if only you'll stop shouting." Sitting up was no small feat as his stomach threatened to expel whatever remained inside.

Thomas stopped, not so much at Reagan's request but at his horrible condition. Never had he seen Reagan's hair so disarrayed or bloodshot eyes, barely open. His jaw wore the growth of a man used to shaving early and it was now nearly noon.

In disgust, Thomas strode to the nightstand and picked up the whiskey bottle. "You've never been one to run from problems and it rankles me to see you now indulge that weakness." He stared out the window as he continued, "I've cancelled your arrangement with the hotel. From now on, you'll return each night to your family, loving or not." Turning, he looked at Reagan with unpitying eyes. "Whatever problems you've created, you'll have to deal with them like any man who's ever wronged his wife. I'll expect you at dinner as well. Katherine had to make excuses to Beauregard last night. Had you been around lately, you would've known he was to be our guest."

Reagan cradled his head with hands that shook. "I worked through dinner until my appointment with the mayor-"

"Sam? What were you doing at the Hampton's last night?" Thomas recalled Reagan mentioning a possible contract through the mayor's cousin, Bertram Hayes. Though he'd been angry to be excluded from the original meeting, Reagan assured him he'd be told if they received a contract. "Why wasn't I informed if a contract was forthcoming?"

Reagan sighed as he clasped his hands between his knees. "Because I received the message late afternoon. I had no indication there was a contract waiting, only a message. Look in my coat pocket." While Thomas retrieved the papers, Reagan pulled the sheet around him and disappeared into the bath chamber.

Thomas scanned the parchment, his eyes dipping to the bottom where the signature remained unsigned. He heard the splashing of water and spoke above the noise. "Why didn't you sign it?"

"Because you hadn't seen it yet," Reagan said around his shaving brush.

Despite his anger, Thomas softened at this show of consideration. It had crossed his mind Reagan might be attempting to override his authority. He'd just been shown the contrary. Folding the contract, he placed it in his pocket. "I'll take it back to the office where I'll expect you within the hour."

"I need coffee," Reagan said, keeping eyes on the mirror while shaving.

"I'll have some sent up," Thomas said. "Oh and Reagan..." He waited until Reagan leaned back and peered at him through the doorway. "Don't ever try this again. I've taken the liberty of informing the hotel that if it makes rooms available to you for any reason, our lumber won't be available for that new wing they want to build."

Long after Thomas had left, Reagan tried piecing together the images that flashed through his mind. He recalled the boring hours spent with the mayor. Then, after returning to the hotel he'd tossed down more than his usual tipple. That should've been it. But something kept tugging at his memory. Dismissing the notion as the by-product of too much liquor, he concentrated on making himself presentable. Thomas was right. He couldn't continue his bouts of excessive drinking for it befuddled his normally keen memory.

Reagan gathered the linens to return them to bed when a curious aroma teased his senses. Astonished, he drew the cloth upward and was no less bewildered when he smelled the faintest scent of roses. He stared at the sheet as if it contained a secret to which he wasn't a party. He sniffed again, thinking his mind was surely playing tricks. Yet, the scent was there, weak but unmistakable. Instantly, images of Amanda formed as he tried making sense of the impossible.

Despite his throbbing head, he retraced in his mind his steps the night before. He then recalled his interaction with Elizabeth. She was wearing this same fragrance. Somehow, he must've gotten her sachet on his clothes and transferred it to the sheets. Relieved at having found the solution, Reagan tossed the linen on the bed and gave it no further thought.

Fortified with a bath and several cups of coffee, he headed for the office, prepared to take whatever punishment Thomas had waiting for him. He imagined it couldn't compare to what he'd receive once he went home to face Amanda. It would be much later that Reagan would wonder how Thomas had been able to enter his suite when he knew he had locked the door.

chapter 69

AMANDA FELT HER emotional turmoil reemerge when Reagan once again occupied their chambers. She worried that after they spent a few nights together, he'd soon demand his husbandly rights. But so far, he played the gentleman and so she in turn, acted cordial but distant. She also noted from the calendar that this was the day she planned meeting Derrick.

Despite believing she had every right to find happiness, she felt suffocated by her agreement to see him. To take her mind off her confusion, she decided she would first spend the morning visiting Gabriella. It would be well into afternoon before Amanda felt enough courage to make the trip to the meadow by the river.

"Thank you, Aunt Ella for a lovely visit," Amanda said, setting down her teacup.

"Oh posh," Gabriella said. "It's you that makes each visit such a joy for this old, useless woman."

Amanda had wanted to talk of another troubling situation, namely, Camilla's birthday party. But at the same time, she couldn't let Gabriella's words go unchallenged.

"Useless? Why, you must be the busiest unworthy I've ever known." She held up her fingers each in turn. "You've recently put together a sewing circle making shirts as well as bandages for soldiers. You provide food and clothing to the Negro settlement, and I know you've sent more than one sick child to Dr. Turner. Whenever a need arises, you step forward."

"You must give this old woman something to fill her time now that her *other* activities have ceased," Gabriella teased. "Poor Ben has become nothing more than a nurserymam, running to the milliner's for scrap cloth."

Amanda smiled at images of Ben collecting fabric that filled Gabriella's parlor. "We must find a woman who'll appreciate his long-suffering," she said. "There are scores of women who would benefit from a man that does what he's told."

"Over my dead body," Gabriella said. "That man has been more than a loyal servant. Why, he's an ally, a dear companion and friend...." Gabriella stopped when she saw Amanda's playful grin. "Naughty child!" She shook her finger. "I should've known you'd learn mischief after all the sport we've had." She sighed, shaking her head. "It seems like only yesterday we were playing hide and seek in the upper rooms and now here you are, a grown woman with a husband of your own."

"My life has indeed, grown more complicated," Amanda said as she smoothed her napkin. "As a matter of fact, I still have reservations about attending Camilla's party. After her last dinner, I've been afraid to accept her invitation, thinking it'd go no better."

"What happened, child?" Gabriella leaned forward. "Did something go wrong?"

Amanda frowned at the memory. "I was openly questioned about the night Reagan and I were caught by those bounty hunters."

"Oh, I see. I suppose Camilla put you on the spot and tried embarrassing you."

"Indeed, she did," she said. "And that's why I have yet to accept."

"But that was before your wedding, wasn't it?" Gabriella said, stacking empty plates. "Reagan would accompany you this time."

"I suppose he would," Amanda said as she looked at her ring. Even to her own ears, she sounded unconvinced. How could she admit that she and her husband barely spoke and just last night, Beauregard found Reagan absent from their dinner table?

"His presence will make all the difference in the world," Gabriella assured. "No one would dare question you now that you're married and certainly not with your husband nearby." She glanced at the clock before grasping her cane to stand. "You did say you had another appointment, didn't you?"

"Yes, I did," Amanda said, rising to kiss Gabriella's cheek. "Thank you, Aunt Ella. Your advice is always good. That's exactly what I'll do. I'll make sure Reagan is nearby."

Gabriella accepted the arm Amanda offered as they walked toward the entranceway. "You can't avoid those that have a malevolent bent, my child. You must face them head on and take back the dignity they're trying to snatch from you."

"I will, I promise."

Gabriella stopped near the door. "George tells me you scarcely visit. I had hoped things would grow better between you and Emily." She stroked Amanda's hair before touching her cheek. "In her own way, your mother loves you. I pray you're not punishing her in some manner."

"Oh no," Amanda said as she drew on her gloves. "It's just been difficult to visit since I've been back. I guess I caused quite a stir with my trip to the lumber camp. Mother was quite upset. She reminded me how important it was to uphold the Bruester reputation even though I'm now married." She gave a short laugh. "She's correct, of course. It was thoughtless of me to do such a thing without letting anyone know my whereabouts. Had anything happened, it could've been disastrous."

"Despite how it seems, I believe Emily is trying to protect you," Gabriella said, tying the strings of Amanda's bonnet. "It's worked for her all these years, and she thinks it'll work for you as well."

"What?" Amanda looked perplexed. "What will work for me?"

"Why, protecting your heart behind a façade," Gabriella said. "To keep from hurt, Emily hides her feelings. One has to discern them through the prism of her temperament and nature."

Amanda considered her own pain, and how she kept it locked away. For the first time, she felt a kinship with how Emily had chosen to deal with disappointment. "Mayhap, mother's right after all. One could certainly feel less vulnerable if a heart could be guarded."

"I tell you these things to give you insight," Gabriella chided, "not to instruct you to imitate them."

Amanda laughed as she stepped outside. The bright sun contrasted against the shade where her horse had been tethered. "Don't worry," she grinned. "I promise I'll visit my parents."

Gabriella watched as Amanda mounted her palfrey. "I had hoped that's who your next appointment was," she whispered.

Retreating to her bedchamber, Gabriella wet a cloth and covered her eyes. As she rested, her thoughts returned to her niece. Despite her good-intentioned interference, it seemed Amanda was destined to mirror Emily's unhappy state. Gabriella mouthed a prayer that fate would intervene, for despite Amanda's lack of candor, Gabriella knew something was troubling the girl, and it wasn't just Camilla's party.

chapter 70

CAMILLA HADN'T THE slightest idea who had responded to her birthday invitations because her mother had planned the party. That she expected an extravagant festivity there was no doubt, as Fay and Emory Muelder gave their daughter anything she wanted. At the age of three, Camilla had discovered she only had to wrap plump little arms around her father's neck and soundly kiss both cheeks to get her way. So charmed by the blond darling, Emory denied her nothing.

The gathering had been planned to serve a twofold purpose. Not only would it be a birthday celebration, but it would also be the time to announce her engagement to Leroy. Camilla recognized the banker's son could provide more lavishly than anyone and felt she alone deserved the Spelding wealth. There was no better way of demonstrating her elevated station than announcing it at her party.

"Mama!" Camilla's voice rang from the upper floor. "Mama, come quick!"

Fay Muelder hastily exited the parlor, adjusting her spectacles as she gazed up the staircase. "What is it, dear?"

"I can't find the ribbon necklace that goes with my dress," Camilla shrilled. "I've searched my room and cannot find it."

Fay started up the stairs. "Don't worry dear. I'm sure it's there somewhere."

Camilla groaned as she stomped into her room. "I simply cannot tolerate the maid's laziness!" she cried, leaving the door wide for her mother. "She was supposed to press my dress, but look at the wrinkles near the hem." She twirled around as Fay entered the room. "And now she's misplaced my necklace!"

Fay looked in bewilderment at clothes littering the floor. "Why darling, your room's a mess. How could this happen?"

"Because the maid only comes twice a week!" Camilla flung her hand toward the dressing table. "She was supposed to leave my necklace on the dresser, but it's not there." Fay began searching through clutter on top of the bureau as Camilla bent to smooth her dress. "I suppose I'll just have to be embarrassed by the puckered skirt. I swear that girl couldn't finish a job if her life depended on it."

Fay opened a drawer, pushing aside broken fans and rumpled kerchiefs. "If you come downstairs to the laundry room, I'll press the hem." She withdrew the missing necklace and held it toward her daughter. "Here it is, dear."

Camilla snatched the ornament from her mother's fingers and approached the mirror. "It's about time someone found it. No doubt, the chit hid it to torment me." Now that her problem was solved, Camilla became completely agreeable. "There," she said, smiling at her reflection. "I'll be the belle of the ball." Turning to cause her dress to sway, Camilla laughed at the vision of delicate beauty looking back at her. "Isn't this the most perfect gown? I mean, look Mother! Don't you think I look like the fiancé of the richest man in the city?" Indeed, the gown was magnificent with varying shades of green that accentuated her eyes and honey-blond hair.

Fay Muelder adjusted her spectacles. "Yes, dear, I think you look lovely." She pressed her hands together as she often did when unsure what to make of her daughter. Even as a child, Camilla had known exactly what she wanted and pursued it relentlessly. Over the years, she'd become increasingly demanding. Fay was no match for the sharp-tongued beauty and fared better if she simply gave in to her daughter's wishes. "Your guests should be arriving within the hour," she reminded Camilla. "You may want to inspect the guest placement to see if it's to your satisfaction."

Camilla tested the security of her hair net, tucking a loose strand. "I only care about Leroy being placed on my left."

Fay smiled tightly. "I wouldn't forget such a formality, dear."

She turned and looked pointedly at her mother. "You *did* keep Beau to my right, didn't you? I know you wanted to put Elizabeth there."

"But it doesn't appear seemly," Fay reasoned. "When one is engaged, one should only be concerned with her intended." She took off her glasses to soften her daughter's frown. "I placed him next to Elizabeth, so he'll be close enough for conversation but not too near to ruin your reputation."

"I don't care one whit what you think, Mama!" Camilla's eyes grew stormy. "Beau makes me laugh, and I want to be happy. Leroy can be so dull. There's nothing wrong with having a dear friend nearby to liven things up. If you don't make sure Beau's beside me, I'll just go down and do it myself."

Fay bit her tongue as she replaced her glasses. "I'll take care of it, dear. Please don't become cross. You know how it forms wrinkles." She departed the room secretly thankful Camilla would soon be married. Her daughter had always been difficult and Fay longed for peace and harmony.

"Don't forget the iron," Camilla called. "I have to be perfect."

chapter 71

AMANDA STRUGGLED TO fasten the back buttons of her sage colored gown. She had chosen the frock for its simple lines as well as being able to forgo her corset. It was one of her favorite dresses, though at the moment she wondered at her selection in light of her maid being ill and unable to assist her. Hoping to see the cause of her difficulty, Amanda twisted in front of the mirror. By craning her neck, she was able to secure two more buttons, but failed to reach those in the middle of her back. Seemingly unaware of her predicament, Reagan faced a small mirror as he knotted his silk necktie. Amanda cleared her throat while stealing glances in his direction, but failed gaining his attention.

At the sound of a frustrated sigh, Reagan looked up. He saw Amanda's arms twisted in unnatural angles as she poked a button with the tip of her finger. "Good Lord, woman," he said, closing the distance between them. "All you had to do was ask if you needed help." He gently unwound her arms before finishing the task. "I wouldn't have refused you," he chided while turning her around. "At least make your request before deciding whether or not I'd oblige."

Amanda dropped her gaze, very much aware of his hands on her. "You seemed intent on your task."

All at once, Reagan wondered if their recent separation had weakened her resolve. Ever since his return to their bedchambers, she'd been cool but decidedly civil. "I say we call a truce," he smiled, giving her shoulders a gentle squeeze before releasing her.

"A truce? What do you mean?"

Reagan reached for his jacket. "What I mean, is that for tonight we should forget about our differences and appreciate the evening for what it is, no pressures, no expectations, just enjoying friends and each other."

"When you say no pressures..." Amanda recalled only too well her trepidation whenever she rebuffed his advances.

"I mean exactly that. I'll be a gentleman for the duration." He grinned, picking up one of her scented fans. Closing his eyes, he waved it near his nose. "But, at the stroke of midnight, when Cinderella loses her magic potion, I too, will turn into a beastly monster, prone to debauchery and rakish behavior."

Despite herself, Amanda laughed. "All right. I'll be certain to be home by midnight," she assured while accepting the fan. "And you need to refresh yourself on fables. You're mixing myths with fairy tales." Though cautious about his motives, Amanda decided to accept his proposal. She recalled a similar truce at the picnic. It seemed to go well, then. It would be refreshing to not worry about her closely guarded emotions. "I believe, I'm ready," she said, giving her hair a final pat.

When Reagan extended his arm, Amanda realized how much his virile good looks still affected her. With effort, she pushed away the thought. She preferred keeping her distance by recalling his treachery. Needing a reminder that he'd dealt with her falsely, Amanda's thoughts turned to her meeting with Derrick. He claimed to have proof that Reagan had married her for money, and with enough time, he could regain her dowry. He assured her that once her fortune was restored, she'd have the power to annul her marriage.

After delicately asking if she were with child, Derrick had strongly urged she leave Reagan to guarantee a swift and unfettered dissolution. But how could she endure yet another scandal? Unable to decide, Amanda had begged for more time. Reluctantly, Derrick had agreed, declaring he wouldn't wait for very long.

As Reagan assisted Amanda down the stairs, he brought her thoughts back to the present. "Beauregard claims Leroy made a purchase at the jewelers. Do you suppose he's asked for Camilla's hand?"

"One can only hope," Amanda blurted. At Reagan's laughter, she blushed. "Oh dear! Did I just say that? I mean-I meant-I'm glad for him."

Reagan glanced at his watch. With several hours between now and midnight, he wondered how he'd endure the evening without making an overture toward his wife. She looked incredibly beautiful and it took all his will power to clamp down on his amorous impulses. As he settled against cushions of the carriage, a stinging pain caused him to shift in his seat. He ignored the discomfort as he turned toward his wife. "How was your visit with Gabriella? I assume she's keeping busy."

"Very well, thank you. She's been active in several projects." She looked at him pointedly. "All of them quite legal, of course."

"Of that I've no doubt," he said. "After one encounter with Jebediah, even the most foolhardy would assume saintly behavior. Besides," he said, stretching out his legs, "since the war began, the papers say few slaves are venturing north." Amanda's gaze dropped to her hands as she recalled the horror of Nell's final moments. She often wondered about the fate of baby Isaiah, but had refrained from asking Gabriella. As if reading her thoughts, Reagan closed a hand over her fingers. "You were very brave that night. Despite what you think, I gained a great deal of respect for your courage."

"And I thank you for not betraying Aunt Ella. Although between the two of us," she said, smiling wickedly, "you've profited the utmost, while I've yet to discover my gain."

"That, my dear, could be satisfied forthwith, if we just ended this discord between us."

She smiled sweetly. "The truce we called, prevents me from responding with the words you deserve." She moved the curtain to view the sunset. "Mayhap, if you ask me on the morrow, I'll be able to explain it—again."

chapter 72

THE SOFT EVENING breezes made the carriage ride to Camilla's home pleasant. Reagan and Amanda had just entered the front entrance when they heard a familiar voice down the hall. "Belle Amie!" Beauregard said, approaching. He had just given his hat to a servant and had yet to enter the parlor. "Ahh, the wolf and the floret!" He raised Amanda's hand to his lips. "You've come to wish Camilla a happy and healthful birthday. How splendid!"

"Splendid for whom?" Reagan said as he handed his hat to the same servant. He shook Beau's hand, wishing the Frenchman wasn't so popular. It seemed he was present at every tea and dinner party in Cantonsville.

"Demoiselle! My paramour, no?"

"That's Madam Burnsfield, my friend," Reagan said through gritted teeth. "You've a failing memory when it comes to a woman's marital status."

"Non Ami, I do not forget," he said, grinning. "I simply cannot resist the bloom you plucked too soon."

"Tis simple," Reagan said. "The better man won the fair lady."

Beauregard dipped his head in acknowledgement. "Oui. It is true. But my friend," he said, making a show of inspecting Amanda's ring. "I have it on good authority you cheated."

Amanda giggled at Beau's lack of concern in raising her husband's ire. "Your company's always appreciated," she said, glancing at Reagan. "Although you seem to have found disfavor with my husband."

"It is no matter." Beauregard winked as he patted Reagan's back. "He's told me many times, what's mine is his, and what's his is mine."

"That was before I had reason to withhold from you my things," Reagan said, annoyed at the Frenchman's needling.

"Perhaps we could find a way to share?" suggested Beau.

To his chagrin, Reagan saw his evening with Amanda diminishing with every moment of Beau's presence. "Some things I won't share. Besides," he nodded toward the parlor door, "I believe you're about to be otherwise detained." From the corner of his eye, he saw Camilla emerging from the parlor.

"There you are," Camilla said, stepping between Amanda and Beauregard. "I thought you'd arrived. Yet, you delayed in coming to wish me happy birthday!"

"My pardon, *d'honneur*." Beau swiftly bestowed a kiss on her fingers. "I've failed in etiquette, please forgive me!"

Camilla's gaze swept Beau's perfectly tailored suit. Leroy, for all his gangling height, could never fill out an ensemble like the compact Frenchman, she thought. If not for the fact the Spelding heir was far richer than Beau could ever hope to be, Camilla doubted she would've given Leroy a moment's notice.

"I'll forgive you this time," she said. "But I insist you make it up to me by entertaining my guests with your witty stories."

"If I have Madame Burnsfield's permission, as we were yet deciding who should be her escort."

Though her smile was pleasant, Camilla's nostrils flared. "Surely my dear, you don't mind if I steal Beauregard, do you?"

"Of course not," Amanda said, forcing a smile. "I'm perfectly content being escorted by my husband." As if to prove her words, Amanda tucked her hand inside Reagan's arm.

"That settles it," Reagan said. "Since this is your celebration Camilla, why don't we join the others?"

As they entered the parlor, Beauregard led Camilla to the sofa. "Monsieur's and demoiselles," he announced. "I've restored the winsome lady into your midst!" He made a show of spreading a napkin across her lap before lifting a tray of confections.

"A sweet pastry for the tempting blossom." Beauregard awaited Camilla's choice before offering the tarts to others. After everyone had taken a treat, he sat and grinned devilishly. "So, ma cherie, what will you *next* sink those pretty little teeth into?" He arched a brow and looked around. "A man, perhaps?"

Reagan stood behind Amanda's chair while everyone laughed at the Frenchman's jest. He rested a hand on her shoulder as she leaned toward Lorelda Hargrove in conversation. With his back to the entrance, he didn't notice the new arrival until he felt a gentle touch.

"Hello, Reagan," Elizabeth said. "So good to see you, again." Hoping to ensnare Reagan's attention, she had worn her most daring gown. Ever since her brazen venture into Reagan's hotel suite, she hadn't been able to think of anything else. Although he'd been in a drunken stupor, he had eagerly accepted her into his bed. Even his words had fortified her belief that he wanted her. Yet, his liquor-tainted speech had chilled her confidence when he murmured Amanda's name. Appalled that his passions had already been spent, Elizabeth now wondered if he recalled anything at all. She had to know if in the heat of the moment, he had merely misspoken. "You must tell me, perhaps over a dance, how your meeting went with father."

"Of course," Reagan said, feeling a strange unease as if a slumbering memory refused to wake. "There should be an opportunity or two, when I'm not dancing with Amanda."

Elizabeth felt a stab of jealousy as she noted his fingers caressing his wife's shoulder. "Until then," she said, forcing a smile before moving away.

"Camilla!" a male voice called from the hallway. All eyes turned when Leroy entered the room. "Why darling," he said, his Adam's apple bobbing above his tightly knotted cravat, "you've started without me."

Camilla accepted his kiss before shifting closer to Beauregard. "Sit here," she said, patting the cushions.

Leroy took the seat, speaking louder than necessary. "I do hope you waited before telling everyone the good news! I wanted to be here when the announcement was made."

Camilla kept her irritation from showing. Once she wed the oaf, she would keep him in check, if not with her well-practiced charms, then with the keen edge of her tongue. "Of course I waited," she said. "I was entertaining our friends." She rested her hand briefly on Beauregard's shoulder. "As you can see, they're all here."

Leroy captured her fingers as he looked around. "Not only have we gathered to celebrate Camilla's birthday," he paused, unaware most already knew of the engagement, "but to announce we are to be wed next spring." The women graciously clapped while the men rose to shake Leroy's hand.

Reagan approached and slapped Leroy's back before offering his hand. "Congratulations on your upcoming wedding. I pray you'll find much happiness."

Leroy barely heard his words while inspecting Reagan's outfit. Never confidant of his own judgment, he usually waited until others sported newer styles before purchasing them. So it seemed fair game to mock the unusual cut of Reagan's attire. "Well, old boy," he fairly sneered at the distinctly narrow lapels, "where on earth did you get *that* bit of frippery?"

"Why, I believe the clothier Ives Du Monde." Reagan winked at Beauregard, one of Ives' most frequent customers. "He seems to have a knack for discovering new styles."

"I've heard the man allows his customers to alter designs," Leroy sniffed. Folding his arms, he studied details of Reagan's clothing. "I dare say, I don't recognize the smaller lapels. Don't tell me," he said, chuckling, "the poor man ran short of cloth."

Reagan smiled tolerantly. He was not unfamiliar with Leroy's habit of sprinkling ridicule when among friends. "Oh, I gave him a request or two," he acknowledged. "However, since Ives has an eye for fashion, I felt confidant in allowing him to guide me. But, perhaps I err," he turned to Beauregard who looked decidedly outraged. "Mr. Barrington has been a fashion authority as long as I can recall. What do you think, Beau?"

Beauregard was at his finest when his ire was raised. Not only had Leroy insulted the clothier's skills, he needlessly slighted his best friend.

"Oui," Beau tapped his chin, as he pondered Reagan's silver-hued ensemble. "One cannot deny the quality, as Monsieur Du Monde imports only the finest materials. And, the cravat accentuates the jacket's color as fine as any I've seen. You must admit, sir, the fit is flawless, is it not?"

"I-I suppose any tailor can cut cloth to measurement," Leroy sputtered, ignoring Camilla's warning glare.

Beau nodded. "You might have a keener eye, but I say the garment perfectly magnifies Monsieur Burnsfield's physique."

From across the room, Elizabeth listened to Beauregard's praise. She secretly agreed the fit looked perfect as she was at that moment, recalling the feel of Reagan's chest against her hands. Although it wasn't the first time she shared a bed with a male, it was the first time she felt possessed by one. In her moment of passion her nails had raked his back. Later, she cursed herself for not staying long enough for Reagan to awaken sober and deal with the reality of her presence. Lowering her gaze, she bit her lip in frustration.

Amanda too, was reliving her own experiences. From her point of view, Reagan was indeed the most attractive man in the room. With the truce between them, she permitted her thoughts to roam even as her eyes rested on Reagan's hands. The memory of what those hands were capable of doing, caused her to blush.

"One has to admire your own taste in clothes, Monsieur Spelding." Beau's eyes were two lit coals. "The splendid suit you are wearing was highlighted in Godey's no more than..." he rubbed his jaw thoughtfully, "...two years ago. While Reagan's attire will not be featured until Godey's spies set their eyes on him." The group laughed nervously as many recognized Beau's hidden jibe.

Camilla touched his arm. "I'm sure Leroy didn't mean to be disagreeable. Let's find our places at the table, shall we? Then, you can tell us the story of your balloon ride." A general enthusiasm arose at the promise of one of Beau's stories.

"Oui," he acquiesced. "My pardon, ma cherie."

Reagan noted Amanda's heightened color when he offered his arm. "My dear, have you taken a fever?"

"No," Amanda whispered as they moved toward the dining room. "'Twas only a thought."

Intrigued by what caused the sudden flushing, Reagan bent toward her ear. "What naughty ideas have crossed that pretty mind of yours?" Aghast at his intuitiveness, she could only stare into his face.

"Surely, not about Beauregard?"

"No," she blurted, "about you."

Reagan chuckled as they neared the table. "Well then. We'll just have to explore that later tonight." Amanda smiled tightly, shocked by what she just admitted. Her fears of being baited were forgotten however, as he dropped the matter. Later, as the birthday cake was being served, Reagan casually captured Amanda's hand. She first thought to snatch it back. But, the wine had a disarming effect and she allowed it to rest in his lap until music signaled the end of dinner.

chapter 73

As strains of music filtered in from the ballroom, Leroy cleared his throat then made a show of withdrawing a box from his pocket. Heir to the Spelding fortune, it was widely accepted he was one of the richest men in Cantonsville. Although he perpetuated that notion, in reality, his father maintained control of his inheritance. As such, Ezra had advanced a far smaller sum for purchasing an engagement ring than many, most notably Camilla, might've imagined befitted the bride-to-be.

"Why, Leroy," Camilla said, touching her throat. "I had no idea you'd be presenting a gift." Well-practiced tears filled her eyes. "Since all our friends are here, I suppose it'd be permissible to let them share the moment."

A warm murmur swept the room as Leroy opened the case with a flourish. Camilla's eyes fell hungrily onto a diamond solitaire nestled between stud earrings. Though obviously worth a goodly sum, the jewels fell far short of the ornate and extravagant jewelry she expected. Camilla looked into Leroy's face in total shock. Real tears of humiliation fell as she recalled her boastful words describing the jewelry she'd have showered upon her once she became Leroy's betrothed.

"It-it's b-beautiful!" she choked.

Lifting her hand, Leroy slipped on the ring. "Why darling," he said. "You're trembling!"

The women gathered round and after a few moments where Camilla tolerated their compliments, she abruptly turned to Leroy. "Darling, the music has started."

"Of course, my love." He nearly tripped in his haste to rise, but paused as he spied the jewelry box. "Camilla dear, the earrings. Don't you wish to put them on?"

"Leave them!" she hissed, taking his arm.

When they entered the ballroom, Leroy grasped Camilla in a rigid embrace. Then nodding to the orchestra, he soon had her spinning in dizzying tempo.

As others joined in, Reagan turned to Amanda. "Milady, would you honor me with a dance?"

She smiled as she watched Leroy's stiff-legged waltz. "Only if you protect my toes should anyone draw near."

"Of course," Reagan said, grinning. Settling a hand on her waist, he offered the other. "But first, you must come closer."

Reasoning she'd be safe enough, Amanda placed her hand in his. However, the moment she entered his embrace, she realized she underestimated his presence and could scarce control her beating heart. She tried resurrecting her anger by recalling his past indignities but to her shock, could barely feel annoyance. Her accusations, which until now had bolstered her resolve, fell silent. It must be the truce, she decided, that caused her weakness. And since he couldn't read her mind, she hoped he wouldn't recognize her vulnerability.

Yet, Reagan saw the struggle in her eyes. Hope surged that this could be the beginning of a permanent reconciliation. He longed to breach her self-imposed barriers and awaited her signal she'd accept his advances. As they swept across the floor, the music soothed Amanda's unease and by degrees, she relaxed. It felt good to be in his arms and had she been of a mind to admit it, she missed the intimacy they once shared.

Emboldened by her softening stance, Reagan repositioned himself to draw her even closer. Her perfume played havoc with his senses as he caressed the small of her back. "You must tell me about those naughty thoughts," he breathed, his lips grazing her temple.

Tiny shivers prickled her skin wherever his fingers moved though it wasn't until they reached her middle back that she found her breasts pressed against his chest. As if coming out of a stupor, Amanda grew rigid. "I beg your pardon," she said, loosening his embrace. "I don't recall our truce including intimate touching."

"Oh, was I doing that? I thought I was being an attentive husband."

"If I recall correctly, our agreement was only to enjoy ourselves."

"But, I was doing just that." His eyes glittered with suppressed desire. "I was enjoying you."

Instead of being outraged, Amanda became amused. "Do I need to remind you of your promise to be a gentleman? Or, should I doubt your sincerity?"

"How haven't I lived up to my promise?"

"Besides fondling me, you've taken liberties with your speech that would've shocked any decent person," she scolded. "With 'naughty' this and 'naughty' that..."

Reagan leaned in so his words only reached her ears. "But these things are permitted, nay expected, among married couples. If we don't display a little intimacy, others might think ought is amiss between us."

Amanda looked around. "No one's paying attention, so there's really no need."

"Ah, except for the truce, you'd be correct milady," Reagan declared. "Didn't you agree that for tonight we'd forget our differences?"

"Yes, but—"

"I'm but fulfilling my end of the bargain," he interrupted. He drew her hand to his lips as the music ended. "But to appease my lady, I'll refrain from further attentions."

After they left the floor he accepted a glass of champagne from a nearby servant. Taking a sip, Reagan checked his watch. He knew better than to rush. Wooing Amanda back to his bed would be a slow and careful process.

As the next dance began, Leroy whisked past with Camilla, his elbows and knees demonstrating his exuberant vigor. Camilla's ribbon headpiece lay askew and if not for her guests, would have shrieked in indignation at his jarring treatment.

Reagan chuckled. "I fear Camilla will have flattened toes before Leroy improves his dancing skills."

"Shhh!" Amanda whispered as Anson Rutledge approached with Elizabeth. "Someone may hear you."

"I say ol' boy," Anson said, slapping Reagan's back. "You caused quite a stir with your fancy suit, didn't you? I thought Leroy was going to pop a vessel," he chortled.

"Leroy was in error," Elizabeth said. "I believe the outfit is complimentary to the man."

Reagan bowed before winking at Amanda. "Why, thank you. My tailor promised the ladies would notice, though, I've yet to receive a compliment from Mrs. Burnsfield."

"That's because it's unseemly to openly flatter the object of one's affections," Elizabeth said, flushing. "Tis better to wait for a private moment for a woman's approval."

"Then your compliment is doubly appreciated," he said with a smile. "I consider it a privilege to have been given insight into a woman's mind."

For some reason, Reagan's banter with Elizabeth pricked Amanda's heart. Though denying herself the pleasure of his favors, she resented his attention being given to another. "Mayhap, one has to witness worthy behavior to receive the flattery you desire," she said, forgetting they weren't alone.

"The lady speaks the truth," Reagan said, holding a hand to his heart. "And, I beg forgiveness. Like many of my gender, I spend more time clothing my frame than choosing words that fall from my lips."

Amanda suddenly realized the impoliteness of her words. She wasn't expecting his blunt admission and felt ashamed of her behavior. "My pardon," she apologized. "I don't know what came over me."

"Twas my fault," Reagan was quick to intercede. "I baited you in sport. And it was a bad joke at that. Please," he said as he gave each a glance, "forgive me."

Anson shoved a hand in his pocket, jingling coins. "Quite all right, ol' boy. Leroy's always saying my jokes lack refinement. Come to think of it," he said, furrowing a brow. "Leroy's ridiculed every witticism I've ever told!"

When the orchestra began playing a popular cotillion, no one noticed the small, sharp kick. "Oh!" Anson winced. "If-if I have your permission," he said, looking at Reagan. "I've yet to have the honor of dancing with your wife." He glanced nervously toward Elizabeth before stiffening his spine. "I-I just realized the last time we were together, I neglected my duty."

Reagan did his best to appear untroubled. "Whatever the lady wishes," he said, smiling at Amanda. "Have you sufficiently rested, my dear?"

Still embarrassed by her outburst, Amanda decided she could use the time to regain her composure.

"Of course," she nodded, "with your permission, Elizabeth?"

"By all means!" Elizabeth released Anson's arm. "A dance or *two*," she suggested brightly.

As Anson and Amanda joined the others, Elizabeth stepped closer and opened her fan. "It's such a lovely party," she sighed while fanning her perfumed bosom. "I was pleased to see you came."

"Yes," Reagan agreed politely. For several moments neither spoke as they watched the dancers perform the quadrille.

Elizabeth inwardly fumed at her inability to gain his attention. Deciding she was being too timid, she leaned over and grasped his glass. "May I?"

Startled, Reagan withdrew his fingers. "Allow me to summon refreshments for you."

"Oh no," she said. "I only need a small sip." After taking a swallow, she passed the glass back, not noticing when Reagan purposely set the drink aside. And though she affected an alluring pose, he gave her no further heed.

Elizabeth's eyes roamed the ballroom with growing frustration. "They do make a handsome couple, don't you think?" she blurted.

"Who?"

"Why, Camilla and Beau. I've often heard Camilla say Latin's are the true masters of the dance floor."

"I wouldn't say that too close to her betrothed," Reagan said with a laugh. "Leroy may take exception to you thinking he's not a good match."

"It wouldn't be the first time two people were ill-suited for each other."

"Are you suggesting their engagement was a mistake?" he asked, looking at Elizabeth.

"I'm merely saying what's obvious to everyone else," she said, shrugging. "Camilla is marrying for ambitious reasons. As for Leroy, he's oblivious to Camilla's schemes. He can't see past her beauty."

Reagan smiled as he shook his head. "I must've missed that bit of intrigue. I thought Leroy had gotten lucky in love."

"Let's just say Leroy is lucky to have wealth or he wouldn't have Camilla's love." She looked intently into his eyes. "Haven't you known two people who shouldn't have married?"

"As a matter of fact, I do." Reagan considered the peculiar coupling of George and Emily. "And yet, together they remain."

Elizabeth slowed her fan, pleased at the turn of conversation. "That's too bad. It's not unheard of in this day and age, to obtain a divorce."

"There's always that option," he conceded. "Let's hope Leroy and Camilla won't need to follow that path."

"But you do agree it's an acceptable choice for those who shouldn't have wed." Her voice grew excited. "I mean, would you consider divorce an option, if marriage became insufferable?"

"I suppose I wouldn't rule it out, if both parties were miserable and there wasn't hope of reconciliation."

As the cotillion ended and a waltz began, Elizabeth's eyes gleamed. "The music sounds inviting, does it not?" When Reagan only nodded, she formed a pretty pout. "Mr. Burnsfield, aren't you *ever* going to ask me to dance?"

"It'd be an honor," he said as his manners came to the fore. Though he preferred awaiting Amanda's return, he obligingly accompanied Elizabeth to the floor. He noticed that where he had to coax Amanda to draw near, Elizabeth had no trouble finding the smallest distance between them.

"So tell me," she ventured, "how did your meeting go with Papa?"

Reagan weighed his words before speaking. If she'd really been the one to arrange his meeting with Mr. Hayes, good breeding demanded his appreciation. "It seems the encounter was mutually beneficial," he said finally. "Still, I'm curious. How'd you know he could further my business?"

Elizabeth felt her importance surge. "Watching Papa has made me aware of how business operates within politics."

"But, why would you intercede on my behalf?"

"Tis better your friends profit than your enemies, Papa always said. Besides, I wanted you to know how special you are to me." She stared at his lips, recalling the intensity of his kisses. "There's so much more I can do. If you let me, I can be very attentive to your needs," she whispered, her fingertips tracing the back of his neck, "especially since you're being neglected by your wife."

Instead of welcoming her offer as she had fantasized, Reagan finally realized what Elizabeth was seeking. "I'm afraid, that's not how I do business," he said, removing her hand. "And, despite what you've heard, Amanda's done nothing to deserve being called anything but a perfect wife."

The shock on Elizabeth's face verified the enormity of her miscalculation. "But, the circumstances of your marriage...you staying at a hotel," she accused. "Surely, it's true..."

"All my doing, I assure you," Reagan spoke low so others wouldn't hear. "And, though your offer is enticing, I've no wish to alter my circumstances."

Elizabeth's face flushed as she stopped dancing. "I must go," she gasped. Fleeing toward the door, Elizabeth was unaware Reagan followed. He reached out, just as she was about to exit. "Elizabeth," he said. "Wait."

Crushed beyond measure, tears formed under her lids. "I'm so sorry. I mistook your behavior as something it obviously wasn't." After years of secretly pining for Reagan's notice, Elizabeth had become encouraged by rumors of a swiftly failing marriage. She had contrived a plan to make Reagan hers, but his outright rejection ended all hope. "Please, forgive me," she mumbled, slipping out the door.

Reagan was about to pursue her, when Beauregard and Camilla approached, followed by Anson and Amanda. "Tiens! Mon Ami," Beau said, tugging his sleeve. "You must settle a wager." He affected a pose, placing hands on his hips. "What say you, monsieur?

Is it not true that *I* am the fleetest of foot in the whole ballroom?" He pointed an accusing finger at Amanda. "Yet, vos épouse claims that *you* are the premier danseur!"

"I only said I find it easier to follow Reagan's lead," Amanda redressed the Frenchman. "I didn't say you were a less excellent dancer."

"This is what happens when I clumsily bump into Camilla," Anson chimed in, "which soon caused Beau to argue about my skills as well as the skills of every other man in the room."

"Beauregard dances like velvet," Camilla raised her voice to Beau's defense. "I've danced with none finer."

"That's only because you've never danced with me," Reagan grinned. He wanted to discover the reason for Elizabeth's overture, but viewing her flight, decided to bide his time until he could speak with her privately. "I believe there's only one way to settle this." He held out his hand to Camilla. "You must allow me the next dance."

chapter 74

WITH THE LAST guests leaving after midnight and except for the early departure of Elizabeth, Camilla considered her party a success. She decided that although her engagement ring fell short of her expectations, Leroy would have the rest of his life to make up for it.

Reagan had mulled over Elizabeth's departure far longer than Camilla, but by the end of the evening his thoughts turned to more important matters. He considered Amanda's outward contentment to be a major accomplishment. That she continued to display a gay mood as they bade Camilla goodnight he deemed a victory.

Once inside the carriage, Amanda sat comfortably near as they laughed about Beauregard's insistence that he and Reagan dance with each other to determine who the better dancer was.

"I thought you were seriously considering his request when he stepped forward with arms outstretched! And then," she giggled, "and then..."

"And then I surprised you all by dancing by myself," Reagan finished with a chuckle.

"Poor Mrs. Muelder must've thought you'd lost your mind."

"Or, had too much to drink," he murmured, bringing his arm to rest on her shoulder.

Her voice turned slightly scolding. "Aside from your antics, I'd have to say it was an enjoyable evening." She snuggled against Reagan's side, stifling a yawn. "Do you suppose Camilla will be happy as Leroy's wife? For some reason she spent most of her time with Beauregard."

"I'm not sure," he said, his chin resting near her temple. "But Leroy certainly seems happy."

In the silence that followed, the carriage's swaying had a hypnotic effect and Amanda's eyelids began to droop. She gradually allowed them to close as a comforting peace settled over her, drifting into light sleep. Reagan enjoyed her nestling against him, but his breath stopped when she accidentally brushed her hand against his groin. He groaned inwardly, unable to control his rapid response to the feather-like caress.

Sitting rigidly, he fought the urge to take her in his arms. He knew her oblivious to the torture she was inflicting and might resist if he touched her. As Amanda rested against his shoulder, a shadowy vision rose with her perfume, oddly out of place with his oft-replayed memories of their love-play. This memory was different, unfamiliar.

But as her face turned toward him, the haunting image faded and her warm body proved too much a temptation. Reaching over, he gently lifted her chin. Amanda's eyes remained closed, but her lips parted invitingly before his hungry gaze. He brushed his lips against hers in a caress that brought no words of reproach but only a soft sigh. Needing no further encouragement, he closed his hand over hers as he pressed her against the cushions and eagerly sought her mouth.

Amanda felt herself being shifted in Reagan's arms. She became aware that he was kissing her and that she was kissing back. She tried lifting her hand but found her fingers pressed tightly against his manhood. Shocked by his obvious arousal, Amanda drew back, aghast. "R-Rea-gan-" she stammered. "What are you doing?"

"Please," he whispered, his lips trailing her throat, "allow me," he slid lower still, "to touch you." He removed his hand from hers and with a knuckle, brushed the lace edge of her bodice. The contact sent chills racing through her body as her senses were fully awakened. Though her heart pounded, Amanda didn't cry out or repulse his amorous maneuver. He took her hesitation as a call to continue. With deft fingers he loosened the front lacings while tracing his tongue over the contour of her lips. Reaching inside, he cupped one of her breasts, feeling an immediate reaction against his palm.

Amanda gasped at the fervor of her response. She wanted to protest but her body rebelled, forcing her to melt helplessly into the cushions. Taking advantage of her vulnerability, he brushed aside the cloth, exploring the other breast until her passions were nearly as strong as his.

"You promised," she accused raggedly, her voice wavering. "This wasn't part of our bargain."

"Dear Amanda," he whispered, "it's now after midnight." As if proving his intentions, his hand found its way beneath her skirt, his fingers inching past her knee.

Amanda hurriedly clamped a hand over the cloth between them. She stopped him short of his intended goal, but her unsated cravings screamed for fulfillment. "We'll be ho-home soon," she stammered, straightening her skirt. "I can't be seen like this!"

"Don't worry, love," he breathed, his fingers creeping up another small degree. "I instructed the driver to use the back entrance. So, you needn't fret." Without removing his hand, Reagan recaptured her lips. With slow deliberation he increased the pressure on her mouth until she yielded. As his tongue found hers, Amanda became lost in a sea of sensations. Her hand gradually ceased its parrying barrier, allowing him to explore her at will. Having spurned his advances so long, she'd nearly forgotten the aching intensity of his touch. Her body begged for the fulfillment she knew to be had, if only she'd allow it. What her pride denied, her heart only wanted. She wanted to be loved as only a cherished wife could. She knew no greater torture as her passions muddied the certainty of her convictions.

Testing the limits of her concession, Reagan fumbled with his trousers then pulled her onto his lap.

She remained soft and pliant as he positioned her legs, certain if he didn't possess her, he'd go mad for want of her. Amanda experienced a myriad of sensations as Reagan's thumb found and teased a peaking breast. She felt consumed, writhing in near ecstasy when his mouth captured a roseate peak, his tongue a hot, flicking firebrand against her skin. Her fingers twined in his hair as she succumbed to the pleasure of his unrelenting seduction. As her breath became labored, Reagan recognized she neared the point of consent. Shifting her skirt, he reached through the opening of her pantalets. He reclaimed her mouth as he gripped her hips, urging her closer. When she felt bare skin next to hers, she wedged a hand against his chest. "Nay!" she whispered. "We mustn't!"

"Love me, Amanda," Reagan pleaded, his hands pressing her against him until she could feel his need. "Please, let me love you." With intentional slowness he began moving against her. The pressure caused shards of pleasure to pulsate in quickening waves until soft whimpering escaped her lips. Amanda's heart raged with indecision. She couldn't give consent when so much lay between them. But neither could she refuse that which she so desperately wanted. At that moment Reagan chose for her, thrusting upwards until completely sheathed in her womanly softness. Shuddering, he clasped her with a grip that prevented retreat. As he began to move, Amanda felt caught in a trap from which she couldn't escape. Time seemed to cease as he thrust against her in quickening tempo and she arched in unbearable pleasure, enjoining his frenetic rhythm with an abandon she didn't know existed. Her rapture soared as pleasure radiated through her loins like wildfire and when a thousand tiny explosions burst within her, she cried out. While still quivering in his arms, Reagan groaned, crushing her against him until his own spasms ceased.

In the aftermath, Amanda was stunned by what she'd just done. Yet, despite the mindset this should've infuriated her, she felt a weight had been lifted. She no longer wanted to feel anger toward her husband. Tears formed in her eyes as Reagan pressed a soft kiss on her throat. If indeed he didn't love her, at least she could pretend he did when he made love to her.

If he intended words of endearment, the sudden turning of the carriage into the driveway lost the moment. Amanda wriggled uselessly as she tried rising from his lap. "Help me!" she entreated. "We mustn't be seen like this!"

"Oh, I don't know," he said, giving her a playful squeeze. "I don't think it's the first time a driver has witnessed an indelicate circumstance."

"Oh no!" She managed to rise a few inches when the carriage suddenly hit a rut, dropping her forcefully.

"Easy woman!" Reagan grunted through stiff lips. "As much as I enjoy the feel of you, you're wreaking havoc on my privates!" Placing both hands around her waist, he lifted Amanda onto the seat where she wasted no time repositioning her skirt and bodice.

"Button your pants!" she urged as the carriage came to a stop. By the time the door opened, Amanda had regained enough composure to be calmly aided from the conveyance.

They climbed the back stairs, not stopping until they reached the safety of their chambers. Reagan grinned wickedly while lighting a lamp. "Milady, you've given new meaning to a man taking a summer's pleasant ride!"

"Shhh!" she whispered, reaching for the back of her dress. "You'll wake your family." After undoing the first few buttons, she turned to Reagan.

"What?" he teased. "Now, you can't wait to get undressed?" After finishing the task, he watched as she shrugged out of the garment, devouring the sight of her exposed bosom. Encircling her waist with his arms, he kissed her neck. "You can't imagine how I've longed to touch you," he murmured before letting go to unbutton his shirt. "I've never been so thankful to be married as I was tonight."

Amanda said nothing as she hung up her gown before removing her hairpins. Though she still felt she'd been wronged, feeding her rage had become too wearying.

Reagan undressed while Amanda opened the bureau to inspect her sleepwear. She decided that after the incautious ride home, a modest nightgown would serve her well. She didn't notice when Reagan slipped behind her until he removed her hand from her intended selection. "No, love. You shan't wear those tonight."

He drew his arms upward until her breasts strained to near bursting against her chemise. "Ah, now there's a sight for sore eyes!" He chuckled as he pressed himself against her backside. "I'm afraid it'd be a waste of time—"

"Reagan," she pleaded as he turned her in his arms. "It seems we've done more than enough..." she looked at him imploringly, "...it's late..."

"Nay, milady!" He ran his hands over her hips before pressing her against him. Her eyes widened as she felt the reason for his eagerness.

"You're worse than a rutting stag!" She tried breaking free but found herself swept up before being carried toward the bed. "Shouldn't you be content with the plunder you secured while my wits weren't about me?"

Reagan grinned as he withdrew his arm, relishing the feel of her while she slid against his naked body. "I've been nigh starved unto death these past months. You can't fault me if I've more pressing needs than sleep." Reaching down, he peeled off her chemise. "Don't worry," he said, flinging the shift over his shoulder. "I should be satisfied come morning."

As his smoldering gaze traversed her body, Amanda thought to remain unresponsive. But when he cupped her face and tasted her lips, her arms somehow found their way around his neck.

"You're so beautiful," he breathed, his gaze dipping to take his fill of silken flesh. A hand traced a path over her flanks as his other captured a breast. It was as if he wanted to memorize every part of her, leaving no place untouched, his mouth once again exploring her body. Amanda trembled from the chill air as well as anticipation and when he lifted her, she nestled against him like melted wax. Then, resting a knee upon the bed, Reagan lowered her before encompassing her with his body.

Amanda sighed in surrender. She would decide her marital position later, for tonight she couldn't think while Reagan slanted his mouth over hers in a penetrating kiss. Leisurely, and with deliberate care, he made love, not yielding to his own mounting ardor until Amanda was fully sated. Then, mindful of the fragile gift he'd just been granted, he lay beside her in a tender embrace. As a blissful contentment settled over him, he determined he wouldn't allow another barrier between them. He decidedly preferred married life, after all.

chapter 75

AMANDA AWAKENED TO sounds of water splashing in the bathing chamber. Groaning, she pulled a pillow over her head to obscure morning sunshine streaming through the window.

"That ought t' do for th' misses," a voice penetrated her pillow. "There's plenty of clean towels and scented soaps she's so fond of."

"Thank you, Lela," Reagan said. "Please tell Mrs. Baker we'd appreciate a breakfast tray to be sent up in about an hour." Closing the door, Reagan approached the bed to give Amanda's bottom a playful slap. When she peeked out with one bleary eye, he chuckled. "Arise, lazybones!"

"Tisn't fair!" she grumbled, covering her eye with the palm of her hand. "You kept me up half the night."

"You weren't complaining last night," he said as he tugged the coverlet. "In fact, you were begging for more."

"I did not," she countered, snatching the blanket and looking warily at her husband. After a night of amorous lovemaking, she presumed there'd be time to reconsider her position. "I'll need my wrapper, if you don't mind."

Reagan was aware that she was totally bare beneath the covers. "Oh, but I *do* mind, milady," he said. "A husband has certain rights, and one of them is to view his wife in various states of undress."

"You used that up last night," she argued, her attention drawn to the tub. She felt an intense desire for a hot, soapy bath. Returning her gaze to her husband, she attempted a stern demeanor. "Now please bring me my wrapper."

Reagan folded his arms and leaned against the bedpost. "No." He lifted a brow, waiting to see what she'd do.

"Then, I'll just stay in bed until you leave."

"Oh, I have all morning," he said, inspecting his fingernails before tucking them under his arm. "And I'm afraid the water's getting cold."

Amanda glared as she pointed at the window. "But, it's broad daylight."

"So it is," he agreed, smiling broadly.

"It's-it's-oohhh!" Throwing back the covers, she scooted to the edge of the bed, giving the linen a hard yank. Wrapping the sheet around her, she entered the bathing chamber and stood at the mirror, pinning her hair. Seeing his intense gaze in the reflection, Amanda had the urge to torment him just a little.

"Will you let me bathe in peace?" she asked. Reagan's eyes were drawn to her fingers as she lifted the tucked end of the linen. When he didn't answer, she released the cloth, letting it fall. Amanda couldn't know the sight of her bare form filled him with such desire; it was as if his passions hadn't been eased. Unaware of his sudden fervor, she stepped into the tub and with her back toward him, vigorously sudsed her cloth.

"I shan't be long," she warbled, "then you can bathe, if you wish." Hearing an unexpected thud, she turned to see him reaching for his other boot.

"What are you doing?" she said as the second boot joined the other. He then began to undo his buttons. As his shirt flew across the floor, her eyes widened. He grinned lecherously while undoing his trousers.

"You can just wait until I finish," Amanda warned when he dropped the last of his clothing.

"I'm not chasing you out," Reagan said, stepping in the water. "I'm joining you." Grasping both edges of the porcelain, he lowered himself until trapping Amanda on either side with his legs.

Amanda scooted as far forward as the tub allowed, and as she hunched forward, she gave him an unobstructed view of her rounded backside. "This is outrageous!" she cried, pinching his toe. "I can't even enjoy a mere bath! This is what I get for allowing you—"

"Allowing me what?" Reagan pulled Amanda toward him, savoring her softness. "The simple pleasures that other married men lay claim to?"

He then took her cloth, lathering it before scrubbing her back. As his fingers worked downward, she ceased her objections, reveling in the impromptu massage. Afterward, he planted a kiss on her neck while reaching around to cup both breasts. Pleasurable sensations coursed through Amanda's body as he leisurely caressed her. With a sigh, she closed her eyes and lay against his chest. There was no use fighting him, she thought. Sooner or later he'd have his fill.

After a few moments, he placed the cloth in her hand. "What am I to do with this?" she asked, giggling.

"Why, you're going to wash *my* back," he said, nuzzling her neck while running hands along her thighs.

"I can't reach it," she said. "I'm in an impossible position."

"Well, then, let me help you," he whispered. Raising her knee, he turned her until her legs girdled him. "There," he said, draping her arms around his neck. "You're now in position." As he waited, his eyes filled with mischief. Not sure what he was about, Amanda laid the soapy cloth on his neck and stroked in a circular motion. As she reached further, she found his lips against hers while he lifted her intimately onto his lap.

Amanda burst into laughter. "That tickles," she protested. "Hold still or I shan't be able to finish."

Reagan luxuriated in the feel of her wet skin under his moving hands. He nibbled her ear before raining kisses down her throat. As Amanda continued to wash, she shifted the cloth to her other hand, stretching to reach his lower back.

With ravishment on his mind, he grabbed her hips, but Amanda dropped the cloth to run bare fingers over his skin. "What *is* that?" she asked. "There's something all over your back." She tried looking over his shoulder but finally rose on her knees. "Let me see," she said, pushing him sideways to lean behind him. "Good Lord, Reagan," she gasped. "You have scratches all over your back!" She sat on her heels as Reagan tried looking over his shoulder.

"I can't see it," he said finally.

"Turn around," she instructed. Both stood and while water ran from their bodies in soapy rivulets, she gently ran fingers over the scabs. "What'd you do?" she asked.

"I don't know. I've felt something, but didn't know what it was."

Amanda examined the strange markings, realizing with a start that they were uniformly scored. Her brow knit in confusion until she glanced at her own fingernails while tracing their pattern. She drew in her breath so suddenly that Reagan twirled in concern, finding himself staring into her furious eyes. "You-you-*bastard!*" she spat, color draining from her face. "You were with another woman!" Amanda stumbled from the tub, splashing great quantities of water.

Reagan was confounded. "What are you talking about? I've *not* been with another woman!" He stepped out as Amanda grabbed a towel.

"Get away!" she sobbed. "Don't touch me!" She ran to the bedroom with Reagan close behind.

"Amanda!" he stormed. "Listen to me!" He yanked her against his chest. "I was *not* with another woman..."

Tears fell as she glared at him. "All those nights at the hotel," she gasped. "How could I have been so stupid?"

Reagan's face became livid. "Dammit woman, you must listen to me!" He gave her a shake, causing her towel to fall. "If I'd been with a woman who raked me, do you think I'd be so lacking in judgment that I'd have you wash my back?"

"How else could you have received those marks? Tis pretty obvious to *me* what they are! If not that," her lips curled with rage, "then what, pray tell, gave you those scratches?"

Reagan stared, looking uncertain. "I don't know," he sighed, bending to retrieve her towel. "I can't say why I'm marked. I only know that while I stayed at the Rochester, I consumed a fair amount of alcohol. Perhaps in my sottish state, I scraped myself."

"I don't know either," she said, gripping her towel. "I only know I have a right to be suspicious when you can't explain such a condition."

"Amanda..."

"What else can it be?" she asked, searching his face.

Reagan's shoulders drooped. "I have no explanation. But I ask you to believe that I've not betrayed you."

Amanda felt more conflicted than ever. She wanted to trust him, yet her mind screamed this was just another example of Reagan playing her false. "I need time to think..."

Seeing her shiver, Reagan took her arm. "If we're going to drip dry, then let's do it on the tile where it can be wiped up." Leading her back to the bath, he folded another towel and placed it on the tub's edge. "Sit here," he said.

Amanda watched Reagan wipe the floor, seemingly unperturbed he was parading naked before her. Her eyes were drawn to his back, then lower, to his exposed flanks as she recalled the feel of him when they made love. She felt anguish that another woman had received that which should've been hers alone. But, to whom did she truly belong? Averting her eyes, Amanda finally dried herself.

"I need to get dressed before Lela returns," she said, tossing the towel she had been sitting on. "Cover yourself before she sees you."

Reagan caught the towel before it hit his face. "Clearly, the sight is offensive to you, as well," he said, scowling darkly.

Amanda adjusted her towel. "I don't know what you're talking about. I simply don't wish to shock the poor girl."

"You don't have to worry, madam," Reagan said as he retrieved his clothes. "I locked the bedroom door."

The pain in his eyes caused Amanda a shard of remorse. She tried thinking of him as anything other than a womanizing scoundrel. "Could you have fallen somehow while drunk?" she asked hopefully.

"It's unlikely we'll ever know." Reagan pulled on his trousers then tucked his shirt. "Unless my recollections become clearer, I don't see how I can shed any more light on the subject."

When Lela brought the breakfast tray they both appeared composed. Yet, they had more on their minds than the meal. Each felt something warm and wonderful had been snatched from their grasp just when they thought they had found it.

chapter 76

"What's yer pleasure, Mister?" Molly sidled up to a soldier at the bar. "Would you be wantin' company?"

The man barely looked at her before lifting his shot glass. "It's a free country," he said. "For most, anyways."

Molly looked admiringly at the sky-blue trousers and dark jacket. Though most soldiers frequenting the saloon were poor, ill-kept lads, this one had an air of authority. And despite having an arm in a sling, his body seemed sturdily robust.

"What's that?" She pointed at half-chevrons on his sleeve. "Look's like snakes with wings." Her eyes grew wide. "Are you a snake charmer?" She smiled in what she hoped was an alluring manner. "You look like a charmer to me."

The soldier gave a brief snort. "No." He swirled the liquor before taking another sip.

Molly frowned at her inability to snare the man's interest. Usually, she could entice a lad to her room where, if the alcohol didn't besot him, a few drops of chloral hydrate would do the job nicely. She'd then go through his pockets before Orville dumped him in the back alley. Later, he'd awaken with a splitting headache and no memory of where he'd lost his money.

"Let's get a better look at you." She reached over and removed his cap, exposing wavy hair and blue eyes that finally looked her way. "Lookee there," she said, smiling. "Ain't you a handsome Yank!" She playfully held the cap away when he tried retrieving it, placing it on her head. "Not so fast, soldier. I want to try it on."

Pulling the cap low, she sashayed before him, giving a view of her tight-fitting frock. The soldier's eyes wandered down her body, stopping briefly where bodice and waist met, then lower, to where her calves were exposed by the shortened hem. "When you're finished," he said patiently, "I'd appreciate if you'd return my hat."

"You got a name, soldier?" Molly asked, raising her chin.

The soldier seemed to consider her request. "Warrant Officer Miles Alexander."

Drawing near, she exaggerated a pout, dropping her eyes to his bandaged arm. "You ain't gonna be needing this ol' cap anytime soon, Warrant Officer Miles Alexander." She pretended to straighten his collar while looking into his eyes. "Why don't you buy me a drink, and then perhaps I'll allow you to escort me to my room?"

Molly licked her lips, thinking she'd soon have a wad of money to give Orville. Of late, he had begun demanding more cash than she could earn. He explained that it was too risky to contact his associates. Once it was safe, he promised to have a large draw with which to repay her. "I'd be very careful of yer wound," she crooned while rubbing his jaw. "It wouldn't be a bother, t'all."

"Aren't you concerned about hurting the baby?"

The unexpected disclosure had the effect of throwing cold water in her face. She looked stunned. "H-how'd you know?"

Miles stepped back before retrieving his hat. "Because, madam, I'm *Doctor* Miles Alexander."

Molly's hands instinctively covered her belly. "I-I didn't think anyone would notice," she whispered.

"Surely, you knew it could be a...hazard...to your occupation," he said, his eyes not unkind.

"Yes, but..." Molly bit her lip as she realized others would soon recognize her condition. "...I can't let anyone know...yet..." She cast a worried look up the stairs where a dapperly dressed gentleman leaned against a post. Chewing on a toothpick, the man surveyed the bar before his eyes came to rest on Molly.

She looked beseechingly at the doctor before forcing a smile. "Look, I can still give you a real good time!" She grabbed his hand and tried pulling him toward the stairs. "I know you soldiers are away from home and-and lonely. I-I could just spend some time talkin' or some such, 'bout yer loved ones."

Miles glanced at the man on the landing before withdrawing his hand. "Look ma'am, I'm on leave because I haven't the full use of my hand. I'm not looking to be permanently disabled by getting my head bashed in." Molly stepped back, her mouth gaping before she turned and fled upstairs. Miles continued to watch until the man pulled her into a room.

Repositioning his cap, Miles motioned for another whiskey. While attending the wounded on the battlefield, a bullet had shattered his hand. Now, he could barely flex his fingers. Despite the disabling wound, he felt determined to regain the use of his hand so he could return to his regiment. He didn't have time for harlots, thieves or scoundrels.

❧

"What do you mean he knew what you were about?" Derrick shoved Molly into the room before slamming the door. "All you have to do is get them up here!" he said, moving toward her. "I don't care what you promise them! That soldier was a good mark. He was worth at least fifty dollars!"

Molly shrank against the bed. "I-I don't know how, but-but he acted as if he knew I was goin' to rob him."

She shielded her face as Derrick shook her. "What'd you say to him?"

"Nothin'!" she screeched. "I didn't tell him nuthin'!"

Holding her, Derrick cuffed a cheek then pulled back to slap her again. "Dammit woman, I need that money!"

"Not my face! I cain't get men, when you bruise me!"

Derrick threw her against the mattress. “Look at you!” he bellowed in disgust. “Why don’t you wear that red gown? It’ll snatch a man’s eye faster than that old rag!”

“Cain’t fit into it anymore,” she sniffed, rubbing her cheek.

“Can’t fit into it?” His gaze traveled her body, stopping at the slight swell in her abdomen. When she shielded the protrusion with her hands, Derrick raised accusing eyes. “So, you got yourself a brat. Who’s the bastard’s father?”

“Since you came back, I ain’t been with no other,” Molly said. “You’ve been here most every night.”

“Not every night,” he corrected.

He paced the floor, rubbing his chin. Finally, he stopped. “My dear, we’re going to find a pappy for your babe,” he said.

“But, you’re the father,” she said warily. “I counted from my last monthly, and figured it ‘bout the time you returned.”

Derrick shook his head. “No, the father of your baby is a rich man. One who’ll provide for you without question.”

Molly dabbed her eyes with the sheet. “I weren’t really with any rich men, like I said before. The girls told me about those who’d pay extra, if I was willin’ to let them do anything they wanted. That way, I wouldn’t have to spend as much time with the lumber slingers. But, that was before you...” she smiled hesitantly. “When you came back, I only did what you told me. I haven’t had enough to buy clothes because you needed the money." She sniffed, looking forlornly at the new suit the man she knew as Orville, wore. He always had enough to dress well, while she had to make do with clothes that would soon be too small.

Derrick allowed his face to soften as he withdrew his wallet. "What you're going to do is tell everybody you've been meeting privately with a rich gentleman." He removed several bills, throwing them onto the bed. "Here, go buy yourself a dress that fits and a fancy ring." He smiled. "I've been neglecting my dove for too long."

Molly gathered the money, wiping her tears with the back of her hand. "I'll buy the prettiest dress in the shop!"

"And everything that goes with it," he said, tossing another bill. "A hat and parasol. You must look your best."

Molly got up from the bed and wrapped her arms around his neck. "Oh, Orville, thank you. I knew you weren't really mad at me."

Derrick ran his hands over her backside, pressing her to him. "Well now," he crooned, his eyes hardening. "Since we're here all by ourselves, why don't you show me how grateful you really are?"

She wavered uneasily. "If'n you're no longer annoyed 'bout that soldier. She paused before continuing, "Sometimes when you're upset, you get a little rough." She looked into his face. "You ain't still mad, are you?"

"Why, no, of course not." Derrick's eyes glinted. "But since this dress is really too small, there's no sense in saving it." With a sudden, downward motion he seized the bodice and ripped the dress.

Molly inhaled sharply, her fears confirmed as she tried breaking free of his grasp. "Orville, no! If you're too rough you'll hurt the babe!" She squirmed as he tore the rest of her clothing.

"Then-don't-fight-me," he panted, pushing her onto the bed. Molly lay quietly, her tears streaming as Derrick removed his coat. When he began unbuttoning his shirt, she removed the pins from her hair, shaking it loose.

"See? I'm not fighting you..." she quaked as he sat on the bed. "...I just don't want you to be angry."

Leaning over, Derrick stroked her face. "I'm no longer cross with you, my dear," he said, his fingers entwining her hair. "But I have a plan, and I must be assured you're going to help me." He studied her lips before lowering his mouth, capturing her lower lip between his teeth. He nipped the tender skin, tasting a drop of blood before kissing her slowly.

"So," he said, raising his gaze, "do I have your word you'll do exactly as I ask?"

"Y-yes," she whispered. "I promise to do exactly as you say."

"That's a good girl," he said. "Because if all goes well, you and I will be rich beyond our wildest dreams."

Molly looked wonderingly into his face. "You... and me? We'll be together...no longer here, at the saloon?"

"If you play your cards right," he said, moving above her. "You'll be a lady of leisure and beholden to no one, but me."

"Do you promise?" she asked, searching his face. Since discovering her pregnancy, she desired nothing more than security for herself and the child.

"As surely as my name is Orville Farnsworth," Derrick said as he positioned himself between her thighs. "You'll share in all my wealth when my mission is complete."

"Oh, Orville," Molly breathed. "That's all I've ever wanted!"

chapter 77

George Bruester arrived at his office and began sorting through the day's receipts when he heard a knock at the door.

"Excuse me, Mr. Bruester," the bank secretary said, entering. "Mr. Schuyler would like a word with you."

"Certainly," George replied. Lucian Schuyler had been his bookkeeper for more than twenty years and as far as George knew, never missed a day of work.

When Lucian entered, George indicated a chair. "Have a seat, Mr. Schuyler."

"Thank you," Lucian said.

"How's your family?" George asked. "I understand your grandson is about to enter college. You must be very proud."

Lucian nodded while he repositioned his spectacles. "Very proud, indeed."

"So, what can I do for you?"

"Due to foul weather, we were late in receiving a batch of outstanding cheques from the bank's private account." Lucian opened his folder and removed a cheque. "Out of all the receipts, this one caught my attention." He leaned forward and extended the document. "Although it bears your signature, it seems different. Also, I cannot find a corresponding entry in our ledgers."

George took the draft. "The recipient is Orville Farnsworth," he said. "Have we ever done business with the man? That name is unfamiliar to me."

"None that I could discover, sir. I took the liberty of going back several years to see if he appeared on our archives and found no such name."

George turned his attention to the cheques' signature. Although it was his name, the penmanship wasn't. The writer must've been familiar with his handwriting, however, for he had done a fair job of imitating the distinctive script.

"It seems we have a thief in our midst," George said, leaning back. "I'm sorry to say, I didn't write this cheque. You were very observant to catch the discrepancy."

Lucian allowed a modest smile. "Thank you, Mr. Bruester. But after all these years, I've become intimately familiar with your signature."

"I suppose we'll need to take a handwriting sample of every employee since this cheque was obviously removed from my desk."

"Of course, sir. I'll inform Mr. Spelding at once."

"No need. I'll do that myself." George paused, deep in thought. "By the way, where did the draft get cashed, Mr. Schuyler?"

"In Turnersville, sir."

"Pennsyl-*vania*? Good God, he crossed the state line?"

"Yes sir," Lucian said. "That's why it took so long for the cheque to get back to us."

"It seems our thief isn't so stupid, after all. I believe we might need the help of a private investigator," he said as he wrote some notes. "Orville Farnsworth may've been smart enough to steal my money, but he made a mistake thinking I'll let him get away with it." He stood, placing the forged cheque into his pocket. "Let's see if my friends at Simon and Helfrich can help in our probe." George grinned. "Between you and me, I'd say Orville Farnsworth hasn't got a prayer!"

chapter 78

MOLLY STOOD ON a path that ran alongside Old Mill Road, near Cantonsville. After questioning a few lumbermen who frequented the saloon, she discovered this was the road Reagan Burnsfield took each morning to the mill. She smoothed her skirt as she waited. The bright yellow dress, patterned with dots had caught her eye while displayed in the dressmaker's window. The seamstress had assured her the pleated silk would certainly be noticed and with its high cut waist, her pregnancy well hidden. She'd chosen a black silk jacket with magenta piping, leaving the front undone to show the snug-fitting bodice. Of late, her bosom had filled out and the tight fit caused her breasts to ache uncomfortably. That morning she had frizzed her bangs and kohled her eyes before applying a small amount of rouge and a light shade of pink to her lips. With her hair curled under her ribboned hat, it was the closest she'd ever come to appearing attractive.

Orville had dropped her from his rented buggy and for an hour Molly paced, concealing her face with her parasol. When she spotted the Burnsfield conveyance, she began walking toward the road with an exaggerated limp, waving frantically. "Yoo-hoo!" she called, reciting her words carefully. "Kind sir, could you give a lady some help?"

The driver slowed, leaning down to talk to someone in the carriage, then came alongside and stopped. Before the driver could descend, the door opened and Reagan stepped out. "May I be of assistance?"

Molly had almost forgotten how handsome the lumberman was. She recalled her pounding heart when she first saw Reagan entering church. From then on, she made a point to sit next to the aisle in the hopes he'd notice her. To her dismay, he never did until that day when she forced the issue.

Reagan seemed to tower over her as she tipped her parasol back. Momentarily speechless, she found her voice when he repeated his query. "Oh-yes!" she breathed. "I was taking my morning walk." She indicated the intersecting road where several modest homes lined the edge of town. "And, seem to have turned my ankle." Lifting the hem, she displayed a lot more than just her booted foot.

"Whoa!" Reagan held up his hand, blocking his view. "That's far enough."

"Oops," she giggled. Dropping her skirt, she rested a gloved hand on his. "Would you be so kind as to give me a lift? I'd be grateful if you could drop me off near the dressmakers."

Reagan led her toward the carriage, considerate of her faltering gait. "Wouldn't you prefer I take you home? Perhaps, your family is wondering where you are."

"Oh no," she hastened to say. "In fact, I'm meeting a-a family member in town. I can go on from there." With her hand on his arm, Molly couldn't help but feel if Reagan could've seen how she looked now, she might've snared the man before he wed the Bruester girl.

By the time they reached the carriage, the driver had the step in place. Closing her parasol, Molly leaned on Reagan's arm as she ascended the step before suddenly losing her footing. "Oh my!" she cried as Reagan caught her. "My ankle pains me so, I can barely put weight on it."

Reagan grimaced, hoisting her into the narrow opening. "That's quite all right. I'm right behind you." After instructing the driver, he took the seat opposite Molly.

She smoothed her gown before smiling invitingly. "Thank you for stopping. I don't know how many passed by without a second look. I thought I'd faint from misery."

"Perhaps you should be taken to a doctor," he suggested. "Your ankle may be sprained and in need of attention."

"With rest, I'm sure it'll be much better."

"As you see fit," he said. "However, I think you should see Doc Turner if there's no improvement."

Warmed by his apparent concern, Molly tried her best to strike a pitying pose. Her job would be much easier if he remained sympathetic toward her plight. "I will," she promised.

When Reagan first saw the girl, he had a nagging idea he'd met her before. Yet, he couldn't recall being introduced, and finally gave in to his curiosity. "Are we acquainted? For some reason, you look familiar to me."

Molly debated whether to remind him of their brief encounter where he'd barely spoken to her. She decided he would never be interested in her unless she portrayed herself as a woman of means. "I believe I've seen you during Sunday services," she articulated her words carefully, as Orville had instructed. "However, I haven't had the pleasure of your acquaintance."

"I see," Reagan said, smiling politely. "That must be it." Yet, the notion he'd spoken to her lingered and after a few moments, he began again. "What's your name? Perhaps, I know your family."

Molly hesitated. Would he have heard of her father, Phineas? Not likely, as the elder scratched out a living several miles from town. Her mother had died when she was only seven, forcing her to do all household chores until she was old enough to hire out as a laundress. "Molly Carnes," she said, lowering her lashes. "*Miss* Molly Carnes."

Reagan searched his memory to no avail. "I'm sorry," he said, shaking his head. "I guess we've not met, after all. I'm Reagan Burnsfield and I'm pleased to make your acquaintance."

Molly could tell by the passing scenery that they were nearing the dressmakers. She didn't have long to execute Orville's plan. If she were going to later accuse

Reagan of fathering her child, she needed to bed him at least once. The timing of the birth wouldn't be as important as the fact he couldn't deny having slept with her.

"Reagan Burnsfield..." she let the name roll off her tongue, "...there's one more thing I'd ask of you."

"Of course," he said. "What else can I do?"

Using her closed parasol like a cane, Molly switched seats. "I'd very much like to repay your kindness," she said, laying the parasol next to her feet. She daringly placed a hand on his thigh. "I can be very appreciative and understand what pleases a man." She leaned forward to let her perfume waft from its liberal application. "As a matter of fact, I have a room at the Rochester. I've found it to be convenient whenever I wish to enjoy an afternoon's repast." She lowered her gaze to his lips. "We could have a nice visit—in private."

Astounded, Reagan could only stare agog at the lady's expectant posture. Never as a bachelor had a woman approached him so boldly. He began to seriously doubt his chivalry, when not once, but now twice, a woman had declared herself willing to bed him with no provocation on his part. "That's quite unnecessary," he said, hastily setting her hand aside. "There's no recompense for what any man would do."

Molly's anxiety grew apace with his rejection and her words reverted to her natural diction. "Surely you ain't afraid of a little gal like me? I wouldn't keep you none too long." Leaning against him, she attempted a kiss. "I promise not to tell..."

Reagan jumped up as the carriage came to a halt. With the alacrity of a much younger man he hopped out, setting the step himself. "Madam," he said as he held out his hand. "Allow me."

Molly wavered, fearful she'd endure Orville's wrath if she failed to entice Reagan to her suite. "At the very least, you could walk me to my room. I may not be able to climb the stairs with my ankle painin' me so."

When Reagan didn't respond, she reluctantly accepted his assistance from the carriage. "I-I think it's hurtin' a little more..." she said, making as if to stumble.

"My conscience wouldn't rest unless it was to *Doctor Turner's,* I escorted you," Reagan said, remaining adamant. "His office is nearby. Otherwise, I must beg your forgiveness in not taking you to the Rochester." He indicated the passersby. "It wouldn't be seemly for a married man to escort a lady anywhere but the most public of places."

Molly pressed a hand to her lips, her eyes welling with tears. "Of course," she murmured as she fumbled for a handkerchief. "I understand."

"Are you well?" He grew alarmed at her sudden change. "Doctor Turner should be in his office."

"No, I..." Molly didn't want another doctor to recognize her condition. "...my brother...will be along soon." She smiled weakly. "He'll take care of me."

"Then, if all is well, I bid you adieu." As Reagan turned, he nearly ran into a middle-aged, diminutive woman. "I beg your pardon!" he said. Looking into the startled face, he recognized the sharply pinched face of Clara Farrington. Reagan couldn't believe his ill luck. "Oh, hello, Mrs. Farrington."

"Hello, Reagan." She looked at him fixedly before settling her eyes on Molly. By all indications, both had just emerged from Reagan's carriage and the woman appeared to be weeping.

Clara was in the forefront of organizing the Ladies Aid Society that sewed uniforms for the Army. Daily, she scoured shops for whatever material the merchants would donate, and when forced by necessity, bartered the lowest price for cloth. It was one such mission she was now on.

"I beg your pardon," Clara said, looking Molly up and down. "I don't believe we've been introduced."

Reagan knew this wasn't going to bode well, but had no choice in making known the two women. "This is Molly Carnes. Molly turned her ankle while on her morning walk and flagged my driver for help. I'm just now dropping her off so she can wait for her brother." He turned to Molly. "Miss Carnes, this is Clara Farrington, one of the busiest ladies in town...with her work in the war effort, that is."

"H-hello, Mrs. F-farrin'ton." Molly didn't know what to do with her hands and began worrying her handkerchief. "Pleased-I'm sure."

Ignoring Molly, Mrs. Farrington turned to Reagan. "Please give my regards to your family. Now, if you'll excuse me, I must be about my business." With that, Clara entered the dressmaker's shop.

Tears spilled down Molly's cheeks in sudden trepidation. Orville had told her many times that a woman with red, puffy eyes was unattractive, and lately he'd been reminding her quite often. If he spied her in that condition, he'd accuse her of undermining his strategy. "Please forgive me," she said, wiping her eyes. "For some reason, I became unnerved when you introduced us."

"That woman could upset the hardiest soul," he said trying to sound reassuring. "Why do you think the Ladies Aid uses her to request donations? With one look, Clara can intimidate the stingiest merchant!"

Despite herself, Molly laughed. She couldn't remember the last time Orville tried making her smile. Rather, he seemed to enjoy pointing out her many faults.

With Reagan's softening demeanor, she wondered if he would change his mind. "I-I don't suppose you'd be willin' to take me to the Rochester? My invitation's still open," she said in a hopeful voice.

"I'm afraid not." Reagan now perceived Molly to be one of the women who earned her living entertaining men. And although he never availed himself of their services, neither did he hold animosity toward those who did. "I must be getting along," he said. "I'm sure your brother will be along shortly." With one last nod, he climbed into his carriage and shut the door.

Molly watched as the conveyance pulled away and though she hoped he would, Reagan didn't once look back. With a sigh, she realized she'd have to face

Orville's anger with another failure. Gathering her skirt, she made her way along the boardwalk.

Unbeknownst to Molly, Clara Farrington was observing her closely through the dressmaker's window. That Molly now walked rapidly and without the slightest limp convinced her Reagan Burnsfield had lied. Not only that, it confirmed the rumors that his hasty marriage wasn't all it was purported to be.

Turning away, Clara's eyes gleamed with righteous indignation at Reagan's brazen lack of prudence. Obviously, he had no qualms about flaunting his indiscretions.

Clara could hardly wait to disgorge this newly obtained tidbit at her next sewing circle.

chapter 79

IN SPITE OF Molly's failure to entice Reagan into a tryst, Derrick had remained remarkably calm. Having been hired as a mill worker at the Burnsfield mill, he had been recently assigned to the new mill when it opened. After working a few days and having accustomed himself to the layout of the building, he quit. He decidedly preferred the anonymity of hiding in Molly's room against the possibility of being recognized elsewhere. It hadn't taken much to convince Molly that he'd be more successful in his mission if he stayed at the saloon with her. Though she never saw them, he had insisted he routinely met with agents who worked to counter acts of suspected espionage. Since his cover portrayed him as a gentleman gambler, he supplemented his wardrobe using her money while reassuring her she would be reimbursed.

With his tie meticulously knotted, Derrick ran his hands over his expensive suit. "What do you think, my dear?" He swiped a finger over the brim of his new derby. "Do I look like a man who's about to obtain a substantial amount of money?"

Clad only in her nightgown, Molly sat at her dresser looking nervously at a satchel. Derrick had been vague about his link to Reagan Burnsfield, claiming it had to do with his undercover work. "D'ya think it'll work? I-I mean, you...stole...papers from his office, and all. What I meant," she said, cringing at his furrowed brow. "He-he won't throw you in jail, or nuthin', will he?"

Derrick stared, thinking before long she'd be useless to him. Yet for now, she still provided a safe haven. "Worried, my dear?" he asked, planting a cold kiss on her lips. "You needn't fret. The last thing Reagan Burnsfield wants is his affairs being exposed."

Molly absently rubbed her arms. "But, what if it doesn't work? I couldn't get him to the hotel. He's not so easy to persuade."

"Our Mr. Burnsfield needs a different kind of persuasion. We'll see if he disregards what I have to say," he said, picking up the satchel. "Put something pretty on, because when I return we're going to celebrate."

She perked up. "You gonna take me someplace fancy? Or, maybe a drive by the river..." Her voice trailed off as he shook his head.

"You know I can't be seen with you." He opened the door, peering out. "I'll bring back some champagne."

After he left, Molly stared in the mirror. "Look at you," she muttered. "You ain't worth more'n two-bits!" Nothing, it seemed, had gone as she imagined. By now, she had expected Orville to rescue her from her life as a harlot. Instead, she was still no better off than when she came. As a sudden, small kick interrupted her reverie, visions of being alone with a babe in her arms taunted her. Tears formed as she pressed a hand against her side. Since her pregnancy was increasingly apparent, none except the most drunken patrons seemed interested in following her up the stairs for the promise of a romp. More and more, she detested her life, believing Orville to be her only escape. Pushing aside fears he might be a double-dealer, Molly concentrated instead on his promise to take care of her and the babe. "You'll see," she crooned to the child within. "Things will get better."

⁂

From his days as a mill worker, Derrick recalled Reagan's penchant for staying in his office while others took their noon break. So with no one to stop him, he entered the outer office and made his way to Reagan's door. Then, after a terse knock, entered.

It took only a moment for Reagan to recognize the man barging into his office. He remained calm, though clearly irritated by the trespass. "To what do I owe this pleasure, Mr. Banning?"

Derrick smiled, clearly in no hurry to satisfy Reagan's curiosity. "I've come to do business with you, Mr. Burnsfield."

"Business?" Reagan snorted derisively. "What kind of business?"

"That which will be mutually beneficial. Before we start, we'll begin with the premise you took something that was rightfully mine. Quite unfairly, I must say," he said, taking a seat.

"I don't know what you're talking about," Reagan said. "I don't make a habit of taking another's property."

"I wouldn't have thought it necessary to spell it out," he said. "But if you insist-"

"Then, let's be quick about it," Reagan said. "I've better things to do than pass time with thumb-twiddlers."

Derrick ignored the insult while unbuckling his satchel. "Let's get back to my premise. I was well on my way to obtaining Amanda as my wife. But while I was gone temporarily, you forced her to marry you. Practically destroyed her reputation, poor girl. Had I been there, I could've saved her from your schemes." His lip curled in remembrance. "I'd say that amounted to thievery, pure and simple. Being a businessman, I expect you to understand my losses and make amends."

"I always knew you were a conniving little weasel. But, even you should recognize it's too late to dispute our marriage."

"Any contract can be nullified if fraud is proven," Derrick smirked as he removed his hat.

"Fraud?" Reagan couldn't believe his ears. "The only fraud I've witnessed is that which you perpetrated on George while you leeched off his good graces."

"I had business dealings," Derrick spat. "If I chose to seek a wife while doing so, what business was it of yours? Amanda was more interested in me before you sullied her name."

"It's too late," repeated Reagan. "So, why are you here?"

"I want Amanda in exchange for keeping me from ruining your precious company," he said. "Which is fair, in light of what you stole from me."

"There's nothing you could do to make me give up my wife," he said, standing. "It's time you left or I'll have the pleasure of throwing you out on your bony little ass."

"Not just yet. You're going to be very interested in what I have to show you, especially if you want to keep your marriage intact, as you profess."

Reagan's eyes narrowed.

"Come, come," Derrick said, stroking his mustache. "Do sit down and act civilized. You'll soon see the advantage of doing business with me. That's better," he said as Reagan finally sat. "There's no reason we can't resolve our differences like gentlemen." Pulling out a document, he tossed it onto the desk.

Reagan unfolded the certificate; shocked to discover it was one of his contracts. "How'd you get this?"

"How I obtained it isn't nearly as interesting as what I plan to do with the other contracts I took. To keep your precious wife, you're going to recompense my loss."

"I didn't steal anything from you. Amanda and I are married because I was the more persistent suitor."

"You were a wily snake, I'll admit," Derrick said, lifting his chin. "Without your interference, I would've been the one to procure her assets." His eyes wandered about the office. "You put it to good use, I see. For that offense, and to keep me from taking my evidence to Mr. Bruester, you'll have to pay me."

"All you have are stolen documents and a vivid imagination," Reagan said. "You can't prove we married for any other reason than the difficult situation we found ourselves in."

"Oh, I can do more than that," Derrick said. "If I were to show this to Amanda, I'm sure she'd find me the better man."

Reagan was stunned. If Amanda, in her present state of upset, became convinced their marriage could be annulled, she just might heed the scoundrel's advice. "So, what you're telling me is you don't really want Amanda," he said. "You just want the money."

"Oh, come now," Derrick chided. "Don't try to tell me you married the chit for any other reason. Although," he shrugged, grinning lecherously, "I'd have to say, she would've been an enjoyable ride-"

In sudden fury, Reagan launched himself over the desk. Seizing Derrick by the throat, he yanked him to his feet while dragging him across the desktop. As the smaller man twisted in his hands, blood lust surged, pounding Reagan's ears. "You swindler!" he ground out, "I ought to kill you!"

Pawing frantically, Derrick pried back Reagan's thumbs and sucked air into his lungs. "It'll d-do you n-no good," he croaked. "There are others..." Finding himself flung away, he stumbled backwards. "That'll cost you!" he wheezed, kicking his overturned chair.

Reagan's fingers still twitched as he watched Derrick cough while rubbing his throat. Though beyond exasperation, he saw no solution other than to submit to the bastard's extortion.

Reagan retook his seat with extreme restraint. Striking a match, he lit a cheroot before withdrawing a leather folio. "How much?" Poising his pen, he blew smoke in Derrick's direction. "A thousand, perhaps? Two thousand?"

Derrick couldn't believe his luck. Reagan was actually complying with his demands. In his arrogance, he believed he had drafted a strategy so flawless the lumberman was forced to acquiesce. With much bravado he picked up his fallen hat. "Nice try," he said hoarsely. "I'd say Amanda's worth at least fifty thousand."

"Fifty-thou-are you out of your mind? My money doesn't just sit in a bank; it's in the lumber you see outside. Until it's shipped, I don't have access to those kinds of funds. Try again."

"Very well," Derrick said, putting on his hat. "I'm a reasonable man. I'll take five thousand now and then I'll accept installments until I'm completely recompensed." He retrieved his satchel. "Remember," he warned, pointing a finger. "I've more evidence hidden away. And if you're thinking to eliminate me, I have a partner who'll expose you. By the way, make the cheque to 'bearer', it's so much easier that way."

Reagan pushed the draft across the desk. "I expect to have all stolen papers returned before you leave Cantonsville for good."

"With every payment, I'll return one of your contracts," Derrick said, snatching up the cheque. "Consider that scrap of paper yours again."

Reagan's face darkened. "Stay away from Amanda. If I find you sniffing around my wife, I won't stop the next time."

"As long as you do your part, I'll not interfere." He paused when he reached the door. "But, if you try crossing me, I'll destroy you."

After he left, Reagan formulated a plan. He would pay a visit to the Simon and Helfrich Detective Agency. Their swift and tenacious ability during a land dispute had proven valuable once before. He determined they must repeat that success once again.

chapter 80

Molly Carnes leaned against the inside of her door, at a loss as to what she should do. Downstairs, the revelry of drunken gamblers and wayward lovers reminded her of all she was missing.

Derrick, whom Molly knew as Orville, displayed his newfound wealth by showering her with baubles and fancy clothes. They ate sumptuously, drank the best liquor and ended the evenings with many a romp. Her happiness was short-lived however, as night after night Orville gambled while eager strumpets leaned on his shoulder. Within a fortnight, he'd resorted to his former self, becoming surly and handling her roughly at the slightest provocation. Lately, despite her growing belly, he began demanding she earn money so he wouldn't have to use all of his.

Rubbing her arms, she fretted over this newest twist of events. She feared Orville would soon cast her aside. Last night, he had come to bed reeking of cheap perfume. She wondered if Phineas, her father, would take her back. If he refused, she could always take up washing clothes in another town. With the war under way, it produced enough widows she could hide the truth of her pregnancy. If she had to fend for herself however, she needed money.

Molly went to the wardrobe and unlatched Orville's satchel. Her eyes widened at the large stack of bills still secured in bank wrappings. In a separate pocket she found the stolen contracts. She didn't understand how they could be used for blackmail, but determined if they could secure wealth for Orville, perhaps she could profit from them as well. Hiding the documents under her shawl, Molly crept down the back stairs.

Later, she returned to her room and packed her valise. After stowing it in the wardrobe, she donned a nightgown and crawled into bed. By tomorrow, she'd decide where to go.

The moon had long since passed its zenith when she heard the door open. "Light the lamp," Derrick ordered as he stumbled inside. It had become his practice to exit the saloon and reenter up the back stairs to avoid being observed from the barroom.

After lighting the wick, Molly watched him remove his shirt and throw it on the bed. "What are you looking at?" he sneered. He grabbed a whiskey bottle from the table. Tipping back his head, he drank deeply before tossing the bottle to the floor.

"Nuthin'," she said. She knew Orville only drank when he lost at gambling. "If you lost all my money, you can pay me back when you get yours." She scooped up the shirt but paused at a familiar scent.

"What money?"

"The money your gittin' from your mission..."

"Good God, woman. Haven't you figured it out yet? *You* were my mission. I needed a reason to hide out," he said, his gaze raking her form. "And some amusement to pass the time."

Shocked by his blunt admission, she let the shirt fall.

"Pick that up," he snarled. "It's French percale. I paid good money for that."

Obediently, Molly plucked the shirt off the floor. "It stinks of Ruby," she challenged as he snatched it from her fingers.

"What do you expect? The brat gets in the way." He turned to hang the shirt in the armoire. "You don't think I'm going to ignore my needs while you grow fat with that bastard, do you?" He looked over his shoulder, unperturbed at her stricken expression. "I've decided once the babe is born, you're going to get rid of it. I won't be a pappy to a whore's son."

Molly was stunned by his brutal words. "But, it's-it's most likely yours..."

"Now, I can't know that for sure, can I?" When his fingers missed the hanger, he dropped the shirt. "Dammit! Now look what you made me do," he said, fumbling through the wardrobe. But instead of finding the shirt, his hand snagged Molly's valise.

She grew fearful when he kicked at the suitcase but it barely moved. "I'll get it," she said, jumping out of bed.

Derrick watched with curiosity as she knelt to straighten the valise. "Why my dear," he said, brushing her hands aside to heft the bag. "This feels heavy. You aren't thinking of leaving me, are you?"

Molly shrank against the wardrobe, her eyes wide. "I-I'm goin' to visit my father. I don't do nuthin' all day, and-and miss my papa..."

"You said your papa threw you out when he discovered you whoring for money," he spat, throwing the valise across the room. "I don't like it when you keep secrets from me."

Molly cringed as Derrick grabbed her hair and yanked cruelly. "Your father won't take back a soiled bitch like yourself. So how'd you plan on feeding your ugly face and the bastard you carry?"

When she didn't answer, Derrick shoved her away. He then pulled out his satchel, doing a quick calculation with his money. When Molly fell, her fingers brushed against the forgotten whiskey bottle. She gripped it tightly while Derrick searched the outer pocket of his bag, finding it empty.

"Where are the contracts?" he demanded, twisting in her direction. "What've you done with them?"

Terrified, Molly rose to her knees. She could only stare helplessly into his eyes as he dragged her to her feet. With deliberate slowness he slid his hand to her throat, shoving her against the wardrobe.

"There are ways to make you talk," he said as his fetid breath filled the air. He braced an elbow under her jaw and dropped his hand to her belly. "I'll hurt the baby," he said, pressing until she groaned. "So, if you want the whelp to live, tell me where the contracts are."

Twisting in pain, Molly swung the whiskey bottle. It struck his head with a sickening thud before falling.

As it splintered against the floor, a sharp explosion burst in Derrick's brain. Stunned, he held her throat in a brutal grip until his vision cleared and his dazed condition passed.

With the force of a gathering storm, his anger turned to full-blown fury. "You bitch!" He slammed her head against the wardrobe with each word. "Tell-me-where-you-hid-the-contracts!"

Molly didn't answer but instead grew limp. As she crumpled forward, Derrick caught her in his arms and eased her to the floor. "Molly!" he said, shaking her and then slapping her roughly. "Molly, wake up!"

When she didn't respond, he placed an ear to her chest, finding no heartbeat. "You bitch!" he said, rising. "Where are they?"

Dumping her valise, Derrick found nothing but clothes. He then ransacked the room, even looking between the mattress and bedsprings. Unable to find the contracts, he paused to think. He knew Reagan would refuse to pay him if he couldn't produce the documents. He viciously kicked Molly's lifeless form. "Look what you've done!"

Yet, Derrick was nothing if not flexible. Whenever one scheme failed, he simply hatched another. If he could no longer use blackmail, then perhaps he could regain his wealth by other means. He began emptying Molly's room of his belongings, leaving no trace of Orville Farnsworth. He would once more become Derrick Banning. If everything went right, there'd soon be a Mrs. Banning to assure he would never be deprived again.

chapter 81

Sheriff Hadley looked forward to Sundays for no other reason than he could be at home with his wife and kids. He had just sat down to enjoy his coffee when he heard a persistent rapping at the door. "Sheriff Hadley!" an excited voice called. "Sheriff Hadley, you're needed at once!"

Opening the door, Jim retrieved his hat. "Slow down Joe, the sun's barely up. What's going on?"

"Sheriff," Deputy Welch panted. "A body's been found. You need to come quick." He yanked off his hat as Mrs. Hadley emerged from the kitchen. "Morning, ma'am."

"Good morning, Joe," Jane said.

"It's a-it's a-woman," the deputy said, lowering his voice while glancing at Jane. "They found the body of a woman at the new mill."

Sheriff Hadley pulled up his suspenders. "Have you sent for the doctor? We'll probably need a death certificate."

"Ed fetched Doc Turner already," the deputy affirmed.

Jim buckled on his holster before kissing his wife's cheek. "Go on to church without me," he said as he shouldered into his coat. "Timmy's old enough to hitch the carriage. I'll be back as soon as I can."

A gathering of onlookers parted to allow Deputy Joe Welch and Sheriff Hadley to enter the mill. Thomas and Reagan Burnsfield stood just inside the office while Deputy Edward McCrae and Doctor Artemus Turner knelt beside a body. Though the woman was obviously dead, the doctor was taking great pains to move her gently as he did an inspection.

"Hello, Thomas, Reagan," Sheriff Hadley nodded before glancing at his deputy. "Ed, what can you tell me so far?"

Deputy McCrae motioned toward a man standing against a wall. "This woman was discovered when the clerk there, Mr. Harris, came in early this morning to retrieve his forgotten paycheck. It seems the office staff has keys to open on workdays, and Mr. Harris thought he could slip in and pick up his check, even though it was Sunday. When he arrived, he said the door was already unlocked."

The sheriff looked at the clerk who was visibly shaken. "Mr. Harris, I'd like you to go with Deputy Welch, here, and give a statement of what you found. Can you do that?"

"Y-yes sir," the clerk nodded, eagerly following the deputy out.

Doctor Turner stood after he had examined the body, prompting Sheriff Hadley to speak. "What do you think, Doc?"

Artemus looked at Reagan and Thomas before turning to the sheriff. "Well, the woman was clearly murdered. She has multiple bruises around her neck as well as a concussion."

"Is she...?" The sheriff pointed to her bulging abdomen.

"I'll have to do a more thorough examination," Doc Turner said. "But it looks like she was pregnant."

Sheriff Hadley turned to the Burnsfields. "Do either of you recognize this girl?"

Thomas shook his head. "I've never seen the lass."

"How about you?" Jim asked, looking at Reagan. "Do you recognize her?"

"Yes, I believe I've met the woman," he said, frowning. "Although I can't be sure, she looks very much like the lady I assisted a couple of weeks ago."

Thomas looked shocked. "You knew her?"

"A woman walking the path beside Old Mill Road had injured her ankle. When our driver spotted her, of course I insisted we stop. I gave her a lift to the dressmakers, where she said her brother would be."

"And you're *sure* that was the only time you met the young woman?" Jim asked. "You didn't know her before or see her afterward?"

"Not that I can recall," he said, staring at Molly's lifeless form. "But, I know I didn't see her afterward."

Jim lifted a pencil and paper from Reagan's desk. "Did she say who she was?" he questioned. "I'm borrowing these, by the way."

"That's perfectly fine," Reagan said, smiling weakly. "If I remember correctly, I believe she said her name was Molly Carnes. And...there was something else..." He tapped his thumbs as he tried recalling their conversation. "She said she lived in one of the houses nearby, and her father's name was..." here Reagan paused as he searched his memory, "...Fin-no-Phineas. Phineas Carnes."

The sheriff rubbed his neck. "Carnes? I don't know of any Carnes living in that area."

"That's what she said," Reagan emphasized. "When I offered to take her home, she declined. Instead, she insisted I take her into town."

"What else did she say?" Jim asked.

Reagan had been dreading this moment from the time he realized the girl appeared pregnant. Unlikely as it seemed, he wondered if in a drunken state, he'd had an encounter with her of the adulterous sort. He'd never been able to recall how he received those marks on his back. Even though the thought repulsed him, his mind kept screaming that these weren't just coincidences. "She also mentioned something about having a room at the Rochester Hotel. And lastly, she also mentioned she frequented the same church as my family."

"That's an awful lot of conversation for two complete strangers," the sheriff noted. "How is it those topics came to be raised?"

Reagan weighed whether or not to reveal the startling proposition he had received from Molly while in the carriage. If he did, it would surely seem strange that now, two weeks later, she suddenly appeared in his office, very pregnant and very dead. He remembered clearly he had done nothing to indicate he was interested in a tryst. "I was simply making conversation, trying to ascertain whether or not we'd ever met," he explained. "In the course of our discussion, I determined we had not. She, in fact, volunteered the information about the hotel." Reagan lifted his hands. "I have no explanation why, and in fact, was quite taken aback by the revelation."

Thomas suddenly took a seat and mopped his brow. "Why would this woman turn up in our office?"

"Not our office," Reagan said gently. "My office. Your office is still at the old mill." He looked at the sheriff. "If there's a connection, it lies solely with me."

Sheriff Hadley nodded grimly as he continued taking notes. "You say you picked her up in your carriage approximately two weeks ago?"

"There or about. I've been using my horse ever since, so that type of thing couldn't occur again. As you can see," Reagan said, gesturing toward the body. "All kinds of suspicions can spring from an innocent encounter."

As the sheriff took notes, Reagan rubbed his brow, wondering how Amanda would take the horrifying news. Although she no longer mentioned the mysterious markings on his back, neither had she signaled her willingness to recapture the familiarity of their night spent in rapturous passion. To compound his troubles, he'd been consumed with finding a way to thwart the bastard, Derrick Banning. As a precaution, he had removed his important papers from both offices and stored them at home. Lastly, he had hired the services of detectives Simon and Helfrich. He'd decided it would be prudent to keep Derrick's blackmail scheme to himself. As yet, Thomas knew nothing.

"Do you have the carriage here?" the sheriff asked. "It's just a formality, but it should be inspected if the deceased recently used it."

"Why, yes it is," said Thomas, glad for a reason to step outside. "Although it didn't look out of the ordinary to me."

The sheriff turned to his deputy. "Ed, fetch my horse and bring it around. Then, stand guard until I return. I don't want anyone tinkering with possible evidence."

"Yes sir!" Deputy McCrae hastened to do his bidding.

"If it's all right with you, I'd like to remove the body to my office," the doctor said. "It's beginning to stiffen, and there are things I need to do."

"Of course," the sheriff said, placing his notes in a pocket. "I'll send a couple of men with a stretcher."

Dr. Turner laid his coat over Molly's face. "Thanks, I should have a report no later than Tuesday."

The sheriff nodded his assent while tucking the pencil behind his ear. "Let's go gentlemen." As the others went outside, Jim pulled Reagan aside. "For the next few days I'm advising you not to go anywhere where I can't easily find you."

"Surely, you don't think I had anything to do with this?" Reagan said. "I mean, how stupid would I be, to kill a woman then leave her body in my office?"

"This has nothing to do with what I believe, Reagan. You should know I'm obligated to follow procedures. Besides," he placed a hand on Reagan's shoulder. "It's the only way to exonerate you. C'mon," he said, grinning. "Let's go take a look at that fine carriage of yours."

Inspecting the carriage, the sheriff found nothing to arouse his curiosity. "It looks pretty normal to me," he said. But just as he began shutting the door, a patch of yellow caught his eye. Reaching in, he felt along the toe-kick and withdrew a parasol. "Does this belong to any of the Burnsfield women?" he asked.

Reagan's eyes clouded as he recognized the sunshade. "No, I believe that belongs to the lady in question."

"I'm going to follow you home to question your driver," Jim said. "It'll ensure for the judge that I'm taking his statement to corroborate the facts."

"Of course," Reagan nodded. "I want this cleared up as soon as possible."

As Thomas and Reagan entered their conveyance, Sheriff Hadley mounted his horse. Even though he believed Reagan wasn't responsible for the terrible crime, his connections with the dead woman didn't look good. Jim's analytical mind ticked off the strikes against the lumberman. Between knowing the victim, having recent contact with her and finding the body in his office, the motive for murder was obvious. A pregnant paramour would be a problem for anyone, particularly a man of means who also happened to be married.

chapter 82

THE DISCOVERY OF a woman's body in the new mill fueled gossip that Reagan Burnsfield had been wantonly indecent with another woman. Within two days of finding Molly's body, Sheriff Hadley had amassed quite a bit of information. He learned that Molly Carnes was a prostitute who'd professed to her co-workers that she was keeping the company of a wealthy man. Her flaunting of jewelry and expensive clothing the last weeks of her life supported her claim. The bartender insisted Molly had kept to herself the past few months, emerging only for an occasional venture into the saloon. Her quarters revealed no information that could explain how or why she entered Reagan's office. A rear window in the mill was open, but Sheriff Hadley doubted the woman could have hoisted herself through, especially in her condition.

Once the news got around, Clara Farrington visited the sheriff, declaring it her civic duty to testify Reagan Burnsfield had indeed, openly courted the harlot. Clara gave a description that matched the dead girl. She embellished her story by saying she could tell right away the strumpet was expecting, though in reality, that news had passed her ears only after the girl's body was discovered.

Even while maintaining such information was circumstantial, Sheriff Hadley experienced a growing dread as he documented each piece of evidence.

After calling on every house on Old Mill Road, the sheriff determined Molly Carnes never lived or worked at any residence, save the saloon. He finally located the home of Phineas Carnes several miles from town. After accompanying him to the undertaker's to identify Molly's body, Sheriff Hadley now had the unpleasant task of taking the man's statement.

"So, there's no doubt she's your daughter?" Jim asked as he sat behind his desk. Phineas Carnes sat slumped in a chair, his hat in his hands.

"None," he said, shaking his head. "I told th' girl no good would come of her living like a hussy!" The man's red-rimmed eyes filled with anguish while Hadley took notes. "But, there weren't no talking sense to th' lass. She done made up her mind. She weren't really a bad girl. She wuz a dreamer, always fixing her sights on what she couldn't git."

"I'm sorry," the sheriff said, having no words to comfort the grieving father. "We're doing everything we can to discover the truth."

"You say she wuz found in a lumber mill? What wuz she doing there?"

"We're not sure," Jim said. "We believe she was either murdered there, or placed there afterward. Doc

Turner determined she couldn't have been dead for very many hours before she was discovered."

Phineas worried the brim of his hat. "I done told her. Why wouldn't she listen?"

Jim set down his pencil. "Is there anything I can do for you, Mr. Carnes? I know this must come as a terrible shock."

"I want you to catch th' brute that done this to my little girl," Phineas choked. "Yer deputy said th' mill weren't locked like normal. Could th' owner have something to do with it?"

"We're looking into all possibilities," Jim said. "I personally know the owners and it's unlikely either of them would do such a thing, although the facts have yet to rule out the son."

"What'ya mean?" Phineas stood, glaring at the sheriff. "Whut kind of facts you talkin' about?"

"Just that there's some circumstantial evidence, nothing conclusive," Jim said, bracing himself. "One of the owners met Molly shortly before she died."

"Don't you figger that's enough proof to lock him up?" He slammed a fist on the desk. "Why ain't he behind bars?"

"He's an upstanding man in the community—"

Phineas's rage now had a target. "I don't care who th' bastard is! I want him locked up until he c'n prove he ain't th' one that kilt my little girl!"

"When my investigation is complete," Jim spoke, his compassion evident, "the judge will determine whether there's enough proof to hold Mr. Burnsfield."

Phineas' eyes narrowed. "Would that be th' lumberman that goes to th' big church in town?"

The sheriff looked startled. "Why do you ask?"

"Cuz Molly told me she wuz fixin' to marry a man by that name when she first took to working in th' saloon. Said she had to look like a fine laidy to snag th' moneybags."

"Sh-she said she *knew* Reagan Burnsfield? She'd met him before?"

"Molly wuz always a moonin' over a man in church named Reagan Burnsfield. Said she talked to him, too. That he made eyes at her," Phineas said. "He must've been leading her on. Telling her lies to git her away from her pappy so he could have his way with her."

Jim struggled to digest this revelation. "But Mr. Carnes," he began. "Reagan got married around Christmas. Both he and his wife were gone til spring. It doesn't seem likely he would've struck up a relationship with Molly after that, even if he had known her."

"Looks like he lied to y'all about knowing Molly. Whut's to say he wouldn't lie about th' rest? Whut wuz his alibi fer that night?"

Jim sat back as he mulled over what Reagan had said of his whereabouts the night of Molly's murder. "According to Reagan and his family, he'd retired early that night," the sheriff recounted. "So far, I've not been able to find anything to the contrary."

"I trust you'll do yer sworn duty," Phineas said, putting on his hat. "And bring Molly's murderer to justice."

"You can depend on that," Sheriff Hadley said. "I serve only justice when it comes to the law." He rose and offered his hand. "I'll do my best Mr. Carnes, to bring the perpetrator to trial."

chapter 83

AFTER THE DISCOVERY of Molly's body and subsequent interview with the sheriff, Amanda had existed in a world devoid of emotion. She had truthfully answered Hadley's questions, giving an account of the evening from the time Reagan had arrived home until they retired. Although left unsaid, it was on Amanda's mind that it was entirely possible he could have arisen during the night, left the house and returned without detection. Shaken to her core, she could only guess why Reagan's office was the scene of a grisly murder. Her only clear determination was to stay with her beloved Aunt Gabriella until the matter was settled.

Though chagrined with her decision, Reagan didn't try to dissuade her. "I'm confident you'll be returning soon," he told Amanda as they stood by the front door.

"It's been a difficult decision," she said, avoiding his eyes. "And very disturbing to say the least. I trust the sheriff will find the culprit."

"I'm sure he will."

"I'm looking forward to that day," she said, forcing a smile. "Though your family's been wonderful, there's no place more comfortable than Aunt Ella's."

Without further words, Reagan escorted Amanda outside. He wanted her to stay; yet how could he make demands while visions of a phantom lover still haunted him? "Will you receive me if I call?" he asked.

Amanda thought Reagan never looked more handsome as he helped her inside the carriage. "I'm not sure. I don't know how I feel about you having an encounter with this girl before she died. Yet, you never mentioned it to me."

"All I can plead was the innocence of it all," he said. "It never occurred to me there'd be repercussions to helping a girl in a time of need."

"It hasn't been explained why she was found in your office," Amanda reminded him. "It seems rather impossible for her to be there by coincidence." Tears slid down her cheeks as she fumbled for a handkerchief. "I don't believe you capable of such a heinous act," she said. "But, I just don't know what to think anymore."

Until this moment, Reagan hadn't accepted his wife was leaving him, perhaps forever. With sudden clarity he realized how much he loved Amanda, indeed had loved her from the first. It felt as if his heart was being torn from his chest. Indeed, his deception had woven itself into a choking vine and, caught in its tentacles, he now ate its bitter fruit.

Closing the door, he signaled the driver and watched as the carriage drove away. Inside, Amanda's tears fell unchecked. She couldn't imagine a worse predicament. Even if she had once contemplated an annulment, the most she could now hope for was a divorce. Like any woman, it was unthinkable to remain married to a murderer.

Amanda regretted her decision to delay breakfast when she felt her stomach protest the swaying carriage. Despite taking deep breaths, her nausea grew until she was forced to pound the roof with her parasol. As soon as the carriage halted, she opened the door and leaned out, retching. By the time the driver reached her, she had a handkerchief pressed to her lips.

He looked at her pale face with concern. "Ma'am, are you all right? Should I take you back?"

"Please, I wish to continue."

"But, you may need a doctor..."

"No, I wish to be taken to my aunt's house. And please," she beseeched. "Say nothing about my distress."

"Very good, ma'am," the driver said. But before shutting the door, he pressed a fresh hanky into her hands. "Just in case," he said, smiling.

Amanda mopped her face, praying Aunt Ella would have a solution to her problem. Only this week, she had become aware that her monthly time hadn't come. Just as she was being forced to think there was no future with Reagan, she discovered she was now carrying his child.

chapter 84

PHINEAS CARNES STOOD at the gravesite of his daughter with his hat in his hands. The minister had spoken prayers for the salvation of her soul but could say nothing to alleviate the pain he felt at having her life taken so brutally.

Reagan had offered to pay for Molly's funeral because she had been found in his mill. But Phineas would have none of it. He viewed the offer as nothing more than an admission of guilt, and declared so, loudly, to whoever would listen. Despite the fact his crops needed tending, Phineas decided to stay in town to observe firsthand the development of Sheriff Hadley's investigation.

As the days passed and finding no one else to blame, a cloud of suspicion grew over Reagan. Particularly outrageous was the unspeakable act of killing a woman who was obviously carrying a child. That she was a lady of ill repute only added to the salaciousness of the deed. With no new evidence coming to light, Sheriff Hadley had the unpleasant task of delving further into Reagan's past. With Judge McCleary's order, he obtained the lumberman's bank records from the last six months. Everything seemed fairly ordinary until he discovered a cheque written out to 'bearer' that was dated two weeks before Molly's death. Turning over the document, 'M. Carnes' was clearly written as the endorsement.

The sheriff stared at the bank note, his heart sinking. Reagan had unmistakably omitted this information when he had been questioned. The cheque itself contradicted Reagan's story of his acquaintance with Molly being based on happenstance. He realized how damaging this would look to a jury. Even to him, it looked awfully damning.

At the Burnsfield home, Jim waited in the parlor while a maid announced his arrival. He had just lowered himself onto a chair when Katherine entered, causing him to bolt to his feet. "Mrs. Burnsfield," he said, taking her hand. "So good of you to see me."

"It's always a pleasure, Jim," Katherine said. "Is there something I can do for you?"

"I'm afraid I've come on official business, Mrs. Burnsfield. I need to speak with Reagan again about Molly Carnes. It'd be best if he came to my office."

It took several dreadful moments before she found her voice. "How can this be? I know Reagan didn't do this."

"I'm sorry." Sheriff Hadley loathed his job at this moment. "There's some evidence that I want Reagan to clarify."

"Can you tell me what it is?" she asked. "Perhaps I can be of some help."

"I'm afraid I'm not at liberty to say."

Katherine stiffened at the sound of the front door. "Well, Sheriff, it sounds like one of my men has arrived." She threaded a hand through his arm. "Let's do what needs to be done."

As they entered the hall, she spied Reagan halfway up the stairs. "Reagan, dear..."

Something in her voice caused Reagan to turn abruptly. "Oh, hello Jim," he said, descending the steps. "Is everything all right?"

"Jim needs you to go with him," Katherine said before directing her next words to the sheriff. "However, I hope you'll let us have supper first."

"Of course," he said.

"I expect you to dine with us as well, Jim."

"That's not necessary, Mrs. Burnsfield."

"Nonsense. I'm going to place another setting. Thomas should be along any moment and I think it important you explain everything to him."

"What is it?" Reagan asked, sensing Jim's discomfort. "Have you found anything?"

"I have a few questions that need answering," Hadley said with a level look. "I believe you'll be better served if we wait until reaching my office to answer them."

"Sure," Reagan said, thumping Jim's shoulder. "Come on, let's have one last meal as friends before you present your evidence."

chapter 85

SAM HAMPTON HAD not missed the oft-repeated gossip about Reagan and Molly Carnes. Though he felt the lumberman was being unfairly accused, the mayor also enjoyed a good story, especially while partaking a sumptuous meal. “As I was saying...”

“Papa, please!” Elizabeth said. “Must you bring up that subject while we’re eating? If you don’t cease, you’re going to make me retch!”

Sam’s fork stopped in mid-air. “My dear, you look positively green.” He picked up the wine bottle. “Here, this should help settle your stomach.” The liquid seemed to mesmerize Elizabeth as he filled her tumbler. “Now, where was I? Oh yes,” he said. “They finally buried the poor lass with her father blubbering the whole time about how it was Reagan that done her in.” Stuffing a piece of ham in his mouth, grease dribbled down his chin. “Just think, we’ve had Reagan at our table. Why, for all we know, we could’ve been entertaining a murderer.”

Elizabeth lifted her wine glass with shaky fingers. Though she sipped many times, the sweet elderberry did nothing to sooth her upset stomach. When she spied oil droplets on her father's chin, her insides rebelled. She dropped her fork and rushed from the room, a napkin over her mouth.

Sam followed his daughter to a hall closet where she was bent over a bucket, gagging. "Are you ill, child?"

"Leave me alone, Father!" She dropped the pail and pushed past him. "I need to lie down."

"Perhaps, I should send for a doctor. It's not like you to be indisposed." He trailed her to the stairway, watching her go upstairs. "I would think he'd have a cure for whatever's ailing you."

Elizabeth stopped outside her room. "I don't need a doctor. Just send up Maggie with some broth." With that, she shut her door.

With each passing day, Elizabeth had grown more uneasy. She recalled one of the maids having a similar malady when she was still a child. When she'd asked if the maid was going to die, the servant had laughed and told her it was nature's way of letting a woman know she was having a blessed event. With the rounding of the maid's belly, Elizabeth finally realized the servant was going to have a baby. If this was so, then truly she had fallen into a trap of her own making.

Nightly, Elizabeth pleaded with God to take her condition away and she'd never again meddle where she didn't belong. Daily, her prayers remained unanswered.

Lying across her bed, she considered what recourses she had left. She could hide the truth temporarily, but eventually she'd show the results of her folly. Surely, God wouldn't allow her to be punished in such a cruel manner! She hoped that if she prayed hard enough, he would save her from this worst of sins.

Elizabeth loosened her dress, allowing the evening breezes to sooth her skin. "Okay, Lord," she whispered. "I've learned my lesson, I promise!"

chapter 86

DEPUTY WELCH STOOD up as Reagan and Sheriff Hadley entered the jailhouse. "Will you be needing me tonight?" he asked.

Jim rested his hat on a peg. "Give me a couple hours," he said while motioning Reagan to sit. "If I decide Mr. Burnsfield is staying, I'll send a message with you to his family." With a nod, the deputy left the room.

Reagan removed his hat. "So, Jim, what is it that has you in such an uproar?"

The sheriff sat behind his desk before propping his jaw against a palm. "You don't seem overly concerned," he said, watching Reagan closely. "I'm just wondering if you realize what a predicament you've gotten yourself into. In particular, why you didn't tell the truth about your involvement with Molly Carnes?"

Reagan looked genuinely surprised. "As far as I know, I have been factual about my encounter with the girl. What have I omitted?"

"You said you only met the girl once," he said, keeping his expression blank. "Are you sure you didn't meet her before or after that particular time?"

"That's right," Reagan nodded. "I don't recall meeting her before, and I most certainly haven't seen her since."

"You're positive you've not had any contact, either in person or in the form of written communication?"

Jim picked up a pencil, tapping his notes. He had read them many times, hoping to find a flaw in Phineas' words. And yet, when combined with the cashed cheque, it was the only thing that made sense. Reagan would absolutely not hand over a large sum of money to a complete stranger.

Reagan folded his arms. "Are you implying that I had some kind of relationship with the girl?"

"The evidence would certainly suggest that," Jim said, looking squarely into Reagan's eyes. "How else can you explain that Molly's father knew all about you and that Molly planned on marrying you?"

"You're out of your mind," Reagan exclaimed. "Do you honestly think I'd pursue, let alone marry a woman like that when I was already courting Amanda?"

"According to her father, Molly was not...employed...at the time. It wasn't until afterward, she began working at the saloon." He dropped the pencil and leaned back. "Supposedly, she needed the coin to make herself look like a woman of means."

"It's a lie," Reagan said, jutting his chin. "I never met her before, nor would I have entertained the notion of marrying her. You know me better than that."

Jim sighed. "I used to think so," he muttered, opening a drawer.

"Used to?" Reagan echoed. "What foolishness did Molly's father spew to cause you to doubt me?"

Jim withdrew the incriminating cheque and held it up. "It wasn't anything Mr. Carnes said so much as what this paper indicates." He placed the cheque on the desk, pushing it toward Reagan.

Immediately, Reagan recognized it as the cheque he had written to Derrick Banning. He looked at the sheriff and smiled. "This I can explain. But, I don't know what it has to do with the girl you found in my office."

"Oh?" Jim voiced as he pulled out a clean sheath of paper. "Why don't you explain it?" He held up his pencil expectantly. "I'm all ears."

Reagan tapped the cheque, realizing he could no longer conceal his thorny predicament. "Well," he said as he lowered his gaze, "as you can see, I was being blackmailed by a scoundrel."

"I had assumed as much," Jim said, his heart sinking. "Tell me how it came about."

"Last spring, we were fortunate enough to garner several large contracts. To fulfill the company's obligations, I needed to build another mill. When my funds ran low, I-uh..." Reagan hesitated, knowing the sheriff would disapprove of his solution. "...married Amanda to procure her dowry." Even to him, it sounded like a poor excuse. To a straight shooter like Jim, it would lack moral integrity. "As you can see," he said, giving the sheriff a lopsided grin, "my mind wouldn't have been on anything or anyone else."

"I'm listening," Jim encouraged.

"Unfortunately, one of Amanda's suitor's felt I'd stolen his rightful place as her intended, and decided to pursue her even after we wed."

"What has that got to do with this cheque?" Jim asked, feeling as if he were being taken on a wild goose chase.

"It has everything to do with it!"

Jim bit his lip. "Go on," he gestured, his pencil poised again.

"This man stole our contracts and threatened to expose why I married Amanda. In order to keep him from going to George and laying bare the truth, he demanded payment before he'd return the contracts." He gestured toward the cheque. "As you can see, this was hush money."

Jim looked at Reagan with something akin to muddled confusion. "That still doesn't explain why you gave this cheque to Molly Carnes."

"Mol-" Reagan burst in exasperation. "-Why would you think I gave it to Molly?"

Jim picked up the cheque and flipped it over. "Because, she's the one who cashed it."

Reagan gaped at the signature. "B-but-I gave this cheque to Derrick Banning."

"Who?"

"Derrick Banning. The jackass who stayed with the Bruesters while I was courting Amanda." Reagan stared at Jim. "How could she have gotten this cheque?"

"That's what I'm trying to find out," he exclaimed. If Reagan was putting on an act, it was a damn good one. "So, you're telling me you gave this cheque to Mr. Banning and not to Molly?"

"That's exactly what I'm saying."

"Do you have any witnesses to corroborate your story?"

"No. He came into my office when I was alone."

"Did you tell anyone immediately afterward? Did you tell your father?"

"I told no one," Reagan said. "The only thing I did was go to Simon and Helfrich's Detective Agency to have the man investigated. I was determined to not pay another cent."

The sheriff looked heartened by this small tidbit. "What did you say to the investigators about Mr. Banning?"

"That the man was costing me a lot of money by having information he shouldn't have."

"Then, it sounds as if you did tell them, in so many words."

"I hope so," Reagan said. "Now I understand why you were so suspicious. I'd appreciate it if you could speak to the detectives yourself."

"I most certainly will," Jim said, smiling. "If I can prove a connection between Derrick and Molly, perhaps we'll find the truth about the death of this poor girl."

"There's got to be a connection."

"But, without proof," the sheriff interjected. "I have nothing to corroborate your story."

"With you leading the investigation," Reagan said, "I've full confidence you'll uncover the whole unsavory plot."

"Perhaps," he said. "But until I can satisfy the judge, I'm keeping you here. There's still the unexplained reason why Molly told her father she intended to marry you."

"I'm truly mystified about that," Reagan said, shaking his head.

"Is it possible she mentioned the hotel room because you were a previous client of hers?" Jim asked delicately.

"I've never been interested in doxies," Reagan said. "My preferences run higher than that."

"I see," the sheriff nodded. "Well, at least I've something to go on. If I find a connection between Molly and Derrick, perhaps I can discover the answer to these other things."

"If you're bound to keep me in jail, then I'd ask that a message be sent to Beauregard Barrington. I need to speak with him immediately."

Jim looked suspiciously at Reagan. "Now why would you need to do that?"

"Because I don't trust Derrick while my wife is staying at Gabriella's and I want someone to keep watch over them."

The sheriff sighed, shaking his head. "Reagan, my friend, you've a talent for attracting trouble. What did you do, to deserve such a fate?"

"Most likely, I'm reaping the harvest of my wicked deeds." Reagan rubbed his eyes, feeling tired. "I suppose I'll now get to sample Jane's cooking, won't I?"

"She'll be mighty displeased it's not at our table," Jim said. "She was looking forward to meeting Amanda."

"Once this situation is resolved, I hope the invitation still stands. Amanda would find Jane charming."

"That's how I found her nearly fifteen years ago," Jim agreed, checking the coffee pot. "And, if you're exonerated, then of course, you're welcome to grace our table."

"So, you still doubt me?" Reagan asked as Jim started a fresh brew.

"I don't get paid to believe you or anyone, my friend." He grinned beneath his mustache. "But of course, I'll be thrilled to discover you've done nothing worse than rescue Amanda from an evil suitor. The rest, with Molly of course, is deplorable. If Derrick Banning had anything to do with it, I hope to set him in front of Judge McCleary with enough proof to ensure a short drop and a quick stop."

Reagan felt an uncomfortable tightness around his neck. "I hope that's not your intent if you can't exonerate me," he said. "Because I can assure you, I had nothing to do with Molly's murder."

Jim motioned Reagan toward the back room. "That remains to be seen."

"That's not funny," Reagan said, scooping up his saddlebag. "You just remember who I am."

"Innocent before proven guilty," quipped Jim, giving Reagan a gentle push.

Now that he had an explanation for the cheque, Jim hoped to prove Reagan innocent of murder. Still, there were many questions to be answered. It would take more than a simple explanation to corroborate Reagan's story. He would start with the hotels and boarding houses that permeated Cantonsville. He was anxious to find this Derrick Banning and see for himself if the man was capable of such acts. If not, it'd be the hardest thing he'd ever have to do to lead Reagan Burnsfield to the hangman's noose.

chapter 87

THE TIME AMANDA spent with Gabriella had done little to resolve her dilemma as she vacillated between ending her marriage and waiting to see if Reagan would be vindicated.

"I don't know what to believe," Amanda said as her teacup rattled against its saucer. "How can I make a decision when I can't tell which story is true?"

Gabriella stirred honey into her tea. "My dear, all I'm asking is that you consider facts, not hearsay. I'd hate for you to make a decision based on what others think."

"I'm not brave, like you," Amanda said, looking at her fingers as if they were the hands of a coward. "I wish I could share your certainty that all will turn out a'right. I'm afraid to trust my own judgment."

"I understand," Gabriella said. "This isn't the first time I've seen lives ruined by the meddling of snooty blatherskites."

Amanda suppressed a smile. "Really, Aunt Ella! Since when do you keep abreast of gossips and snoops?"

"Hmmph!" Gabriella took a sip. "One doesn't have to look very far, even in one's own family."

"What do you mean?"

"I think it's high time I spoke up," Gabriella said, setting down her cup. "I've been quiet these many years, and all it's gotten me is severe indigestion." She gave her niece a meaningful look. "Once before, I mentioned I'd reveal the reasons for your mother's ill temper. I thought to wait until your life was settled with children of your own. However, since it appears that possibility may be in jeopardy, the time has come." Amanda dropped her gaze at Gabriella's words for she had yet to divulge her condition.

"This may come as a shock, my dear, but long before Emily showed an interest in my brother, she was secretly engaged to Thomas Burnsfield." She paused, allowing her niece to grasp the significance of her words. "At that time, Thomas wasn't nearly as prosperous as he is now, but he was well on his way."

"Your mother was very beautiful and Thomas loved her. For that reason he worked hard to obtain the kind of wealth necessary to ask for her hand." Reaching over, Gabriella gently lifted Amanda's sagging jaw. "I know, 'tis a shock to hear this, for Emily has treated Mr. Burnsfield with contempt since before you were born. But, it was when Thomas petitioned for Emily's hand that her father forbade the union. Of course, Thomas demanded that they marry without her father's consent. She refused, thinking Thomas would persist until he could change her father's mind. Yet, she misjudged Thomas's pride. It wasn't long after that he began courting Katherine. Emily never forgave him, and rather than admitting her mistake, confirmed it by chasing after my brother, George. The poor man was smitten by Emily's beauty, and quite helpless, I might add. Within a year of Thomas's marriage, George and Emily were wed."

Amanda's eyes grew wide. "Do you mean to say my mother only married father because Mr. Burnsfield didn't wait for her?"

"It would seem so," Gabriella nodded. "Instead of being happy as any new bride should, Emily was miserable and treated George accordingly. It's a wonder you were even conceived, my dear, all things considered."

"Why do you think father stayed all these years? It doesn't seem right for a person to suffer so."

"Because he loves you," Gabriella said, giving Amanda's hand a gentle squeeze. "And believe it or not, he continues to love Emily."

"I see." Amanda rose and gazed out the window. "Although this explains mother's behavior, it doesn't make clear which path I should take."

"What I'm trying to say is that things aren't always what they seem."

Amanda wrung her hands. By refusing Reagan's husbandly rights, did she cause his first unsavory step toward infidelity? Did that start a chain of events that led to another's death? She turned from the window. "I'll think about it, I promise."

"There's one more thing," Gabriella said as she reached for her cane. "And then this old woman will forever butt out."

"Don't say that," Amanda said. "You know I always listen to your advice."

"I have a bad feeling about that Mr. Banning who called on you yesterday." Her eyes lit at the memory of the nattily dressed dandy who seemed anxious to dismiss Gabriella from her own parlor. "I know it's none of my business, but it seems mighty peculiar he should be making suggestions about ending your marriage even before the sheriff's had a chance to clear Reagan's name."

"Why, Aunt Ella! Were you eavesdropping while Mr. Banning was here?"

Gabriella thumped her cane before shaking a finger. "I'll be stone cold before I let that kind of chicanery go on in my own home! I hope you set the coxcomb on his ear, for proposing such outlandish ideas."

Amanda raised an inquisitive brow. "Since you're so well informed, why don't you tell me what I said?"

"I can't," Gabriella said, frowning.

"And, why's that?"

"Because that's when Ben came in," she complained with another thump. "I couldn't let him see me listening at the door."

"I told Mr. Banning I'd make no decision for the time being," Amanda said.

"Well, thank God for that!" Gabriella said. "The fact your mother preferred Derrick over Reagan causes me to distrust him."

"In case you forgot, Reagan *has* been accused of a very serious crime."

"As long as there's breath in this old shell," Gabriella said, tapping her chest, "I'll never believe him capable of such a despicable act."

chapter 88

AS THE DAYS passed, Elizabeth Hampton found herself burdened with recurring bouts of retching, which she hid from her father. After counting for the hundredth time the days since her last monthly, she felt the walls closing about her. No longer uncertain about her condition, Elizabeth decided to arrange an extended vacation. She would send a letter to her Aunt Emmaline who lived in a neighboring state. The distance wasn't too far for a journey, but far enough to prevent the travel of errant news. She would then explain to her father that the change would surely cure her ailment. Lastly, she'd need to engage in a conspiracy with Aunt Emmaline to not inform her brother of his daughter's shameful condition.

Elizabeth had few memories of her mother. Josephine Hamilton died when Elizabeth was nine years old. What she did recall was her Aunt Emmaline coming to live with them the months following her mother's funeral. As Sam's older sister, she had taken over the household much the same way she had while raising Sammy when their parents died. Young Emmaline had girded herself with an implacable nature in order to be a steadying force in raising her younger brother. That same nature had come to the fore when Elizabeth's mother had fallen ill and died shortly thereafter. As Emmaline seemed no stranger to adversity, Elizabeth clung to the belief her aunt would know what to do. With her new course of action and some luck, she hoped to escape being branded a loose woman.

With insight usually reserved for those of greater age, Elizabeth determined her child wouldn't be sullied with a label. To that end, she would undertake whatever was needed to protect the babe.

"That much I can do," she murmured to herself. "Even if it takes my last breath.

chapter 89

A SATCHEL-CLAD messenger entered the cool interior of the Bruester Bank and Trust and approached the bank officer's desk. "I have a communication for George Bruester," he said.

The bank officer looked over the courier, recalling him to be the young man who had opened a savings account less than a year ago. At that time, he had listed his employer as Simon and Helfrich Detective Agency and since then made weekly deposits of five dollars. "Hello, Johnny," the officer smiled.

"Hello, sir. I have an important message for Mr. Bruester."

"Could I deliver the message?" the officer asked. "Mr. Bruester's in a meeting with Mr. Spelding."

Johnny shook his head. "No, sir, I was instructed to deliver the message straightaway, or wait until he could see me. Those were my orders, sir."

"Very well. If you'd be so kind as to wait here, I'll be right back." Within moments he returned, ushering the currier to the office.

Johnny had never met the owners of the bank and fumbled with his satchel as he looked from one to the other. "I-I have a message for George Bruester."

George held out his hand. "I'm George Bruester."

Johnny handed him a note. "I'm to await your answer, sir."

George quickly read the missive.

"It seems Mr. Simon has information about the stolen cheque I told you about and desires an immediate audience." He looked at his partner. "It looks as if he means right now."

Ezra frowned as he glanced at his watch. "I really have some pressing matters to attend. Let's finish our meeting at another time."

"Very well, then," George said as he closed his folder. "We can go over these figures tomorrow." Rising, he reached for his hat. "After you, young man."

chapter 90

SHERIFF HADLEY HAD spent the greater part of his morning traversing between boardinghouses and hotels, seeking the man Reagan claimed blackmailed him. It wasn't until the sheriff inquired at the Rochester Hotel that he found someone familiar with the name Derrick Banning. "I believe the gentleman has been our guest for two to three weeks," the clerk said, flipping through the registry. He then turned the ledger around. Jim's neck prickled, for the signature bore a striking resemblance to the strokes that penned 'M. Carnes' on Reagan's cheque.

"I'll need to appropriate this ledger," Jim said. "But, until I send for it, could you please keep it secured?"

"Our vault should be safe enough," the clerk said, closing the book.

Jim leaned on the counter as he viewed the stairway. "Would Mr. Banning be in his room right now?"

"I'm not sure. He usually leaves during the day."

"If you'd be kind enough to direct me to his door, I'll see for myself."

Jim went to the top floor and knocked at the door registered to Derrick Banning. A man with suspenders riding over his bare, compact chest threw open the door. "May I help you?" he asked.

"I hope so," Jim said. "I'm Sheriff Hadley, and I'm investigating the murder of Molly Carnes." He watched for signs of recognition, but if the man knew the girl, he hid it well. "I have a few questions I'd like to ask, Mr. Banning. May I come in?"

"But, of course," Derrick said, stepping back. "I hope you'll excuse my appearance. I was just about to finish my toilet."

Spotting the coat rack, the sheriff hung his hat. "Looks like a mighty fine place," he commented. "I suppose luxury like this costs a pretty penny, eh?"

Derrick studied the sheriff while closing the door. He believed the lawman displayed too mild a manner to hold damning information. "I find the charge to be appropriate for the accommodations."

Jim noted a silk shirt draped across a chair. "Just out of curiosity, how can you afford it?"

"I'm not sure what you mean, sheriff."

"Well, you don't appear to be employed, and I was wondering if, within the past few weeks, you might've come into a large sum of money?"

"I hope you don't mind, but I'm in a bit of a hurry," Derrick said, indicating a washstand. If you'd like, you can continue your questions while I ready myself."

"Go right ahead," Jim said. "Don't let me interrupt." He watched Derrick fill a shaving mug and stir the brush. "You were about to tell me how you can afford this suite," the sheriff cued.

Derrick took a long time lathering his face. "Oh yes, I was about to explain that, wasn't I?" He picked up a razor and tested the blade's edge. "I happen to do very well at the gaming tables, and as it often happens, I'm having an extremely successful run of luck."

"Oh?" The sheriff crossed his arms. "Whatever happened to the business deal you were trying to do with George Bruester?"

A drop of blood glistened on Derrick's finger as he eyed the sheriff. "My, my, you seem to know quite a bit about me." Turning to the mirror, he spoke smoothly. "As one might expect, the war has put a temporary halt on my plans," he said, scraping a cheek. "I'm cautious by nature, and don't like taking unnecessary risks." Lifting his chin, Derrick began moving the blade in careful descent. "However, since I believe the venture will be successful once the war is over, I've decided to stick around."

Though his words had a ring of truth, Jim felt Derrick had prepared himself for the possibility of being questioned. "I understand you still have an interest in Amanda Burnsfield."

Swishing the blade in water, Derrick chuckled. "I've made no secret about my desire for Amanda. In fact, already this week I've had the pleasure of her company." Giving it his full attention, Derrick worked the razor around his thin mustache. "And, once the matter of her husband is decided, I intend to correct Amanda's choice of mate."

"How would you respond if someone suggested you pilfered information to blackmail Reagan out of the way?"

Derrick splashed his face before toweling dry. "What?" he snorted. "Am I now being accused of coercing my way into his marriage?" He placed the linen around his neck. "I can't believe Reagan would stoop so low to accuse me of that. From what I understand, he's losing Amanda all by himself."

"What do you say to the accusation?" Jim persisted.

Derrick lowered his chin like a cornered turtle. "I'd say it'd be the desperate act of a desperate man. Unless of course, you have some proof."

Sheriff Hadley realized he couldn't shake the man's aplomb. "No, not that I've discovered."

"I see." Derrick tugged the towel back and forth. "Is there anything else I can help you with?"

"Molly Carnes was murdered two weeks ago," the sheriff said, saving his thorniest questions for last. "What were your whereabouts the night before Molly was found?"

"Most likely, I was gambling at the saloon or in a nearby town." Derrick crossed the floor and put on his shirt. After tucking in his shirttail, he reset his suspenders. "Unfortunately, one day seems pretty much like another for someone like myself, so I can't be more accurate than that."

"If you frequented the saloon, then surely you knew Molly."

"No more than any man who'd pay for a few hours pleasure," he said, opening the wardrobe. "On any account, I don't recall the wench." Donning a vest and jacket, he inspected himself in the mirror. "I, of course, would have no reason to kill a helpless strumpet, but from what I hear, Reagan Burnsfield did." Pleased with his reflection, Derrick grasped his lapels. "I do hope you're finished because I have an appointment to keep with Amanda."

"For a man who doesn't know much about this crime, you seem pretty certain of the outcome," Jim said.

"I've every confidence you've found the real perpetrator," Derrick said, forcing a smile. "Although I do realize it's your duty to examine all possibilities."

"So, you'd have no problem if I were to question George Bruester about your employer, and confirm your associations in New York?"

"There's no need to disturb Mr. Bruester," Derrick said. "I'm happy to give you all the information you need. Do you wish to write it down?"

Though there was no outward appearance, Jim felt something had changed in Derrick's demeanor. "Sure," he said as he pulled out a pad and pencil. "Here, I'll let you write it down as I'm liable to spell it wrong."

Derrick quickly scribbled a name of a different bank, calculating how much time he'd have before the lawman would receive word he wasn't employed there.

"Don't be surprised," he said, "if at first they don't remember me. After all, I've been gone for nearly a year."

The sheriff glanced at the handwriting. The bold strokes were clearly similar to the signature on the cheque. Once he verified the bank's name with George, he'd send as many telegraphs as necessary to get the answers he needed from New York.

"Thank you very much, Mr. Banning, you've been most cooperative."

"Anything to help bring a killer to justice," Derrick said. With luck, the sheriff would be put off long enough for him to alter his plans. After escorting the sheriff to the door, Derrick leaned against the wooden panels. "Well, well," he said, tapping his wounded finger against a lip. "Amanda may be of use to me, yet."

chapter 91

WHEN GEORGE WAS ushered into the office of Barnabus Simon, the investigator, he was more than a little surprised to see Thomas sitting beside the only other empty chair. Barnabus rose from behind his desk, extending his hand. "So pleased you could come on such short notice. I hope you don't mind my asking Mr. Burnsfield to join us because this affects you both."

George nodded stiffly before settling into the chair. Ever since the horrifying murder of Molly Carnes, he'd suffered guilt, thinking his daughter had wed a dangerous man. On the other hand, he'd known the Burnsfields most of his life, and fretted equally that he was misjudging his son-in-law before the facts were known. One thing he did know, Thomas had to be suffering even more than he. George laid a hand on Thomas's shoulder and gave a comforting squeeze.

Barnabus opened a portfolio with several pages inside. "I have to tell each of you, how extraordinary this case has been. Never before have two separate investigations intertwined."

"Two?" George looked at Thomas. "Did you have a cheque stolen too?"

Thomas shook his head. "Until this morning, I had no idea Reagan had hired Mr. Simon. In fact, the only reason I was summoned was because Reagan is unable to come."

"That's correct," the detective said crisply. "When the junior Burnsfield came to us, it was before the tragic occurrence of a few weeks ago."

"Does this have anything to do with that terrible murder?" asked Thomas.

"We don't know if it does, Mr. Burnsfield. We're only certain of what we found. The rest must be determined by the law." The detective held up his hand. "You both look confused, so let's start at the beginning. Mr. Bruester came to me several weeks ago to investigate a cheque that had been stolen, forged, and then cashed out of town." He lifted the document from between the pages and set it on his desk. "When his bookkeeper reported the discrepancy, George believed he'd uncovered a thief. All we had to go on was the name of the person to whom the cheque was made out, and that was Orville Farnsworth."

"I take it you've found something," George said, leaning forward. "Did you locate him?"

"Yes and no," Barnabus answered. "But for you to understand this fully, I need to explain it as it unfolded." He looked at Thomas. "Not long after we began our probe into the stolen cheque, Reagan secured our services to investigate a man he all but admitted was blackmailing him."

Both men gasped. "Am I to understand that your son didn't inform you?" the detective asked.

Thomas's face turned ashen. "No. He never said a word."

"Reagan wasn't specific about the nature of the extortion," Barnabus continued. "Except to say it had something to do with his wife, Amanda."

Now it was George who turned pale. "Amanda! How could she be involved?"

"Did Reagan say who was blackmailing him?" asked Thomas.

The detective glanced at the papers before him. "Reagan claimed it was Derrick Banning."

"Derrick Banning!" both men said in unison.

After a stunned silence, George spoke first. "What connection does this have with the man who stole my cheque?"

"I'm getting to that," Barnabus said. "Periodically during each investigation, my men would report their findings." He folded his hands, looking from George to Thomas. "And this is where it becomes interesting. We hadn't found much about Mr. Farnsworth, except to confirm he'd cashed the cheque and deposited the money in a bank across state lines. Soon after, he withdrew the cash. However, our investigation of Derrick Banning took our man to New York, where our subject originally met Mr. Bruester."

"That he did," George nodded. "In fact, he was my escort while in the city."

"We began at the largest banks, intending to question them all, if necessary." The detective shuffled the papers, removing one before laying it on top. "We did discover where Mr. Banning was employed," Barnabus said. "But in addition to that, we found they had a warrant against him for embezzlement."

"What?" George said, rubbing his forehead.

"Apparently Mr. Banning made a hasty departure from New York because he stole a payroll deposit instead of entering it into an account he handled. And that's not all." Barnabus looked pointedly at George. "They did some investigating of their own, and unearthed a few of his cronies. At that time, he went by the name Orville Farnsworth."

"Can this help Reagan?" asked Thomas.

"I'm not sure. All I can say is it shows this man's a criminal. If he were blackmailing Reagan, it's possible he may've had access to Reagan's office, which would put him within the realm of being able to place a body there." He held up a hand at Thomas's elated look. "Now, it doesn't prove anything," Barnabus pointed out. "All it shows is a connection. As soon as my man reported what he found, I put two and two together. Derrick Banning, who was blackmailing Reagan, was also the same man who stole a cheque from Mr. Bruester."

"He very well could've taken the cheque while in my office," George volunteered. "All this time, I never suspected."

"I've all the documents you need to prosecute him for theft," Barnabus said, placing papers inside the portfolio and handing it to George. "I'd recommend you inform the sheriff immediately. If Derrick

Banning is indeed Orville Farnsworth, I'd have to say he's been a very busy man."

"Thank you very much." George said, standing. "What you've uncovered is truly unbelievable."

Barnabus smiled good-naturedly. "I hope you'll still say that when you receive my bill."

Thomas grinned at the banker. "What do you say we pay a visit to Sheriff Hadley?"

George slapped Thomas's back. "I can't get there soon enough."

chapter 92

AMANDA BELIEVED STAYING with Gabriella was the best choice she could've made. Though she hadn't revealed she was expecting, she felt a calmness of spirit within the comfortable house.

While Gabriella spent the day visiting friends, Amanda stayed home, keeping busy with needlework. And, though she didn't feel up to traveling herself, she encouraged her Aunt to spend afternoon tea with Emily before returning home. Amanda had just carried a tray into the parlor when she heard a knock at the door. She went to the entrance to find Beauregard standing there with a big smile on his face.

"Why Beau," she said. "What brings you here?"

"Tiens!" Beauregard extended a fistful of pink and red geraniums. "For you, demoiselle."

Pleased at the unexpected visit, Amanda opened the door fully. "Do come in," she said, finding a nearby vase. Arranging the blossoms, she spoke over her shoulder. "Where ever did you get these? They look just like Aunt Ella's."

Beau stepped near, his hands behind his back. "They do?" he voiced warmly. "That's strange..."

"Beauregard Barrington!" Amanda said, wagging a finger. "You picked these flowers from the front yard, didn't you?"

"Ah," he touched his chest. "I'm wounded to the heart. Even demoiselle thinks me larron of le fleur."

"Oh Beau," she said as she kissed his cheek. "It's good to see you. I thought I'd lost my friends."

"Non, ma chéri, " he said, cupping her chin. "Fair weather friends are not worth having."

"You have indeed been a good friend," she said. "Would you like a cup of tea? I just brewed a fresh pot."

"And crumpets? Warm and crisp crumpets?"

Amanda drew him toward the parlor. "How would gingersnaps and butter cookies do?"

"That's sounds magnifique!"

Once settled on the sofa, Beauregard's concern was evident. "How've you been? I've been distressed for Reagan these past weeks. It must be doubly so for you."

Amanda stirred her tea before taking a sip. "It's been extremely difficult. I feel as if I've fallen into a pit and can't get out." She laughed at Beau's stricken expression. "I'm sure I sound quite morose. Please, forgive me."

"Surely, you don't believe the accusations?" he asked.

"I don't want to believe Reagan capable of murder or the...other..." she admitted. "Yet, the girl was-a-was-a-" Amanda couldn't speak for fear it was she who pushed Reagan to that desperate need.

"A fille de joie," Beau finished. "Yes, I know demoiselle. However, even if he *had* fallen into that trap," he said, "Reagan could never raise a hand against les femmes."

A tear slid down her cheek. "But, it may have been my fault! I-I was not always-receptive-"

"Shhh!" Beauregard pressed a hanky into her hand. "It is not so, Reagan loved you too much to be a traître."

"Love?" Amanda shook her head. "I'd venture to say he found advantage only."

Beauregard looked adamant. "If you don't believe another word I say, believe that Reagan loves you. I've seen it. Accept, ma chéri, the man has eyes only for you."

"Then why has it only gone from bad to worse?" she asked, daubing her tears.

"Tis true," Beauregard laughed. "Misfortune arrives on horseback, but departs on foot." He patted her hand. "But what of you? How do you feel about him?"

Amanda searched her heart. Did she still love Reagan? The ache in her breast seemed to indicate so, even as Derrick's offer had presented an appealing escape. When she considered being another man's wife, her emotions had splintered into a thousand broken pieces. "I..."

A sharp rapping drew their attention. Amanda set down her teacup. "Who could that be?"

"Perhaps, someone is calling on Gabriella," Beauregard said.

"If so, they'll be disappointed. Ben took her to visit my mother this afternoon."

As Amanda entered the foyer, Beauregard strained his ears. He soon heard voices and then Amanda entered the parlor with none other than Derrick Banning.

"Oh," Derrick said. "I didn't realize you had company."

"Derrick, you remember Beauregard, don't you?" Amanda prompted. "We were just having tea."

Derrick appeared pained. "But, my dear, I promised you a ride in the country. I'm sure Mr. Barrington will understand."

"But, Beau has just arrived," Amanda said. "Please, have a seat." She tried withdrawing, but found her hand trapped in Derrick's.

"My dear, I really must insist. What I mean, is," he smiled over gritted teeth, "I have a surprise, and it requires that we leave immediately."

"Not to worry," Beauregard said, rising. "I can return another time." He approached Amanda, bringing her free hand to his lips. "Rest assured, milady, I shall soon return." Then, touching his brow stiffly, he hurriedly left the room.

chapter 93

SHERIFF HADLEY HAD been studying the Rochester Hotel ledger when he heard an insistent rapping on the jailhouse door. Suddenly, George burst into the room followed by Thomas. Both men began talking at once as the sheriff looked on in bewilderment. "Hold on!" Jim placed a marker between pages of the ledger. "I can't understand unless you speak one at a time."

George's breath came in short gasps as he fumbled with the flap of a satchel. "Sheriff, we have some information..."

Thomas squeezed past, interrupting George. "Release my son at once! Reagan is being blackmailed by a man who might be involved with that girls' murder..."

"Men!" Jim held up his hands. "Stop! My ears can only digest one thing at a time." He pointed to George. "Mr. Bruester, I actually sent for you, but you'd already left the bank. So, why don't you begin? But please," he said, "at least have a seat so I can understand what you're saying."

George hurriedly took a chair, withdrawing several papers from a satchel. "We just left Simon and Helfrich's," he began. "I received information about a man who stole a cheque from my office. His name is Orville Farnsworth. But, I knew the man as Derrick Banning."

"Derrick Banning?"

"Yes," Thomas broke in. "And that's not all. Derrick Banning is blackmailing Reagan. Due to the circumstances, I think he may have something to do with the murder of that girl."

"Molly Carnes," Jim said, holding out his hand. "Let me see those papers." As he scanned them, he continued to speak. "You may be surprised to know I'm already investigating Mr. Banning. As a matter of fact, I spoke to him only an hour or so ago." He looked at Thomas whose knuckles were turning white gripping his knees. "Just yesterday, Reagan informed me of a cheque he'd written to keep Derrick from spreading information about his marriage." He gave an apologetic glance toward George. "In fact, I was going to verify Reagan's story about hiring a detective later this afternoon." Neither man noticed how nervous Thomas looked as he realized what damning information Derrick had discovered.

"At the moment, that's not my concern," George said, believing the sheriff was about to reveal his sister was accused of transporting slaves. "Right now, it appears this man Banning isn't who he portrays himself to be and may be dangerous."

Thomas couldn't hold back. "If Derrick Banning is blackmailing Reagan, I believe he'd have had access to Reagan's office, which places him under suspicion of murder just as much as my son."

The sheriff flipped through several pages, stopping when he encountered the purloined cheque. "Gentlemen!" He looked up, his voice filled with excitement. "We may have evidence to link him to both crimes." Dropping all but the cheque, Jim opened a drawer and removed another cheque.

"What do you mean?" asked Thomas.

Sheriff Hadley laid both cheques on the edge of his desk. "Look at the handwriting. If you notice, the inscription 'M. Carnes' on this document looks identical to the handwriting on the cheque made out to Orville Farnsworth. And not only that," Jim flipped around the ledger, opening it to the marked page, "it looks just like the signature on the register from the Rochester Hotel, signed by Derrick Banning." He tapped the cheques. "It appears that Derrick Banning has just implicated himself with Molly Carnes."

"Does this mean that Reagan can be released from jail?" asked Thomas.

Sheriff Hadley grinned. "That depends on whether or not you want to punish him further. It sounds as if Reagan has committed a few sins."

"By all means, let him go!"

"I heartily concur," George said, immensely relieved that Reagan wasn't a murderer. He could hardly wait to go home and report the news to Emily. The poor woman hadn't been the same since the wedding.

She had lost much weight from worry, which accelerated after Amanda's trip to the lumber camp. By the time Reagan was arrested, she had become a shell of her former self. If not for his concern over her lack of nourishment, George could've appreciated how much his wife now resembled her former self.

Jim reached for the keys when the door burst open and a rather breathless Frenchman ran in. "I must speak to Reagan immédiatement!" He skidded to a stop. "Monsieur Sheriff!" Beauregard took in a few ragged breaths, pointing toward the open door. "There's outré chose amiss! The knave Banning, is acting most ètrange when he came to see Madame Burnsfield..."

"Hold your horses! I didn't understand a word you said," Jim said. "Speak English!"

"Eh Bien!" Beauregard said, gripping a chair. "Why does no one learn the French tongue except Reagan?"

"What about Madam Burnsfield?" Thomas had caught that much of Beau's words. "Were you visiting Katherine?"

"Écouter-Listen," Beauregard looked imploringly at the sheriff. "Monsieur Banning is at Dame Gabriella's, and is acting most strangely..."

Jim's jaw dropped as he slapped his forehead. "Good Lord! I completely forgot. Derrick said he was seeing Amanda today."

He grabbed the keys and hurried toward the back room, emerging seconds later with Reagan close behind. "Dammit Reagan," he said, slapping on his holster and buckling it in one motion. "I couldn't do anything else with the evidence I had. You had to be locked up."

"You could've believed me..." Reagan stopped when he saw the others. "Beau, what's going on? And what are you two doing here?"

"Calm down," the sheriff urged. "First of all, I need to fill you in on what's going on." He quickly went over the information Thomas and George had given him and then continued. "Beauregard's just come from Gabriella's..."

"That's because I asked him to watch over Amanda," Reagan said, interrupting. "I wouldn't put it past that snake to try something while I was in jail."

"I'm afraid Derrick's wasted no time," Jim said. "And he's at this moment plying your wife with promises of becoming her new husband-after your demise, that is."

"Tis true," Beauregard said, motioning toward the door. "Monsieur Banning says he has a surprise. He took Amanda for a ride."

"I need a horse and a gun," Reagan said. "I'm going to Gabriella's."

Hadley pulled a rifle from a rack, tossing it to Reagan. "Take this, and take my horse. He's already saddled. I'll round up a few men once I saddle your horse. He's still in the pen out back. The sheriff turned. "George, I need you to go to Madam Stroebel's boardinghouse and ask for Joe. His cap's set for her daughter and that's where he is when he isn't here."

As George hurriedly left, Reagan grabbed Beauregard's arm. "Come with me. We've got vermin to hunt down."

"Bon ami," Beauregard opened his coat. "I have non armé." He looked to the sheriff. "Do you have a small weapon? My hands do not do so well with grand piéce d'artillerie."

"I believe I've just the thing." Jim opened a drawer and removed a derringer. "I took this off a gambler who liked recovering his losses in back alleys." Scooping up a handful of bullets, he handed them to the Frenchman.

"Merci." Beau pocketed the bullets as he gingerly handled the gun. "I'll do my best not to shoot myself."

"I'm coming too!" Thomas insisted. "I'm pretty handy when it comes to shooting rats. I always keep a gun in my buggy."

"Is Gabriella home?" Jim asked the Frenchman.

"Non," Beauregard assured. "She's not there."

"Let's go then. I'll rendezvous back here in one hour with any men I can muster. We'll split the posse to cover all roads leading from town. Reagan, if you haven't returned by then, my group will head directly to Gabriella's. Be careful until we get there."

"Come with me!" Thomas tugged Beauregard's sleeve as they went outdoors. They turned the Phaeton around and followed dust kicked up by Reagan who rode Jim's horse to its swiftest gait.

chapter 94

AFTER BEAUREGARD LEFT Gabriella's, Amanda wanted to scold Derrick for the way he had ordered Beau from her parlor. To that end, she insisted she needed to change before taking a ride. When she descended the stairs with her parasol, the mantel clock had long since chimed the half hour.

"There you are, my dear." Derrick rushed forward to take her arm before opening the front door. "It's such a beautiful day, don't you think?"

"It is, indeed," Amanda agreed, trying to shake the feeling something was amiss. Derrick seemed nervous, which awakened reservations about leaving the protection of Gabriella's home. "You've raised my curiosity," she said. "Why do we need to go somewhere else? Can't you give me your news here?"

"You'll know very soon," Derrick said as he led Amanda to his rented livery, helping her inside. "Yet, let me delay a little longer, so I can give you the grand news in the perfect setting."

"Where are we going?"

"Somewhere peaceful," he said, setting the buggy in motion. "And private."

They rode in silence until they reached the willows along the river. Halting the conveyance, he set the brake and took her hand before speaking in a rush. "My dear, I've found a way set you free!"

"What do you mean?" Amanda felt uncomfortable with his tight grip on her fingers. "The investigation isn't over yet..."

"Why don't we go for a stroll?" Derrick suggested. "I know a perfect place where we can enjoy the river while we talk."

Suppressing her growing anxiety, Amanda accepted his assistance, deciding she'd remain agreeable until regaining the safety of Gabriella's home. Afterward, she'd rid herself of all distractions until Reagan's fate was resolved. It was the least she could do, considering the life growing within her.

Because of the carriage's design, Amanda couldn't see the valise tucked in the storage compartment behind the seat. As she opened her parasol, Derrick reached inside and removed a snub nosed revolver before dropping it into his pocket. "Are you ready?" he asked pleasantly. "There's a nicely secluded spot just around that thistle patch."

chapter 95

George rushed past a vagrant dozing on a bench as he entered Stroebel's boardinghouse. "I must speak to Joe Welch immediately!" he demanded of the woman behind the counter.

"May I ask who's calling?"

"I'm George Bruester," he said impatiently. "My daughter, Amanda, is in the company of a suspected murderer! The sheriff sent me for Joe while he rounds up a posse."

Mrs. Stroebel set down her pen. "I'll get him right away. He's in the garden with my daughter."

George paced the floor, unaware he had caught the vagrant's interest. "Did'ya say your daughter was Amanda?" the man asked. "Amanda Burnsfield?"

George mopped his brow, looking surprised. "Y-yes," he stammered. "Do you know Amanda?"

"My name's Hogan. Last winter, she hired me as a guide." He stood, gripping a knife beneath his jerkin. "Is she in some kind of danger?"

Just then Joe entered the room, followed closely by a young woman and a concerned Mrs. Stroebel. "You're to come with me," George grabbed the deputy's arm. "Amanda may be in peril!" Needing no further incentive, Joe hurried toward the door as Mrs. Stroebel handed him his hat.

"I'm a'comin' with you," Hogan growled. "No one's gonna hurt that girlie whilst I'm around."

By the time George, Joe and Hogan returned to jail, the sheriff had sworn in several volunteers with newly dispatched badges. Among them was Reuben Kincaid who had grabbed a pitchfork when he left the dry goods store. A large wagon was brought around for those on foot while others clustered on mounts, awaiting the sheriff's instructions.

"Men!" Hadley raised his voice above the excited babble. "We're looking for a man who may be responsible for the murder of Molly Carnes." He held up his hand as fresh murmurings swept the crowd. "He's gone by the name of Derrick Banning, but we believe his real name to be Orville Farnsworth. We believe he may've kidnapped Amanda Burnsfield to make good his escape. In view of the evidence against him, I've released Reagan Burnsfield to help in the search. Understandably, he's gone ahead of us to find his wife. Now, we don't know which way our suspect has gone. I want some of you to go with Ed, who's going south toward Rock Creek, and some with Joe, who's going west. The rest of you come with me. Each group will be looking for a well-dressed man in a buggy with a young woman. Do not," he emphasized, "attempt to apprehend the man. Instead, I want you to send someone from your party to get me. I'm heading to Gabriella Bruesters, where our suspect was last seen. If he's not there, I intend on going east toward Giddings. Once we find out where he is, we'll formulate a plan of action." As the men broke into groups, the sheriff signaled to the buckboard, "C'mon men, let's go find us a skunk."

chapter 96

AMANDA FOLLOWED DERRICK down an obscure path that led to a little-used stretch of riverbank. "There, my dear," he said, dusting off a large, flat rock inside a hidden alcove. "It's now tidy enough for you to sit on."

As Amanda sat on the makeshift seat, Derrick stood and admired the river's view. "Isn't this a beautiful spot? When I found this recess, I knew this to be the perfect place to give you my grand idea." Facing her, he quickly assumed an air of concern. "It's weighed upon my mind how your circumstances have grown steadily more dreadful. With your husband all but convicted of a heinous crime, I can no longer watch your honor be destroyed." He knelt, placing his hands over hers. "So, I've taken it upon myself to seek a solution." Smiling at her perplexed expression, Derrick continued. "Ever since you accepted my proposal..."

"Derrick," Amanda broke in. "I've already told you, I must wait until I know what's to become of Reagan."

"You'll not want to do that, once I give you my news," he said as irritation crept into his voice.

Swallowing, Amanda determined she would hear him out before declining whatever it was he was about to say. The more time she spent with the dandy, the more she realized she could never consider Derrick for a husband. He simply annoyed her too much! "All right," she said. "I'm listening."

"I've retained the services of a lawyer who can have your marriage dissolved. However, it must be done before Reagan's trial so you can free yourself from the slur of his name."

Derrick placed a finger over Amanda's opened lips as he braced himself for the lies he was about to say. "I told the lawyer we'd start divorce proceedings immediately. Furthermore, I told him I'd pay for it, myself. It's the least I can do," he said, giving what he hoped was an adoring look. "I planned on having money wired from New York. But, the lawyer insisted he needed the funds today." He took a deep breath before hurrying to finish. "So, I'm asking for an advance until my funds arrive, whereas I can then repay you. Since I knew you'd want to start right away, I told him I'd procure the money this afternoon."

Amanda was stunned. "You told him," she choked, "I'd pay..."

"It would only be a thousand or so dollars," he said, frowning. "Nothing you can't afford."

"I'm not ready to forego my marriage," Amanda said, yanking her hands free. "At least until I know whether or not I'm wed to a-a murderer." She searched his eyes. "That's not asking too much, is it?"

Derrick's agitation grew with her resistance. "But, *dear*, I think I know what's best for you."

"This time, I think not," she snapped.

He stood to avoid glaring at her. Placing his hands behind his back, he gazed at the swift moving current. "I suppose you could be right," he sighed, glancing from the corner of his eye. "After all, there is the outside chance Reagan is innocent, even though the girl *was* found in his office. Tell me," he said, looking over his shoulder. "Was the mill broken into, or were the locks intact? Surely, that would indicate whether or not an intruder committed the crime, don't you think?" Derrick recalled how he'd opened a window, and after entering the dark interior, had unlocked the entrance from the inside. He knew Amanda was unaware of his brief employment and his familiarity with the building.

"The lock was undamaged," Amanda admitted. "The mystery has yet to be solved."

"I hear the slain girl's father has no such uncertainties," he said. "He's convinced Reagan killed his daughter. He says there's no other explanation for her body to be found there. I say the man has a valid point." Derrick felt he was near to crushing her resistance and spoke before considering his words. "If you want proof your husband was involved with the trollop, consider that he paid her a large sum of money to keep quiet about the bastard she carried." Seeing the bewildering hurt in her eyes, Derrick delivered his final blow. "Just weeks before she was killed, Molly cashed a cheque that your husband wrote for five thousand dollars." Amanda became speechless as her last vestige of hope vanished. If Reagan gave money to Molly, that meant he knew her and was most likely guilty of her murder. Retrieving her hanky, she quietly wept as he continued. "She must've demanded more, and he had to get rid of her. Don't you see?" he cajoled. "Divorce is the only solution you have left."

Troubled by the image of Reagan paying the girl in secret, Amanda stared into her handkerchief. "Derrick," she said, raising her eyes. "How'd *you* know Reagan gave money to Molly?"

Suddenly, a loud snap sounded beyond the briars. With a growl, Derrick withdrew his gun and at the same time snatched Amanda to her feet.

"Who's there?" he demanded, holding her in front of him. "Come out!"

"*You* had something to do with Molly," Amanda accused, twisting in his grip. "You knew her...you knew Molly."

Derrick pulled her tighter against him. "Don't struggle, my sweet," he whispered, rubbing his cheek against hers. "She meant nothing to me. It was you I wanted, not that bitch."

Amanda's struggles only seemed to arouse him more. He pressed his lips against her neck while groping her bosom, evoking an indignant screech as she fought to free herself. With a mighty backward thrust of her elbow, she knocked his arm from around her waist. As Derrick teetered on his heels, he lifted the hand holding the revolver and slammed it against her head. Amanda's last thoughts were that a sudden burst of a thousand stars had shattered the daylight. The sun's light slowly shrank until it resembled a flickering candle before even that fluttered into merciful, oblivious darkness.

chapter 97

THOMAS AND BEAUREGARD took positions outside Gabriella's home while Reagan entered the front parlor, calling Amanda's name. When nothing but a ticking clock answered, he made a hasty but thorough search of the house. Dashing onto the porch, Reagan signaled the men before crossing the property to study recently made wheel prints in the lane. "It seems you were right, Beau," he said, looking eastward, "these tracts head toward the river." He mounted his horse while Thomas brought the buggy from where he had hidden it. "Did Derrick say where he was going?"

"Non," Beauregard said grimly as he climbed into the conveyance. "Le loup only say that he had a surprise for her."

At that moment, one of the new newly sworn deputies galloped toward them, reining in outside Gabriella's gate. "Have you any news?" he called.

Reagan urged his horse forward and met him on the road. "We think Derrick's headed east with Amanda. Tell the sheriff we're going after them."

Signaling his understanding, the man whirled and galloped out of sight. Reagan then headed in the opposite direction with Thomas and Beauregard trailing in the buggy.

Once they reached the meadow, Thomas pulled alongside Reagan who had halted to examine the ground.

Beau mopped his face. "Have they gone to the river?"

"It's hard to tell. But, we can't continue on without making sure. C'mon, let's go," said Reagan, kicking his mount.

Beau grew excited when he spotted a rented livery near the willows. "That's the de voiture I see at Madame Gabriella's!"

Thomas guided his buggy behind tall bushes and climbed down. As Beau followed at a slower pace, the elder withdrew a shotgun from the rear compartment. Reagan joined them after tying his horse and checking his weapon.

"What am I to do?" Beau asked. His hands shook as he loaded his gun. "My weaponry skills are not so good as yours."

"Perhaps, you should stay and guard the livery," Reagan suggested. "If they return, you can whistle a warning."

The Frenchman seemed relieved. "Oui, I'll hide thus," he said, stepping behind a tree and peering through its branches, "and watch without being seen."

"I'm afraid we'll have to split up," Reagan said to Thomas. "I can't tell if they've gone up river or down."

He gave Reagan's shoulder a quick squeeze. "Don't worry," he said. "We'll find her." Neither made a sound as they moved through the copse in opposite directions.

Reagan looked for footprints near a briar patch when he thought he heard a muffled sob. When he advanced, he stepped on a dry branch and it snapped. Suddenly, he heard angry voices before a loud screech rent the air. Raising his rifle, Reagan rushed forward, coming upon a sight that nearly stopped his heart.

Amanda lay limply across Derrick's arm as that one pointed a revolver toward the hedge opening. "So, that milksop let you out of jail!" Derrick snarled. "Tis a pity! I was looking forward to seeing your neck stretched!"

"What've you done to Amanda?" Reagan demanded. "I swear, if you've hurt her..."

"She's not seriously hurt," Derrick interrupted, signaling for the lumberman to back up, "unless you do something which forces me to change that."

Reagan stepped back as Derrick advanced. "I won't try stopping you," he said, his gun lowered. "Just let Amanda go."

"You think me a fool? I've no intention of letting her go."

"She'll only hinder your escape," Reagan said. He saw Amanda's eyelids flutter. "She needs a doctor."

"A hunk of ice would work just as well," Derrick said, shifting his burden. "See?" he jeered. "Your lady arises."

Amanda wobbled unsteadily until Derrick cruelly bit her earlobe. "Arise, my sweet, you need to walk now." She roused with a pained cry as her captor swung his gun toward her head. "Now, don't try anything stupid," he warned Reagan. "I guarantee you aren't faster than a bullet."

Amanda could hear voices as if from a distance. As they grew louder, a painful throbbing at the back of her head kept her from slipping back into oblivion. With effort, she opened her eyes but couldn't make sense of the confusing images. She thought she saw Reagan and heard his voice, but the last she knew, he was still in jail. Yet, who was keeping her upright when she felt a great need to lie down?

"Take me instead," Reagan said. "I'll go wherever you want."

"Are you kidding? She's my ticket out of here. Besides, you haven't repaid your debt. Now, put down your weapon and get back."

Reagan lay down his rifle and backed away, watching as Derrick retrieved the weapon and tossed it over the riverbank.

"Well, Mr. Burnsfield, I must insist you stay in front of us so I can keep my eye on you." The dandy then grasped a handful of Amanda's hair beneath her hat. "Come, my dear," he said, pushing her forward. "It's time to go."

All of Amanda's efforts were used in staying on her feet with none left to discern the cause of her pain. When she stumbled, she found herself yanked against a hard chest, which only intensified the hammer-like pounding.

Derrick ignored Amanda's distress as he forced her up the path and toward the livery. Reagan continued to back up, keeping Derrick from getting a clear view of the meadow. When the trio neared the clearing, Reagan raised his voice to an unnatural pitch.

"Derrick! If you let Amanda go, I won't tell the sheriff which way you went. Please leave Amanda with me!"

Sensing his strategy, Derrick scrutinized the surrounding area before glaring at Reagan. "I swear, if anyone tries to stop me, I'll kill her!"

"No!"

Derrick smirked. "So, you've feelings for the wench, after all. I suppose, she's comely enough to satisfy most appetites. And when I'm through with her, perhaps I'll leave a lasting legacy for you both." He laughed when Reagan's face contorted with rage. "As much as I'm enjoying our conversation," he said, reaching the livery, "it's time for us to go." He yanked on the tether before retaking Amanda's arm. "I'm afraid you must climb in yourself, my dear."

Though Amanda's pain overwhelmed her senses, she understood enough to know she didn't want to go with the one who held her captive. With a sudden, downward motion, she jerked from his grasp.

At that moment, Beauregard stepped from behind a willow tree. "Monsieur Bad Man!" He held both hands to his weapon. "Let go of demoiselle!"

With an enraged growl, Derrick caught Amanda's arm while firing at the Frenchman. He then pointed the gun at her temple, halting Reagan who had nearly reached Amanda's side. "If you come any closer, the last thing she'll ever see is your ugly face!" His lips twisted in hatred. "Now get back!"

Thomas came crashing through the brush to see Reagan retreating with his hands held high.

"Drop your weapon," Derrick snarled. "Or, I'll shoot you too." Thomas complied, dropping his shotgun as Beauregard slowly crumpled to the ground. Screaming, Amanda covered her eyes as blood spread over the Frenchman's chest.

"Get in!" Derrick thrust her savagely into the livery before scrambling in behind. Amanda fell in a corner as he lashed the horse into a frenzied gallop across the meadow.

"Get the buggy!" Reagan shouted to Thomas as he ran to Beau. Kneeling down, he tore open Beau's shirt and stuffed a handkerchief against the wound. "Hang on, Beau," he said, taking Beauregard's hand and pressing it tight to the kerchief. "I need you to help me keep my best friend alive."

"Je-" he panted, "je vous plains-" He grimaced as he endured a spasm. "I-I am sorry, Mon Ami-"

"It's all right," Reagan said while Thomas brought the Phaeton alongside. "You didn't do anything wrong."

"Non-" Beau shook his head. "I hesitated...demoiselle may be lost..." he said weakly, "-mon fault-"

Reagan leaned over until his lips neared Beau's ear. "Une bonne action ne reste jamais sans rècompense," he whispered, gently wiping away Beau's tears.

"Oui," Beauregard tried to smile. "A good deed is never lost."

Jumping from the buggy, Thomas paled at the sight of so much blood. "We must get him to a doctor!"

"*You* get him to a doctor. I'm getting Amanda!" Reagan said as Thomas picked up Beau's feet. Together, they hoisted him into the buggy.

Climbing inside, Thomas gathered the reins while Reagan mounted his horse. As Thomas urged the courser to a speed worthy of saving a man's life, Reagan kicked his mount into a full gallop. Leaning over, he scooped up Thomas's forgotten shotgun before racing toward the road.

Within seconds, the only sounds heard in the willows were the soft rustle of leaves and the trilling of a bird as it called to its mate.

chapter 98

Sheriff Hadley and his newly sworn deputies were just reaching the meadow when Thomas's carriage flew past. Moment's later, Reagan reined in sharply when he saw the band of men. "Derrick's taken Amanda," he informed them. "Since you didn't pass him, he must be going east."

George pulled up beside him. "Was that Beau who was injured?"

"Father's taking him to the doctor," Reagan said. "Derrick shot him." He turned to the sheriff. "I'm guessing he's heading to the nearest town."

"Dammit!" The lawman looked guardedly at Reagan. "He probably won't take Amanda where she could call for help."

Reagan nodded, speaking so low that even George's straining ears failed to hear. "I know."

"What are we going to do?" George said, raising his voice. "Amanda's still in the company of that vile man!"

The sheriff backed his horse until alongside George's buggy. "We're trying to determine how to apprehend Derrick without harming Amanda," he explained.

"Can't we somehow get ahead of him?" George shaded his eyes as he looked down the road. "Didn't there used to be a road that cut through the gorge near here?"

"If there was, I never heard of it." The sheriff turned toward the others. "Does anyone know of a short cut through the gorge?"

"I know the road," Hogan said, urging his horse forward. "It's about another mile down, and then cuts north, instead of the southern route the road now takes."

"How much time can we gain by taking it?"

"About two hours," Hogan calculated. "But no more. Don't figure the wagon c'n make the steeper places lest the men get out and run alongside."

"That won't be a problem," Jim said. "But what about Mr. Bruester's buggy, can he make it?"

"I'll go on foot if need be," George vowed. "There's no way I'm not coming."

"If he's that determined, he'll make it," the tracker said.

"Then, let's go!" Hadley said. "Hogan, you show us the way."

❧

Derrick had whipped the horse to its fastest speed and it wasn't until the road entered a patch of trees that he hid the livery among bushes. "Well, my dear, it appears we're not being followed." He glanced over his shoulder and then at Amanda, noting her queasy expression. "Once we're safely away, I'll grant you time to rest. After all, I'm not an unreasonable man."

"Where are we going?" she asked, touching where blood seeped from a head wound, stickying her fingers.

"That depends on whether or not you behave. If you remain cooperative, you'll stay with me until we can safely part ways."

"And if I don't?"

"Then, I'll have the unfortunate duty to leave you where no one can find you. But first, I'd have the pleasure of sampling what should've been mine all along," he said, his eyes raking her form. "The choice is yours."

"Why should I trust you? You're not an honorable man."

"We can have an understanding, not unlike the arrangement I had with your husband. No harm will come to you if I get what I want. And right now, all I want is to get away with my hide intact."

"I heard you say Reagan owed you a debt. Does that have anything to do with the cheque you claim Molly received?"

"In a way, yes. Molly was a simpleton. She needed someone to manage her life. I provided that service."

"You knew the poor girl!"

"So what?" he growled. "Molly knew a lot of men. It's how she made her living."

"Then, how could she accuse Reagan of fathering her child?"

"Well, Molly tried bedding him once, to validate her claims. But, your husband wasn't interested in a tryst. I should've expected it, seeing he had you to come home to every night."

"But, I don't understand. If Reagan wasn't the father, how could she blackmail him? Why would he write a cheque to someone he'd met only once?"

"I suppose there's no harm in telling you," he said, flicking the reins, prompting the horse forward. "After that bastard stole you away, I broke into his safe and took documents that proved he married you for your dowry. When Molly failed to entrap him, I went to him and threatened to expose the documents instead. I didn't care how I got my money, as long as I got it. When Reagan wrote me that cheque, he was simply paying for the return of one of his contracts. I used Molly's name to endorse it so I couldn't be linked to the transaction."

"Did Molly know?"

"Not any more than she knew who got her with child," Derrick snorted. "She claimed the brat was mine, but in truth, I didn't care. Had I gotten the rest of my money, I wouldn't have stayed long enough to find out."

"So, when you said you'd regain my dowry for me, that was just another lic, wasn't it?"

"Only the part about giving it back. I would've had it, too, if that wench hadn't stuck her nose where it didn't belong!" His face contorted. "She hid the documents. I couldn't find them. After that, I decided I'd have to marry you."

Turning toward him too quickly, Amanda was rewarded with a fresh stab of pain. "Is that when you killed her?"

"I didn't murder the bitch! It was an accident! How was I to know the tramp would hit her head?"

"Then, why blame Reagan for her death?"

"I had to dump her somewhere. What better place than on Reagan's doorstep? It got him out of the way. That was, until the sheriff started snooping around."

"Why don't you just let me go? Surely, I can be no further use to you."

"You're as mad as your husband, if you think me that foolish."

"But, why?" Amanda pressed. "You've already escaped."

"I told you, my dear. Your presence will ensure my continued good health."

"When will you release me?"

"I haven't decided," he said, mopping the back of his neck. "Most likely, when I'm sure I'm out of harm's way."

Amanda believed she couldn't outrun him, even if she jumped from the conveyance. She decided to look for an escape with better odds. Feigning fatigue, she pressed herself into the seat and on the pretext of touching her wound, she felt for the long, sharp pin that secured her hat. Grateful for that small bit of security, Amanda awaited her chance.

chapter 99

HOGAN LED THE posse through a boulder-strewn gorge, grown even narrower from lack of use. At one point they unloaded the wagon and lifted it over a rocky patch. "Once we're back on the road, there's a bend in the woods a feller cain't see around," he explained. "That's where we can catch him unawares."

"I know that area," Reagan replied, "although, I never knew about this shortcut."

Hogan spat a stream of tobacco juice. "That's cuz it's a pain in the arse."

By late afternoon, the men had reached their destination and were strategically hidden on both sides of a hairpin curve. Minutes turned into an hour then stretched into two before they heard the soft clop of a horse coming down the road. As Reagan peered through weeds, he could see a livery with Amanda slumped against the seat. He rose off his belly only to be halted by a hand on his shoulder.

"Stay down, you damn fool!" Hogan hissed. "You cain't be seen yet."

Reluctantly, he hunkered down as Hogan melted into the woods. Moment's later, Reagan saw two men hurry from the trees, one on horseback. Once they gained the road, both turned toward the approaching livery, as yet unseen beyond the bend. When the buggy navigated the turn, Reagan and the others began creeping forward.

Derrick swerved to avoid the man on horseback and his companion who had a pitchfork slung over his shoulder.

"Hullo!" Hogan said, stopping his horse in the center of the road. Standing next to him, Reuben rested the tines of his pitchfork in the dirt. "Can you tell me how far the next town is? We're looking for work."

"You're two hours away," Derrick snapped. "Now, if you'd be so kind as to step aside, the lady and I have business to attend."

Amanda sucked in her breath when she heard the familiar voice and lifting her eyes, was even more surprised to see Reuben Kincaid. Too late, she tried hiding her mistake by suddenly coughing. Yet, Derrick's quick glance caught the moment of recognition in her eyes.

As he groped for his weapon, Amanda seized her hatpin and stabbed the back of his hand. He bellowed, yanking the pin free to slap her brutally. Amanda's hat flew when she fell against the seat. She immediately righted herself, gripping the sides as Derrick tried forcing the livery between the men on the road. But Reuben, emitting a loud cry, brandished his pitchfork in a back and forth motion until the terrified animal swerved. As the livery pitched sideways, Hogan pressed his horse close, pulling Amanda over his saddle before galloping away.

With his hostage now gone, Derrick panicked. Snatching up his gun, he jumped free of the buggy only to trip and fall. Reagan dashed toward the livery while Derrick scrambled to his feet, unknowingly running in his direction. In one motion, Reagan leaped upon Derrick and slammed him to the ground. The forest exploded with swarming men as the two men tumbled among weeds. Reagan grabbed Derrick's throat, but he wrested free, aiming his weapon at Reagan's head. Reagan seized the gun, thrusting it upward as a shot rang out. Squeezing Derrick's wrist, he pressed his forearm under the man's jaw until he dropped the revolver.

Without a weapon, Derrick quickly reverted to his street thug mentality and lunging forward, viciously bit Reagan's ear. His fingers probed for Reagan's eyes, but the lumberman bent his hand backwards until Derrick screamed.

Rolling onto his knees, Reagan slammed his fist into Derrick's belly. "You sniveling coward!" he spat as Derrick scrambled away. "Fight like a man!" Seeing other men circling around, Derrick turned back only to have Reagan's knuckles ram his jaw.

Derrick spit blood, stumbling back into the sheriff's arms. "Whoa," Jim said. "I don't want you yet. You've got a score to settle." As he flung Derrick back, Reagan braced his feet, sinking his fist into the outlaw's middle.

When Derrick crumpled to the ground, he spied his gun amongst weeds. Scores of feet surrounded him as he crawled toward it. “I yield!” he panted. “I surrender.”

Reagan was clearly in no mood to end the beating. “Get up,” he growled. “I’m not done.”

“Stop! Please, stop!” Derrick writhed snakelike on the ground, covering the gun. “Don’t let him hurt me!”

“Now Reagan, you’ve had your revenge,” Sheriff Hadley said, stepping between them. “There’s not a man here that doesn’t think he hasn’t gotten what he deserved. But, we have laws. Besides, we found the money he stole from you,” he indicated the valise held by a deputy. “As much as I’d enjoy it, I can’t allow you to beat him to death.”

Reagan stepped back as the sheriff held up a hand. “I suppose it’s better to let the bastard suffer the fate he tried pawning on me,” he said, panting. “I’ll settle for watching him wear a noose.”

No one noticed Derrick’s fingers curl around the revolver until he sat up and pointed it directly at Reagan. “You son-of-a-bitch!” he snarled. “I’d a had it all, if not for you!” He pulled back the hammer, his bloody lips twisting. “Naught what you do to me matters anymore! I’ll see you in hell-”

Jim grabbed Reagan and threw him to the ground the same time a gun discharged. Derrick screamed, dropping his weapon while blood spurted from his shoulder. All eyes turned to see George holding a rifle.

"Damned if I'm going to let you kill my son-in-law." He grinned at Reagan's astounded expression. "After everything that's happened," he shrugged, "I owed you one."

The sheriff hauled Derrick to his feet while Amanda rushed up and threw her arms around Reagan's neck before breaking down in sobs. "Shhh," he murmured, holding her close. "It's all right."

After awhile, he lifted her chin and inspected her cheek. "I should've gelded him for touching you."

"It's nothing," she said, sniffling. "I barely feel it." She stroked his face. "It was Derrick who killed Molly. I'm sorry I doubted you."

Reagan chuckled. "You made it up to me when you stabbed that bastard with your hatpin."

"If only I'd believed you," she said. "None of this would've happened."

"You had plenty to consider," he said. "There were times when I even doubted myself."

Twilight had fallen by the time the sheriff dispersed the posse. Two men assigned to guard Derrick tied his hands and placed him on a horse while Reagan led Amanda to George's buggy. Her father had already lit the lanterns when Reuben approached.

"Sorry, about your hat bein' squashed, Miss Amanda," he said, holding it out. "I couldn't get the dents out."

"Don't worry, Papa promised me a new one, didn't you Papa?"

George grinned as Amanda snuggled close. "If necessary, I'll buy a hundred hats, with bigger pins."

"You won't have to worry about any hats for at least a fortnight," she said, touching her bruised scalp.

"We'll send for Doc Turner as soon as we get home," Reagan said. "Perhaps, he can give you something for the pain."

"I felt better the moment I saw Hogan and Reuben standing in the road," she said. "I can't think of a better salve than dear friends coming to one's aid."

"Huh!" Hogan said as he mounted his horse. "I expect there'll come a time when you'll be needing me again." He gave both a knowing look. "A woman's a curse. You cain't predict whut she'll do, and you sure as hell cain't control her." Grinning suddenly, he tipped his hat before heading into the dark. "Until we meet again."

Sheriff Hadley joined the group. "I'd like Reagan and George to come by my office tomorrow and give their statements. I'm filing charges against this derelict for theft, extortion and kidnapping." Tipping his hat, he winked at Amanda. "And, please let me know if your husband ever neglects his duties," he said, waggling a thumb at Reagan. "I've got plenty more empty cells."

Amanda glanced at her husband. "I'll keep that in mind, sheriff."

chapter 100

"AMANDA," GEORGE MURMURED, touching his daughter's cheek. "You're home, honey." As comforting as it was to have her curled against him, it was time to return her to her husband. Reagan and George eased Amanda from the buggy and holding her between them entered the foyer of the Burnsfield home. It didn't help Amanda's headache when the hall resounded with excited shouts as Thomas and Katherine followed by Amy, Emily, and Gabriella rushed from the parlor.

"Oh, my baby!" Emily nearly knocked George over in her haste to embrace Amanda. "Are you all right?"

Emily had almost fainted when word had reached her about Amanda's abduction and not knowing where else to go, hastened to the Burnsfield home with Gabriella in tow. Her fears intensified when Thomas later burst in with a badly injured Beau. Having summoned Doctor Turner, they gathered round as Thomas recounted his discoveries about Derrick. Emily couldn't stop weeping when she realized how the scoundrel had tricked her and slipping away, sat alone in the parlor. She thought long and hard about the decisions she had made over the years. How many other times had her judgment been wrong? Emily felt a crushing shame and as regret ravaged her soul, she wept. Later, Katherine had found her and brought her back to the parlor to wait with the others.

"Reagan, thank God you've all returned safely," Thomas said. "Did you apprehend that swindler?"

"He should be sitting in jail, awaiting the doctor," Reagan replied before describing Derrick's capture.

Katherine gently turned his face as she viewed his cut temple. "Are you hurt badly?"

"I've never felt better. In fact, it's one of the best days of my life."

"Just in case, Doc Turner's still attending Beau. I'm sure he'll want to check you both."

"How is Beau? I worried about him all day," asked Reagan.

"With a little care, he'll be as good as new," she said.

Having waited long enough for her turn, Gabriella hugged Amanda then kissed her cheek. "We're so thankful you're home, dear. Although, you do look a little worse for the wear."

"I'm fine," Amanda said. "Just terribly messy."

"We don't care about that," Emily stated. "We just want to know if that terrible man hurt you."

"Now Emily," George said. "Amanda's had quite an ordeal. Let Amanda go upstairs so the doctor can examine her. There'll be plenty of time for explanations later."

"Of course, you must all stay," insisted Katherine. "I've had guest rooms prepared. Amy, I'm putting you in charge of bringing refreshments while I show the Bruesters their room." She turned to Gabriella. "If it's satisfactory, the room you rested in earlier should accommodate you nicely."

"I know where it is," Gabriella said, reaching for the banister. "It'll be just perfect."

Reagan reclaimed Amanda's arm, amazed at the obvious similarity between his wife and Emily now that the elder had lost girth. Indeed, in her youth, Emily must've been a very beautiful woman, and of a sudden, he felt compelled to make peace with her. "We'd be honored if you'd join us for breakfast," he said, smiling at Emily.

She smiled in return. "It'd be a pleasure."

Amanda too, sensed a shift between them. "I'm happy you're staying, Mother. It'll give us time to speak tomorrow, for I'm afraid I'm very tired now."

Reagan headed upstairs with Amanda while Katherine looped her fingers around George's arm, leaving Thomas to escort Emily. As the elder Burnsfield offered his arm, she accepted, though she slowed her step until there was a distance between them and the others.

"I have a confession to make," Emily began, keeping her eyes on the stairs. "Ever since our broken engagement, I've held a grudge against you. Furthermore, I've stupidly allowed it to spill over onto Reagan." She hushed Thomas's attempt to interrupt. "No, please, let me finish," she said, giving him an apologetic look. "All this time I've only thought about how angry I was, believing it was you who betrayed our love. I never considered how painful my rejection would've been to a man who offered all he had, only to find it wasn't enough. I now realize what a fool I've been. First, for allowing others to govern my decisions, and second, for not appreciating George for the blessing he is." Tears moistened her eyes as she looked at him. "All I want now, is to tell you how sorry I am, Thomas, for treating you so badly. You didn't deserve it, and neither did Reagan."

Thomas halted. "There's no need to apologize. Back then, my pride exceeded my sense. Had I loved you as a man ought, I wouldn't have allowed your father to stop me. I thought if I tried again, I'd be proving I was pursuing your wealth. It wasn't until later that I understood what real love was. So, it was just as much my fault as yours. Besides," he said grinning. "We were always involved in one squabble or another. It probably would've been our undoing."

Emily laughed, recalling how each had more than a fair amount of will. "I suppose you're right," she said allowing Thomas to continue leading her up the stairs. "George possesses the gentlest spirit. I don't know if another man could've put up with me."

"I think he's the better man, by far," he said, smiling. "And, he's got a streak of bravery a mile wide."

"Are you saying it would take a brave man to marry me?" Emily asked.

"No," Thomas said. "He only has to love you. And that's evident to anyone who sees George look at you."

"Thank you Thomas," she said as she neared her door. "And good night."

"Good night, Emily."

By the time she entered her room, Emily felt a renewed appreciation for her husband. She determined to repair the harm she had caused him, starting tomorrow.

After examining Amanda, Doctor Turner mixed a potent pain remedy, insisting she drink it. "I'll return in the morning to check on you and Beauregard." He then looked to Reagan who had earlier refused his attempt to minister his wounds. "When that medicine hits, she'll feel dizzy," he warned, shutting his bag. "You might want to stay nearby."

Reagan followed him to the hall while Amanda changed her clothes. "Don't worry. I don't plan on going anywhere except showing you the door."

"Stay. I can see myself out. It sounds like I'm going to the jail next anyway. By the way," he paused, extending his hand, "congratulations on becoming a free man. It looks like the sheriff has the real murderer."

"Thanks." Reagan clasped his hand before grinning. "And if you must medicate our jailed friend, don't let him sleep too well."

Later, while undressing, Reagan could hear Amanda's frustrated sighs as she sat at her vanity. Within moments, he was there, gently taking her hands from the tangled mess of her hair. "Here, let me," he said. Amanda closed her eyes as he removed her pins and then taking a comb, spent several minutes working through snarls.

"There," he said, kissing the top of her head. "Milady's toilet is complete.

Though Amanda had every intention of rising, her lids felt heavy and she wavered on her seat. Reagan recognized the medicine was having an effect and gently scooped her up before easing her into bed.

As she lay slumbering, he marveled at the chain of events that had taken him from accused killer to free man. In the process, he had regained his wife. Finally, he blew out the lamp and joined Amanda under the quilts, vowing never to lose her again.

chapter 101

THE SUN HAD nearly reached its zenith by the time Amanda awakened to a knock on the door. "Come in," she called. The maid entered, carrying buckets of hot water.

"Good morning, Mrs. Burnsfield," Lela greeted. "Mr. Burnsfield felt you'd be wanting a bath."

Amanda struggled to sit up. "That sounds wonderful. I could use a good soaking," she said.

As Lela went into the bathing chamber, Reagan stuck his head in the room. "Good morning, sleepyhead." He entered, holding a vase of fresh flowers. "Mother insisted I bring these to you."

"They're lovely." She looked happily about the room while Reagan set the vase nearby and Lela departed. It felt good to be home. Throwing back the covers, a familiar sourness began in the pit of her stomach. Amanda paused, hoping the sensation would pass, but when the affliction grew stronger, she grew mortified she'd be sick in front of her husband.

When Reagan saw her paleness, he tried getting her back into bed, but Amanda stubbornly refused. "You must leave!" she insisted as she groped under the bed, grasping an empty pan. "Please, leave now."

Reagan hurried to the room where Katherine and Doctor Turner were tending Beau. "Amanda's ill!" he sputtered.

"She's ill?" Katherine looked toward the doctor. "May I check on her?"

"Of course," he said, taking bandages from her hands. "I'll be there as soon as I finish."

Kneeling over the bedpan, Amanda didn't see Katherine keep Reagan at the door so she could enter first. After wetting a cloth, she handed it to Amanda.

"Thank you," Amanda murmured, pressing its coolness against her face.

Katherine looked into the pan before turning to Reagan. "She's all right now." She touched Amanda's shoulder while removing the pan. "I'll take care of this, dear. And Reagan, I think you better get Amanda her wrapper before the doctor comes."

Reagan hurried to the wardrobe. "What if he needs to examine her? Perhaps, she's taken a turn for the worse." Helping Amanda into the housecoat, he missed her wry expression.

Doctor Turner came to the door where Katherine still held the pan. "Beauregard insisted I see to Amanda before I could change his dressings. Oh!" His brows shot up when he spied the contents of the bedpan.

"We heard Amanda's ill!" Emily barged in, followed closely by George. "Is something the matter?" She looked around fearfully until she realized nobody but Reagan appeared to be upset.

Amanda sat on the bed. "No, Mama, I just had an upset stomach, that's all."

"Doc, don't you think you should examine her? I mean," Reagan motioned toward the bedpan. "It's not normal to become ill like this, is it?"

The doctor set down his bag. "Oh, I'd say it's very normal, actually." Opening his jacket, he withdrew a wrapped cigar. "I didn't expect I'd be using this," he said, holding it up. "But it looks like we'll have to."

Reagan's perplexed expression grew even more so as he stared at the rolled tobacco. "Amanda has to smoke a *cigar*?"

"No, you idiot," he said, tucking it into Reagan's pocket. "You're smoking it." Artemus grinned as he patted the pocket. "You're going to be a father. Congratulations."

Reagan's jaw dropped. He stared at Amanda who was now giggling. "Is it true?" he asked. "Are you going to have a baby?"

Everyone waited breathlessly until she nodded. A gleeful clamoring erupted as Reagan knelt and took her hand. "My darling," he breathed, pressing his lips to her palm. "This is just too wonderful!" Amanda laid a hand on his shoulder as Katherine quietly motioned for everyone to leave.

"At first, I was afraid to say anything," she said smiling. "But now, I don't mind if the whole world knows."

"My love," Reagan suddenly choked. "You've given me a gift beyond my wildest imaginings!"

"Does this mean our marriage is legitimate in every sense of the word?" Amanda raised a brow. "After all, you did marry me for my dowry."

Reagan pulled her to her feet and touched her face. "That's what I told myself. But in truth, you captured my heart and I couldn't live without you. I think I've loved you from the start."

"You had a funny way of showing it," she said. "After I discovered your chicanery, you became sour as an old drunk and twice as crotchety."

Reagan grinned, dropping a hand to her derriere. "That's because I was mad with lust. How else could I be in your presence and not ravage you?"

"If you suffered, you deserved it twice over," she said. She pushed away his hand and made her way to the bath chamber.

A knock prevented his reply and Reagan opened the portal to Lela who was holding two more buckets. "I'll take those," he said relieving her of her burden before shutting the door. By the time he entered the chamber, Amanda had disrobed and was lowering herself into the tub.

"Mmmm," she sighed. "This feels wonderful!" Seemingly unconcerned Reagan was viewing her nakedness, Amanda lay against the rim and closed her eyes. Reagan took several moments to admire her perfectly shaped body before pouring the remaining buckets into the tub. A few drops splattered her face, causing Amanda to open an accusing eye. "Hey," she said, flicking water at him. "You did that on purpose."

"No," he laughed, splashing back. "*That* was on purpose."

Soon, their playful antics had water covering the floor as well as Reagan's clothes. "Well, my dear," he said, unbuttoning his shirt. "I see you're itching for a fight!"

Amanda observed his garments fall one by one. "What are you doing? Don't you dare get into this tub," she said, bracing her arms. "This bath is mine and I'm not sharing it."

Reagan pried her fingers loose before stepping in and when she tried standing, he grasped her shoulders. "Oh, no you don't," he said, pressing her back. "You escaped from my bath once before. You shan't do it again." After settling in front of her, he picked up the soap.

"But Reagan," she protested. "Our parents are awaiting breakfast."

His eyes danced as he lathered his hands. "Then let's get going, my love." Amanda sighed but remained still while he ran soapy fingers down her back. Inching closer, he placed her arms around his neck so he could better reach her waist, and when she didn't resist, he lifted her onto his lap. He then wrapped her legs around his waist and pressed her against him. "That's better," he murmured, nuzzling her ear.

Amanda wriggled pleasurably at the intimate contact. "Oh, you devil," she said, playfully biting his neck. As his lips found hers, he pressed her even closer, seeking that place where he felt complete and Amanda's love filled his heart.

chapter 102

A LIGHT BUT determined knock interrupted Sheriff Hadley as he wrote a report on the investigation and capture of Orville Farnsworth, alias Derrick Banning. Though there were gaps in the story, Jim believed he had more than enough evidence to exonerate Reagan. He would present his evidence before the court, where Judge McCleary would determine whether Orville should be tried for murder before returning to New York to face embezzlement charges.

Opening the door, he looked expectantly at a young woman. "May I help you?" he asked.

Clutching papers to her bosom, she gazed hesitantly at his badge. "Are ye th' sheriff?"

Hadley stepped back. "I am. Please, come in and have a seat." After she sat, he retook his chair. "What can I do for you?"

"M' name's Agnes McGregor, but most o' me friends call me Aggie," she said, setting her papers down. "I've got something you'd be wanting. Something I held for a friend o' mine."

"What are they?"

"They're documents that were given t' me for safekeeping."

He unfolded the topmost item and then looked up in surprise. "Where'd you get these?"

Aggie swallowed several times before opening her mouth. "Not that long ago, a girl I knew, came t' me home. Her name wuz Molly-"

"Molly Carnes?" Hadley was instantly interested.

"That be her name," Aggie nodded. "We had a falling out, and I told her I wuzn't gonna be her friend no more. But she came a'knocking, late one night."

Jim unfolded the other papers, scanning their contents. "Did Molly say how she came to be in possession of these documents?"

Agnes dropped her eyes. "Molly worked in th' saloon so she could snag herself a rich man. I told her no gentleman would take t' th' likes o' a saloon gal, but Molly eventually became a-a-" Agnes turned pink as she struggled to utter words forbidden to her.

"Let's just say a lady of the evening," Jim offered kindly.

Agnes wiped away a tear. "That night she wuz real scared. She said she had t' git away from a man she'd been living with. She wuz carrying his babe-"

Jim could scarce believe his luck. "Did she say who the father was?"

"Orville Farns-" Agnes struggled to recall, "-Farnsworth."

The sheriff sat back, amazed. "Why didn't you come forward sooner?"

"Molly told me t' hide th' papers afore I wuz t' meet her at her pappy's farm. When she didn't show up, I came back home and heard she wuz dead. I wuz scared t' tell anyone, not knowing who kilt Molly. I waited t' see if Orville got pinched. But, when Mister Burnsfield wuz put in jail, I knew I had t' give th' papers t' you, because Molly weren't afraid o' him." She raised tearful eyes. "I just got them out o' hiding, and come straight away."

"You've been a good friend, Aggie," he said gently. "Molly was lucky to have someone like you."

Tears spilled down Agnes's cheeks as she pulled out a hanky. "She weren't really a bad girl, just stupid, is all. Molly wanted better for her baby. She said she took th' papers t' start over."

Jim rose. "These documents will be extremely valuable in bringing to justice the man we believe killed Molly. I'd very much appreciate it if you could return tomorrow to give your statement to the judge."

"I'd be most happy to," Agnes said.

After she left, Jim placed the contracts in a small safe. He then sat down to rewrite the report, a smile about his lips.

chapter 103

Beauregard looked wounded as Reagan placed the spoon back in his fingers. "But, Mon Ami, I'm going home today. And though I love ma mère with all my heart, she's not so fair to look upon as chéri."

Reagan smiled, placing both hands on Amanda's shoulders as she sat near Beau's bed. "I really think you can feed yourself, my friend. You've been doing it for nearly a week."

"True," Beauregard said, stirring his soup before winking. "But, there are times when I feel weak. And that is when I'm in need of the services of a beauteous demoiselle."

"Then I must have Doctor Turner return for another examination," Reagan said, feigning concern, "because you've had a weak spell every day this week."

Beauregard jabbed his spoon in the air. "Non, only when certain les fleurs come to visit."

Amanda smiled in amusement, for Beauregard had rapidly improved the last two weeks. Just this morning, the doctor declared the Frenchman fit enough to travel. Once his noon meal was over, he was going home. "I'd have to say," she said, "I never realized how many women know you. Every day, there's a steady stream of female visitors from breakfast to dinnertime. You'd have thought there wasn't another man within fifty miles."

Beau settled his eyes on Amanda. "That's because Madame has never fully experienced mon's charms."

"I'm afraid it's too late," she said as she patted his hand, "since I'm already taken."

"Oui!" Beauregard sighed, setting aside his tray. "It's always the beautiful bird that gets caged. But, I don't think I'll be as quickly shackled as my friend," he said, eying Reagan.

Amanda was quick to object. "Oh, I don't know. Of all the young ladies, surely, you could find one or two to your liking."

"I'd have to say, he's rather enjoying the attention," Reagan interjected. "I've never known the French to seek one female, when a cluster would better do."

"Ahh," Beauregard clasped hands behind his head. "Spoken like a true Parisian. 'Qui se marie à la hâte se repent à loisir.'"

"What did he say?" she asked. "And don't lie. He's too smug to have said anything nice."

"If my French doesn't fail me, he said marry in haste, repent at leisure."

"Oh!" Amanda slapped Beauregard's leg. "Are you saying my husband regrets marrying me?"

Beau's eyes shone. "Actually, it is I, who most regrets Monsieur Burnsfield has married you. But, since you're not available, I must distract myself with many other demoiselles."

Reagan looked sternly at Beau as he helped Amanda from her chair. "Don't let your pea-sized brain forget that, either," he said, placing an arm around her waist. "I still don't share my most prized possessions, not even with you."

"I shan't forget," Beau said, looking fondly at the couple. "Even though wise men are sometimes foolish, I won't play the fool."

Reagan and Amanda nearly made it to the door when Beauregard quipped wickedly under his breath. "But only a fool never changes his mind!"

Epilogue

ELIZABETH SAT BY the fireplace sipping fresh tea. A new quilt covered her knees, evidence of her Aunt Emmaline's belief that idle hands were the devil's workshop. A letter lay on her lap she had written to her father, claiming the weather too cold for travel and explaining that perhaps she needed an extended vacation after all. His dear sister, Emmaline, was a bit lonely and quite anxious to have her stay for the winter.

As Elizabeth stared into the fire, Emmaline concentrated on her needlework. Though she disapproved of her niece's conduct, she would take care of Elizabeth just as she'd always taken care of her brother, Sam. Still, she detested lying to her friends about her war-widowed niece who was expecting late this winter. Emmaline felt it her duty to instruct her niece on the vices of a hell-bound life and insisted Elizabeth read from the Bible, loud enough for Emmaline to hear while about her tasks. It was a small price to pay, Elizabeth decided, for having a secure place to stay until her babe was born.

As Emmaline stitched a colorful tapestry, Elizabeth felt her life equally stained with her own threads of betrayal. She rested a hand upon her unborn child as it moved beneath her fingers.

Reagan's child.

Made in the USA
Charleston, SC
23 October 2012